GROUNDED

Spellkeeper Flight – Book Three

Ken Hughes

Windward Road Press

Los Angeles, CA

Windward Road Press
11923 NE Sumner St Ste 879426
Portland, OR 97250-9601

Publisher's Note: This is a work of fiction. Names, characters, places, and incidents are a product of the author's imagination. Locales and public names are sometimes used for atmospheric purposes. Any resemblance to actual people, living or dead, or to businesses, companies, events, institutions, or locales is completely coincidental.

Book Layout © 2017 BookDesignTemplates.com

Grounded/ Ken Hughes. -- 1st ed.
ISBN paperback: 979-8-2019736-7-4
ISBN ebook: 978-0-9850484-7-1

For Ace, who said we should all set writing goals for that summer.

And Leslie and Sarah and Hilary who already had them. For Robin and the chorus of Carols, that never stop writing, for Tag who makes starting look so good, and for Scott and Garrett and Carmen and all the rest.

A series is a whole world, but a writing group is more than a universe.

CONTENTS

CHAPTER ONE

NINE POINTS OF THE LAW

Dammit, Angie! None of this is helping you!

Mark Petrie took another glance back up the police station corridor, but with all the cops moving about he couldn't even see the door they'd taken Olivia Nolan and her lawyers through.

Silently, he focused on the magic in his belt again to search for her power. The weather energy Nolan carried was a primal force his gravity power could barely feel at the best of times… and using any more magic now stretched his frayed nerves and made the dull, shifting roar of the police station's constant crowd beat against his head. At least he could sense Henry's own gravity belt up the other way, in the room the cops had taken him to.

"We should be done with him soon."

Mark snapped his head forward again. Was that *satisfaction* in the rail-thin detective's voice, about how shaken Mark's cousin had been when they led him off, and how much he might let slip? *We can't even let them guess what's got us so wired: the effects of our magic.*

One risk of that secret getting out would bring Winton down on them all.

The cop was still blocking the corridor they'd taken Henry up, and he swept his gaze between the remaining three of them. "Tell me again. It was Olivia Nolan who kidnapped you two," and he looked at Angie's father Joe Dennard, and Henry's girlfriend Christa, "and murdered this deep-freeze corpse you found. That's your story about yesterday—

"And then this morning she chased *you,*" and he looked at Mark, "and Henry Maes through the blizzard, and she broke into a mausoleum? And one of that place's next of kin, Sasha Lawrence, can't be found now. And yet, none of it's got a connection to the gang bloodbath this week at Henry Maes's house, that we already had *you* in for," and he glared right at Dennard, "and you still say Henry wasn't even there when that happened—"

He broke into another round of his spluttering coughs, but Mark thought he saw those eyes watching Christa. Henry's prim corporate girlfriend had shown a brittle kind of stillness ever since she'd been dragged into their struggle, and she'd still only had a glimpse of what they and now Henry had faced.

"And Henry wasn't." Dennard's steady, ex-cop confidence broke the detective's insinuations apart.

—But it's a lie, Mark thought, *and even that was because we couldn't risk being in custody and at Winton's mercy. And yet now here we are with the police again.* What was keeping their lawyer, Todd Gilbert?

Dennard went on "You've heard all our separate statements, except you're dragging out Henry's. But Irene is still dead, Sasha is missing, and I woke up in Ms. Nolan's garage in handcuffs."

He held up his wrist to show the bruises around it. The motion was so quick Mark wondered how many times he'd done it today— Dennard had always been the one hoping that this once the police could lock up one of their enemies even without the whole truth.

What had Nolan done with Sasha's book, and Mark's coat? Had she caught up with Sasha again, before the police brought her in? Or had Winton himself stopped pretending to protect her, and taken Sasha himself?

The detective snuffled once, then glared back at them. "But then there was that other time... you keep saying the gang came to Henry

Maes's house," and he hooked a thumb back up the corridor where they'd taken Henry, "and the person they found there wasn't him, and it wasn't his cousin—" he looked at Mark— "it was the cousin's friend—" and he turned to Dennard. "And now it's Mark Petrie's boss Nolan who's kidnapped Petrie's friend—" Dennard again— "and his cousin's girlfriend—" to Christa. Then his eyes locked on Christa and he snapped "So, which of these 'cousins' really dragged you into this tangle—Mark? or was it your Henry?"

Christa didn't move, pinned by the detective's gaze. How had she kept quiet so long, just to protect a boyfriend she'd only thought she'd known? For one instant Mark felt nothing but the cold fan humming away above them, loud in a sudden pocket of quiet after the cop's question.

Then Christa said, "Olivia Nolan drugged the two of us, and your tests will prove it. Along with the *dead body,* Irene." Her voice wavered only on the last words.

But the detective's eyes were looking past her now, right on Mark, probably seeing how the nineteen-year-old kid in the weather-battered clothes must be the one that connected them all. *What was Henry telling them? How can he keep* anything *in after he saw the magic get me so crazy he had to side with Nolan against me, at least until he saw how deadly she could be? And now he has to keep his story straight in an interrogation twice as long as I got through...*

The chatter of voices around the police station pressed at Mark worse than the walls, all those people ready to throw Henry in the madhouse if he had said one word about magic. Henry didn't even have much magic left; he'd already swapped his own belt for Mark's nearly drained one. But just one flex of the power Mark wore could float himself upward and throw all the lies away...

"Please, can you let me see him?" Christa asked, and her voice wavered again.

"When we're done. These things can take… as long as they take," and the detective gave the tiniest smile. A bluff, it had to be.

"So you're stalling until the blood tests come back, and seeing if we change our statements," and Dennard chuckled. "When they do come, you'll see Christa and I were drugged. Probably Irene too, before Nolan had her frozen."

"With what?" The cop coughed again, and that rasp added to his voice's contempt when he went on "An industrial freezer in her back pocket?"

"After all the deep cold snaps we've had?" Dennard shot back. "How is that a mystery?"

Except, it was Nolan's weather magic at the heart of these crazy months, that and Winton's possession and flying talismans like Mark's.

Just one push upward, to float him up against that damn fan's downdraft...

Mark could hear the regret in Dennard's voice, wanting to come clean with the police force he'd served with long ago. *But I'm the one who restarted the lies, just like I left Henry with Nolan, when she killed Irene, now she maybe killed Sasha...* I *trusted her, just like I trusted Winton—*

And got Angie trapped—

He drew in a slow, steadying breath. One moment of magic could prove it all, but then they'd lose control of the hunt for Winton. He drew on the belt's power again to feel for any other magic it would resonate with.

Angie was there. He caught no trace of Nolan's power brewing up some escape, but he could feel the solid gravity magic on Henry off in his own room, and the rough-edged flicker of the energy that let Angie hold onto the body she had left. His sense placed her far above the building, just where a watchful owl should be winging by.

Her presence centered him, even better than floating in the sky himself. Mark turned to the detective again and let the frustration slip away from his jaw, his fingers. *I'll fight for Henry, for Dennard, but* nothing *will make me say one word that could take us away from the hunt for Winton. For the magic to help Angie.*

The detective was studying Christa again. "Look, your boyfriend's been asking to see you. But he can't remember why you were both at Ms. Nolan's home—what, some all-night brainstorming about her business?"

"Yes," was all Christa said.

Dennard added "We already told you—"

"You *did,*" and the cop stabbed a finger right at Christa. "Henry needs a doctor soon, but even he didn't pretend he'd drag you out to see his cousin's boss to talk promotion tips."

"What doctor? Is Henry—" Christa began. Mark opened his mouth to break in, saw Dennard move to step between her and the cop—

A buzz swept through the corridor. A whisper of voices, low but everywhere, and a ripple of movement as heads turned toward the space behind Mark.

Nolan was walking out.

Mark only caught a glimpse of the small, squat woman surrounded by the three sharp-suited lawyers. But none of the police pressed close enough to be keeping her in custody. She wore no handcuffs.

A shocked gasp came from Christa behind him. Some other voice slipped above the corridor's murmur with "Is that the one—" and broke off.

Nolan paused at the far end of the wide area, talking to one of the police. She didn't look at Mark or the others, across the open space and the currents of startled cops and staff and visitors and all, but she didn't flinch away either. Instead Mark saw her motion one of her lawyers away from her, and the suit drew a step back, keeping the ring around her spread wide even as she kept talking with the cop.

What was she doing? Mark stared at her; Nolan never hesitated, but was there something... uncertain about the way she looked between the officer and her lawyers? Or her assistant at her side, Zeke Brent?

No: she was simply watchful. Keeping a safe distance from anyone Winton might use to touch her.

One grim-faced cop turned from her group and strode across to Mark's side of the area. He stepped past them, whispered in the coughing detective's ear, and then moved on beyond them toward where Henry was.

Christa tried to slip in behind him, but she only moved a few steps before their own detective moved to block her.

"So you're letting Nolan out?" Dennard said. "What about the evidence?"

The detective laughed coldly. "The toc screens came back. You two weren't drugged, you were drunk."

"We were *not!*" Christa's voice rose.

"Drunk, the lab says. And the prelims say the dead girl may have stumbled out into the snow—" He coughed again. "Exposure can do worse to a body. The files show other cases like it, even someone drunk enough to take shelter in a car trunk."

A human popsicle, just from a crazy winter in Lavine? Of course that was Nolan hiding the body she'd killed. Mark felt his feet moving to edge him clear of Dennard and Christa's sides, his eyes back on Nolan—as if his muscles expected to have to leap across the room to stop some counterattack of hers at any moment.

She still didn't look at her accusers. Mark felt for her magic, and for a touch of Angie's presence outside…

Off there! Just for an instant Mark felt it, not the soft power that might be Nolan's magic but a fleeting familiar *twitch* off across the corridor like an enemy eye peeking out. Which was what it had to be.

"So I imagined this?" Dennard was growling, waving his bruised wrists again.

"Those tiny marks, are those toy cuffs? Sounds more like you want to blame your host for the party you had."

"Party? What are you implying?" came Christa's outraged voice.

But all those sounds were back behind Mark, pushed away by the strain of keeping his face calm, his focus on the magic that he should have been watching for every second. He felt the presence spark up and vanish again, gone too fast for even its victim to feel Winton peeping through his eyes.

Like Winton did with me, when he planted one of his talismans on me. Like when he used me to kill.

Mark kept his face toward Nolan, as if he'd never sensed the killer's will lurking somewhere among the dozens of unsuspecting cops. Another flicker came, and from the corner of his eyes he tried to pick out the face that matched it—

For one moment he thought he could see Winton's own eyes watching him, before the presence hid again behind the uneasy face of Osborn, the same M.E. who'd once examined... Angie's body...

Think! Mark tore his eyes back to Nolan, away from the puppet, before the red rage could fill his vision. The tests and the evidence should've nailed Nolan... but Winton had controlled Osborn before, he could be using him again, and other tools like Osborn to cover the truth up...

He's protecting Nolan? *After she chased Sasha all over town?* But Mark felt himself breathe again. Winton must be covering for Nolan just to keep attention away from any hint of magic, same as ever. He'd killed police to keep the secret, once.

"Is that—Christa?"

Henry's voice was hoarse, but still firm, and Mark saw Christa dash up the corridor to meet him and give him her shoulder to lean on. Henry was fine, of course he'd faced the police down and stuck with their story after all.

"You, you're letting her *go?!*" Henry stared straight across at Nolan, and his voice rang off the ceiling. "Where's Sasha?"

Nolan never turned away from her lawyers. But Mark saw Zeke at her side spin and glare a challenge back at them, and he could hear a hush tensing all through the precinct as if the police were waiting, watching for what they'd let slip now. And Henry hadn't even thought to sense Winton's power coiling here.

Dennard snapped "They're letting Nolan go, because Lavine's Finest have barely looked at their evidence. Not even how an 'accidental death' crawled into a car trunk to die. We can file a complaint for that."

Mark glanced from him back to Nolan—

At the corner of his eye, something moved. A shape slipping through the crowd, closing in—

"Osborn—" Mark gasped, a warning he would have shouted if he dared, but—

The possessed man reached through the crowd. He touched Dennard's back.

Mark felt the magic shift, and he saw Osborn pull back a step, mouth half-open as he woke and found himself across the corridor from where he'd been. Dennard's possessed face didn't even twitch, but Mark had to choke down a scream of *let him go!*

One second later, Christa said "Filing a complaint sounds appropriate. We were *not* drunk."

And Dennard… slumped. His measured resistance was wiped away as the puppetmaster spoke through him: "No, we might as well admit it. Drunk."

"What?" Christa's shout burst across the space. "You were just demanding, how did Irene really get in that car?"

She stopped then, and Henry whispered in her ear. This time he must have sensed what was pulling the strings.

But Dennard, Winton, took a slow step toward Nolan and her group. "Irene's death was a tragedy. But…"

Mark stared. He felt his side brush the heavy table there, and knew it would only take a moment to press it against the ceiling and prove magic was real, to *try* to stop whatever Winton was about to unleash. All useless.

Dennard's voice settled at a strong, low tone, almost like his real voice at the times when Mark had heard him exhausted. "We regret this happened. I suppose you want to sue us for false accusations next? You've got your lawyers right here."

And he clapped the lawyer in front of him on the shoulder.

Power jumped, leaving Dennard and seizing that lawyer and then moving on to the colleague brushing against him, to make that man pull back and reach toward Nolan.

His hand touched her.

Nobody else could have felt it, only Mark and Henry, from the soft brush of Winton's magic resonating against their belts. The simple touch, the flick of power—and the faintest curve of Olivia Nolan's lips—as a second flicker of the same energy threw Winton's control back and left the lawyer drawing away as if nothing had happened.

"Ms. Nolan?"

The lawyer was free. Mark felt the power wink out, and saw Dennard staring at the two but only edging away, in control of himself again as well.

Nolan had… her own possession magic now? God, *what was in that book of Winton's?*

Mark glanced back to Osborn, the one Winton must have planted a control talisman on. Sure enough, the power gripped him again, and his gaze slid to watch Winton's enemy.

"I think," came Nolan's slow, confident voice—and Mark saw her eyes flicking toward him, and then to Winton in Osborn, before turning back to Dennard and the crowd—"I think that my life isn't as easy to ruin as you think."

Dennard took another step back. "And that's it? You just walk away?" The tight words were more challenge than thanks.

Stillness hung thick around them, but then the cops' murmurs began eddying and swelling in reaction. A smothered cough came from the police detective.

Mark forced the words out, stepping toward Dennard. "It's no use. If the evidence isn't helping us, we should just go, and be glad it wasn't worse."

Dennard froze with his mouth in an *O* of surprise. Then his eyes darted past Mark—toward Osborn—and settled back on Mark with barely a hint that he'd noticed the man their enemy had used in the past.

Then the ex-cop let out a loud sigh. "All right. For now."

"You can't!" Henry's voice was rising again, his control slipping away.

"Are you both out of your minds?" the detective said. "You think you can make murder accusations and then just wipe them away?"

Nolan nodded. "I think I'd be happy to leave things where they are. I have too much to get back to."

"Then, thank you," Dennard said. He turned to the detective. "Looks like that's all there is to it."

The detective coughed, and spat to clear his throat. "For now, like you said. You know this is just Round One, and we'll keep digging into you and her both. Don't do something stupid."

Dennard grunted something back to him, and then raised his arms to herd their group down the corridor. Henry and Christa started dazedly across it, Mark and Dennard behind them, through the forest of watching eyes and whispers.

Mark felt his thoughts clearing from the shock. Of course, of course, Nolan wouldn't want to double down on public attention to their fight, any more than Winton would.

Walking just ahead, Christa looked back to Dennard. "How could you back down like that? It was just one blood test and a cop who saw only what he expected to."

"It wasn't that," Mark said. "Please, just keep walking…"

The human currents were moving around them now, and Mark's glance back could only catch a glimpse of Nolan's knot of people. He forced his thoughts away from what she must be saying about them, and all the eyes watching. *One step at a time, steady as Angie balancing on the winds outside...*

Winton's magic moved. It moved to follow them—not by walking, Mark felt the energy pulsing as it closed the gap, jumping from one person to the next to weave through the crowd like a spark moving up a twisting fuse.

Mark scrambled a step to stay with the others. And Henry's eyes went wide.

"You feel that moving? It's *him*—"

"Come on," Dennard cut in, low and controlled.

They pushed for the door—and the sudden briskness in their step made an officer up ahead turn to watch, suspicious. Winton's presence worked its way closer.

Mark brushed Henry's shoulder. "Easy..." and he held himself down to a quick walk. Winton could only jump along paths where people were clustered together. That had to slow him down, didn't it?

Still, it only took one touch. Winton could kill with one touch from a possessed body, and he might have done worse to Sasha, and nobody watching would even know what they'd seen.

Henry's face was pale and twitching trying to steal glances back. Christa kept her hand on his arm, but she couldn't *know* how it hurt him to use the magic too long.

Then Winton's presence fell back, and Mark realized they'd passed a wide room, where the people spread out and thinned Winton's supply of stepping stones. The crowd was tighter up ahead, but that was right by the door outside.

Mark strode forward and slid boldly between the people in their path, and the others kept pace behind him. The door stood so close now, Winton was still hanging back, Angie's owl presence waited in the air outside—

He felt Angie being flung across the sky, two steps before he shoved the door open, open into the blast of arctic air.

The clouds piled above the station were a heavy gray stacked as high as his eyes could see. The air bit into his lungs, and wind rolled against his face as the afternoon light darkened with a growing whirl of snow.

God, Nolan had hours *to gather this storm, and I missed it all!*

A young woman behind them called "Trust me, you don't want to go out in—"

They pushed across the parking lot, wrapping their coats against the whistling wind. Mark could feel Angie struggling back across the block above them. Out there Nolan could only freeze them slowly, but in the crowd Winton could still send a puppet after them at any moment. Or Nolan had the power to do that herself.

Mark's phone buzzed in his pocket.

He glanced down, as Henry gasped "It hurts… to breathe…"

Was Nolan *focusing* her cold on Henry? Mark clawed out his phone with numbed fingers, to see Nolan's text on the screen:

we shouldn't be enemies

And Henry heaved in a breath, then another, smoother now. Nolan had let him go.

Mark looked back across the pavement. Just behind the glass door, he could see a knot of people there—what had to be lawyers, an oblivious cop or two, and the woman who held their lives in her hands.

Two uniforms trotted past them, heads down as they made for the shelter of the station. The air was growing dark.

wheres sasha? Mark threw back at Nolan.

I'd still welcome your help Nolan answered.

Help? She had her weather magic, and now she'd blocked Winton's attack too. What did she need with them? Mark felt Winton's own grip hanging back beyond the entrance, watching too.

Wind slammed against them again, fiercer than ever, and Henry gasped.

Christa yelled "Get to the car!" She pulled Henry forward, wobbling a moment on the slick pavement.

"No, back to the police!" Dennard said. "Winton let us go once."

Mark looked between them, and back across to Nolan, untouchable with her untraceable weapon. His belt was *useless*—everything about canceling gravity only made them easy prey for Nolan's winds, ideal for allying with her but suicidal against her.

I could increase my weight to help me push through to get to her... no, down is the wrong direction...

The wind was blowing right in his face, leaving no shelter from the cars at his back. He took a step toward Nolan, then with a flex of thought he cut most his weight to let himself skip backward within the blast, twisting around and flinging up his arms as he *slammed* into a van.

Then, where he leaned against its grill, he sent power through his touch.

The van *lurched* upward—just for one creaking instant before the wind pulled it from his grip and it slammed down with its full weight again, suspension straining to take in the impact. Car alarms ripped through the howling air, and Mark saw figures all around the lot spin to stare at where it had slid whole feet across the snow.

Mark's phone was still in his hand, and his stiff fingers managed to text:

dont make me go over the top

Only two icy breaths later, the winds eased off.

He slid the phone away and stumbled toward the others. Dennard had wrenched open the back door of his Ford, waving Henry and Christa in.

Mark dove into the blessed warm shelter, and found his hands had closed on the seat belt and the ignition before his mind finished savoring being out of the storm. He eased the car out of its space and through the mostly-still lot, with all the care of a driver who'd had too much practice driving in a city under Nolan's power.

"Did that van *float?*" Christa said, sounding out the words. "That was you, Mark?"

One car? Angie knocked over a whole junkyard stack of cars, once, Mark thought. The memory stabbed at him, and kept him silent until he felt Angie soaring safely above them again. Along the street he saw cars pulled over to the roadside, drivers leaving more of the street open to the fast-gathering snow.

Then he said "The threat made Nolan back down. Just like everyone did with the arrest—she'd never let anyone realize magic is real. I think keeping that edge hidden is the only thing she won't stomp over if it gets in her way. Her and Winton both." Even her texts had been careful, nothing the police could have proved were threats.

"They'll still be watching her, and us," Dennard said. "We need to get out of sight. Keep an eye on that car that pulled out behind us."

Mark glanced in the mirror and saw Henry take a startled look back. A shape moved through the snow behind them, but the outline looked too trim and elegant for a police vehicle.

Coldness brushed through the enclosed air around them.

Dennard twisted the heat up to roaring, but his voice was tight: "So she's keeping eyes on us. If she's taking that risk, she'll ice up the police tails on us both, and keep on us to convince us we can't get away." He looked back at Mark, then at Henry behind them. "Because she can't let us get away. She'd lose the only two people who can trace Winton's magic."

"Unless she can do it herself now," Mark sighed. "I felt it, she knows some of his secret too."

"She what?" Dennard said. "Tell me exactly: what did you sense?"

Christa added "So that was what happened? Someone was possessed?"

"Dennard was," Mark said.

Dennard's eyes only flickered, nothing more.

Mark went on "You were. Just long enough to announce we'd changed our minds about accusing Nolan—I know how that sounds, but you were. Then Winton jumped from you to Nolan, but she *stopped* him."

"She what?"

"Blocked him from grabbing her. I guess all that really was in that book Sasha got from Winton, and Nolan took it. The one thing we needed, and we lost it."

"But Nolan's got that power," Christa said slowly. "And she's still trying to kill Winton, isn't she? And we know too much? And Winton is… is he still waiting to catch how you make these belts work?"

Henry muttered "He was protecting Sasha. She was our last link to finding him—you think Nolan got her before the police brought her in?"

A wind slapped against the car, useless against its weight. Mark's knuckles tightened on the wheel, but he only had to keep their course steady and assume the whole road was iced. Nolan couldn't hurt them this way.

He tried to picture the streets around them, and the way he should drive with such skeletal traffic and Nolan battering at them. *How do I shake her off? I thought I knew every twist in Lavine after all my cab driving and my flying.*

Another wind buffeted them, and this time Mark sensed Angie—

being smashed downward, helpless, *NO*—

and sweeping clear, somehow the mental presence of the tiny barn owl spun safely through the gust and slipped away from the unforgiving hard street and he felt his heart start up again.

"Look out!"

Dennard's words yanked Mark's eyes forward, to the truck that had stopped at the light ahead of them. He braked and the car *slid*... he could only hold on as it glided up and settled and halted half a length from the trunk's bumper.

The dark sports car that must be Nolan's stopped behind them, cutting through the storm as if the winds never touched it.

Mark counted only five wild heartbeats before the light changed and the truck lumbered forward again, but for a moment he saw frost on his breath. The car's heater chugged and labored as he edged them over to pass the truck in front.

"Outrunning her is suicide," Dennard said. *"Can* you lose her? It'll take more than getting out of her sight for a minute. This snow's leaving tracks."

"Take… take me back!"

Henry's voice was a moan of despair. Mark saw his face in the mirror, half-hidden behind his hands.

"Take me back to her, let me look for Winton for her again! All she wants is me—"

"You can't!" Christa was grabbing at Henry, whispering what had to pleadings and reassurances in his ear.

Mark brought the car around a turn, as quick as he dared, then up a sidestreet. Nolan only glided along behind them.

Dennard asked "Is Angie still…"

His voice died away. Was he weighing his daughter's chances to be human through bargaining with Nolan, instead of them finding Winton and the mind-magic's secrets themselves? But he couldn't track how every twist of the air made her struggle to keep from crashing.

"The winds!" Dennard said.

"Angie's handling them—"

"No, our tracks! When Nolan throws a wind at us, it covers up our tracks. If you can find a spot to use that."

Mark nodded, and stared harder at the half-hidden lines of the buildings ahead.

It had to be a sudden turn at some place Nolan wouldn't spot it, if they couldn't outrun her in the ice. And the road where they left had to be one with some traffic on it, enough to make her think they were still hiding in the middle of the cars. Not Riverside, not Evans, they'd never make it to Grayton… streets and patterns flashed through his head, but he fought to picture how those familiar routes would *look* to Nolan behind him in the blizzard…

One turn, and another; street names fell away leaving only the anxious sliding of the cars along them. Sound and cold faded, but he felt every buffet of air, every time Angie struggled to stay in the sky. He eased the pedal down, down, and pulled into what had to be the industrial traffic of Mormont Street.

Another wind smashed at them, Nolan pressing her attack for the moment they were out of her sight. And Mark spun the wheel to dive back for the rightmost lane and a tiny alley, dragging his foot back from the gas and his thoughts away from Angie, slowing the world to the floating, helpless instants of skidding the car toward the tiny escape—no, the van behind him was too close—and shoving the pedal once to dart past it and feel his tires slide, start to spin…

The crash felt like the whole world jarring loose, rattling teeth and flaring the air-bag out to fill his sight. But the noise faded, and he shoved the bag away and glanced back to see his riders awake. The car's back corner had only banged against the brick wall.

The wall of the alley, a good thirty feet out of sight of Mormont, and Angie soared away up that street. Nolan must still be moving on that way. They'd fooled her.

He took one more slow breath, before Dennard said "Everyone alright?"

"Just get us out of here!" Christa begged.

Mark turned the key… and the engine wheezed once and died. He tried again, heard it struggle and struggle but not turn over. The roar of the heater was gone too.

"So she's got us?" Dennard asked.

"No. Angie's heading on up the main street; I think she's staying on Nolan. And… maybe Nolan's giving up?" The tight alley cut most of the sound from the winds, but Mark thought he could hear them growing fainter.

"Please be gone, please be gone—" Henry broke off, and caught at his coat trying to straighten it. "My hands are shaking. Why can't I make them stop?"

Dennard gave a small, sad smile. "Welcome to the club, I guess. It's more than adrenaline this time. All that shaking, and the fear, and the feeling like you had something torn away from you—I went through it, and Mark did, when we let the magic get to us. And, weren't you the one who got him through that?"

"He's right," Mark added, and he tried coaxing the engine again with the key and pedal. "You just need time for—"

Magic moved above them. Not the ragged feel of Angie clinging to her owl, but the smooth, sinister energy of some bird under Winton's own control. Mark twisted the key over hard, still useless.

"What is it?" Henry gasped, his voice going shrill.

"Nothing." It popped out before Mark could catch it, and Henry's gasp proved his lie had only fed their fear.

Winton was still a block away, and Mark felt him shifting from side to side—still looking for them. But they were *stranded,* in a dead car in the remains of a snowstorm… Mark looked around at the dim, empty alley he'd crashed them in, and let the ignition key go. All the floundering engine did was announce their helplessness.

"It's Winton, isn't it? Or Nolan?" Henry said. "Don't scream, Christa, you can't scream… Can he hear us?"

Christa's voice was low and level, but it trembled. "But… you said his creatures had to touch someone to control them, didn't you? Unless he put a talisman on us? So, does that mean we're safe in the car?"

Not with that killer, he always finds someone he can use. Mark reached for the door handle—already cooling without the heater—but stopped. Running left them exposed, and floating all of them out… he pictured himself trying to hold onto three people in the snowstorm, trapped high over the city by wherever the winds went, just hoping the bird had lost sight of them…

Winton, or Nolan, veered closer. The presence swung toward Mormont, with a clear view up the alley. The narrow space of the car felt tighter by the second, hemmed in by seats and straps.

"How close?" Even Dennard's voice sounded shaken now. "Do we run or duck down? Mark?"

Then it came—the other presence, flying back above the street, rushing straight at the enemy bird. And the enemy only closed in on the car, blind to Angie's attack.

Mark caught his breath, held up his hand to halt the others' rush of questions. He tracked the two forces drawing closer… leave it to Angie to turn being an owl into the perfect weapon against her enemy's tools… if her claws could strike before Winton's magic touched her…

"How *close?*" Henry's gasp came, far away.

"Shh! Angie's almost—"

He felt her dive.

Mark yanked himself around to stare through the back window where the two presences would collide. Somewhere in the shadows of the alley walls, a flash of color moved through the snow, right in the invisible-gray Angie's path…

But she swung aside. He felt Angie roll aside and spin down past her target. Winton must have seen her, she must have known it was a trap, but still—

"She let him go??" Mark heard his voice crack, spilling his shock into the world.

Angie only watched, as the other bird flew closer. Mark had a glimpse of it before it passed over the car: a parrot. After all the nimble creatures and inconspicuous people Winton had used, now he sent a gaudy green parrot that could barely flap its way through the storm?

And it flew blindly into Angie's ambush?

That last fact settled it. The bird settled on the car's hood, and Henry growled in rage. But Mark reached over and slid the window down a crack.

Just a crack, enough to let the frozen air slip in. Enough for the one thing a parrot could do:

It croaked "It's me, Sasha. We have to talk."

CHAPTER TWO

PARROTING

Valens Street again... Mark crouched on a roof at one end of the neighborhood, looking over the dim maze of apartment buildings, as the last of the sunset faded behind the clouds.

Meeting here. He felt his anger tightening all over again. Sure, a crashed car that Nolan had just missed was no place for them to talk, but the parrot simply told him to come here? And still, Mark trotted into the trap.

And it had to be a trap. Even though Sasha's mother lived here, and last night Mark—and Winton—had saved her from Nolan and Rafe. It would still be just like Winton to bring him back to a place Sasha knew, one more way to pretend the mind behind the parrot actually was her. *All I could sense was that there was someone controlling it, something besides an accident like Angie being trapped.*

Cars and voices around the neighborhood were scattered, softer than the low breeze around him. He took out his phone, and his whispered words pushed those sounds back as well:

"I'm here. The parrot never tried to shake me off—and it came to the meeting place anyway, and then he, or she, must have released the control on it. No magic to track now."

"Too easy," came Dennard's answer. "Winton pretending to hide himself could be just more bait, so you wouldn't be thinking about the trap."

"You just get Henry and Christa out of sight. I'm only looking around, at a safe distance. Maybe there's still a reason to meet."

Dennard didn't answer that.

Sure, any meeting had to be somewhere. But… this was the puppetmaster, the killer, or else it was a frightened girl who thought Winton was a saint.

The cold of the roof tiles was seeping into his hands and knees. Mark leaped forward.

The breeze pushed against him, but he tightened his belt's magic to hold that momentum and push him through. As he did, he drew his arms and legs in, forming a ball of warmth against the cold—and to let anyone below who might look up see something less obvious than a human silhouette.

One of Angie's tricks—where is she? Mark couldn't feel her presence in the nearest blocks. Had she gone off to watch Nolan or some whole other plan instead of following the parrot? The owl's help was never something to get used to.

He drifted low over the next roof, letting him peer down into the shadows behind it. Those dim shapes at the end *could* be the pocket playground that "Sasha" had mentioned, but he guessed it would be deeper within the neighborhood. At least the lack of noises and streetlights hinted he wouldn't be stepping into another crowd Winton could use against him.

If he had any reason to go down there at all. Even if that parrot was Sasha, she was only a housemaid of Winton's that the manipulator had tried to give a book of his magic to, and Winton might not even need her alive much longer. *But I was just a friend of Joe Dennard's daughter who saw Dennard trying to destroy a belt.* Mark gritted his teeth.

As he passed the next building, he glanced over at a tangle of gray lines off to the side—could that be the meeting place? He pulled at gravity again to catch at his position and slow himself. But he held the anchoring pull too long, and felt all his momentum slip away, leaving him hanging immobile in the air.

"Stupid!" Once all his motion ended the magic had nothing to extend. With nothing his feet could push off from either, he could only let go of his grip in place to let the wind float him back, or else drop—or rise—for something he could touch or ride. He spat a curse and looked down at the dim, silent shapes below.

Blocks away, he felt a ripple of magic: Angie flying into his reach again.

Her presence—invisible-gray somewhere in the night, but a clear flicker to his sense of her energy—traced a wide arc along his left, and in towards him. She didn't search for the address the parrot had given.

Mark searched through his memories of the last three months. Angie as an owl had followed their words when she wanted, so the body couldn't be weakening her whipcrack-fast human mind. And why should it, just because that happened in folk tales? None of the other legends they'd squeezed out of the internet had matched how magical secrets and talismans actually worked.

Instead, Angie's silent presence swung smoothly, gracefully toward him. The last time she'd tried communicating with him, mind to mind, it had used up some of the mind energy that held her in the bird and kept her alive—

His shivering fingers clenched. *The parrot might be Sasha or Winton or anyone, but it still gets me one step closer to tracking down the possession magic that can get Angie back.*

"Mark?"

The voice on the phone made him bring it to his ear again. "I'm here." And he let his grip on space around him slacken so the wind could push him back—as if he hadn't been hanging in midair like an idiot.

This time it was Henry. "Just saying, we're all settled in at the hotel. And, I think I've got a text from your father."

"Don't you—"

Mark stopped and heaved in a breath, and let himself drop to the roof below. His feet slipped and scrabbled on the slope before he caught himself.

"Don't even joke about that," he managed to say. Wasn't the bastard in prison again?

"Sorry, sorry," Henry said. "I only… well, we needed to see if you were still you."

"A *test?* I go silent out here, and you think Winton got control of me? Well, again?" he had to add. Now that he said it, the words started to make sense, more sense than the old wounds clenching up his voice.

"Sorry," his cousin said again. "And… about everything else too, since yesterday. I, I've been jumping at shadows and hearing myself panic and…"

And trying to chase Winton without him, until Henry had seen how far Nolan would go to catch their enemy.

At least he didn't see how I risked Sasha's life too.

"We've all… been through a lot," was the most he could reply.

Henry didn't answer. The moment stretched, filled with the breeze along the roofs and the sense of Angie circling nearer.

Off to the side… he felt a low, faint pressure. Not the single flicker of Winton's magic in use, but a wider ripple of the same power. Like he'd once felt right at the edge of where Winton had hidden one talisman away to gather energy. That sense would grow painfully strong if Mark went closer.

Dennard's voice came in then. "You're about a block from where Sasha's mother lives, Elizabeth Lawrence. And, she's the superintendent around there."

Christa added "Nolan and Rafe already took this woman hostage once. Do you think Winton's using Sasha, and now he's gotten hooks into her mother too? Like the way he used me?" Her voice sounded sharp, angry.

Mark looked around. The streets were silent, but he thought he saw a patch of light in the sky, where the clouds must be letting a scrap of starlight peek through.

Just then, Winton's magic *winked* into place again. It took control of something on the path below, and Mark felt it moving toward the jumbled shapes he'd guessed were the tiny playground. That flutter in the shadows had to be the parrot settling on what looked like the edge of a bench.

Still just the parrot, no glimpse of Sasha herself that would let him sense if she were possessed too. If Winton had left her alive.

So… wait? Crouch on the roof and soak up the cold, hoping the bird did something besides sit there? Creep around the streets and let Winton think he was afraid?

"He's there. I'm going in," Mark heard himself say.

"No—" Dennard began, but he was already diving into the air.

Dim walls and a handful of lights in storm-shuttered windows slid by, and the bench swept toward him. He stole a moment to glance up at the bit of starlight in the sky, before focusing on the parrot as it looked up at his approach. His leap should put him right on the bench itself, dangerously close to the bird—

The bench! If he sat on it, and Winton had hidden a talisman in the bench's slats—

The wooden shape rushed up, and he wrenched at power to catch himself, and slammed to a bone-wrenching midair stop with his knees tucked up just inches from the bench.

The parrot squawked and flapped up—*away,* not rushing at him. Mark went weightless for an instant and tapped his hand high up on the side of the bench, enough to push off and step down onto the snow a few feet from it. Not *too* clumsy.

The pressure of a charging talisman was stronger here, like he'd dived into a tugging breeze that could grow into an invisible vortex somewhere further on. But he kept his eyes on the parrot itself, where Winton's or Sasha's power lurked all too close.

The parrot flew toward the playground's swing and settled on the spare tire. It passed a slow look over him. "Showoff."

Showoff? Was that what a killer said to an enemy who might have dodged his trap? It sounded too… petty for a body-hopping business-man who'd lived at least two lives.

Mark drew himself up, watching the parrot for any sign of it trying to close in on him. The corner of his eye stayed on the nearest door in the building; he felt Angie moving around too, better than anyone at spotting an ambush. A silvery lump glinted on the parrot's leg, the talisman that made it its controller's tool and weapon.

"Just practice. Sasha," Mark added, but he could hear his doubt as he said the name. Winton had manipulated them, pushed them, nearly killed them again and again trying to trick the secret of gravity magic out of them…

"I've been practicing too. That's why I wanted to meet here. I've got stones powering up all around here."

"I know." *Did I have to say that? Why admit I can sense the threat?*

But the parrot only looked at him a moment, an un-birdlike still-ness to its head. Then it said "Oh. Well, I remember the right words from Mr. Winton's book. Soon I'll have all the devices I need."

Would Winton tell him all that, so casually? "Talismans."

"Of course," it said. "Back when I had one of the talismans he made, he had to take me over whenever I was in trouble. Now I won't need any of that."

"Then… what do you want now?"

"More."

"Sure you do." He shifted a foot in the snow, readying a fraction more to leap away, and tilted his head to watch the side door better. Winton could have put those talismans out to tempt him and Angie, or just distract him. To sound the parrot out, Mark added "Here I thought you were more worried about Nolan hunting you."

"Yes!" The parrot bobbed its head, a wide motion that made the tire sway a fraction under it. "She— she chased me, she stole the book from me, and she's the one who's after us all. We both want to shut her down, don't we?"

"Right…" *Don't you ask me to kill Nolan—I'd crush* you *to bloody feathers if you didn't see it coming—*

"And we could stop her, I know we could! But I can't do it with the magic I have."

This time Mark didn't say a word, couldn't pull a moment's attention from tensing for the attack that had to be coming, and the dazed, distracting thought *did Winton just* tell *me he's going to grab the belt—*

"So I figured it out. What we need is to get the secret of her weather magic."

"What?" The word slipped out on its own. What was Winton playing, what kind of impossible trick was this?

The parrot chattered on "Don't you see, it's the deal we all need. We get my book back too, before she can learn to use it. And we get our hands on her magic, words and all. Think, you'll be able to fly without fighting through the wind—we both get to throw her storms right back at her. And after we've gotten that secret, I'll use my own magic to get your owl a real body—"

his heartbeat thundered—

he felt Angie *twitch* on her perch, right at that instant, *she understood that alright—*

"—but only after we get that woman's power. And, maybe we all learn more about why she's hunting Roger Winton."

It had to be a trick.

Mark's eyes stayed locked on the parrot, his knees stayed ready to fling him away even with his thoughts whirling with the confusing, impossible hope. But, what came out of his mouth was *"Why* she's hunting you?"

"Me?" The parrot's beak fell open, and hung there, a perfectly human expression that lasted for two wild heartbeats before the bird said "Hunting me? You think *I'm* Mr. Winton? Why would you think that?"

If he was wrong, if he'd thrown away a chance at someone *not* their enemy who could simply hand him everything he'd fought for… He could only say "After all the lies, you can really ask that?"

The parrot only stared at him, for long, measuring moments, with no sound and no expression reaching its un-human face. Finally it turned away and flapped once, to settle to the ground.

It slumped into sleep.

Mark crouched an inch lower, ready to dodge wherever the attack came from. But he didn't feel Winton switching his control to another pawn, anywhere around.

The parrot *had* sounded like Sasha… hell, the way it had talked about showing off, it could have been her trying to impress *him*. But Sasha could be the trap herself, if she still trusted Winton the way she always had.

If I let my guard down Winton makes me a murderer again, or whatever else he's after. Mark thought of simply leaping away, maybe risking grabbing some of the talismans here.

Angie took flight. He felt her presence loop out to circle around the night, in a low, slow glide she'd used before when she kept watch.

Up the walkway, he heard footsteps. A figure stepped around the corner: Sasha.

And with no magic controlling her. At least it was still her—unless Winton had hollowed her mind out and moved permanently into her.

Mark edged back as she walked up past him and gathered up the sleeping parrot in her hands. With her close, he had the moment he needed to strain his full concentration, and catch the faintest flicker of an unused talisman in her pocket along with the one on the parrot. The girl had the same pale face, same dark hair under the winter cap, and the same awkward way of blinking as she turned to look at him.

"It's really *me,* Mark—or Marty, or whatever your real name is. Is that what that Nolan woman's tricks did to you? Make you think everyone is someone else?"

"Sometimes they can be. I've seen it." He sighed. "So, after you put us and the cops to sleep, and ran away from the graveyard, what happened? Nolan didn't find you? Did Winton contact you?"

"No. I don't know why he hasn't."

Her gaze dropped, and her hands folded around her bird. For a moment she looked smaller.

"He… Mark, why would he use my aunt's tomb to hide the book? We weren't even sure she was dead. Does that mean you think you were right, that when Roger Winton's father knew her… that man was my father too? And my aunt was my real mother?"

"Maybe."

Or the Winton she worked for and the one her 'aunt' did were the same man, because he stole his son's body. *If that's true, she has a father who's a monster like mine wishes he could be.* Mark felt his jaw, his hands trembling; how could he warn her when the man had played her friend for years? *He fooled her worse than he did me, and he even steals his children's bodies.*

"I think," he said slowly, "I think you should remember how I was lying to you, back when Nolan had me fooled."

"Until she wanted to torture me. To hunt down Mr. Winton—I mean, my brother, or maybe not—well, she kept chasing *him,* and you saved me. But she still hates him, doesn't she?"

The trembling tightened. They *all* had reasons to want Winton dead, but Sasha didn't even believe…

But instead of that warning, he forced out: "What I mean is, I'd be glad to make that trade of yours, Nolan's magic for Angie's body. But if I were you, I'd be careful about family, and friends, and what you're told about anyone—Nolan, or me, or Winton," and he tried to make the last just another word. "When you have power like this, you're setting yourself up for dangers you don't even understand." Like naïvely letting Winton into her life.

But she was offering him Angie.

"Mr. Winton's always protected me before. A little like you did, when you turned against that woman because you found you couldn't hurt me." And she took a step closer.

Now she thinks I'm attracted to her? "Well, don't get the wrong idea."

He took a step back, and looked away. How could it not be all over his face, that moment on the way the graveyard when he found he'd rather send her body to Winton if it meant a chance at helping Angie? He had to live with what that moment meant, about how far he could go.

He added "I mean—"

Angie's low, shrill cry floated through the night. She followed her muted shriek by swooping along the walkway, the same way Sasha had approached.

"Someone's coming."

Sasha twisted her head toward the corner, and back. "How do you know— That's my mother! I have to go."

"Okay. But…" The warnings and reasons he'd been lining up fell into place, and the best one poured out of his mouth. "If you want to see why I'm doing this, be at the front of Grace Hospital at six tomorrow night."

"Grace—was that where we went to ask where Mr. Winton was taken—"

"Not that place. This one is different."

He turned and sprang for the side of the nearest building. Light, long steps swept him around the corner and out of sight in moments, to let him pause and lean against the cold wall.

Footsteps marched up the walkway.

Sasha called "I, I found the poor bird."

She started toward the other person, but those steps only accelerated and reached Sasha. "Is it hurt?" said the woman, her mother.

"Just asleep, really."

"What about you?" Her tone was tight, contained, but firm enough that Mark could just make it out. "Why ask me to hide you here after that thug's attack, if you're just going to let your pet get out?"

"I can handle—"

"By running out here alone? A man came after us with a gun—and this morning I find my sister really was dead all along. All these years, I was right."

"You thought she was dead?" Sasha's voice sharpened into outrage. "You only told me not to work for Mr. Winton, you never said you thought his father had…"

Mark leaned closer. Was Sasha finally starting to see?

"I didn't say he was a murderer. I know Isabel worked for him and left on her own, because I still heard from her for another month. But the Wintons ended up *burying* her, and never telling us?"

"Did you ever think… they tried to protect her? And Mr. Winton saw something in me too. But now I can't get in touch with him."

"Saw what in you? You said nothing was going on with him."

"Not like that! But I think we were friends—"

"I said the son of Edward Winton couldn't be someone to get involved with. I told you how many maids Edward went through—he must have done *something* to them, but Izzy never talked about it. And then that man's son wants to hire her niece—"

"Have you heard from my brother or not?"

"No! And Winton's not your brother, he's only a creep with money."

"If he was anything else, would you even tell me?"

Her footsteps broke into a run, with her mother's after her. Both sounds echoed and faded into the stillness of the neighborhood.

Mark straightened up from the wall. He began walking along the path, at a slow, easy pace that felt like a luxury now.

He brought up the phone, still in his hand.

"Did you hear all that? About Sasha and Winton, we still don't know what he wants with her, but she just *offered* us Angie's cure, and help against Nolan." The words came out more eager than he meant, and he added, "If we can keep Winton from snapping up the secrets of Nolan's magic. She'll give it to him in a heartbeat if he just asks."

"So you do think this girl is still Sasha," Christa said.

"But… could it work?" Henry asked. "If you beat Nolan and get Sasha's book back, is that everything we need? Could we use the book to deal with Winton too?"

"Keep your eyes open out there," Dennard cut in. "I told you, the better the bait, the more we could talk ourselves into the trap. Winton has his reasons, don't forget that."

Christa added "If it's too good to be true, it usually is—basic negotiation, I agree. But…" and her voice softened, "it could simply be that Sasha can offer what would be the best for all of us. And, I thought you said Winton's real body was bedridden, even when he escaped from you last time. Because Angie killed the bird he was inside, wasn't it?"

"Right," Mark said. "Since he had to be carried out of his house, right after that fight."

"Then, is it so impossible that he thinks he's dying, and wanted to pass something on to his daughter—or if she's not, she's still a friend?"

"Or he's still doing whatever it is to set her up as his next ticket out of death. Or something." Mark sighed. "And she thinks her biggest problem is she can't contact him."

"The man took over my body to get at Henry, and you," Christa snapped. "I'll never *trust* he's not up to something, but I'm just saying it's possible this offer isn't his doing."

"Possible, sure. Well, Sasha needs to know what else is possible. Tomorrow we can show her how far we'll go to bring Angie back, and tell her whose fault—"

Magic was flying, somewhere in the area behind him. The two presences caught Mark's attention, as one of Sasha's—or Winton's—birds flew deeper into the complex, and Angie swooped and twisted along behind it in what had to be keeping herself low and out of its sight.

He looked up at the small two-story building beside him. The complex had enough shapes like these to shelter him from the bird's view, but he couldn't launch with the busy street humming off to his left side… He broke into a quick walk, trying to picture how the buildings jammed together. Then, one quiet nook gave him the privacy to leap up to the frigid roof.

Pressing low and watching for people, he loped on all fours along the tiles and sprang to the next little clump of apartments. The bird was two clusters away, one cluster… Mark crawled backward to press himself flat on the roof's slope, down behind the rooftree. The parrot's stocky shape flapped through the air.

He felt Angie too, still keeping out of its sight. And… what had to be a block away, where the parrot almost melted into the background cobwebs of energy, lay the faintest edge of another wide field of a talisman gathering power. He saw the parrot headed straight for that space.

The next building ahead blocked Mark's view. He scuttled sideways along his roof's slope, and felt the bird's presence dimming, the deeper it flew into the magic's zone. Was that what those were, jamming fields put up against his sense of magic?

The parrot's presence was completely lost when Mark reached the side of his roof. He leaned around its edge, but all he saw was a shadowy canyon between two buildings out there; even Angie's presence had grown fuzzy.

Then the pressure dwindled, ebbed, faded away and left the birds clear as pinpricks on his awareness again. Mark's eyes narrowed, trying to place where the parrot lurked... somewhere in the shadows along that roof, or clinging under its eave?

And... another pool of power rippled and took shape, a tiny one barely larger than the bird itself must be. He felt the parrot glide out of it, and flap away.

"What is it? Mark?"

Dennard's voice in the phone was faint, but Mark realized it had been asking ever since he'd felt the parrot again.

"It's... one of those pools of energy, like the time Angie showed me Winton's talisman in that factory. Sasha said she was collecting power..."

"Can you get it?" Christa asked. "Is that what Angie needs?"

"Risky; the talisman's owner still controls it, maybe with bigger talismans. I tried using one of Winton's once, and he almost got me."

But why had this field vanished, and then a smaller one formed, why send out the parrot to it...

"The parrot can speak," Mark said, and he felt his own whispers leading his thoughts into place. "It can say any words, even magic ones—and this magic does use words, same as ours does, Sasha said she's doing this with words she remembered from the book. Did the parrot fly up there to start charging a new talisman? Was that it collecting one and starting another, and we almost heard..."

Angie was flying toward him.

He stared into the dim air, as her stubborn, battered power drew closer until he saw the gray barn owl take shape out of the shadows. She must have heard him, she knew what they both might have glimpsed, and what it might mean for her.

He clung to the roof's frozen side—knowing it was barely a taste of what she'd lived as an owl—and looked at the pale disk of her face, and tried to dig through desperate, tumbling thoughts.

"We almost heard the words. And we know the mind talismans use silver and jade… if we spied out the words we *could* be that close to working out the rest of it, and making our own talismans that they can't control…"

She shifted in the air above him, a beating wingspan shorter than his arm holding up a wind-frail body that must weigh less than a pound. The night air felt colder now.

"We could, *maybe* we could build you the power to hold on to yourself—and then start trying you in other bodies… but, we don't know, how'd we learn to control it? and there's so much that could go wrong if we just grabbed the secret, Sasha would never trust us again… but how hard can it be, if she's learned all this in a day…"

Winton would have spied out the secret; he'd turn lives inside out to get what he needed. And Nolan would force it, *and I already gave Winton one chance to take Sasha over… We can't.*

"We can't, can we?" His voice broke as he said it to her. "We can't risk you now, we don't know *anything* about what it really takes to bring you back… and she said she knew how. Angie, we might just need to hear one more whisper to save you… but I don't think it's that easy. Can we just keep our guard up, but give Sasha a chance?"

She circled in the air. *Angie, how much do you know what I'm saying, after all these months?*

It might have been a trick of the starlight. But he thought he saw her face dip in a nod… or else it was the first motion as she shifted in the air to fly away.

CHAPTER THREE

DREAMS BEFORE SLEEP

The hotel was cleaner than Mark expected. He heard scattered voices and one drunken fight from the doors he passed, and rumbles from the highway just outside, but the corridor was spotless enough that he felt all too aware of the skyload of snow and moisture dripping off his clothes.

And they'd be untraceable here—not like how Sasha had run only as far as the homes her mother managed, not like the dive Mark had once gone to where Winton himself had tracked him down. Dennard had picked this place himself, to keep them out of sight. He wished Angie had stayed with him to see it.

The invisible pulse of their talismans told Mark the room would be right near the back stairs. He stepped onto the second floor, and saw Dennard himself standing outside the door.

Am I betting right? Is working on Sasha really the way to get Angie back? Catching Angie's father alone made the question rise up inside him.

But, something in how Dennard leaned against the wall… like it was all that was holding up his weight…

All he said to Mark was "We've got just the one room, for tonight. Two rooms would be easier to trace."

As if he wasn't tired at all, or it made no difference. Mark felt his throat go tight, and covered it with a simple nod as he took the offered key card. Dennard stayed where he was.

The lights were out, and the room looked tiny. The low glow from behind Mark was just enough to pick out what would be Henry and Christa slumped on the floor with their backs against the bed, as if they'd fallen asleep waiting up for him.

Henry lurched awake, and his hand shot out to seize the other magic-charged belt where it lay. *I have that reflex too, any time I start getting addicted to the magic.*

The motion jolted Christa, and Henry turned to her. "Sorry."

"Stop *apologizing,*" she sighed. She stood up enough to reach the lamp on the nightstand. "Mark?" Light flooded the room.

"But we *are* sorry." Mark crouched down beside the two, the wall forcing him too close to the strange, makeup-smeared face of his cousin's girlfriend. He had to whisper: "All you did was care about Henry, and Winton dragged you into this fight. It's not right, or fair."

Christa's eyes shifted from bleariness to focus as they settled on him. "You mean, the same unfairness of how you care about Joe Dennard's daughter? You aren't complaining."

Mark fought the urge to edge away from her; the wall behind him wouldn't let him. The moment stretched, and somewhere from a room or two away came a burst of cursing from someone watching some late-night game…

The best Mark could do was force a smile. "At least I get to fly."

"So if you teach me how that works, then I'll think it's all worth it too?" Christa tilted her head. "Don't get me wrong, I'd love to know how that feels. But it seems like all of this power takes away more of our lives than it gives."

"I know." Mark's stomach churned. *I barely know her, how could I tell her how much I owe the Dennards?* And Angie's father was so close outside.

Then Henry said "One thing first." And he reached down to the belt beside him.

"Hey—" Mark's hand went out to stop him, too late. "You need to stay away from magic until you—"

"And we need to be sure nobody brushed against your back, froze your mind, and slipped a tiny bit of Winton's jade into your pocket. Isn't that what you keep telling us?"

His eyes on Mark slipped out of focus... then he let his breath out an eloquent sigh of relief.

Christa's fingers closed on the end of the belt, and for one moment Mark saw Henry's muscles tense before he let her take the talisman. In the narrow quarters, the motion looked oddly intimate.

I used to ask Henry to keep watch that I wasn't giving in to the magic again. But I still ran off and would have lost myself again, and I did it again last night... Mark swallowed, and peeled off his own belt. Setting it down felt like letting go of a lifeline, but holding it in the face of Henry's self-control felt worse. At least he'd been able to come back to them without the detour that would have brought the belt's energy up to its full, tempting strength.

Dennard stepped into the room, tucking his phone away as he did. "You still want to plan this tonight?"

Henry only said "Sit."

Besides the bed, the room had only one chair, and Mark was surprised to see Dennard motion him to it—until he realized his sides were still shivering from the cold flight. Still, he waved the offer off.

"So." Dennard settled down on the floor next to them; even his whisper carried a reassuring calm. But he didn't start with saving Angie, instead he said "We have two enemies, Roger Winton and Olivia Nolan. Both murderers. And we already tried having one arrested."

Christa added *"She* keeps saying she was trying to save us from Winton. And save herself, when that girl Irene tried to blackmail her, I suppose. Not that that excuses anything," and she glanced at Henry. "And, Winton wants to take control of every kind of magic?"

"Right," Mark said. "Winton used to be sending street gangs after Dennard, trying to force him to use the belt again. And he'll kill to get it, and to stop police or anyone from getting too close to the fact that it's real. For most of this time he's been too hungry for a look at how our magic works to really go after me, even though I can sense him enough to be a threat." And dodging Winton's spies had to be easier than facing the full-on assaults he threw at Nolan.

"He didn't go after me either," Henry added. "Even when Nolan had me driving around probing for his magic in every corner of the city. And last night she was trying to hack traffic cameras and dig through reports, about the time before when you almost caught his real body. You said he looked like he couldn't walk by himself—he must be too weak to really abandon that body—so maybe he hasn't gone far. All of those might tell us what parts of the city to go scan."

If it were that easy, we'd have Angie back by now... But there was an eagerness in Henry's voice that made Mark frown.

Christa's hand touched Henry's shoulder. "Might? What you're saying is, you'd go out there with all this power and hope you found him before you lost yourself."

Now Mark leaned forward. "That's one more reason to focus on Sasha instead. She has some connection to Winton, and she says she has enough magic to help Angie. Maybe she can, or at least it has to be worth something. We just don't know how much Sasha is really under Winton's influence—she thinks he's just giving his secrets away to her, but maybe we can convince her what that man is."

Christa spoke again: "And she'll help us if we get her book back, and... get her Nolan's magic too? How would we do that?"

"You heard the offer." Mark felt his fingers tapping on his arm, faster now as he explained. "I think it would mean breaking into Nolan's home, that's where she'd keep it all. We get the book, and anything like it that Nolan keeps about herself—and get our coat back too before she uses all its flying power against us. We just might get the power to match Nolan wind for wind, and in exchange for a share of it, Sasha actually puts Angie back in a real body… it's a perfect deal, with a huge *if,*" he added, trying to throttle back the excitement in his voice. "It's all *If,* Sasha can go through with it when we know Winton has to be using her."

"The whole trade sounds like his idea," Dennard said softly. "He gets Nolan's power from Sasha, and a shot at ours too if we don't watch our backs."

"I know, but…" Mark took in a breath. "How do we *not* try to warn her she's trusting a monster? Hell, a wounded monster, who has to be working toward getting a new body, probably hers. Do we ignore that? And it does something about our other enemy too—unless you want to beg Nolan to take us back, no matter who she kills next?"

Henry frowned. "Not her. But, a deal this good does sound too much like Winton's behind it. It may be the only way someone's willing to help Angie, but that doesn't mean the chance is real. We may have to face that."

"I *know.*" He pushed the word out before the bitterness could twist his whole mouth up; this was no time to snap at them. "Winton used to tease me with hints that he could bring her back, remember? Of course it sounds like him. That's why we watch our step, and look around every corner when we go into this. Because that book still looks like our best chance at getting more of Angie's cure than what Sasha learned from it, and watching Sasha is our closest line on catching Winton. And, on getting Sasha out of his grip."

"Still… Mark, you've already made up your mind?" Henry shook his head. "You could have gone back and taken those talismans—"

"I can't risk using them, remember? She made them, so if I stole them she might just take control of them—or Winton would—"

"No, Mark. I mean… you didn't ask us about them, you just decided yourself to leave them? You're not the only one in this now."

"But…"

He choked back the words *I'm not doing it for me* and met his friends' warning, too-close gaze. They were *right,* but he had to show them, convince them that this was the best chance for all of them.

Then Dennard said "But he *didn't* make a choice. Besides jumping in to talk with the parrot—and that was a rookie move, admit it," he added with a smile, "what Mark's done is keep our options open. We can still hunt Winton or try to use those talismans. But we can't leave Sasha out there alone. Working with her might protect her. And stop Nolan. It just might trap Winton."

Mark noticed he didn't mention Angie herself. But this gave them a chance at getting her Sasha's help, and the book Nolan had, or even getting Winton himself and the rest of his secrets. Mark waited, looking from Dennard to Henry and Christa. The roar of the highway filled the moment, stretching it out, but he saw their faces soften.

Henry said "You mean, we put the evidence together about how Winton uses people—like how he controlled Christa, and Mark? And we work on getting that ready for Sasha while we look for ways to get at her book and Nolan's magic?"

"That's right. See which works." Dennard's smile widened; he must know he'd convinced them.

Christa said "How *do* you get Nolan's magic and trade it? You don't mean stealing one of these magic gadgets from her. How does getting her magic work, can you spell it out—" She broke off. "Oh, sorry, I didn't see that pun."

" 'Spell'? I've heard worse," Mark said, glad he could laugh again.

"It's the same way Nolan and Sasha started making talismans like Winton's," Dennard said. "Winton must have put the process in his book, and Nolan should have something like that about her own magic. Or we catch her making them, the way Mark got a peek at Sasha tonight. But I expect there'll be notes somewhere—Kate, my ex, used to tell me magic's keys were too important to ever leave in your head."

Mark added "But once we know the secret, I think anyone can make them. Rafe stole the secret from me and had a whole gang jumping off bridges, and now it looks like Winton's got Sasha making his kind of magic. Nolan called herself a 'spellkeeper,' and said she got her own magic from her father. Dennard got it from Kate and her family."

And I took it from him, because the magic words are on the original belt itself, or something close enough is: "Made in Sha Ta Ruath." That and Dennard kept it right across from the street from the park where it recharges... but Winton and Sasha don't go to a single place—

Christa sighed. "So Winton has been stalking us all to learn your secret, and now you want to learn his by stealing Nolan's. I suppose that's beating him at his own game, unless it still *is* his game all along."

Dennard sighed too, deeper. "It might be easier to search Sasha's place, not Nolan's. Or watch her with those talismans. But we'll find out."

"Or we could take the book back from Nolan on our own, wouldn't that be safer—" Christa stopped. Then she said "I'm saying *we,* when I didn't know a thing about this yesterday. I think I've been pushing and challenging all of you all night. And I don't even have a reason to be here."

"Except staying alive," Henry said.

"That, and—" and she leaned against his shoulder.

Mark glanced away from the couple, down to his phone. "Sasha's mother said something else, about this Winton's father, that we think was just the last body the same man used. She said he went through a lot of maids like Sasha's aunt, so if he was using them for something, and we convince Sasha… Or it could just mean Sasha really is Winton's daughter from his last body. Not that that would save her."

"Fathers. About that…" Henry shifted where he leaned against the bed. "Before we go on, there's something else we may have to deal with. Mark, when we grabbed a few things from your apartment, I took…"

From under a pile of his clothes, he drew out a stack of envelopes tied together.

Mark stared. Heartbeats hammered like his pulse could crack open his skull. He heard Dennard's warning hiss of *Henry* before he gasped in the breath for:

"You took those?"

The shout blasted through the tight space, and he caught his breath and forced himself down to a savage whisper.

"You never thought there was a *reason* I never opened his prison letters? When you mentioned him on the phone, you weren't joking, were you?"

"Mark, he's my uncle, and your father. I wanted these safe in case you wanted to see him again, and he's out now—"

"Have you been talking to him?" Mark was on his feet, fist raised.

"No!" Henry lowered the bundle, but the bastard still glared back at him. "But… we may need to find him, because Winton or Nolan may go after him to get at you—"

"Don't you say it." For an instant Mark could see his mother again, her last breath slipping away from the drugs Bryan Petrie had left lying around while he was out dealing them… "We are not slowing down, we are not taking one step to worry about that man."

"And that's another decision you get to make yourself?" Henry said.

"We've almost got a plan, and now you want to stop and… *no!*"

He lurched away from Henry, toward the door. His feet tangled and he slapped a hand to the wall to catch himself.

Then Dennard was saying "It's alright. Besides, Winton and Nolan won't know to look for him anyway."

All three of them were watching Mark, with what had to be shock in their eyes. He pushed his hands down back to his sides.

Softly, Christa said "Did you ever think that this idea of warning Sasha about someone who might be her father could be—"

"Don't—"

He choked his voice off before it could rise.

Clenching his teeth, he tried again. "Don't start the head games with me. I've *seen* Winton do that, playing he was some kind of father figure when he bought my sketches, all as a way to use me. He doesn't need to be Sasha's father either, she's got no idea what danger she's in. At least she still has a mother—"

her hand going cold in mine—

"and Winton doesn't have her yet. And I need some air."

He scooped up the belt and clawed at the door, trying to twist it open.

"Slow down..." came Henry's voice. But Mark couldn't bear to look back, he yanked the door wide and dashed into the corridor.

One pull from the belt's magic let him leap down the stairs, and run on without a sound... *no.* He let the weightlessness slip away before he lost himself in that speed. Instead, each hard stamp echoing in the muffled corridor held him down on the floor.

Then the half-lit ceiling gave way to the endless, open sky. He lurched to a stop, before he could take another step that would fling him into that welcoming dimness, and let the magic dig deeper into his head. The sounds of the highway filled the air.

He sagged against the hotel wall—colder than the night air, but at least his head was clear enough to still feel cold.

And none of it changed anything.

"They don't get it." He clenched the belt tighter, banged his fist against the wall.

Kee-yak!

The soft call made him look up at the gray-brown shape gliding by. One thought flashed *Of course Angie would find us here,* but he only went on aloud:

"Well, they don't get it. They say I'm taking risks just to pull Sasha out of this, or else I'm stuck on getting revenge for Winton and his lies… I don't *care,* Winton's already done the worst thing there is."

She glided downward, wings spread to settle right toward him. Too close.

"No more mind-touches!" He dodged out of her path and let her sink past him. "We got lucky last time. You need what power you've got to keep yourself in that owl."

She landed on a hotel windowsill, just steps away. He moved closer, and her head cocked.

"And, I know none of the others will give up," he tried again. "We *will* find the answer for you, either from Sasha or taking it from Nolan or Winton. Your father's fighting for you, and Kate, wherever she is. Henry's all in, and I think Christa's tougher than she looks. And just knowing you're out there keeping watch, and how you spot trouble better than any of us, you always do…"

He broke off. That wasn't what he meant either.

Angie shook herself, and her feathers fluffed up as she shifted on her feet. Then she hopped into the air to beat upward, so slowly.

"Something to show me?" He moved after her, calling the magic to track her presence in the dark and take the step up to follow—

No, no more magic tonight. He slumped to a halt, helpless.

Angie only flipped around in the air and turned back toward him.

"Sorry," he said. "But… what I mean is, don't you give up. I don't care how long it takes or what it costs. We'll bring you back—"

She landed on his elbow. A single pound of weight, barely more than the air that carried her—

Her face filled his sight. He should be warning her, stopping her from spending any more of herself trying to speak to his thoughts, but all he could see was the disk of her face, a white heart-shape against brown and gray feathers.

"We'll get you back…"

She leaned closer.

Her beak twitched out, to give his nose the faintest, gentlest *nip*.

Then a rush of air and she was gone, soaring into the night and the street noises and the cold. He couldn't seem to move.

His face flushed hot.

* * *

"I don't like what you're getting at. Some kind of harassment, you mean? There *was* nothing like that. Edward Winton never did a thing to me."

The aging housewife brushed the blue streak in her hair and glared back at Christa from the doorway, and at the glowering Sasha behind her. Mark watched them from the rear, feeling the belt's power for any moment that Winton might peek through Sasha.

"I'm sure it can't be easy to talk about," Christa said. She took a step closer, and from the corner of his eye Mark saw an older couple on the sidewalk slow as they passed. Christa went on "Certainly after so many years. But tell me, would it make a difference if we had talked to the other women he'd hired, and they all said he'd tried to abuse them?"

That's a good what-if to offer, at least if any others had still been in town for us to reach. Mark wished he could join in, but this was still better coming from a woman.

"Said what? That they took a rest from cleaning his home, and fell asleep? Is that all?"

"Anyone could doze off," Christa said, but Mark heard her interest spark; she'd felt moments like that under Winton's power too. Her fingers gave her own hair a brush, matching what the older woman had done. "Still, did that happen to you at any other house you worked at?"

"I…"

Just the faintest hesitation. But he knew the sound of someone doubting themselves.

Then she answered "Nothing happened. And I'm sure the others didn't say it had either. You've got nothing to sue him for." The woman pulled her blouse tighter against the outside air; her patience was fraying.

And Sasha breathed a slow, angry hiss. He hadn't expected her to take these questions well, but he'd hoped she'd recognize something.

"You're sure? Just the fact that he had so many maids in three years— No, I see what you mean." Christa shook her head. "I apologize for taking your time."

"Thank you. I hope you're wrong." The woman closed the door.

They started down the fresh-shoveled walkway out, and Mark could feel Sasha's fuming with every step they took. Four steps, five—

"What was that about?" she demanded. "Are you trying to blame Mr. Winton for what his father did, the same as my mom does? Something that didn't even happen?"

"Did I ask about her falling asleep?" Christa slowed, and glanced at the strolling couple on the sidewalk drawing further ahead of them. More quietly she said "She's the one who thought of that. And she's an innocent person 'falling asleep' around someone with mind magic. Doesn't that sound familiar to you?"

Sasha's eyes only tightened. "Who are you anyway? Another friend of Mark's that he thinks is a victim?" She stepped around Mark to glare fully at Christa.

"Is that how you see us?"

But Christa edged back out of Sasha's reach. He could see her fear: Winton had gotten a talisman onto Christa before, and if he could use Sasha's to see through her eyes, any moment could turn dangerous.

Mark moved between them. "We're only trying to build a sense of how all of this really is. And, it did sound like a sign that Winton— Winton senior, I mean," he added, "was using some influence on people. And he did go through a lot of them." As if he was preparing something, a lifetime before he hired Sasha.

"Well, she said nothing happened." Sasha tossed her head. "And I'm sure I never blacked out or dozed off or anything, except when Mr. Winton needed to save me from that Nolan woman. Now I know what you're really asking about."

"Oh? And what is that?" Christa was almost hiding the taut frustration in her tone.

Sasha folded her arms against her tan coat, and Mark saw her take a slow glance around the neighborhood. Snow-coated trees and the stillness of the streets gave the block a quiet, idyllic look. The couple that had passed them on the sidewalk was already heading into another house.

"It's back to my parents again. You're looking for signs that Mr. Winton's father did more than that with those women. You still think I'm his daughter, his and Aunt Isabel's, and now Mr. Winton's my brother."

"It's one possibility—"

"I don't believe it. I think the man I know wanted to share his magic with a friend. And there's an easy way to be sure."

Mark said "There is?"

"My mother—my real mother—keeps saying I'm not any of theirs. And we did DNA tests years ago to get my real father's benefits when he died. Well, I just asked for another copy of their report. You wanted to meet me at the hospital anyway—let's go there now."

Christa said "Why don't the two of you go, then. I'm not being much help here."

"I'm sure it's not your fault." Sasha's voice had a touch of smugness in it. "Mark asked you to get to the truth here, when there was nothing to find."

Christa's lips curved in a smile, just barely. "Like that woman said, I hope it is nothing." She turned and marched away.

Mark watched her go, at a rapid pace that barely counted as a walk. He glanced back to Sasha: "Can you give us a minute? I'll catch up with you."

"Okay. But… do you think I was too hard on her?"

He swallowed. "It's fine, I'm sure."

Christa already halfway up the block. Mark scrambled after her, fighting the urge to cut his weight and skim faster over the slushy pavement. He tried not to think about her walking alone, blind to any of Winton's tricks that might spring up around her.

She had her phone up when he reached her.

"Henry says Nolan's dropping off some kind of package."

"What?"

She switched it to speaker, and he heard "She must have left it there. I can sense one of the bits of gravity magic still back there—"

Mark pushed the phone away, finger to his lips—at least nobody had been walking close enough to hear it.

Christa flushed, and switched the phone off speaker. "Sorry, Henry. And you two are alright?"

Dennard was speaking just as Mark joined the call: "—don't think she's spotted us. I don't see any police on her either—could be that watching her's not a priority, could be Winton pulling more strings."

Mark added "But, why's she leaving a bit of our… stuff there? What did she do, cut it off the coat I made?"

"Probably," and Henry actually growled. "Well, every bit cut away is less power left in that one brain-melting chunk."

Dennard said "She's on the move now. Anything else? If not, better let us stay focused—we'll check in next time."

"I'll remember," Christa said. "Good luck."

They hung up.

Then she looked at Mark, hands tight on the phone. "In a few minutes, I've alienated what could have been a lead, and Sasha in the bargain. And now I almost gave away our secrets on the street. You'd tell me if I was getting in the way, wouldn't you?"

Angie would. And then I'd have to apologize for her. "I… it's fine. Just, try to stay in the subway until Henry can pick you up."

"Because it's one place Winton can't search by air, isn't that what you said? Since only you and Henry can know if he's watching us, so I should concentrate on not letting him spot me at all."

"Right. And, I'm sorry if Sasha treated you…" He trailed off.

"Really, I suppose that's how we expected she'd react. When someone trusts her with a secret like this, of course she hates to believe he only did it to use her. All the same," she added, "I think if a stranger took the time to warn me about that, I would have shown them a little more kindness."

"We'll make her listen."

* * *

Mark and Sasha took the subway themselves. Sasha gave him a hurt look when he asked her to ride in the far end of the car, out of the line of sight of him. It did look less and less likely that Winton would even try peeking through her eyes, if he could.

Still, when they reached Grace Hospital, she was eager to let him hang back when she met her mother. The two of them in their matching tan coats moved inside, and Mark kept at a distance behind a huge family that trailed chattering children, peeping around them to watch the pair.

Then he felt Winton's power moving.

It didn't grip Sasha or her mother, instead he sensed it advancing through the building ahead, closing in from what had to be a corridor to the side. The two women were just approaching a door with a logo of a figure embracing two children—maybe the "family testing" Sasha had mentioned. And Winton's pawn was closing in on that.

Mark clenched his teeth, and told himself Winton wouldn't strike at Sasha right here. Before the killer could reach the main corridor, Mark ducked up a side turn out of view.

People filtered past him, trailing muted, professional voices or the rattle of a supply cart. One nurse gave him a curious look, and he pulled out his phone to deflect questions about himself standing around. Beyond the corner, he felt Winton's puppet reach where Sasha and her mother had been, and that door with the logo.

He settled in to wait, and think. Even now that Winton did steal a look at Sasha, the puppetmaster didn't tap into her own mind again? But… Winton still had to have a talisman somewhere here already, and that meant he'd known they were coming.

The phone at Mark's ear buzzed. Somehow he kept from jumping.

"Is there anything new on our enemy?"

Kate's voice. Angie's mother, calling from… wherever she and her son had gone into hiding.

"I'm… watching him now." He edged back down the corridor, slowly enough to feel for any sign of Winton heading out into view. "And he's watching Sasha and her mother. I think this time I sensed him in time to stay out of his sight. Unless he already knows I'm here too."

"And, you're afraid anything you do could trigger something drastic from him." Kate spoke as firmly as if her guess was certain.

"It's a hospital full of people, I *have* to hope he won't go past watching them. We just found a hint that he might have been practicing—"

He stepped around the corner to see the door again. His gaze fell straight on a stocky orderly who gave him a narrow, suspicious look.

Mark eased to a stop, not risking pulling back at once. More softly he said "—practicing his magic on those girls when he was Edward Winton, and Sasha didn't believe us. She thinks it's all about whether she's his daughter—I'm trying to tell her, it didn't save his *son* from him stealing his body."

"It… may not be that clear." Hesitation edged into Kate's voice, that Mark rarely heard from her. "I've finished my investigation into the town where Roger Winton grew up."

"Wait, you mean where the father's body died? Did you get any evidence of him taking over? Or who started the fire—all part of the father's plan, or was it the son trying to defend himself?" Mark heard his words hissing now, more fierce the more he forced his tone to a whisper.

"I said it's not that clear. For one thing, the pictures of both—"

The deadly flicker of Winton's influence moved, out toward the room's door. About to see him.

This time Mark lunged back around the corner, ignoring the startled look from the orderly. He marched up the corridor, quick as he could without breaking into a jog. He felt Winton's pawn moving toward the branch at his back. All Mark could do was slow, and hope the killer had no reason to glance over sideways.

Winton moved on past his corridor, not even slowing.

Mark gasped for breath, and let the enemy pass further out of view before he pulled the phone in again.

"Sorry, just dodged Winton again." He turned back; Winton was drawing deeper into the building now. "At least he's left Sasha and her mother. And if he's concentrating here, he's not going after Henry—or Batiste."

"Batiste?"

"Well, Batiste was the first one to notice that this Winton acted too much like his father. But Sasha's not ready to meet him yet. Unless you found out something more that'll open their eyes."

"What we found… is this really the time you can stop and listen, Mark?"

Just as Kate said it, Mark saw Sasha and her mother walking away past his corridor.

"Oh." He sighed, let out a breath. "No more pushing my luck, sorry. So, later?"

"When we can. You be careful."

Mark shut the phone down, and moved after the two women. Winton's presence was further away than ever—he had to have some other plan for that body, or just a way to keep its owner from noticing any memory gaps. That left Mark free to draw closer to Sasha and her mother.

The two moved with a brisk pace, trading sharp looks between them. He could just catch Elizabeth Lawrence's words:

"—hope you're satisfied. The truth is the same as when I sued your father. I'm still your mother, your father's still a soldier and still long dead. And you questioned that again, why?"

"I just… had to." Sasha's voice was lower, but it had a firmness that held its own in the hospital murmurs.

Mark frowned. So Sasha wasn't a Winton… or had Winton looked in because he'd been covering up the test results?

The older woman went on "But you picked right now to ask again. One day after a man with a gun came looking for you. After finding Isabel's…" She whispered a word that might have been *grave*. "Admit it: you're hoping to make some kind of inheritance claim with the Wintons. About being their child and my sister's."

Winton's attention was still far away, good.

"Mom, I'm *glad* I'm not related to them. Of course you didn't lie to me. Plus, it means Mr. Winton didn't either—"

She broke off, and her gaze flicked back to Mark behind them. He saw her eyebrows begin to rise… and stop, holding in her reaction.

Then her mother stepped ahead of her, blocking her off. Her gaze speared into her daughter. "So it's about the *Mister* Winton you know? What did he really do to you, and what are you trying to get out of it—and who sent *you?*"

Her eyes locked on Mark, too close.

"Sorry." Heat flooded his face, and he turned away. *Please, let her not remember her glimpse of me from stopping Rafe.* "I didn't mean anything, I've got to get to—"

She stepped in front of him, arms crossed. "No, don't go. We've had too many strangers interested in my daughter. One pointed a gun at my head a couple of nights ago, until someone else killed him. And now you? You tell me, right now, what she's gotten mixed up in."

"Mom!" Sasha stepped around her. "Mark's a friend of mine. He's not in some conspiracy—and we're leaving before you embarrass us more than you just did." She grabbed at his arm.

"Don't you walk out on—"

But Sasha tugged Mark away in what fell into a quick trot down the hall.

Behind them, he heard a shout of "You call that nothing? No trouble, no schemes? Sasha!" and then the layered murmurs of the corridor sounds swallowed her voice up.

The hospital entrance was in sight before Sasha let his arm go, and they slowed to a quick walk. But the outside in the twilight was where Mark had wanted them to meet all along.

"Sorry, Sasha. I didn't mean to overhear all that."

"Didn't you? You were creeping up behind us, but not spying on us?"

Sure I was, but not like Winton did. But Sasha wouldn't listen to how deceptive Winton was, not just yet. "Well I, I wasn't sure if you'd told her about all this." They stepped out into the fading light and the people at the entrance.

"Mom thinks I can't..." Sasha's eyes lowered for a moment, then back to him. "Anyway, I'm not related to the Wintons. He gave me his magic for *my* sake."

"It looks like it. Except, he hid it at your aunt's grave? Did he ever tell you why he picked that spot to leave the book? Or, told you anything since then?"

"What's that mean? What are you hinting at now?"

"Just... please, did you tell him you were coming here? That it was my idea?"

"Isn't that my business?" Sasha waggled a warning finger at him. "I don't need to tell you."

So maybe she already has. Can I even trust her with anything?

He had to.

"Please…" Mark managed a calming grin. "I didn't ask you here to fight. But please, don't tell him any more, until I've shown you enough so you can make up your own mind about all this. I wanted to show you the reason I'm taking on Nolan and the rest of them. It's this way."

The main building would be ringed by people all the way around. So Mark led her past its corner and toward a side structure, a research wing squeezed in among several other towers of glass. This complex would be a maze for someone who'd only seen it from the ground.

When they stepped in among those shapes and left the main crowd behind, Sasha turned to him. "Listen. I don't see what difference it makes if I'm related to the Wintons or not. I know my mother loves me, and I know that now I've got this magic, that makes me stronger than Nolan or that Rafe muscle of hers. Maybe I could… do what Mr. Winton did, that made sure Rafe won't be bothering me again." She smiled, but there was a quaver of fear in her voice.

"So you feel like you're invincible now?"

Sasha simply raised her hand and reached toward his arm again.

Don't flinch, she wouldn't do it, except she did it before—

"I can knock someone out by just brushing against him." Her smile widened, and her fingers closed lightly on his elbow. "I don't even need to, well, shut him down like Rafe was. And I can use someone, or some animal, to see through their eyes. And I can put your owl into a real body, but only when we finish our deal. Like you said, I didn't come here to fight."

Was it that easy for her to talk about Angie, and withholding her cure? Sasha was posturing, that had to be it.

This stretch of walkway between the buildings had nobody in view, not at this hour. Mark drew the belt's power through himself and through Sasha's grip to float them upward.

Sasha flinched back in the air, but he caught her hand before she fell away. Good, he'd broken through her screen of false confidence.

"Well, the magic's scared me sometimes," he went on. "And I don't mind saying Rafe used to scare me before this, all through school—"

"Don't... don't you try to rattle me." Sasha stared at the ground falling away.

"I mean, Rafe was bad, and Nolan's worse. And you think you're just stronger now that you've got the best magic?"

"I wouldn't say it like that, but..." Sasha glared back at him. "It *is* better than this flying. So whatever you're showing me, I've already seen it."

"You haven't seen this."

The touch of breeze announced they'd passed the upper rim of the building. Mark loosened the magic to let them drift freely, and they wafted over to its roof and dropped to clatter down on asphalt. Sasha barely kept her balance.

He went on "It all takes practice. You didn't start using Winton's talisman as soon as you grabbed it—first you saw *me* use it to help Angie, or I tried to. But once you took it, it was Winton possessing you through it that let you make it to his book."

Sasha looked away, and seemed to pull into herself. "I... know. Look, I'm still trying to find all the ways I can use this. But it gives me so many tricks—that means I'm stronger than anyone now, except Mr. Winton. And maybe that woman who stole the book."

"More uses, it certainly has that," Mark nodded. "And sometimes I think doing any of this is about realizing how much of the world just opened up to us." He motioned across the rooftop, through the tangle of generators and pipes.

Sasha's grin came back, so fast Mark knew he was right. She *was* trying to prove herself—no wonder she wanted to get her hands on Nolan's magic too. *She might give it to Winton just to show off to him!*

He led her on past the humming metal shapes. Even in the dimness, the machines had enough space to walk easily between, and he knew the way. Almost there.

"And the more we get to know our power," he went on, softer now, "the more we have to make some hard choices. Nolan used Rafe to do some of her dirty work, but before that it was Winton was using him."

"No… And then Rafe betrayed him, right?"

"You could say that." *After Winton didn't deliver the gang leadership he promised, and after he possessed Rafe as part of fooling me.* "Rafe was part of a street gang, that Winton took control of." *And later Winton used me to murder some of them.* "Another time there was the sniper that Winton used. And before that—"

They reached the far edge of the roof.

Mark handed her a small set of binoculars and motioned out toward the wall of glass across from them. "Second floor from the top, on the corner. They leave the curtains open."

Sasha aimed the lenses, and he heard her gasp.

He knew what she was seeing: the sunken, shrunken figure in bed trailing thin wires and thicker tubes to the banks of machines. But Sasha wouldn't know the woman was still in her thirties, she wouldn't pick out the smoothness in her face where it hadn't sagged over the bones, ringed inside the limp brown hair. Sasha couldn't hear the soft, rubbery breathing that would fill the room.

"Is… that… your Angie?"

"No! Her name's Melissa Davis. The records say—" Mark took the binoculars and searched for the rows of flowers on the table beyond the window; two bright bundles of silk petals and one old, drooping shape half-hidden behind them. "There's no medical chance she has any mind left. But we think we can move Angie into her and wake her body up."

"Wake her?"

Sasha spoke in the faintest whisper, as if she was afraid her words might stir the patient herself.

"We've checked every way we know; this woman is gone. But I've seen Winton's power pull drugged people awake, so that's a start."

Sasha turned away. "You can't... you want me to... and if it worked, then she'd have to get better, inside *that?*"

Mark leaned closer; finally, Sasha was starting to see what they fought for. "Angie should have been *dead,* so she's already beating all the odds. Or if this body is too far gone, we know there are other patients, in other cities."

"You'd try it again and again... what if she gets *stuck?*" The last word caught in Sasha's throat.

"Angie can—" Mark smiled. "You *really* don't know her."

"But I..." She stumbled back from the roof, from the view below. Then she straightened up. "I'm... sure I can fix her, it'll be easy. But we get Mr. Winton's book back, first, a deal's a deal." Her voice quavered with doubt, but she went on. "We get the book, we save her and we get that Nolan woman's weather secrets too. That'll show Mr. Winton what we can do."

I knew it. " 'Show' him? Was going after Nolan's power his idea?"

"No! That was me!" She reached out toward Mark's arm, but halted. "I haven't heard from him since the graveyard. But... you never told me, how did Angie get in the owl?"

Sasha's hand was so close, close enough to strike at him. Mark concentrated on her pale face. "You know how. Winton."

She shrank away. "But... it was an accident, right?"

"No." *Except that she survived. And that it wasn't me instead.*

"But... it must have been..."

Sasha's hand twitched toward him again. Mark held still, and felt for her magic, to sense if she readied it.

Something else moved, gliding out through the open night. The delicate, deadly power of the enemy.

Sasha's voice was only a breath now. "I, I don't believe Mr. Winton did what you said. Can we... can we just go get the books—"

"Get down."

He pulled her back toward the humming of the largest generator, and Sasha staggered after him and they crouched down behind it.

How long had he let his guard down, if Winton's bird had gotten that close? Or had Winton only just taken control of it—because he had a bird with a talisman waiting here?

"What is it? Are we hiding from Mr. Winton?" Sasha's voice spiked in anger. "Or is it Nolan using—"

"Shh."

Mark pressed them lower, hoping the generator's hum could cover their voices. No need to peep out; he tracked the bird's magic passing over the opposite building, holding his breath until it moved right by that window. It didn't slow, as if it had no reason to watch that one particular patient.

"I said, is it Nolan—"

"Please!"

His word must have gotten through this time, because she went silent. The bird swung around in a wide, high circle, and Mark glanced up at the dim metal shape they crouched behind. Could Winton see them, how hard was the bird searching?

Angie would have sliced it out of the sky if she were here.

Finally, it moved on to the far end of the hospital complex, and the magic vanished from it. Mark let out a slow, deep breath.

Sasha edged back from him. "So it's over? *Was* it that Nolan woman?" Her voice was trembling.

"I can't sense who controls them, except when it's Angie." Mark stood up. "But getting a bird out here seems like fast learning, even for Nolan. And you told Winton you were coming here?"

"I said I didn't. But what would it matter if I did?"

Winton lies and murders, and we think he stole his own son's body, and you won't even hear it!

Sasha was drawing another step back from him. Mark tried to let the anger fade from his face.

He settled for saying "What if," so softly, "just what if, Winton wasn't innocent. You say going after the books is your idea. But if it's

Winton's plan, he could watch us and then step in and grab Nolan's tools and your book, and never let you help Angie."

"He wouldn't—stop saying he—"

"But what if he did? Don't give him the chance—"

Mark's phone vibrated.

He glanced down at it. After Kate, hadn't he set it not to signal him at all? No, Dennard would still be the exception, in case there was trouble with Nolan, but *now?* He pulled it out.

On the screen was a video, marked as a live stream from Dennard:

The Lavine university commons, looking up broad stairs to a young woman fighting to hold a snarling black dog back by its leash. The animal was straining toward the steps—but not toward Dennard, the camera's view was from somewhere off to the side, and the dog's gaze was on something else out of frame.

The *possessed* dog, it had to be, trying to reach its target. Just a minute after a bird had been searching the roofs here all the way across town.

Startled, confused voices spilled from the phone, sounds with the muffled, out-of-reach quality that kept the desperate tiny figures on-screen from being as close as some real-world window. Motion rippled through the people as they backed away from the "maddened" dog, with one or two moving forward to help.

The dog tore free and leaped down the stairs… and slipped, skidded, tumbled to the pavement below and scrabbled up. As the camera followed the attack it caught a glimpse of the woman stumbling away from the dog—Nolan, with her assistant Zeke stepping between them. Something glimmered under the dog's paws that must be one of Nolan's ice slicks.

Mark couldn't breathe. One enemy attacked another before his eyes, and Zeke fought loyally to defend the murderess.

"Is *he*… doing that?" Sasha crowded in beside Mark.

As the dog lunged forward, a big man stepped out of the crowd, a cardboard box of books in his arms. He charged into the dog's path and swung the box in a sweeping, awkward blow, and the beast tumbled away—

It went limp where it fell, just as Mark saw the box fall from the rescuer's fingers and him casting a look around. Not following the threat but to get his bearings—and his gaze went straight to Nolan. The dog had *touched* him, and Winton's control had jumped.

"I think it's down," the puppet said, his young voice sounding eager to help. "Are you alright?" He started toward Nolan.

"Thank you, fine," and Nolan spun and walked away.

"Olivia? what—" Zeke began.

"Here, just let me—"

Winton's puppet advanced, but Nolan broke into an open run down the campus. Zeke stared after her, and her pursuer ran a few steps before slowing.

Something blurred in the air. Snow, maybe to go with more ice slicks to protect her—the image already looked grayer. Could all those people really watch yet another sudden cold snap and never suspect?

"Did you get that?" came Dennard's voice. The video cut off.

Mark brought the phone up, forcing his eyes not to flinch away from Sasha's shocked face. "Got it. Can you catch up with her?"

"Can't. I have to get Batiste away—Winton's going to figure out who she came to campus to see."

"Oh." Mark felt cold rushing through him, as if he could feel Nolan's blizzard through the phone. Dr. Batiste knew a little about Edward Winton and his similarity to his "son"… before, Mark had taken care to approach him without Winton knowing… but now Nolan had led Winton right to him—

"Miss Nolan was right there," Sasha breathed. "So who was here with us just a minute ago?"

"Probably Winton too. His real body is somewhere safe, so he can switch between different talismans as fast as he wants, anywhere he's put them."

"You mean he can be everywhere at once. I can do that too, right?" That was a tremble in her voice, fading.

"Sure. And look how he used that power."

"Of course he went after her, that woman keeps chasing us. She almost froze me solid last time… and you, you had a friend watching her all this time?"

"Well, yes, we had to—"

A thought tumbled forward from the back of his mind.

"Sasha, Nolan's on the run for now. She might be calling up a full-sized snowstorm to stop Winton from chasing her, and that can cover *us.*" He flipped the phone to its weather app, checking the spread of the snow. "Ready to make our move?"

"You mean… now?"

"Her home's empty, she's distracted, we've got a storm to sneak in through. If she comes back, we trap her there. You know a better time to get your book back, and the rest of it?" Mark felt his smile growing.

Then he looked at Sasha. She was huddled back against the generator, huddled in on herself. "I can… I want to, but watching those two… Mr. Winton could have killed her…"

Mark's phone buzzed in his hand.

For whole heartbeats he stared at it, before he flipped away from the weather app to the video.

"Too late," Dennard's voice came.

On the screen, Dr. Timothy Batiste lay slumped in a classroom in the middle of a crowd, shocked young students and two dazed older men trying to wave them to calm. At least the old professor's wrinkled neck seemed to have breath stirring through it… an angry face glared into Dennard's lens, and the view pulled back.

"Who is that? Who?" Sasha whispered.

Mark's throat tightened grimly. "Someone who knew the old Winton. If that's mind magic putting him to sleep, I don't know if he'll wake up at all."

"You mean…" Sasha's pale face was ashen, bloodless. "It's as bad as a coma, like that woman you showed me, but this time the power *made* it happen? Nolan's just… *perverting* it all!"

"Or… it wasn't her. Batiste knew the Wintons." Mark laid each out word slowly, inevitably, trying to think how Dennard would put it. "That's knowledge that Nolan could use. Knowledge Winton could want silenced. Like he silenced Rafe, but at least the doctor's alive."

"No… he wouldn't… I mean, the book had whole things about how we had to keep it all secret, but—"

"But I knew a cop who got too close to Winton, Detective Lee— dead now. Nolan did this kind of thing too, when a friend tried to blackmail her. But Winton—"

"It's. Not. True."

Winton killed Rafe's thugs using my own hands. *He played the gangs, he got Angie, and we need to—*

Sasha was shrinking away from him, the desperate denial on her face cracking with what looked like the beginnings of crushing fear.

Mark shook his head, let his fingers relax. She wasn't ready for it all.

He said "The rest of us can take this tonight. If Nolan keeps the storm up enough to give us cover, I can get in, maybe before she gets back at all. If we're right about this, we can get what we need to block Nolan with her own magic. Just don't tell Winton until it's done, don't give him a chance to grab—"

"So *I* don't get a chance at the magic? You grab it yourself and you're all set to keep it all?" Sasha pulled herself upright, though her knees were still shaking. "This was my plan! And I have to be there!"

"Have to be?"

"That woman tricked me, and she chased me all over town. And I let her take the book that was supposed to change my life! This is my chance to stand up to her, finally—no, better!"

A slow smile started over her face.

She laughed. "With power like mine, I don't even have to go near her. You just help me with some of the parts, and that's how we'll beat her. It'll be easy."

CHAPTER FOUR

SCISSORS CUTS PAPER

Setting it up took longer than he liked.

The blizzard faded, by the time Mark's ride brought him out to the hills above Nolan's home. Every minute raised the risk that Nolan had gotten there before them. Until…

"There! That's Sasha, flying in!" Mark stared out the car window through the trees, trying to match the sensation in his head with the night-softened curves of Nolan's Orchard Heights hills. Had Angie spotted the bird yet? "Unless it's Winton."

"This is about when Sasha's parrot should be reaching you," came Henry's voice through the phone. "And there's been no magic from anywhere around Sasha's room since she sent it out."

"And if Nolan looks for her here, Henry and I'll be ready," Dennard's voice added.

From the seat beside Mark, Christa asked "Do you really think this will work? Can we get the weather secret, and Sasha's book for Angie, and—"

She stopped, but he knew what she couldn't say with the phone line open: *and keep it all away from Winton?* That was the other danger that Henry's senses would be watching Sasha for.

"We have to make it work— The bird's gone."

The magic in the approaching bird had vanished. He felt only Angie circling above.

Then Sasha's voice came on the line:

"There's nothing around her house. I'll keep watching—the parrot's eyes don't see too well in the dark. But we'll have the books and fix Angie in no time."

"Thanks," Mark began, but her magic had already reappeared in the sky, and he knew her human body with the phone couldn't hear him.

She sounded too confident. Like now that she didn't have to come anywhere near Nolan in person, or leave her body unprotected since Henry and Dennard were there, she thought nothing could go wrong. Or else she was trying to push through her doubts about this world of magic and danger—he knew all about that need.

He stirred his chilled, stiff limbs from the car seat, and glanced over at Christa, huddled tight in a second coat and blanket, rather than turning the heat on and risk any wisps of steam someone might see. "Are *you* sure you want to stay here alone?"

She nodded. "Do you really think 'keeping the car ready, just in case' is so hard? You three can't take all the risks here. And I don't need to see an enemy coming, I just have to stay awake."

"As long as they don't see us here." *If they do it's because I'm stalling, when I should be going out to keep any attention away from the car.* "Stay safe."

He caught up the pack with the tools they'd picked, and stepped out into the night. One leap and then another swept him up the dirt road, before he turned to plunge in among the trees. The bird was still closing on Nolan's estate below, but Mark had to be far away from Christa's car before he stepped into the open.

Then he twisted around one last tree and shot along the pavement. The long walls and open grounds spread around him; he was already too deep in Nolan's neighborhood to stay unseen forever. Sasha still didn't pull back from her bird, so she had no way to hear his phone.

Instead he leaped upward. The air was warmer than he expected, and he soared up fifty, a hundred feet… sure enough, the bird must have seen him against the sky, because he felt it turn to meet him.

Mark sank back to the ground—*I'm actually reaching out to a possessed creature that isn't Angie?* The blocky shape of Sasha's parrot flapped out of the dimness.

It flew past Mark to settle in a tree across the road, above his head but five whole paces away. He moved to meet it, and it said "Nolan's lights are on, but that could be a trick to make us think she's back. Are you ready to show her what we can do?"

"Oh yes." His words rushed out to match the bird's eagerness; that *couldn't* be Winton inside it. Mark swung the pack of tools into his hands, and reined in his voice to start weighing the details. "So, I think we've worked it out—"

"It's simple. Think about it, Mark. The books could be anywhere there. The thing is, she doesn't know we're working together. How could she?"

Oh, maybe because we fought her off together before? "All right. And you're thinking…"

"You let me in a window. I crawl around there, and if I find her here I put her to sleep, and the whole place is ours."

What? Mark lunged forward a step, then gasped out "She'll kill you!"

"Kill me? I'm not even here." The Sasha-parrot leaned forward on the branch, and her wings beat once to catch her balance. "She could be hiding her magic anywhere there. But I catch her and we win. Even if we can't find it, we can make her talk—it's what she wanted to do to me—"

"Sasha, *think.* If she's there, you're betting everything that she's asleep. But I tried sneaking in there once, and she almost shot me. But for you…" He waved at her, and tried to keep the words calm and clear. "Don't forget, tonight you're a bird—think, how many downdrafts did you have to fight that fragile body through to fly out here? Now, what would one of Nolan's hurricanes do to you if you're trapped inside the house? Most of her walls are solid stone. And if she kills the bird while you're inside it, the shock might kill *you.*"

He'd thought about it too many times, the moment Angie had flown in there to save him. If Nolan had been a few seconds faster with her magic, Angie would be lying dead in a corner before he ever knew who the owl was. He looked up toward the sky where she flew now, hoped the owl's ears could follow the warning too.

"I… of course I can sneak up on her." The parrot only hesitated a moment, and then its squawk sharpened into anger. "Or I can let the bird go in time. You're trying to keep me out again? I told you I'm doing this! Don't think you can stop me!"

"I think…" He drew a deep breath, and reached out a hand trying to calm her. "I think you nailed it, the trick is that she doesn't know there are two of us. But you don't have to go inside that bird-trap."

Dennard's voice—quiet so long—came from the phone: "The alarms! Remind her, we know how they work."

"And," Mark added before the parrot could go on, "Sasha, we lived in that house for days. We saw how many ways Nolan defends it."

"You did?" This time the parrot was listening.

"We did. She knows what one bird can do with a touch, and she's had months to put up grates and motion sensors and more. And we're only guessing she can't have changed the system too far from what we saw. What we need is for you to keep her busy, without getting yourself killed."

The bird leaned forward again. "Like how?"

* * *

The ski mask covered his face, and with it the last pretense that he could risk anyone in the neighborhood spotting him. He floated upward along the utility pole, gloved hands on the wood guiding him up.

The power lines buzzed like shrill rattlesnakes hidden in the shadows above, most of them deadly to touch. Careful, careful…

Out behind him, several of the lines ran down toward Nolan's home, where a single golden light shone in a squat block of stone amid the grounds. And clearer than any light, he could feel the gravity-charged coat she'd stolen pulsing in one corner of it. His pack hung against his chest with the tools in easy reach.

"The setup looks just like we thought." Could the others even hear him over the wires? "If Nolan isn't in there, her alarms have got to have a remote alert for this. Either way, Sasha knows what to do."

Then Henry's voice came in his ear. "I was just thinking, Mark. About the weakness that Nolan's magic has, and the one yours has."

"What?" He could feel Sasha moving restlessly at the far side of the estate, still keeping her distance from it. But, Henry wanted to talk *now?*

"You said possessed creatures have to stay away from Nolan's winds, but that's when she has her house to protect her. Outside, Winton's magic can come at her from anywhere, because she has no way to see it. But possession shouldn't catch you and me, because our magic *can* sense it. And if we try flying at Nolan we just give her a bigger weightless target to toss around. Did you ever think that when the three magics fight, Nolan is rock, possession is paper, and we're scissors?"

For a moment Mark couldn't answer, only hung beside the pole. And stare at the insulated cutters peeking out from his pack. *Scissors, maybe.*

"So… what does that mean, my scissors are going to break on Nolan's rock, if we don't bring Sasha's paper inside to save us? Thanks for the vote of confidence."

"I just… just be careful in there. Go tear the place apart. Or if she's in there, don't let her see you coming."

This time I'd have to take her down. He swallowed. "Right. Thanks."

He felt Sasha, still ready—and Angie, passing high above in a wide arc that should raise no suspicion on Nolan's radar. Of course.

"Here goes."

He tucked the phone away and drew on gravity to hold himself in place, to free both hands. Then he set the massive, rubber-sheathed clippers around the first wire, and stared down at Nolan's home.

Scissors against rock... the cable held, the shears refused to close, only trembled as his hands strained to find the force, to make that first small crack in the metal's defense that might mean...

The blades moved, then moved again. The cable parted and fell away... and the house behind him went dark.

Mark heaved in a breath and kicked off from the pole into a long straight-line leap toward where that light lingered in his eyes. Air whooshed by his face, and he sensed Sasha flying in—*cutting the power is Nolan's own trick, if she's there she'll be waiting*—

The dark block of the house swept up to fill his vision. At the last moment he caught at his magic, halted in the air, and dropped to the grass just steps from the small back window. When his feet touched down, his hands dove into the pack for the crowbar.

A scream of wind tore across the grounds.

So Nolan's here? Mark found himself crouching and braced against the gust—what did he expect she'd do when her alarms went blind?—but he felt Sasha spinning away. Still, the parrot struggled safely upward, and the wind swung around a quarter.

So much for "search the place all night in peace." No way around it now.

He dove for the house and jammed the crowbar under the window. Dennard called this the best place to break in, but Mark still had to move while the wind covered the sound, before the power came back.

Wood splintered, the window slid up. He slid inside, then fumbled with his aching hands to find the wires Dennard had described: one in the frame, one in the window he'd wrenched up. The broken window didn't align right but the upper and lower wires had to meet—

Somewhere in the house, something *hummed* to life. Nolan's back-up generator.

Mark looked around, at the huge clotheswasher in the faint light from the window, the even fainter glow beyond the door. So, he was back to creeping through Olivia Nolan's home again—this time not trying to avenge Angie here, but to take the power to bring her back.

Power lay pooling around him. The same thick ripples of mind magic he'd felt outside Sasha's—the feel of those talismans gathering energy. Sasha's and Angie's magic above was still clear, but the closer he got to this energy the more he'd lose track of what was outside. None of it masked the mass of gravity power where Nolan must be keeping the coat.

Footsteps. The still corridors drummed with the echoes of that march, a quick pace as clear as Nolan's signature. Mark tensed, trying to place how close those feet were to him.

Then another blast of wind howled against the walls, and he felt Sasha flung from one side of the house toward another—she'd made *another* try to distract Nolan?

Sasha's presence outside grew dimmer, muted by the gathering energy she'd flown near. The footsteps moved toward her; the house sensors must track her better than Mark's magic could now. But the motion detectors were only on the outside, and the echoes put Nolan somewhere in the corridors ahead.

This time I have to beat her. One grab and one wrench of his magic, if he was fast enough... Nolan was a murderer too, but not a monster like Winton... and the thought of rushing in and crushing her under his power... even for Angie... He stared at his shaking hands, and his heart pounded louder than the footsteps.

No, those footsteps were softening. Nolan was slowing; her sound faded away.

Mark drifted up onto tiptoe. Even on this hard floor he could make less noise than a cat, when he weighed less. But with each step the pool of power beat harder against his senses—every other magic but the raw strength of the coat faded away. And his eyes and ears showed only dim, silent turns and doorways, where any step could open onto Nolan blasting cold or possession or a bullet into him.

Just one more thing, before I face my fear.

He sank down to sit on the wooden floor. The magic in his belt pounded with the hunger of the talisman Nolan had set charging, only that and the pulse of all the coat's power. But still…

Under the clamor, he caught one flicker that would be Sasha, fluttering around the walls, and the ragged power of Angie up in the sky. And, somewhere in his awareness, there had to be the talismans Nolan carried too.

Breathe and pause, my sense is like my breath air mingling around the home, with the flow of it all. Feel it and the static as steady warmth on all sides, everywhere, nothing like the thrumming at my waist or the coat's room, or the shifting that waits at the wall, or up in the sky, or out at the gate—

The gate? Mark started up, legs cold against the concrete as the senses faded. He *had* felt it through the pressure, a third piece of mind-magic in actual use, far out near what had to be the grounds' gate. Winton.

Just when Nolan's own feet were marching toward Mark.

Another sound broke through that. A tapping against glass, and Nolan's footsteps turning toward it.

In the stillness came a moment's groan of wood, and then a muffled hint of the night stirrings through what had to be a window just cracked open.

Sasha's parrot-voice croaked "This time tell me the truth. It was always you hunting Roger Winton, wasn't it? Why are you after him?"

"Is that… Sasha?"

Nolan's voice made the guess all in the course of one breath, with only a small rise in pitch for surprise.

She went on "I'm 'after' that man because he's attacked *me* with gangs, killers, and everyone on the street I can see—and their 'little' dog too," and Nolan actually paused as if she expected the parrot to laugh. "Or didn't Mark tell you about his girl Angie? Winton has been tearing all of us apart one life at a time, all to steal our magic. Or just eliminate us for what we might do to him."

—But Winton himself had to be the presence out at the gate…

"Just like you're hunting him!" Sasha snapped.

Mark ghosted forward. If Sasha was trying to distract their enemy, he'd never have a better chance to close in.

Nolan's answer was calm, certain. "I didn't start the war. But what can I do? He had a man with a rifle shooting at me from right across the street from here—and then made him jump to his death to cover his tracks. That's how Winton can come at me, again and again."

The sounds came from the next room, the library.

Sasha's voice rose. "And you lied to me, all this time! You said you were looking for him to protect him!"

"To save us all from him? Yes, I lied. But how many secrets did he keep from you? You worked for him for years, but suddenly he sends you to visit your own aunt's tomb?"

Through the doorway he saw Nolan, her back to him as she spoke to the cracked-open window between the bookcases. If he could just close the distance… and she didn't use his touch to take control of him… then he could get her…

How could I stop her from touching me? Blocking that could save me from all of it. He looked around at the library, and remembered how he used to use the belt to block his own apartment window. Maybe nobody had to get hurt.

"Your own aunt," Nolan said softly. "Did you ever think Winton killed her?"

"No. Never—"

Mark charged.

He dove for the towering oak bookcase closest to her; part of him heard the gasp that meant Nolan had spotted him, but none of that mattered for another instant. His leap let him seize the shelving and yank it upward—glass doors over the books flapped in confusion, but Mark spun around swinging the shape like some huge, weightless screen door in his hands, and rushed at Nolan with it as his battering ram.

It's such a broad shape, and it's cobweb-light now—one of Nolan's winds would fling this away like a sail—

But instead the woman dodged away, two steps that might have been pure reflex, toward the clearer space toward the room's back, just where Mark could pivot a step around her and shove the case against her until it forced her back right where the two walls met behind her. It trapped her in the corner.

He pushed weight into the shelf again, enough crushing weight to seal it in place. The wood groaned, but Olivia Nolan made no sound. Finally, he grabbed a quarter-height bookcase and shoved it onto the first case's top. More weight sealed that in place to stop her climbing over it.

"Your hands can't reach me, and your winds can't push this much weight off you. You're… trapped." Mark looked at their enemy and felt the truth sinking in.

"You *did* it!?" Sasha's bird-voice came from the window. "We got her!"

Mark let his hands drop to his sides. "My scissors caught your rock, this time. Even if it had to be behind a whole shelf of paper."

Paper... The library's shelves drew his gaze up, all around him. Any of those hundreds of books could have Winton's book tucked behind it, or whatever notes Nolan might keep about her own magic, and then he had the whole rest of the house to search. If she didn't simply keep them on her person.

"Is that your plan?" Nolan's voice had a forced sound as if she didn't have space to draw a full breath, but there was no hesitation in her words. "A trap?"

"Did you want me to kill you? Maybe hold the shelf over your head and drop it?" Mark tried to smile. She wasn't Winton, she didn't *need* to be wiped out—

Winton. I felt him out there too, we may not have much time. They had to find the books, fast, but the only shortcut to that was making Nolan tell them.

Sasha laughed "How's it feel to be helpless? After you had me chased all over town?"

Mark added "And I know you'd never bring the police into this, so it's just between us." He looked around the library again, trying to sort through plans. "Sasha, remind me if she stays quiet long enough to be controlling something out there."

Nolan only said "I wouldn't waste my time. Sasha, did you ever think that the Wintons killed your aunt? After all, they were the only ones who knew she was dead."

"And Winton Senior was my father? I remember all the lies you tried to confuse me with," Sasha flung back. "My aunt was fine when she left the Wintons, my mother said so. She died later, and Mr. Winton's father just respected her enough to have her buried well, same as his son chose me to learn the best magic there is."

Mark glared at the walls of shelves. The others' words pulled at his thoughts, and the pool of gathering magic and the clamor of the coat muffled his senses.

Nolan was saying "Chose you? Winton handed you a loaded gun and left you to shoot yourself."

"He told me everything I needed!" Sasha snapped. "He's been preparing me for this for years."

"And you say I'm the liar? Sasha, I *grew up* with magic. My parents trained and tested me every day to be certain I was ready. And they made sure I'd never think to attack an enemy if I had only mastered one trick, that couldn't even get me in through a window. You don't even know how a spellkeeper has to think. Of course your friend's doing all the work—"

"Says the 'expert' pinned under her own shelf—"

Mark lunged for the doorway.

The coat's beacon of gravity power led him into an easy jump down the dim, bare corridor. The faint shapes of the walls in the dimness were enough to steer him through his memories of it; he could picture what cabinet Nolan had "hidden" it in before he came in sight of the room.

Remembering the others, he pulled out his phone. "Did you get all that? We caught Nolan."

"Caught her?" Christa said.

"Don't sound so surprised," he laughed. "We only have a little time, though. That has to be Winton outside too, and I don't know how puppet-proof this place really is without her defending it. I have to start scooping up every paper in sight, or make Nolan tell us where the magic ones are, and do it fast. Either way, I could use more power."

Dennard said "Fast sounds good. If you're careful."

"Got it."

The cabinet drawer was locked—like some kind of joke, with all the fierce, ready magic he sensed just inside it. Mark laid a hand over the drawer and pushed weight from his belt into it, until the wood creaked and splintered and tore downward to rip the cabinet open.

Then the coat was in his hands. It had enough power-charged leather to maybe bring Nolan's stone fortress down around her. *Or burn away my self-control long before then.*

Mark's fingers lingered on one edge of the coat. That edge was jagged, with pieces cut away… Henry had felt Nolan leaving pieces of leather in some kind of dropbox today. What had she been doing?

He took a deep breath. The gathering mind-magic felt further away in this room—he could sense the other possessed creature still out near the gate. But not Angie, unless she was back toward Sasha and hidden in the static.

Mark rushed back for the library. The coat's power felt eager to be used.

Sasha's parrot-voice was still speaking at the window. "—tell you again, it doesn't matter if he's my father or not. He wanted me to have this magic."

Mark looked around the library. The single desk's drawers didn't look big enough to carry all the books if he yanked them out.

Nolan's voice cut in: "But I think it does matter. And I think he still killed your real mother."

"I told you, she was my aunt, and she was fine! Now you're just throwing all your lies at me all at once."

If I start smashing *the house, will Nolan tell me where the books are? Will it stop her taunting Sasha?*

"But that's how it all fits." The coldness in Nolan's words made Mark's gut tighten. "If it was part of the same plan Edward Winton did with his son Roger—to take *permanent* possession of him. To wipe the boy out, and be young again."

"He *stole his son's body?*" This time Sasha had no denials, only shock.

"You know it's possible. Like Angie taking over the owl."

Mark's fists clenched. And yet, Nolan was showing Sasha the same evil about her "mentor"—the same enemy scheming at the gate—that Mark hadn't dared to tell her yet...

Nolan pressed on. "And you're the old Winton's child too. That might be why he *had* a second child, if the transfer works best between relatives. And, I've seen his current body is broken—he couldn't even walk to fight for his life.

"He must be desperate, Sasha. He gave you a book of tricks to keep you loyal, until he's ready to move into your head. Ask Dr. Batiste; he's seen how it was the old Winton inside the new one—"

"Batiste? The man in the... the coma? No, no! Mark, you never—"

Something buzzed against Mark's hip.

"—said that he—"

He grabbed for the phone.

"—used his son—"

Henry's words were sharp, tight enough to push back the protests in the room. "There's another belt out here," he was saying.

Here? Where they were watching Sasha's place? "What? One of Rafe's belts?" Mark said.

"Rafe is dead," came Dennard's answer. "But he might have—"

Something *banged*. Something at Mark's elbow, shrill, sharp, so fierce that it sent him diving away before the thought *gunshot* could form. Before he heard the next shot tear another blind hole out from behind the bookshelf. Nolan had a gun ready all this time.

Mark rolled to his feet, and his gaze swung from the doorway behind him to the enemy in front. The shelf tipped, fell forward, boomed and clattered down.

Its weight must have worn off—

Nolan had been stalling, and someone else was at Sasha's—

Somewhere between those thoughts and the sight of Nolan's gun swinging toward him, Mark lunged away and up the corridor.

At the turn he halted. Why was he running, he'd beaten Nolan once tonight, and now he hugged all the coat's raw power in his arms…

Back at the library doorway, Nolan's arm lashed around the door frame to feel along the wall. *If I had tried crouching there to catch her as she stepped out, she'd have possessed me now—she's always ready, I have to survive to help Henry—*

He flung himself up the turn, hearing a shot crack behind him, but he saw the next turn ahead and dove around it to arrow toward the front door. For frantic heartbeats he scrabbled with one latch, another… and at last twisted free into the outside. Just as the winds hit.

*—Slam the door first, don't let Winton just fly in—*and then Mark wrenched himself into the dizzying, icy rush straight up at the sky.

Long frozen moments later he settled into a position in the heights, and the whipping air of his flight resolved into the fierce wind lingering from Nolan's rage. He swept his blurry gaze downward. Angie's presence was gone, missing—and Sasha's too—but he felt Winton moving slowly on what must be the ground. That presence showed which black space below him was Nolan's estate.

The winds hadn't even tossed him a block… and they couldn't be too strong, there was still a faint graying of fog on the horizon… *fog?*

He raised his phone again, and his eyes picked out the direction toward where Henry and Dennard were keeping watch over Sasha. East, the same as the fog.

The phone reached his ear:

"—answer me, Dennard! Hell, how'd they even *find* you in this soup?" Henry's words were gathering speed, stampeding toward shrill fear.

Christa added "It's not her, Nolan never left her house. I don't know what she's doing—"

Mark managed to say "Henry? You okay?"

"Mark? You're back?" Henry gasped. "I don't know what okay means now. Dennard went silent after this fog came up. And I can't sense Winton or Sasha moving any magic in it. But if someone found where Dennard was keeping watch… and that was after Angie flew on past him too…"

Angie's there? *She could have seen the fog Nolan sent from up here… but somehow Nolan still reached out and got Dennard…* Mark dropped for the ground, the motion roiling his stomach.

"Stay back," he said, but when he broke off he heard Christa still calling "—are you alright—"

"I'm going to check on him," came Henry's words.

"Get out of there!" But Mark knew his warning was only garbled in the middle of Christa's pleas: "Henry! Don't, don't you—"

His feet came down on concrete; the fringe of some estate's pool, a glance he took in as he dashed for the wall. No time to float across town, no time at all.

The voice on his phone brought his hand to his ear again. "Henry! Mark, where are you!" Christa was saying.

He flung himself into a quick leap over the wall, landing in the empty street beyond, and shot her a location ping on their app. Then he was bolting up the street fighting the urge to tear free of the ground again.

Nolan sent that fog… she must have been stalling them all through their encounter, somehow she'd found where Sasha had hidden… *and we thought as long as Nolan was holed up in her house she couldn't strike out at us…*

The empty night split as a car roared behind him. Mark ran on, ignoring the small thought that his speed was only drawing more attention. But when the headlights washed past him he heard a sharp *beep* and a familiar car pulled over to let him dive in beside Christa.

"We're coming, Henry!" she said. Mark saw her phone set up on her dashboard, then he slammed back in the seat as she raced the car forward.

The next turn on the winding street loomed ahead and she barreled around it with a screech of rubber. *She'll crash us—* Mark opened his mouth to stop her.

"I've got him!" Henry's voice came, half-lost in the engine's roar. Christa cut their speed as Henry went on "He's been hurt!"

"Dennard? How bad?" Mark said. Their motion was more controlled now but he felt his head spinning, helpless.

"Someone hit him, he won't wake up. I can't see anything—Angie's still circling—"

Calm, he needed a calmer voice. "Henry… please, get out of there. Use the magic, it can let you carry Dennard, you can both be safe." How had those words gotten so steady while he strained to brace himself in the seat?

"The door to Sasha's place is broken. Someone got in, I'll try to help her—"

"Henry!" Christa screamed.

Snatches of hard, running breathing came through the phone, in the gaps between her pleading. *He can't hear now, not if he slid the volume down like I do whenever I go into danger—like now when I took on Nolan and* never noticed *the real danger across town—*

An owl's shriek blasted through the phone, Angie was warning Henry too. But, Mark thought he heard the creak of a door.

Then, a silenced gunshot, that low metallic *cough.* A thump.

Christa was still calling "Henry? Henry?"

Then: "Henry??" A single low word through the phone. And the line went silent.

There was something about that voice, and it almost sounded surprised too... it was a small thought, under the pounding *how could I let him get shot?* And Dennard was hurt, and Angie was right there like she could be next, and Sasha, *how—*

Then Christa sent the car forward again, this time with a smoothness to the turns as if her hands had lost all connection to her pale, trembling face. Mark swallowed his pleas about taking the wheel and only let the street maps' routes fill his mind. One more left turn, out into the city and the speed of the straighter, open streets by night, then edge to the north and keep going, slower and slower as the fog stole more of their sight the closer they came...

Once he wondered if Winton was still creeping around back at Nolan's, playing his own patient game. And if Angie had been hurt— *don't think that—*

The low lines of Valens Street apartments loomed out of the grayness, and Mark caught his friends' magic pulsing within, leading them toward Sasha's home. But he sensed one gravity talisman, not two, and no trace of Angie. Sasha's talismans were still drawing power around the area, but those currents would never hide anything as strong as a belt out here.

Christa pulled over and they rushed out. Mark dashed up the walkway between the buildings, knowing he should slow down and watch for whatever threat wasn't long gone, but the one bit of their own magic was too close ahead.

A stack of boxes by the back wall—it was a spot with a clear view of Sasha's door, and piled so close to the wall that a man could be almost invisible behind them in the fog. And yet Dennard lay sprawled beside them, still.

Mark's knees didn't want to bend to look. That was *blood* over the side of Dennard's head.

But he was breathing, Mark's fingers felt the man's chest moving in the dimness. His hands moved on their own to push Dennard, shake him, and his voice whispered some kind of plea.

Christa's footsteps behind him almost hid Dennard's groan. "Heh.. Henr..."

Was that what a concussion sounded like? Dennard was trying to lift himself up, and Mark pressed him down; even the lightest touch stopped him. "We're here. Don't you move."

"Where's Henry?" Christa's control bled away as she spoke.

"Not here," Mark said. Henry had to be alright, if he'd taken his talisman away, and Angie would be with him; that had to be it. It had to be.

"Ambulance." The one heavy word was all Christa said, as she tapped on her phone for help.

Right. Mark stared around, trying to think. What had happened, what could he find out before the police arrived? His eyes went to Sasha's door just down the row.

A few steps—his trembling knees wouldn't leap—brought him to the door Dennard had been watching, the place Henry had been heading. A small, neat gap hung in the wood around where the knob had been.

Even in the wet of the fog, he smelled the blood.

He grabbed for the door. Inside lay shadow, the fogged-out light from outside only slanting in a few steps into the dim corridor.

Something in the back of his head kept telling him to go slower, to watch each room he entered for a gunman in the shadows. But the wild ride in and the sight of Dennard and the sickening truth of being *too late* shoved him forward to rush through one room after another of the bare, empty apartment Sasha had tried to take refuge in. Nobody was there.

He could only sink down to the floor just inside the entrance, staring at the spatters of blood where Henry must have been shot. Only dabs of it, but so many of them…

A ruffling of feathers made him look back. Angie settled on the step behind him.

The sight of her, safe, tore the barrier open inside him and the words came tumbling out. "How, how? Was it one of Rafe's men? How'd he spot Dennard—how'd they do this?"

Out of breath, he turned back to stare at Henry's blood.

Something brushed his back, and brushed his mind.

No, she can't risk it, Angie needs her power to stay alive—

The world spun away, swept away in a whirl of her magic and memory—*fight, have to push her back*—but, shapes came crashing through the vortex—too fast, too many—the memory of herself beating at glass and shrieking at the faces inside, useless, ignored—two faces shouting at each other—following above a masked figure with a gun, marching away two women and a man clutching an injured arm—their car moving below—then the four disappearing down into the subway, Sasha and her mother and Henry all herded along by—

The face, the gunman's face that looked up and homed in through all the night sky to pick out the hidden owl and meet its gaze, and that image that made him, Mark, fling the owl away and break the memory trance.

Too late. He'd seen his father's face.

CHAPTER FIVE

DESCENDED

This time it wasn't a hospital. He watched them walk Dennard into the police station, wobbly but awake—and this time Mark's worst fears were for Henry and the two women taken away under *that man's* gun. But even that didn't keep him from seeing the night he'd first blundered into the belt, and how that had led to Dennard rolling up an emergency room corridor, no matter how far that night's dreadful stillness was from these currents of sullen, frustrated faces.

He still smelled the blood, even just the spatters he'd found that must be Henry's.

All he could hear now was the pounding of his heartbeat. This time there was no Angie beside him to share a secret with, only the police who'd taken the injured Dennard off for questioning one way, and Christa another. Two uniforms and an aging woman detective stood around Mark.

And they watched him, like some kind of angry ghosts waiting for his resolve to crumble. The detective had only asked him a handful of questions so far, but the way they stood always blocked him from racing off to find Christa, or even following the pulse of the talisman that could lead him right to Dennard again.

Henry had to be fine. Dennard had to be.

But... Mark couldn't hold himself up straight. He kept seeing the look of fury Christa had shot him as the police took her aside... and that after the shriek Angie gave when she flew away with God-knew-what on her mind.

All he could do was clench his arms around himself. In one night, his father had struck at *everyone* good in his life… and the tighter he huddled, the more he crushed the burning, useless power of the coat closer to himself. Useless, all because he had left everyone that mattered alone to watch Sasha.

My father shot his own nephew, he took the woman who could make Angie human again…

Mark tried to picture the glimpse Angie had shown him—Henry as only a prisoner—and how Dennard could still speak after his blow, halting but clear. Both could have been hurt much worse.

I should be fighting past those police vultures to be sure Dennard's recovering. I can feel the talisman with him right there in the next wing… Angie can't come to him indoors…

Mark couldn't move. The most he could do was try to think.

How had his father known, how had Nolan found out where they were? How could the man *do* it—Mark remembered him as a petty, destructive thing that dragged people down around him, nothing like these spellkeepers and masterminds. Mark could still see him through Angie's eyes when that gaze swung unerringly up to spot her in the darkness…

So he could track magic too, if he got his hands on some power. Nolan must be behind it, since she had sent the fog there. She must have recruited him with a piece of the coat and the guess that a blood relative of Mark's and Henry's could sense energy too.

His blood, in Mark's veins too, and Henry's spattered on Sasha's floor…

When one cop whispered a message to the detective, he almost missed it.

Then she stepped right to where Mark huddled and snapped "Did you do it?"

"Whaaa—"

"Did you shoot him? Your friend Christa said—" And she broke off.

Mark choked down the *She said what?* he knew the detective wanted to get from him, and locked his eyes on her. A small woman with gray hair wrapped up tight; he had a sudden thought that someone from a more normal family might have called her an angry grandmother.

"You've already been seen," and she stabbed her finger at him, "in public, with Sasha Lawrence. Now she and her mother are missing, and your friends are found staking out the place she'd gone to hide. And they were attacked by someone who got close. Did your friends come to talk *you* out of doing something stupid, and it all went wrong?"

"No! It—" He caught himself.

She only waited. Her lip clenched pale, tight with accusation. The two uniforms still hung back. Mark tried to remember what else the police must know.

Instead, he glared back at the detective. "What were they telling you? Did they find Henry?"

She didn't answer. Didn't move.

"Did they? Or is something wrong with Dennard?"

Not a sound.

"Alright, I'll—" He took a step around her toward the wing where he sensed Dennard. She moved to block him.

He studied the lines etched in her face, the way her arms folded, one hand's fingers just inside the edge of her coat, where her gun would be.

He tried to soften the accusation out of his voice. "What is this? Am I under arrest?"

"You're a person of interest." Her voice was softer too. "Whether tonight makes you a witness, a target, or a murderer."

Murderer?

Henry had been led away, alive, Angie had shown him that much—and the detective's voice had hitched just an instant, part of a lie. *They're always trying to bluff secrets out of us, that had to be it, same as when they dragged out Henry's interview before.*

He said "Dennard's going to be fine. Henry must be a prisoner, he's not dead. He can't be."

The damn woman raised a mocking eyebrow.

Lies. Or else they'd arrest him, or show him the body to break him… Henry wasn't dead. "You're lying," he said, and he locked his eyes on hers.

"You'd know, if you shot him."

There, that flicker in her tone had to be the lie. He took another step to the side, and she still moved to keep in front of him, and behind her the others moved closer—

His fingers clenched. *She's so* close, *one quick grab and the magic could pin her to the floor, or let me toss her right into the other cops—*

"Two friends of yours staked out a woman's house," she said. "As if they knew she and her mother would go missing. And you keep turning up on the edge of gangs, hostages, graveyards, you call Olivia Nolan a murderer but you never give us a story a baby would believe. Who the hell are you protecting?"

"My goddamn father."

The end of the word came out as a low growl. The thought had floated up inside him so easily, it only ripped him open when he said it aloud. Behind the words came more ideas—*focus the hunt on him, find Henry and Sasha and her mother, get Angie's cure back—and they'll believe it was all him—*

"Him," Mark said. "He's who attacked—"

"If you're wasting my time—"

"Bryan Oscar Petrie, my father, small-time drug dealer and all-around crook, and they tell me you just let him out of prison again. He'd do anything for a price—"

"And this tiny fish just happens to be the one who came after your friends? He pulled off such a perfect snatch and grab? You need a better story than that."

"It *has* to be him!" Mark snapped. "We had a tip that—"

"Tip?" she prompted.

"Tip."

A little bird told me... the thought whispered in his head, tried to loosen his lungs into crazy laughter.

"And," he forced out before the laughter could start, taking a step closer to her now, "I might have an idea why he went after Sasha too. And why..."

What could he say—why Sasha's patron Winton hadn't been seen in months? Why Nolan was always surrounded by unexpected fogs and storms, and how Mark could prove it? He clamped down on the rest, not sure how much he could lie about.

"I've given you a start," he said. "Before I go on, let me see Dennard and Christa!"

And the detective started up the corridor, with a motion for him to follow. She said "If Christa wants to see you."

What did that mean? Mark scrambled after the detective, but her pace was so slow; he had to hold his feet down when he ached to rocket on past her.

The way Christa had looked at him—that memory came clearer with every hobbled step they took. The same way Dennard had looked at him after Angie, or Angie's shriek about her injured father tonight: rage that needed a target. People milled about in the corridor, and uniformed or not they *all* walked like he was the one who needed to get out of *their* way. Now he could hear the PA speakers jabbering some "code."

Just be sure Dennard's recovering. Then... there had to be a way to send the police after his father, to track down Henry and Sasha and everything else that man had taken. Or Mark would find him and...

His magic *thrummed* around him, so ready to smash. The power and the rage clenching his fingers made his head swim. He stumbled between a uniform and a ragged man who smelled like a six-pack of spilled beer.

When the detective stopped, she made him skid a moment before he dodged around her and looked through the doorway she'd halted at.

Christa was leaping to her feet and spinning toward him, with a startled-animal look on her face that hardened an instant later as her eyes locked on his. But beyond her… she'd been whispering to someone inside, out of Mark's view. *Henry?*

"You need to go." Her voice was empty of expression, and her eyes only flicked toward the detective a moment before settling back on him, watching him as if he was something other than human.

He moved forward. "Is Henry—"

She blocked him. He couldn't even see if Henry was back there, and Christa *blocked* him.

His hands shot up to catch her arms and snatch away her weight, and he lunged forward and swept her along in a step, motion flowing into motion so easily, ready for the next step that would fling her away—

He froze. His hands trembled as he set her down.

Her gasp of breath broke the silence, as Mark turned to look into the room. It wasn't Henry, simply an older man in a fine suit with crisp lines and eyes wide awake even at this hour. Not Henry, not some cop with news of him—

"You—" Christa's voice snapped Mark's gaze back around to her, and he saw her glance past him to the detective just as she cut her words off. Then, "Get out."

"Ma'am?" The man in the suit edged around, and Mark knew he had to be a lawyer even before he went on "If your plan is to keep charges from being filed against your boyfriend, I suggest you ask your friend to explain why he sent him out there—"

"GET OUT!" Her words smashed into Mark, ringing off the walls and out beyond the room. "Don't you pretend you give a damn about anyone human."

"But I…"

What could he do, promise to save Henry? Say he never wanted him to be part of this? And even now Christa was still keeping their secrets with the detective watching.

"Sorry," he sighed.

Christa's eyes clenched shut. She slumped where she stood.

Mark floundered back into the hallway, and kept moving.

It's all *my fault. I pulled Henry into this when I needed a place to rest—then Winton grabs control of Christa to watch me, Rafe attacks Henry, Nolan wears him out searching for Winton—now this, and Dennard's hurt too,* again, *and Angie… I was shot once, but for all of them it happens again and again—*

God, what did I think *would happen when they went to Sasha's alone?* Henry could barely risk touching the magic after what Nolan put him through, and Dennard could never sense enemy power at all. And still Mark had let them go off alone and forgotten them, because *he'd* always been able to fly away from the worst—

Footsteps behind him made him look back at the detective, closing in behind him with the two uniforms at her heels.

Mark tried to drag his thoughts away from where he'd gone wrong. The lawyer's words came back to him, and he said "You're not going to charge Henry for this. When you find him."

Huffing for breath, she said "He disappeared from the site of a possible kidnapping. If none of you can give a real reason for that, I may have to."

Always trying to pressure us! "I told you, we had a tip that my father was headed there."

"What 'tip'? That doesn't cut it."

"Look, can you take just me to Dennard?" The moment Mark said it, he realized he was already marching toward the room where Dennard's talisman waited.

But the detective said "I'll make a deal with you. I'll keep leading you to where he is, for as long as you keep explaining." And she slowed, threatening to stop.

"My father—" Mark began.

In the moment she moved up ahead of him, he tried to think. Getting everyone back was what mattered. Could he tie Sasha to how her boss Winton had disappeared for months? No, too risky to point at Winton and start him killing whoever knew too much—

The detective was already slowing again, eyes on him. He had to say something.

"My father tracked down Sasha. I think he was working for Olivia Nolan."

A group clustered around a uniformed cop on crutches blocked the path ahead. Mark and the detective edged to the side.

Dennard saw Nolan sending out pieces of this coat—was that testing my father, to teach him to find one talisman using another? Was she so desperate to sniff out magic again that she'd give it to the lowest lowlife in the city? He heard his breathing growing harsh, and reminded himself who could get caught in the crossfire. The crowd passed.

"Look, can you find my father? Henry, Sasha, and her mother are out there somewhere, and he has to be the one who took them."

"And it's Olivia Nolan's fault, again?" She leaned closer. "What's your issue with her? You called her a murderer already."

"Nolan's more dangerous than she looks. I think the woman she killed, Irene, tried to blackmail her. So Sasha might have been a threat to her too."

"To her? Or to Roger Winton?"

"But—"

Mark's phone vibrated.

He glanced down, just for an instant. "Maybe—" *No, Winton's too dangerous to mention!* And if the police somehow did catch him themselves, he'd never see the books that could have Angie's cure.

But the detective's words came faster. "Winton got you a job as a cab driver, and Sasha Lawrence worked for him too, before he dropped out of sight. Now she's gone, and it's you and your friends on the scene…"

Mark stole a glance at his phone; was that code from *Kate?* Well, Angie's mother was thousands of miles away; he focused on the detective again.

Admit Nolan had a feud with Winton? Or say how often freak storms and fog sprang up around Nolan, and then show the belt's power to finally break through that wall of doubt on the detective's face?

He pushed those thoughts away. "Look, can you find them or not? You've got my father's face and everything you know about him on file, you can keep watch over Nolan—"

"Nolan again? Did you see her at the kidnapping?"

"No." Not her, she'd never need to be there.

A white coat beside a black uniform caught his eye, a doctor and a cop standing outside a closed door. About where he'd sensed Dennard's energy. He felt for it again.

Winton!

The soft twitch of possession in the same room with Dennard's talisman sent Mark charging forward. The police shouted behind him. Was that Angie up there too, did that rougher magic mean she was flapping outside just beyond that room?

He rushed up to the door.

The cop was already blocking the doctor there, thick arms folded. "The lieutenant said nobody goes—"

The doctor countered "Will you just—"

Then the officer flinched, and stumbled backward staring past Mark's shoulder. Mark grabbed for the door, and from the corner of his eye he saw the "move-aside" wave from the aging woman he'd taken for just another detective. He dove on in.

The room felt *cramped,* filled up with the oversized wood desk in the middle and pressed in with walls of dry erase boards and shelved plants and the curtained window where Angie must be beating helpless outside. And the haggard, blond man under Winton's control, bending over the corner where Dennard slumped in his chair.

"Let me sleep. But don't I... know you?" Dennard's words were low and wavering, knocked loose by his injury.

"You might," the possessed cop said. "But, your friend already told us about Roger Winton."

"But, he wouldn't—"

The door slammed shut behind Mark, and he heard the old woman bark "Interrogating a witness when he's half-conscious, Jennings? Explain. Now."

Mark edged to the side to put the desk between him and Winton's body. Worthless protection in such a cramped room, and the enemy was already right in front of Dennard.

"Sorry," the man said. "I only meant to—" He took a small step *toward* his accuser.

Mark snapped "Keep back!"

Angie's warning *shreeeee* burst outside.

The older cop's startled eyes swung to the window, then Mark. "What?"

Winton went on "I was only trying to—" He took another step, and then he seemed to trip and topple forward.

It was over in a moment. The old woman stepped away but her back thumped against the door, her arms went up to ward him off, and the possessed man fell across them. Those arms stiffened as the man's body went limp. He slumped down the wall with a soft rustle.

And she, Winton, called out "Clear everyone away from this door! Nobody comes in, on my order!"

A voice from outside said "But... yes, Captain."

Captain. The word froze Mark, just as his feet had been shifting to let him reach toward the desk. He had an image of a full police captain waking up pinned under the furniture he would have thrown at her— He hesitated, again.

"You…" Dennard's groan shook off some of its muzziness, and he tried to rise from the chair.

Winton stepped toward him, stolen eyes watching Mark for any moves. The woman's voice said softly "You're all so reckless."

"I know!" Mark gasped. "I won't let them get hurt again. And don't you—"

"I didn't mean what happened to your friends." He reached a slow hand toward Dennard.

Somehow Mark still couldn't move. Winton's touch had left Dr. Batiste barely breathing—and snuffed out Rafe's life. Now it was Dennard's turn, with Angie trapped right outside to watch?

"Don't!" This time the word came a fraction louder, and he added "I'll shout—"

"Pass your phone over here." Winton let his hand hung in the air over Dennard.

Mark yanked out his phone and tossed it over. He was halfway through the motion before he realized he could have tried recording his elusive enemy.

Winton caught it, glanced at it, and set it aside, always keeping the captain's eyes at an angle that covered Mark and Dennard both. Mark edged another step back.

Winton whispered "This isn't a duel over whose words can control who comes through that door. Whatever you do to stop me now, I only need to come back again in an hour, or a day."

Why can't I move, why can't I think?

"But I meant," Winton went on, "you've been careless about being noticed. What did you tell them?"

Mark stared at the face that wasn't Winton's, and tried to will away the woman's features and the higher-pitched voice, to imagine the brusque, impatient sound of the man he'd thought was his friend. All he could do was say "And then you'll just kill them? Everyone who saw a hint of magic?"

"Too clumsy. But if you compare the ripples made by one 'cop gone mad,' against living in a world that knows any strange twitch could be my pulling their strings… or where authorities search through every satellite trace that could show someone flying…" The woman's lips thinned in a smile.

Dennard slurred out "So you picked Lieutenant Jennings. He hated how I tried to stay in touch with the police… so he's who you used to catch me. All set to wipe us out so nobody would get it." He edged the chair back from Winton, gaze still out of focus.

I have to jump Winton. But the captain would be caught in that too, even if I was fast enough to crush him before he moved into me… think!

"You think I'm a monster?" Winton's smile twisted up to one side. "Someone needs to make these choices. At least Miss Nolan understands that. But you don't, and you're the ones that have the hardest power to hide." His hand settled to just over Dennard's chest. "What did you tell them?"

What could he say: all of Winton's secrets? Or Nolan, or the magic? But he didn't dare slow down enough to pick a lie. "I said *he* took Henry, Sasha, and her mother."

Unless Sasha's your *daughter, not hers,* he thought of adding. Would that put a crack in the calm that gripped the captain's face? Instead Mark pushed on, ready to say whatever it took:

"I told them my father did it."

"Your father?" The puppetmaster paused, and Mark could hear the thought settling in his voice: another relative like Henry, so the sense for magic must run in the family.

Dennard groaned "Mark, no—"

"And you said why he took them? You told them about Nolan?"

" 'Told' them?" Mark flung back. "We already accused her once, they won't forget that no matter how you make us change our story. They'll put it together. And what you did to Dr. Batiste too!"

"Will they?" Winton's smile widened. "Then I should remove this captain first."

More victims? Somehow Mark's thoughts went to Angie again, the small presence outside forced to listen, while his eyes bored into the possessed officer's. "No!"

"Or…" Winton added, "you put the blame on your father, but how did you say you already knew he'd be coming after the Lawrences?"

"You think explaining that is easy?" What answer would keep Winton satisfied… but he had no time— "I just said we had a tip. That's all, just a tip that my father was after them."

And Winton nodded, slowly. "I can work with that. Your father could have promised you he'd come after your girlfriend."

You mean Sasha, dating me? The thought was *wrong*... but of course it fit with how Mark had lived in the years before he stopped dancing around Angie… all things Winton knew from those scattered conversations of pretending to care about Mark's life. All those years waiting for a chance at the Dennards…

"So that's it? Lies are that damn easy for you?" Mark spat.

Winton shrugged. "What you are, all of you, is dangerous. You're loose cannons in what should be a private battle between myself and Nolan."

Then Dennard's voice cut in, and the last of his dazed sound slipped away in mid-syllable: "You, Nolan, and Sasha, you mean."

"What?" For a moment the puppetmaster sounded as surprised as any human.

Dennard's voice was low and certain. "You spend your time making threats. Instead of taking action. That tells me you need us."

"Is that what you think?" The woman's voice settled into a chuckle.

Mark joined in with "You *do* need us, to find Sasha if you can't. And you want the police too—so shooting up cops here would slow them down in looking for her too, right? And you can't risk that. Not with *your own daughter* out there."

He threw the last point in that smug face, carried on by the rush of reasons that fell into place, afraid to slow down—even though Winton made no reaction.

Mark swept on "Your daughter. Or maybe you just see her as a body you're preparing for yourself to use. But she's out there right now, in the hands of a man who almost killed two people tonight to grab her. He's got the magic to see any tricks she plays, and to sense yours too—if you could even find where he's got her. And tonight Nolan already had Sasha thinking you abandoned her."

The chain of arguments rattled to an end and left him gasping for breath. Winton still didn't answer, and Mark thought of flinging something else at him, some warning about the lives his father had destroyed…

Winton looked slowly from Mark to Dennard and back. "Believe what you want. But if she dies, keep in mind how many ways I can come back for any of you. And… be careful when you talk about fathers."

The captain's eyes locked straight on Mark, and tightened with Winton's malice.

"So now your own father is a threat to me too… He's able to see my work, as well as expose us all if he soars up where someone can see him? Then you want to put a stop to him, or I'll have another reason to take it out on you."

He stretched his hand over Dennard.

"And you'd best deal with your father quickly, before I do that my own way."

"What?" Mark felt his head whirling.

"You know he will, Mark," Dennard sighed.

Did Winton just warn me to find a harmless way to stop my father, to save my father?

Mark stumbled back a step, his shoulder grazed the wall and sent him swaying on his feet. What was the schemer *thinking*… if they got a chance to save Henry and Sasha—and Angie's cure—they could never stop to worry about who was in the way, least of all *him*…

"Now get going."

And the old captain's body edged to the side, and squatted down and wrestled the sleeping "Lieutenant Jennings" up along the wall to his feet—Mark saw the woman's hands shaking from the weight, but Winton's will forced her onward. She paused there and gave one warning glance to Mark and Dennard.

The magic jumped, from the captain back into Jennings, and the two staggered apart. The captain fell against the closed door, her eyes open, blinking to focus.

Jennings, Winton again, hissed at her, and his face twisted more with every word. "It's him, you know it is!" He waved to Dennard behind him. "Him at that gang war, him stirring up the Blades again, and now here he is in the middle of this!"

What was Winton doing now? His performance had to be more than just covering up Jennings coming here.

The captain took a sharp step toward the man. "Did you just *hit* me—"

"Don't you get in my way!" He shoved her back, slamming her against the door again. "Dennard asking questions like he's still police, and then all the bodies around—this time you're going to answer me—" He turned toward Dennard and brought up a fist.

"Lieutenant, *stand down! now!*" The words shrilled like a whistle in the room.

Voices began to blare beyond the wall, but the possessed man tried to close in on his "prisoner."

Mark lunged between them, with a fleeting thought of *Winton doesn't need Dennard, but he needs* me *intact*. "Jennings" shook his fists and roared something at him, something too lost in the pretended rage to settle into words.

Then the voices and the pounding footsteps flooded in, and Mark drew back to let the police drag their lieutenant to the ground, still ranting. *Don't think about the real man trapped inside all this, the life that's being ruined—if Winton leaves him alive—all to give me an excuse...*

Instead Mark found himself shouting down the captain's apologies with words about *is this your idea of protecting us* followed by *let us out of here now.*

All building on the puppetmaster's opening. Because Winton needed them outside.

CHAPTER SIX

PREY

It took until morning before the police and their doctor released them. The guards around him and Dennard—and probably on Christa, in her own room—didn't vanish at once, but every hint they made about lingering over more protection, questions, or accusations shriveled when Mark or Dennard mentioned how the department's own man had come after them.

Mark only had to channel a fraction of his own anger to push back against any pressure that came. Dennard was recovering, but Winton could be back at any time if Mark couldn't rescue Sasha and her mother. He felt Angie coming and going at the window all night, but he tried not to guess how far across the city she flew between her visits, or how desperate she was for an answer. For himself, all he had was what little sleep he could get, and the rage that right now he owed to Nolan, and to Bryan Petrie, for turning Henry and Sasha and her mother into bargaining chips.

When the doctor finished examining Dennard, Mark barely noticed his summary, only the cautious smile on her face. Then Mark was leading the injured man outside.

Dennard didn't say a word, not on all the long way out past the police, and Mark could only walk with him and wince at any wobble in his step.

When they stood under the open air, Dennard finally said "Next step: I try to take Christa and get where Winton can't find us, but that'll take time. Any more news from Kate?"

"Kate?" Well, that was *one* side that had stayed quiet. "Not a sound, after that message that I missed because of… everything."

"She'll call back. Whenever she's free."

Dennard's words were simple, quiet things, that ended at once and left the silence between them again, growing, stretching—

"I could have stopped all this," Mark had to say.

"Don't you start—no," Dennard broke off, and he folded his arms. "On second thought, just how is this your fault?"

"How?" Mark glanced around the street, keeping his eyes on the busy, untroubled people nearby instead of meeting that gaze. "Because you got hurt, *again.* I let Sasha run back to her 'hiding' place that was on the same block as her mother, when I should have demanded she move somewhere Nolan hadn't already seen her. And I missed our chance at the book Angie needed, and we lost Sasha herself and Henry in the same night! *And* Winton's threatening you, with Angie stuck outside the window watching, and I have to defend *him.* All because my father… this is a man who just shot his own sister's son, and marched him off with the others!"

"And that's your fault too?" Dennard's voice sharpened.

"Not that, just… I'll fix it." His hands tightened on the coat. "This is only until I get Henry and Sasha and her mother out, while you and Christa get somewhere Winton can't find you. And I can handle Bryan Petrie. Nolan must have given him talismans she cut from this coat. He spotted both of you by sensing the magic you had on you, but I can look for his too. And he can't know much about flying—trust me, I'll *make* him tell me where Henry and the rest are. Whatever it takes."

He stopped then, felt his fingers kneading at the coat, too eager for the throb of power waiting in it.

Dennard took a long, slow glance at his grip on the leather. "You're ready to chase around Lavine until you find an answer? I know a better way. But first, I want to know that you'll keep that under control."

Mark nodded. "I know. I have to watch the magic—"

"And your temper. I want your word here. Think, what would Henry say if you pushed yourself off the edge, trying to save him?"

"I… yeah." He sighed, and met Dennard's knowing eyes. "Control. I promise."

Dennard studied him a moment. "Then keep an eye on Nolan herself. Or go after that assistant of hers, Zeke Brent—Nolan doesn't let many people in, but he has to have seen something. Also, the police won't forget how we accused her, or us either. Watch for that, and you might be able to use it."

"Right." The word was easy, too little for how Dennard's judgment took a tangle of threats and still pulled out the best answer. After a concussion.

Dennard's eyes turned up the street, and for a moment they closed. He went on:

"Don't forget that promise. Keep the magic under control, and the rest of it too. If I weren't so shaky I'd be right there with you, but now all the real calls have to be yours. Because you'll be the guy on the ground. Sort of," and he smiled tightly.

A laugh broke out of Mark, one quick sound before he caught it.

I won't let you down. I can't. He swallowed, and his hand lifted from the coat wanting to reach toward Dennard's arm.

Dennard looked back, and Mark's hand settled to his side. Again, "Right," was all he could say.

* * *

Henry's BMW was still outside the apartments where he'd been taken. Mark started it up with the spare key fob, and tried to move it gently over the streets' last traces of slush. He couldn't help Henry, or anyone, by roaring this car into a wall like he had Dennard's. And Angie still came and went above him, making her own searches but always coming back to follow where he drove.

He even managed to shut the door without slamming it, when he left the car by the curb and moved up the block to view Nolan's home again.

The estate always looked different in daylight. The long stone wall still meant something at these hours when passing cars and curious eyes could see him if he leaped over.

The police car changed it even more.

The cops must have gone on inside, but they'd left their car parked outside the gate like some brand of shame for the wealthy neighborhood to see. Mark tried to hold the layout of Nolan's cameras and scanners in his head... but staying back made his gut ache now. He moved up to a tree outside the wall, that gave some cover from the motion sensors beyond it, and hopped up to steal one glance over.

Two cops were walking out toward the gate, with an angry wave back at Nolan in her doorway. And... that had to be Zeke walking behind them, shooing them out. And going to his own car that sat just inside the gate.

Did she keep them out of the house? Are Henry and the rest hidden inside there? Except, would Nolan really have risked everything on keeping the police out—when Irene's body had been found there already?

The squat manor was a tiny fortress, complete with its wall around the grounds. Olivia Nolan had set the place up to keep herself safe... and even before Mark had first come here, she'd tried tailing *him* when the news had hinted about people falling from the sky, to head off whether he was a magical threat. That was what she did— responded to threats to herself. No, she'd never bring her prisoners here.

She had both possession magic and weather magic, two ways to reach out to the world without leaving her shelter at all. And now she had *his father* to hold her prisoners, or that man and Winton could be closing in on each other at any moment. While he was staring at walls.

By the gate, the police pulled their car over. To block Zeke's tiny blue car in the driveway.

Zeke shook his fist, tried to speak to them through the window. Too far away to notice Mark, or for him to hear.

Mark's hands grabbed at cold stone. The coat's power smoldered around him, and he vaulted the wall and dashed along its inner side just ahead of the fears of how Nolan's security must be lighting up. The police and the always-loyal Zeke would be stuck outside the gate ahead, and the wall hid him from them.

"And where are you going now?" demanded one voice.

"To work. But try to search me if you want—her lawyer would love filing a harassment suit."

Search him? Mark halted just behind the gate and tried to reach for any of the small stillness of Nolan's talismans in the car. But the coat's power thrummed through his veins and swallowed his focus.

Instead, their words kept pushing into his attention.

"—was a dead body found here, Mr. Brent. And now accusations of kidnapping—"

"—need that lawyer now? Ms. Nolan was attacked by a mad dog yesterday. Be grateful she's giving any respect to this circus at all!"

Circus? That had been Kate's word for public attention too. But, *focus, dammit.*

The cop's voice pushed on "A dead body, I said! You think you can ignore that?"

"Your own investigators called it an accident. Isn't it time *you* stopped Mark Petrie and his friends from making senseless accusations?"

"And if it's more than accusations?"

Mark strained. If there were just one touch of Nolan's talismans there, it would tell him how much Zeke was trusted…

The cold wall brushed his side and jolted his eyes open—he'd been swaying on his feet. A car was roaring away into the distance.

But only one car. He moved in on the closed gate and peeped out through it.

Zeke was still there. He sat with his hands on the wheel, slumped and shaken. Like a man weighed down by something he knew. *Or suspected.*

Mark vaulted the gate in a moment, before he even thought who might see him move. Then he was standing next to Zeke's open window.

"You! Stay away from me, I'll call the police—" Zeke grabbed a button and the window snapped up.

"I'm not going to hurt you. The killer's not me, it's the woman you're protecting!" The words came out as a growl.

"Stop *lying!"*

I promised Dennard, calm. Mark had to clench his teeth shut, and took a long look at Zeke's face, at the tanned, smooth lines tightened up by worry and frustration. He had to make him understand.

"Irene died. Right here," he tried again. "You want to tell me you never asked why? Or when that gang attacked Nolan's banquet, don't forget I saw they were coming. You had no idea, but I knew, didn't I? And I know what Nolan and I did to stop them that night... we *killed* some of them, to save more lives. And now some of those lives we saved are being held hostage. By her."

Henry... his fingers clenched.

"Hostage. Right." Zeke's voice was tight, more contained than Mark's sounded in his ears. "Can't you leave us alone? Ms. Nolan never did a thing to you, all she wants is to get through a day without something attacking her—"

"That's what I want too. But someone dived out of the sky and *took* that—he took it from me, and he took it from Nolan too. But she's the one who fought back by holding hostages and hiring a thug that's..."

Mark halted. It was all he could do to keep from shouting. Instead he leaned over the car—the blue vehicle was so small he might not need magic to push it over.

"Zeke, remember this number." He flashed a letter-based phone number on his phone, a tip line they'd tried using in the past. "You'll need it someday. Remember, Irene worked for Nolan. And she still killed her when she saw too much. You have to know you could be next—"

Zeke snapped a fierce shake of his head. "You don't know her at all."

"And you know her so well? Do you know why she went to the campus yesterday? I do. Or think about this: does she have places away from here that would be safe to keep prisoners? Somewhere she never paid much attention to before, but now it's where she's hold-ing—"

"You're insane! If I see you one more time I'm calling the cops, no matter what she tells me!" He grabbed for the key.

"Listen to me! You know too much—"

The engine snarled and the car squealed away down the road.

Mark stared after it. *I wanted to persuade him, not scream at him— I said I wouldn't let this get to me!*

Still… he held where he stood, trying to let his breath slow, until Zeke passed out of sight around the corner. Then he dashed for his own car as fast as he could keep his feet on the ground.

Zeke couldn't get away. Nolan's winding streets were a maze Mark had solved long ago—he knew when to gun the engine to keep the blue car just in view as it made the important turns, and how to fall back out of sight when there was only one route Zeke could take.

Partway out, he felt Angie slide into place above Zeke. He drew back, grinning—with her presence over Zeke's car he didn't even need to see it.

They moved from the winding streets into the city in only minutes. He tried to hold down his hope, that Zeke might be rushing straight to some secret, suspicious place of Nolan's. The full city traffic and Angie's guidance let Mark hang back among the other cars, only creeping forward now and then to steal an occasional glance at his blue guide. He set the coat aside on the passenger seat; the amount of power in his belt was all his head could handle now.

He'd just edged up for another glimpse at Zeke, when Angie pulled back. She wheeled and dove low, again and again above one particular gray sedan a few cars ahead of him. How long had that car been there, behind Zeke…

The police. Sure, if they'd seen Zeke peel out from Nolan's, they'd want to know where he was headed too. *And me, are there more cops watching me too?* Mark eased further back within the traffic to put more distance from them. Still, Angie only warned him of the one car, then moved back up to where Zeke must be.

So that was it, let the police find whatever Zeke had suspected? Mark tried to let out a slow, calming breath. He couldn't stop them, couldn't risk racing ahead of them—and if they found Henry and the rest, they should be better than him at freeing hostages. At least it would keep him away from his father.

His phone chimed. He saw Kate's number and dodged into the slow lane before he dug it out.

"I'm driving—do we make this quick?" Tracking Angie made keeping the car on course easy, but splitting his attention that far was enough. "I'm following Zeke, and so are the cops."

"You're what?" Angie's mother had the same cold, unshakable tone it did on most days, so close to judging him.

"He could be about to lead them to Nolan's hostages. Maybe the cops get my father."

"And Winton gets what he wants?"

"It's just till Dennard and Christa get out of his sight—or you want him to come after them again? Or let my father *keep* Henry? This way everyone goes free, nobody has to get hurt."

"I see."

What was she hinting at now? Mark opened his mouth…

Angie swerved away, streaking up a side street. Mark's gaze jerked after her before he locked it back on the street in front of him. The cops' gray car wasn't turning, did that mean Zeke hadn't changed course either? So what had Angie seen?

Her presence was already a block away and fading fast. Mark swung up the side street after her.

A block later he caught it: the distant, solid pulse of a gravity talisman ahead.

It was already twisting away up the road—he pressed his foot down and felt the engine growl softly. Someone up there had his own gravity magic, someone not far from where Zeke had been heading, someone who might have spotted Zeke and the police just in time to run. *Or sensed* our *power…*

That's my father up there.

Mark wrenched the wheel left to sidestep two hesitant drivers, before diving back and swinging on into the crowded business street after it.

Cars swam through the street in front of him, too many to see past to which one *he* was in, but Mark felt a grin growing on his face. *The more cars in the way, the more pains it makes for the amateur driver.* Angie soared up beyond him, faster than him and closing in on the magic.

Mark twisted around a lumbering truck, ignoring the honks behind him. Which car was the magic in? Would he spot some kidnapper-sized van with Henry and the rest neatly in the back, one 911 call away from rescue?

Or they could be back at whatever place Zeke had been checking on, and the police could be freeing them right now without anyone's help. Not that it ever seemed to be that simple.

He shot past an underground parking's ramp. No sign of a van in view, even though he could feel magic where some car ahead was struggling for the fastest lane; the prisoners might not be here at all.

And his father could sense him coming too, so he couldn't try tailing him to Henry and Sasha. That left… it left forcing the answers out of him.

Of course it does.

Mark's fingers locked on the wheel, and his eyes narrowed to sweep the cars he closed in on.

A tiny yellow VW lurched out of the speed lane and swerved through a reckless, mid-block U-turn—the car with the magic. Mark fought his way left after it, but the Bug had already rushed on past him, and twisted onto Juneau toward the overpass.

Mark banged a fist on the wheel and watched for an opening to turn after him.

Just how had that car been moving, back when he first sensed it, had it been just finishing a turn away from him? *Did he sense me be-*fore *I was close enough to spot him?*

Angie darted into range ahead of him, and swept on past him after the target… Mark pumped the brakes at a glimpse of a tailgate rushing up at him, and felt Henry's unfamiliar car skid for one breathless moment before it settled.

He pulled in a steadying breath and edged the car to a bare patch of curb, a loading zone. Send the police? he reached for the phone.

A voice snapped out from it, *Kate.* "Are you alright?" She was still on.

"Fine—" But, what would the police do if he called, if he said he'd gone after the kidnapper himself? Or could he chase his father straight down Juneau, or guess which way he'd get off…

Kate said "You need to let your father go."

"What??" The raggedness in his voice made him wince.

"Think past what happened last night," she said, steady, calming. "Winton made his threats, but I know my ex is already getting out of his sight, so you can't live in fear of his retaliation. And this could be your last chance to reconnect with the strongest ally we've ever found. Think: you and Nolan almost caught Winton's real body before, and now he's making you defend him—does that mean he's desperate? And the simplest way to help Nolan's prisoners, and restore Angie, could be to search out our common enemy together again. And now she's got one more person who can search—"

"I *know!*" But, not after Winton's threats, and never beside his father. Mark glared at the stream of cars for some gap he could slip into. "They could be hunting Winton right now—my God, the park!"

He shoved the phone in a pocket and yanked the car back into the lane, barely sliding in behind an SUV.

"If he stays on Juneau," he gasped, more to himself than for what Kate might hear, "if he cuts left… he could get just blocks away from the park, and he could sense the secret…"

The engine roared at his touch. The streets formed in his mind; not the simple lines of maps but living channels like blood vessels, each pulsing at their own speed. Which way would cut that Bug off from Rosewood Park?

Unless he'd already passed it. *I kept thinking what my father would mean for the search for Winton, I forgot he could find the location of our magic first!* At least Nolan couldn't tell him the words to keep recharging a talisman, but for Bryan Petrie to know his son always had to go back to that spot in the park… or if Winton got hold of him…

Mark forced his hands to move gently on the delicate little BMW gearshift. He let the stoplights and the pace of traffic fill him; he was *driving*, not fighting for every inch of street. *But, this is the man who left his drug supply out and killed my mother as sure as any bullet. And last night he* did *put a bullet in the only person who gave me a real home.* And he stole Angie's hope.

The gearshift strained as Mark slammed it over.

But, the VW could have gone the other way and missed the park completely. He swung onto the next street, faster now. As long as he locked out the idea of who he was chasing, and focused on the roads and how to convince the cops, he could keep his head clear enough to catch him.

When he sensed the talisman ahead, he kept his thoughts on the traffic.

—The trucks and vans jutting through the stream of cars ahead; where was that glint of yellow?

—The hope of feeling it angling away from the park, still five blocks short of the source of magic.

—The *joy* of sensing Angie ahead and knowing she had lured his father away from it.

Mark eased the engine back. Now they only had to pin him down, trap him, to save the prisoners and everyone.

Or let him go up against Winton. Mark's foot lifted from the gas at the thought. Like Kate said, his father might find their real enemy… and he and Nolan just might finish the puppetmaster at last. Or else Winton could erase this newest spellkeeper with a touch.

Mark's heart pounded to swallow the car's roar. He held onto the image of Henry and Sasha and her mother still caught between them.

But if I only wanted to save them, why didn't I call the cops long ago? His fingers locked and couldn't seem to let the gearshift go.

Then, he sensed Winton behind him.

Mark spun the car around in the still eddy between a pair of vans. Winton, it had to be Winton, had grabbed control of someone *just now,* more than a block behind where he'd passed? And not another spybird: this magic was at street level, so the killer had some plan that brought him down from the air.

Mark slowed to match the traffic's speed, stalking instead of chasing. Just to have a clean shot at the killer instead of dodging Nolan's paranoia and his own father… The puppet lurked somewhere on the street ahead.

Was it moving as part of the traffic, like one of the cars? As Mark thought that, he sensed the magic drifting right and slowing to a stop, like pulling up at a curb.

It vanished—and he felt it reappear high above, in what had to be Winton shifting his control to another talisman, on one of his birds. Mark kept the wheel steady; Winton might be searching, but why would he recognize him in Henry's car? And the human body had to be in one of the parked cars ahead…

Then Mark felt what he'd missed. The other gravity talisman, his father, closing in behind at the edge of his range. He wrenched his head around and felt Angie swinging by above, veering up a side street.

Like she was trying to lead his father away again, he realized. But the talisman only bore in closer.

Up ahead, a white van sat among the cars pulled up along the road. A white van with a staff-and-snakes medical emblem on the side.

Mark's mouth went dry. Of course it would be a medical van—just days ago Winton had needed help to move his real body, even possessing a man to drag it away from Mark and Nolan. And now Winton had shifted from his driver up to a watchful bird… and maybe left his own body helpless inside *there*.

A yellow shape glinted in Mark's mirror.

There was no magic in the van he could track, not while Winton kept his focus in the sky. But Mark had still led his father right to the obvious target, and Nolan could be sending her raw power to join the attack at any moment, the same as she'd sent that fog cover last night.

The Bug moved out ready to pass him.

In one cold instant, two thoughts twined in Mark's head: *Winton can't even move without his power painting a target on him,* and *My father can take him on and at least we'll be rid of one of them.*

But that could leave Henry and Sasha trapped—and Angie—

That alley ahead. Mark slowed, then ripped the wheel around and slammed his car over as the VW moved by. Tires squealed, horns blared as echoes to the thunder in his head. *Damn, damn, dammitall—*

But the yellow Bug spun away right up the alley, the dead end. Mark wrestled his fishtailing car to a halt, and felt his lips split in a fierce grin.

Behind him the talisman moved. Mark matched the energy to the skinny shape springing away from the Bug—the *only* person who'd been inside it—and racing from the alley up the sidewalk toward the people ahead. Moving in a bouncing, ground-eating magical gait toward the edge of a crowd.

What was that, the closed-down farmer's market? Was some band trying to hold a pocket *concert* before they took down the canopy for the winter?

Mark wrenched open his own door.

As he did, Winton's bird plummeted from the sky, striking straight for his father.

In the instant Mark's foot touched the street he thought, *but Winton said he'd give me a chance to stop him first—*

His father leaped away. A clumsy long leap that left people staring, but it launched at the moment the bird dove and swept him straight to the edge of the concert's crowd and under the market's canopies.

He went into the crowd? *Idiot!* Mark flung himself forward, his eyes taking in how many people Winton's power could skip between to close in on his target. *Save him or Winton, him or Winton, which one saves my family trapped between them?*

Mark twisted between onlookers, using only a hint of magic to keep his step light. Voices rumbled around him, only a few here and there. The music beat at his ears, some rock number too off-key to place, as he stepped under the canopy.

The "concert space" had more space than people, and he saw the lean shape in brown huddled near one of the support beams. Pressing buttons on his phone.

With a shriek like a passing train, a blast of wind smashed into the market. Canvas strained and flapped all above their heads, and some startled musician let his guitar strings *sproing*. Worried voices clamored louder than the howl of the windstorm.

They think it's the last freakish months' weather getting freakier. This weather has a name, *and Nolan could be close by.*

His father looked up from his phone and turned toward the stage, the thick of the crowd. Mark arrowed forward to cut him off, and saw him spin and make for the edge of the canopy.

Winton's bird was sweeping down again, how could his target not *notice* it—

A second bird struck at the first, Angie's shriek mingling with the winds. Winton veered off, and Mark felt both flung away in a surge of the gale.

Mark closed in on his target. Somewhere behind him the band began pounding out their clumsy beat again, as if they could drown out the frightened voices or push back the wind before it split the canvas. That wind was stronger now—as if Nolan herself was drawing closer too.

He reached his father.

Bryan Petrie's face was like a reflection in a window, if the glass were lined with streaks of raindrops and washed away with a pale, wasted tone. In the years since Mark had seen him, it hadn't changed a line—or there had been no space left to damage anymore. And he gazed right back, waiting.

Mark pushed himself in close, enough to hide his words from the people around. What came out was:

"How can you *do* that?!" He sucked in a breath and tried again. "You just *grabbed* Sasha and her mother? And Henry, Henry! Are they even alive?"

"How could you not tell me about this… power?"

His father spread his hands, and smiled. And those hands trembled, his eyes were wide and dark. *Is the bastard on* drugs, *in the middle of all this?*

Those dilated eyes tilted straight toward the belt at Mark's waist. "How did you make that belt so strong? This is what those ex-Blades had, isn't it? But I bet you can run faster, you can jump over the moon!"

Mark struggled to keep his fists from clenching, and failed. "Are… they… alive?"

The man waved a hand to brush that aside. "You really think I'd kill them? Nolan said you'd hate me. You never answered my letters."

Canvas cracked in the rising wind. *"Hate* you? Where are they?"

"I'll take you to them. They aren't back where those cops almost caught me, but we still have to be quick—"

Mark stepped in front of him. "If you say they're fine, they must be dead and cold!" He meant the words as a test—his father's drug-tightened voice gave him so little to read—but the rage in his own tone flooded his ears. "You shot Henry!"

His father's eyes closed, for a moment. "Someone was coming in the door, so I put the lights out—how'd I know it would be family?"

That voice halted, almost as if he felt something.

Then he leaned toward Mark. "But I said, quick! Winton's body feels like it's right up there—" He waved back toward the street. "If we join up with him in time I bet we get even more power."

"Join…"

The word came out as a shocked wheeze, before Mark caught his breath.

"You, you *just* joined Nolan and you want to turn on her, for *that killer?*" He glanced up toward where the van had been—would it still be there?

His father tilted his head in surprise. "You mean you aren't with him? Why the hell not?"

"I didn't—" *Who am I protecting from who again?* He gritted his teeth, tried to think of Henry and the rest, and what might shake their captor's confidence. "You go to Winton and he'll stab you in the back.

But so will Nolan. You know she used to have a hacker with her, Irene, until she killed her?"

The man sighed, he actually sighed, and for the first time some of his uncaring manner seeped from him. "Nolan didn't give me a choice—"

"There's always a way!" Angie's rule came to his lips, but the words came out like a curse with his father here. Where was Angie, where was Winton now?

"You think so?" Bryan Petrie took a slow step toward him. "Our time's running out. Soon the only way left will be to stick with Nolan—and there's a bonus for me if I bring you back to her side. Or a bigger one if I find how you make your magic and bring her that."

Tricks on top of tricks... "There's no way I'd trust you, or her," he spat back.

"So you're just leaving Henry, and those two women?" His glittering eyes narrowed then, locked onto Mark. "A minute ago they were all you talk about. When I left them, Sasha was so scared she can't talk straight. Doesn't matter what we say, she won't buy that we don't want to hurt them, Nolan just wants to take Winton down."

There's a lie in there, I heard it somewhere...

Mark glared back, but all he wanted was to shout him down. He opened his mouth.

The phone in his father's hand buzzed.

Mark stared, his heard pounding in his ears louder than the faltering music, as his father actually stopped to listen to the call. Like he was *expecting* it, like someone was watching. His face was unreadable.

The phone came down. "Nolan says this place is too crowded. And, I brought one of the prisoners along in the car for leverage—I'll show you."

He started through the crowd. Mark forced out a breath and moved after him, thoughts whirling.

Keep my eyes wide open, those two could be planning anything. Probably all a lie, how could they keep Henry or Sasha out of sight in that tiny car? Mark watched the crowd they moved through for any glimpse of Nolan closing in on them, and then they stepped out into the worst of her wind. At least his belt had his father's tiny talisman outmuscled.

Winton was moving. The bastard's bird was diving down through the storm to position itself for another rush at them. Bryan Petrie yelped and jumped backward.

Can't one thing leave me alone for one damn minute?? Mark flung a scream of "This is for Sasha!" into the wind.

The bird twisted away. Mark felt it spin away in the wind, gone. His father's head turned to follow it, then gave Mark a startled glance before moving on up the blind alley.

The space was empty except for the yellow car. Mark kept his hands ready to strike, and one eye on the alley's entrance behind him, as they walked closer.

His father drew out the keys. But instead of moving to the door, he unlocked the trunk. "Here."

Was Henry stuffed in *there? And I could have crashed the car with him in it!*

Mark stepped closer. His eyes locked on the rising lid, but his ears waited for that one footfall at his back—

The trunk was empty.

Sure enough, he heard his father lunge toward him, and he was already diving away clear of that touch. He caught one glimpse of a stern expression and a flicker of power running all through his father. One of Nolan's talismans on him, Nolan's ambush striking through him.

Mark dove forward. His hands lashed out, grabbed the traitor—

Ready power and blood thundered in his veins, deafening—

A simple shove and a twist of magic sent the helpless old man crashing into the open, waiting trunk. Mark heard the keys clatter on the pavement. He shoved a sprawling foot inside with the rest of the man and slammed the lid down.

It might be the exact trap they'd meant for him. Instead he locked the trunk, then slapped a hand on its rim and poured weight into that one spot until the car's suspension strained, metal buckled to seal the lid… and he could hear his own savage breathing slow again.

I just touched a possessed man. Nolan could have grabbed me, *if she was faster with this magic.*

But we just captured the man Nolan needs to track Winton. Who's got "leverage" now?!

And then there's Winton himself.

Mark raced up the street. Winton's attention was still in his bird battling back through the winds, and Mark saw the medical van still waiting at the curb. He dodged between people, leaping and twisting for every frantic step to close in on their true enemy.

The magic shifted to grip the van's driver.

Mark could see every line of every figure on the sidewalk ahead, every glint of paint where the car still didn't move, in the moments that he flung himself across space and onto its back bumper. The glass of the rear window lay right in front of him.

The back of the van was empty. No injured Winton, nothing but rows of shelves.

He lunged around the pavement to the van's front, to stare in the passenger window.

His eyes found only a tiny, dark man at the wheel. Winton's twisted thoughts looked back at him through those eyes.

Then the puppetmaster's grip vanished. The driver stared out, stared around, and began a torrent of curses about waking up in a strange place.

Mark staggered back from the van, unsteady on his feet.

Winton had forced him to catch his pursuer… and the schemer had taken this driver onto the street to draw them all out, but his real, crippled body had never been there at all. *All this fighting over a decoy.*

Except this time, Mark had a prisoner of his own.

CHAPTER SEVEN

LINKS OF THE CHAIN

For some reason, Bryan Petrie wasn't shouting for help. By the time Mark grabbed his coat and circled back, the Beetle still stood alone in the alley, and he heard only a faint rustling beneath the jammed trunk lid. Still there, along with that feeble gravity talisman and a possession talisman too.

Mark took the key he'd caught up and backed the Bug out of the alley. His fingers were shaking from the aftermath of the chase and the confrontation, furies that wouldn't release him even while Nolan's gale over the block faded to a whisper.

Go easy on the gas, I'm just one more car pulling away from this attempt at a concert, don't think about anything more—

Winton's bird swung into his awareness. He felt it two blocks to the—north?—and moving closer, and then Angie not so far from there. Both searching, for Nolan, in case she'd snuck out here after all?

Their directions aligned to streets in his mind, and Mark twisted up a block before he saw the underground parking entrance he was searching for. Winton was too close, too close… he stabbed the ticket button, pulled his foot off the pedal to keep from ramming the Bug through the slowly, slowly rising gate… but it did rise, and freed him to jolt down the ramp and out of sight of Winton's bird.

Winton. Nolan's body never had to come out here at all, any more than Winton's had. But Winton's eye was out there searching for her anyway.

Mark rolled along the lot's well-lit gray slope and the ranks of cars, feeling Winton pass on by above. Angie and Winton still crisscrossed the sky, ignoring each other as if the owl and the man who'd put her there had some accidental truce.

The longer we keep Winton searching here, the deeper Dennard can get himself and Christa into hiding. That would leave Mark free to focus on Henry and the rest of Nolan's hostages—

and my father.

Somehow he kept his grip light on the wheel until the car reached a clear space. He parked, climbed out to check the trunk lid again, and walked a few bumpers away as he got out his phone.

Dennard needed to be safe; he should check on him before he opened that trunk. But his fingers were trembling again, and his speed dial brought up Kate.

She answered with "Mark. I see you're alright."

"Better than I thought. Winton got away—well, I think the real Winton was never here—but I caught my father, and he's the only other one who can track him." A grin spread over Mark's face, as he glanced around for anyone passing by. "Plus, the cops might have already found Henry and Sasha, if they're at wherever my father made his break away from. But I bet it's not that easy."

" 'Caught' your father?"

"Trapped him. He hasn't even tried to escape—but I think he's still got his phone in there. Don't know what he's playing at now."

"Mark…" Kate's voice was tight, hard. "If he was chasing Winton, and you interfered, do you know what you put at risk?"

"I know! But Winton wasn't even here. This way he won't be taking it out on Dennard and Christa, and they have more time to get out of sight."

And Winton doesn't have to kill my father, whispered a thought.

He rushed on "It's not like my father or Nolan would call the police on me. Not those two."

"I suppose not. You should be more worried about her tracking that phone of his herself. But at least that would make her come to you."

"You mean now I have to protect that man from her too? Well, he does sound like he'd stab her in the back for half a promise. Or stab anyone, and skip the promise." He winced; had he said that out loud?

"No, Mark. I mean, Nolan needs him to search for Winton. And you have a prisoner to trade for the ones she has, and that puts the focus back on what each of you wants. Which is, stopping Winton."

He frowned, then paused to let a car roll by. When had moved on outside, he added "You said something about that before. You think we can work with Nolan again even when she's killing people? Or do you just mean we can trade our people for hers?" *My father for Henry and Sasha?*

"We can't trust her, no. But it may be our goals aren't so different."

He shook his head. "She killed her own friend, Irene. Of course we're different!"

"You introduced yourself to her by breaking into her home; we've all made choices in this. And Nolan is holding Winton's book, *and* Sasha, the two best ways to bring Angie back."

"Careful," and Mark heard a sharpness in his voice. "Don't just go there after all the times you said that was impossible."

"We'll see. If we can stay out of Winton's reach for a while, you might get a chance to see what Nolan's really made of. In fact, I'm putting together something that might help with that."

"What's that?"

"It should be ready any time now. You'll see."

* * *

Mark drove slowly, dreading the moment he might sense Winton looking for him again, or Nolan's ice closing around him. Dennard and Christa might be having an easier time shaking off any tails than him, even doing it blind to Winton's presence. At least they weren't tied down to the same bright yellow car by the man locked in its trunk.

But Winton didn't spot him again, and nothing behind him seemed like police surveillance either. Instead Mark worked his way out through city concrete to suburban lawns to the widening spaces of the highway beyond Lavine, trying not to think of how they were only searching for the privacy to tear today's wounds in him even wider.

The clear lands outside the city streets felt too rough. Couldn't Dennard know some good solid parking lot that was far enough out of earshot, somewhere Mark had seen a dozen times? Instead he had only his phone's vague description of "woodlands" when he turned off the highway, and into side roads that only got narrower and narrower. Trees taller and stouter than in any city park pressed around him.

Somehow Dennard and Christa were there ahead of him. He pulled the Beetle over into the brush beside the gray Chevy they'd rented, and they climbed out to meet him.

Christa's gaze stabbed at him the moment she stepped out, silent and unflinching. Dennard looked the same as ever... *but this will be the first time he's met my father, except for being ambushed by him last night.* That would have told Dennard all he needed to know about Bryan Petrie.

Mark turned away from them and forced his steps toward the trunk. His shoes crunched through some kind of high grass. The coat folded over his arm burned with ready power.

"So today you took Henry's BMW," Christa said, "and you bring back a Beetle?"

"Sorry." What was that, another accusation, or a joke?

Christa looked at the ground. "I... shouldn't have blamed you for this, Mark. I know Henry made a decision to help you, and I'm sorry. But right now—the police still haven't found Henry and the others. So stop telling me to get out," and she glared at Dennard beside her. "Not while she has him."

"I understand that," Dennard said, "but—"

She waved him aside. "But right now we have the person who took him, and we have to make the most of that. Mark, I know he's your father—"

Dennard muttered "I don't think you know those two at all—"

"Look, Mark, you can position yourself as the 'good cop' here if you want. But please don't try getting in my way."

And she picked up a branch—a short, heavy branch lying beside their car, stubbled where twigs had already been stripped off. She hefted it awkwardly, but she planted her feet ready to swing it hard.

My magic can crush metal with a touch, and she wants a club?

Mark breathed out some of the tension in his chest. "Okay," he managed.

They spread out around the back of the Bug, each keeping well out of reach of it.

Dennard drew out a gun, and all expression faded from his face. "We're going to open the trunk," he called. "When we do, throw out your talisman and your weapons."

"The mind talisman too," Mark added. "I'll know."

"It's… not that easy." The muffled voice sounded cramped, or in pain. Or wanted them to think he was.

"We'll be watching you." Christa drew the club back and up like a baseball bat.

Mark gripped the trunk where he'd bent it to seal it shut. The coat's energy crashed into it, eager to fling the car high above the forest or crumple it like an empty can… *so easy, so much simpler than pulling one piece of metal up and the other down just enough…* he clenched his teeth and held the power contained until the lid creaked open.

A gun arced out, bouncing off the bumper to land in the brush. Then a scrap of leather with a hint of magic.

Mark peered inside the shallow trunk. Was that trembling shape huddled in there what the long cold drive had done to his father?

Christa snapped "Now toss out the silver one. We know what a possession talisman looks like too."

"I… told you, she didn't make it that easy."

Bryan Petrie stretched one leg out of the trunk, and he slid his pants cuff back. A sturdy plastic loop ringed his ankle; on it was a heavy lock, fused to a lump of grayer metal that would be the talisman. *Fastened on like the electronic bracelets they use for parole— makes it about right for him.*

Mark remembered what the others relied on him for, and held his breath. Just looking at that man—and the shivering, frozen look on that face—made his nerves crawl, but he strained for calmness, for the stillness to sense any other waiting magic…

"It's the only talisman left on him," he sighed. "He's powerless if he can't touch us." He stepped back, as his father began fumbling his way out of the trunk.

"And you keep your hands where we can see them," Dennard added, gun ready. "So, Nolan must have had that whole device ordered as soon as she saw what Winton made talismans out of. Before she knew how to activate them. That really is the kind of enemy we're dealing with."

His voice had a grimness that made Bryan Petrie flinch—a glimpse of weakness.

Mark added "And she doesn't trust you either. Maybe you can use her weapon, but she's got her magic tied to it so her weapon can use *you,* and you can't take it off."

"But she's not listening now," Dennard said, with a glance at Mark to confirm it. "How'd you meet her anyway?" he added. It was the first question in the interrogation, slipped in so calmly it could have been nothing.

"Oh, you know how it is," the shivering man said. "You're out a few weeks, you need money. You get a package with a wad of cash and a bit of leather that says there's more money if you can *feel* another piece of the same stuff. Then you get a job."

Packages? Mark glanced at Dennard. "Those must be what you saw her setting out, before Winton sent the dog at her. Henry said there was magic in them. So that was her testing him."

"And then that night—" Christa leveled the branch at their prisoner, and took a step closer. When you say 'job,' you mean kidnapping. You crept up on our friends and attacked them."

Mark's father—*Bryan, his name's Bryan*—looked at her, then over at Dennard and his gun. "Um, that was you hiding outside the girl's place? Look, it was just a job. I sensed you, I came up behind you… I could have shot you instead, y'know. Don't blame me if your head hurts, it was a *job.*"

Dennard's face didn't stir.

"Did you apologize to Henry too?" Mark snapped, and his fingers kneaded the coat over his arm. "After you shot your nephew?"

"Nolan didn't say he'd be there—"

"Liar! You already said you know I was in this!" Mark flung back.

Christa poked the branch toward Bryan's face. "Is. Henry. Alright? Are the others? *Convince* me!" She stepped nearer, but Dennard waved her back.

Bryan said "We bandaged his arm up, he's fine, fine! The girl and her mother too. All I had to do was take them to where Nolan wants them kept."

Was that a new quaver in his trembling voice, like *regret?*

Mark's fingers tightened on the coat. "And now you can take us to them, is that it? You think we're that stupid?"

He heard what might have been a low groan from Dennard, and realized he'd been dragging them off from whatever approach Dennard had planned.

But his father just went on "Hey, you and me had our chance back there, before she checked in and noticed we were talking. Now I *have* to do what she says—you saw what she did to me!"

He waved at his ankle, at Nolan's magic leash.

"She could grab me any time! Look, you think I want to go against *you?*" and he motioned toward Mark. "You know I—"

He took a step closer, and Mark drew back.

Christa said "So you're keeping Nolan's secrets because she scares you."

"I got no choice! You people can run and all, but she bosses *storms* around! She's got a back door in my head! How do you beat that?"

"Maybe the way I beat *you,*" Mark said, and the satisfaction rang in his voice.

"You're all dead, if you take her on. Unless you got something better than floating to back you up."

—There he is again, asking if we went over to Winton's side. Why, so he could betray him and us all at once? Mark clenched his teeth, kept silent.

"Then we have a problem," Dennard said. "We need to know where you took the prisoners."

"Like they're still there? I bet she moved them by now."

Dennard smiled, faintly. "You think so? The police didn't find anything at the shop you fled from, but I think that was always a wrong trail. Nolan can't go out easily, not with the police *and* Winton watching her. So I think they're right where you really left them."

Bryan Petrie shook his head, stumbled back. "I can't! Think, man—she could take me over, any time!"

"It's just an anklet," Christa said. "We can cut it off."

"Yeah? And what about the poison? She stuck a needle in me, said I'd need some antidote from her every day. Or I'm dead."

More lies, it has to be... Mark locked his eyes on the shivering shape, at the darting eyes that would fit so well with him taking some drug. He forced out "So if we don't let you go, we're killing you? And we should believe that?"

His father's head tilted downward, but his gaze stayed on them. Still, his voice had wavered when he'd said his lies, hadn't it?

Mark glanced to the others. Christa took one hand from her branch to wave him and Dennard toward her. Dennard edged to the side to join her but still keep his eyes and gun trained on the prisoner. Mark drew in among them, suddenly relieved to take his eyes off his father and what he claimed.

Christa whispered "It's a lie, isn't it? He's only saying he's poisoned. Nolan isn't making us choose between that and losing our chance at finding Henry."

Dennard said "She's used drugs before, on me and Irene, and Sasha too. Don't forget how dangerous she's proven she is. But, that doesn't mean we have to believe this story either."

Mark had to add "But Nolan wouldn't trust him either, not with power like this, not without every way she could find to control him. Not her." *My father could be* dying *if we keep him here, but it has to be a lie—*

"You wanted to talk to me?"

The cold, crisp words in his father's voice yanked Mark's gaze around. The half-frozen man was standing straight as if his body no longer cared about the temperature, and possession magic coiled through him.

"Nolan," Mark muttered, in case the others had any doubts.

Christa hefted the branch in her hands. "Have you been listening the whole time? Or were you too *busy* to talk about all the people you kidnapped?" Her knuckles were white on the wood, but her voice managed to stay level, though the strain in it made Mark's fists tighten as well.

Dennard's teeth clenched too, Mark saw from the corner of his eye. Then that anger smoothed away as the ex-cop asked "So why are you taking hostages now? How does that get you what you want?" Calm as if he dealt with this every day.

"Why are *you* interfering with my search? We're all enemies of Winton—or you were until today," and the possessed face twisted in one of Nolan's scowls.

"We only—" Mark began, but Dennard waved him silent. What, they couldn't tell her how Winton had threatened them?

Dennard answered "This trouble between us keeps escalating. Winton's the one who twists lives left and right, and has to be put down. If we do have the same enemy, we need to walk our own dispute back before more people get caught in it."

" 'If' we have the same enemy?" she said. "I didn't hear a denial there."

Mark snapped "Of *course* we're not on the killer's side!" Nolan couldn't be *that* paranoid.

"You know we aren't," Dennard added. "And you don't have the body count that he does—not quite, not yet," and his tone tightened to a warning, just for a moment. "So why don't we stop this from getting any worse? If Winton's the real enemy, we both have every reason to make a trade, Bryan Petrie here for Henry. That way we each have one more person with a scanning sense back with us, so we can both put more pressure on Winton. Better for everyone."

"That sounds… reasonable."

At Mark's elbow, a breath whooshed out of Christa.

"But," Nolan went on, "it also sounds like I'd be rewarding your grabbing something of mine as a bargaining play. Or it sounds like he's told you about the poison, and you want to trade someone you're afraid to hold onto. If you want to force a deal with me, you're going to need more determination than that."

"What??" Christa gasped.

The possessed body didn't answer. Instead it lowered itself to the ground, and laid his phone out beside him. Then it slumped over. Not just abandoned, but forced into sleep in the brush.

Mark stared, but his father didn't move. Low wind ruffled through the trees… somewhere a car moved on the road…

"What's she mean?" Christa said. "Did she just dump his body?"

Mark opened his mouth to answer—but the phone on the ground chimed.

"I don't get it," he said. "Why switch to the phone?"

Dennard scooped it up and put it on speaker. "Alright. We're all listening."

Sasha's voice, tight and anxious, spilled into the forest air. "Who's that? Who's there?"

"I'm here," Mark said. "Me and my friends."

"Mark? She's got me and Mom—and your friend Henry. But, she had Henry locked up with us, and now he just unlocked his chains and he's holding the phone…"

Henry. Nolan must be controlling Henry right now, using him to let the other prisoners speak to them in their own words.

The distant car's rumble grew louder.

"It's okay," Mark tried.

Before he could say more, a rasping voice on the phone whispered "They're fine."

It was Henry's voice, but Nolan's measured words, it had to be. Speaking in a low whisper now, maybe too low for Sasha to follow.

That possessed voice went on "Mark, your father isn't so useful if I have to worry about him using up your power when he searches. And you had to take that coat. If I wanted to force a better deal, I might give you ten seconds to tell me the words for your magic, before I shot one of these people."

"No! You can't!" Mark flung the words at the phone, too loud with the car closing in but he had no time to care—

His cousin's stolen voice swelled. "Now, do you want to match wills with *me?* "

A voice behind them said "It's not your will that's the problem."

The car, the car that had been rolling up, had halted beside them—window down and its door swinging open, as Kate stepped out to join them.

She went on "The problem is trusting you. The more you push at us, the harder it is for us to believe there are lines you won't cross."

She stood beside the group now, looking straight past them to the phone in her ex-husband's hand. Her suit had the precise look as if she'd stepped straight off of a first-class airline seat ready to take on some boardroom. Kate Woodward was a small woman, like Angie had been, but the control in her bearing made her seem bigger than Dennard right now.

And Dennard only nodded at her, not surprised at all to see her here in person again.

"Kate Fletcher Woodward."

The voice wasn't from the phone, it was Mark's father again. Nolan's control drew him to his feet again and locked those eyes on Kate.

Nolan went on "So the runaway spellkeeper is back. Who's in charge there?"

Christa answered *"All* of us. You turned all of us against you, when you started talking about shooting our captive friends. In case you missed that part," she added to Kate.

Kate took a long look at the possessed body, then cocked her head to the side. "Can you tell me, why do you even need Sasha or Henry?"

A faint smile etched the stolen face. "Besides the fact that they got you talking? Even you, back in town."

Mark felt the thoughts starting to flow in his head again. "It's not just that, is it?" he said. "Holding Henry means you could force him to search for Winton again, if my father can't help you. If magic can't control him all the time."

Dennard added "And having Sasha and her mother to threaten gives you something else on Henry. Or else you still think you can convince Sasha that Winton's the real danger to her."

Nolan shook her, his, head. "I *think* Winton takes permanent new bodies to stay young, and his daughter here would have been next, if he'd been ready to jump to her. And I think as long as I have her, Winton will have to come out and get her."

"That could be true," Kate said. "We spent most of yesterday try-ing to convince Sasha of the dangers she was in. On the other hand, what if Winton's plans for her are something different?"

"Trying to make me second-guess myself? Don't bother. This is how I read the facts, but it doesn't matter as long as he needs her—and he does. Let me guess, he told you to come save her too, didn't he? Notice that he never used you as hostages to do his dirty work until I got Sasha."

Nobody answered. Even Kate only looked back, still.

"As for Henry and Bryan," Nolan went on, "I need them to find Winton. So I don't think I'll be letting anyone go."

"Except," and Christa's voice swelled with fresh confidence, "you need them alive." She tossed the branch aside, and it clattered and rus-tled away through the brush. "Do you really want to make threats—"

"Want? You think I *want* to be fighting all of you?" The man's voice cracked as Nolan's tone screeched upward. *"Winton's* the one after me!"

"And you want your life back." Kate nodded slowly. "You want a simple, safe life of throwing banquets and using your magic to 'find' days that the skies are clear—not a bad way to use your magic secret-ly, either."

Under his breath, Mark added "Except when she killed Irene for figuring it out."

Kate must have heard that, but she went on "So what do you tell yourself? That you're only protecting the life you built? But these people you're holding aren't Winton, and they didn't threaten you first—they're simply people that got in your way by accident. Wouldn't killing them be Winton's kind of response?"

Dennard cut in "But killing Irene over blackmail is fine?"

His objection rang out and rolled across the open, empty country-side. Mark stared at him, at Kate... but Kate's face held itself impassive, as if she'd never heard the objection at all.

"Accusations are easy," Nolan's stolen voice said.

"Questions aren't, if you decide to answer them," Kate replied. "The more I understood my magic's consequences, the less I liked them either. The best answer I could make was to run away from my heritage."

Nolan flung back "And let your husband keep it instead, and then Mark, until a bunch of street punks were floating off bridges and about to show the whole world what they had! If you want to talk about how much you have in common with me, you shouldn't *run away.*"

Did Kate's head lower, a little? "You may be right. When Winton started making his moves, I got my son to safety. My daughter… wasn't so lucky."

"Now you get it. There's no room for mistakes in this. Or are you back in town talking to me again because now I have the magic that owl needs? Are you bargaining for that too?"

Mark's teeth clenched. That would have been the perfect offer, if they could trust it.

Christa shook her head. "More threats, more promises—"

"It does sound too easy," Kate added. "We'd have to believe all the damage you've done and the threats you've made are nothing more than ways to fight back against Winton's attacks, and that you still have lines you won't cross. Can you make me believe that?"

Nolan's, Bryan Petrie's, eyes narrowed. "You'll *believe* it when I get Winton!"

Dennard stepped past Kate, drawing what looked like a momentary frown from her. He said "Then we're all after the same thing. So we need to let your man here go, and you can give us Henry. That way whatever else we decide, we both have another way to hunt down Winton—now that he's not holding *us* hostage."

"Please," Christa added. "It's what you want."

"That does sound fair," Nolan said. "We can make that trade, and we can talk about the rest in person, where we can actually see each other."

"Fair," Kate nodded.

"—If," Nolan added, "you let Bryan here go first."

"No!" Christa snapped. "Not until Henry's safe."

Mark swallowed, sighed. "I think… I think this is a better offer than Nolan really has to make." *Or else we let the poison get my father.* "Think, what if we really didn't have to be enemies?"

"We set him free," Kate nodded, "but we keep his gravity talisman until we have Henry."

"But—" Christa began.

Kate glanced at her. Their eyes locked.

"…okay." Christa turned back to face Nolan.

The enemy was gone. Instead, across from them, Bryan Petrie was huddling and staring at them as her control released him.

"Wha… how did… she did it to me again? What happened?"

Mark felt a tension ease in his neck, and it freed his mouth for a slow smile. "We… saved your life."

CHAPTER EIGHT

TRADING MASKS

By the time Bryan Petrie called back with directions, rush hour traffic waited for them on the city streets. Mark squinted in the lowering sun and tried to keep his hands clear of the extra controls of the high-end Subaru Kate had rented.

He wondered why Christa had asked to come in their car instead of driving with Dennard again, at a distance behind them. But suddenly Christa burst out:

"This has to be a trap. Kate, *please* tell me you brought a gun too. Or magic."

Kate shook her head. "I'd be more likely to hurt one of us. With either of them."

"I suppose you're right."

She fell silent. The car crawled through another block of traffic, and another. The eager power of the coat in Mark's lap didn't make the slow pace any easier.

Then Christa added "I am so tired of feeling helpless. But it feels worse than that now: I was so close to beating that man bloody with the stick, and it scares me. And it's your father, Mark—I never should have gone that far."

Mark squinted tighter. "I… know all about letting anger get to me. So does Dennard."

He caught a flicker of something at the edge of his senses, drawing closer in the air behind them. Toward where Dennard's car was following.

"That's Winton! Behind us!" He glanced at Kate and saw her holding up her phone to pass his words to Dennard. "The bird's a block away on your left, closing in, don't know if he'll see you—what are you doing?" The talisman in the other car had *slowed.*

"You pull ahead before he spots you too," Dennard's answer came. "Finish this, I'll keep him distracted. Or, you know anywhere I can lose him? I think Josephine Court's coming up."

We can't leave him behind again! Mark edged the car forward and glared fury at the sea of bumpers ahead, and wracked his memory for all the details of the streets he'd just passed.

"Watch for the red Fixit sign," he decided. "I think that store's got enough exits that a spybird can't watch them all."

"Understood." And Dennard's talisman pulled off the road, with Winton's bird circling above it.

Mark pulled ahead, then into a slow turn around the block. Why'd it have to happen now? If Winton stayed on them the killer would get his chance to grab Sasha and attack Nolan—just when they might be coming to terms with them. Or he'd trap Dennard again and demand something worse than he had before.

"I'm going into the crowd," Dennard reported.

"He's staying in the air. Maybe he *can* see you when you leave." Damn, damn…

Mark pulled the car over, still most of a block away from the building. Too far from Dennard, too close to Winton in the sky.

"Do you see what you're doing here? You three worked through all that without even blinking." Christa leaned forward, toward Kate in the front passenger seat, and her wide-eyed gaze filled the mirror. "If this is really a chance to save Henry and the others—please, please, don't let me screw it up."

Kate's eyes closed, for a moment, before she answered. "I wish I could promise you some easy answer. But I haven't been fighting enemy 'spellkeepers'... I never knew there were others. I didn't know there was a word for them."

"But you were raised with magic, and secrets and knowing how dangerous they are. I'm a corporate marketing girl."

"Christa... I was about your age when I lost control of myself with the belt. I almost..." She shook her head. "Then my husband decided to keep the belt anyway, and he hid it and said he'd only use it in an emergency. I couldn't trust Joe, and I couldn't trust myself either. I had no choice but to leave him, and our daughter. That's what magic can do."

"Oh."

"Honestly, you know the hope that keeps me going? –Mark, I don't suppose Angie is with us by now," she added.

Was that open regret in her voice? "No—"

Winton's presence had moved.

"He's on the ground! I think he grabbed someone, he's still near the store's front—get out of there!"

"Out the back," was all Dennard said.

Mark slammed the car forward. He twisted between bumpers and strained to match Dennard's and Winton's magic to where the building's walls would be. Winton moved slowly, and that might mean he was still searching for Dennard in the crowds, but Dennard would be trying to hide from an enemy he couldn't recognize...

"Careful!" Christa said, then cut herself off with a gasp as they ducked in ahead of a clumsy van. All they had were moments, one chance to hang onto the advantage where he had tracked Winton and the enemy didn't have his eyes on them. *Scissors cuts paper, but only if we're in time.*

The door burst open, Dennard jumped inside, Mark roared away.

Winton's presence... stayed in the store. Mark tore around the next corner and slowed to a normal speed.

He forced himself to breathe then, deep and steady. Behind him Christa shifted her seat to let Dennard buckle up.

Finally Kate said "If it's any comfort, Christa: the one thing I hope is that we can restore Angie and save Nolan's prisoners—and then get away and let Nolan and Winton kill each other, and never have to deal with magic again."

Christa shook her head. "You make it sound… so easy."

They didn't sense Winton again, even when they swung five extra blocks to the side before they closed on the address they'd been given. Even then, they left the car two blocks short of it and walked the final distance.

That address was a real, genuine warehouse. It was clear across town from the shop Zeke had been heading to this afternoon, but looking at the long brown block of a building, Mark could see why people might choose it for secret meetings. The parking lot—empty— stretched wide enough around it to give it privacy, even with the industrial traffic rolling past in front. The open lot and the dirtiness of the *Theater Supplies* sign showed it could be closed down.

And it had magic.

"There's a bit of gravity power in there," Mark said as they eyed it. "A small talisman, maybe another that Nolan took from the coat. Or it could be the one Henry had."

Dennard said "They said to wait. I don't see the door open for us yet."

Christa stared up and down the street, the buildings around it. "Wait? What if this *is* where they have Henry—why would they take the time to move his things here without the prisoners themselves? Could you sneak in and find out?"

"She wants to negotiate. Or at least, there's a chance she does," Kate said. "Breaking that truce isn't worth the risk."

When did Kate get to be in charge? But, they had agreed to try talking with Nolan.

At Dennard's suggestion, Mark and Christa settled back to watch from behind a building's corner, where the stream of people around the bus stop would camouflage them. Dennard and Kate moved inside a fast-food spot on the block's other end.

Which put those two indoors, and left Mark and Christa standing in the deepening cold as the crowds thinned. Christa rubbed her hands and vibrated in place, not speaking. Mark fought to balance the restless power of the coat around him with the creeping chill in his hands; just feeling cold proved the magic hadn't eaten into his self-control yet.

The shadows were still growing and pushing more and more of the traffic from the street, when he felt the magic. "That's Angie!" he said, the first words on the phone since they'd taken their positions.

"Where?" Kate said at once.

"Closing in, high over your end of the street." Where had she gone after they'd trapped his father? Mark waved Christa back and peeped around the corner.

"One car coming in, slowing," Dennard said.

A tiny block of a car turned into the warehouse lot, pale in the fading light. A small figure stepped out, that had to be Nolan. She moved for the building, and the car headed back along the street.

Mark smiled. "I bet she never knew Angie's on her. Maybe followed her all the way from her home."

Then Nolan stopped, whirled away from the warehouse. Instead she marched out to the street.

"What's she doing *now?*" Christa muttered.

Unruffled, Dennard said "She saw the police tail."

Police, now? Mark saw Nolan step directly in front of a slowly-approaching car. It could have swerved, but instead it jerked to a stop in front of her challenge.

He ducked back around the corner. The cops were this close to the meeting place, and she was confronting them?

"Can you still see them?" Christa asked the others. "You're sure they're police?"

Kate answered "She knows they're watching her. And she's used to magic that lets her work without exposing herself. If she risked coming to us in person, it's because she thought she could slip past them."

"But they're right here," Christa said. "And you think that's Henry's talisman in there… Do we tell them the missing people must be right inside? No, that would only make it all worse."

"Look again," Dennard said.

Mark risked another look around the corner. Another car—the small one that had dropped Nolan off—had stopped behind the surveillance car, and the driver stepped out to join the argument. From his height and hair, and the car's size, maybe…

"That's Zeke again," Mark said. "You were right before, he suspected *something*, enough to lead him close to where my father was hiding. But he doesn't know about all this, he's just her right-hand negotiator for her business. Or he was."

"He's good, though," Dennard chuckled. "The police are pulling out. Better get out of view."

Mark and Christa pulled back from the corner and began walking away. The police would be driving past them… and he tracked Angie moving with them now, above the sound of a car passing behind them, gone.

"Angie's watching *them* now," he reported, grinning. "I bet if I sense her circling around, it means they're sneaking back again."

"Look at Nolan and Zeke now," Kate said.

Back up the street, the man and the small woman were facing each other, with Zeke's arm motioning wildly toward where the police had gone. Confused, frustrated.

"Too many secrets," Kate added.

For long moments more they seemed to argue, until Zeke stepped back into his car with what looked like a fierce slam of the door. He headed on down the street, and Nolan walked to the warehouse's little office door.

She left it open behind her.

"Now?" Christa said.

"Now," Dennard answered. "And she has to own that building, so be ready for anything."

Christa rushed the first steps forward, then held herself back to keep to Mark's pace. Dennard and Kate approached from the far end. The lot's open pavement, that Mark could have leaped in seconds in the dark, seemed to take forever to walk across now.

The gravity talisman inside moved to the front door. Bryan Petrie swung it open, waving them in with a smile. He kept himself close enough to the doorway to test each of them for Winton's talismans as they filed past.

Mark entered last and angled himself to never let his father out of view. They hadn't risked removing the anklet talisman, so he—or she—would only need one thought for him to lunge in and seize any of their minds with it.

Olivia Nolan was waiting. They crowded into a shabby office lined with faded movie posters, too small to let six people stand in without the tension between them seething. Mark settled in the back beside a file cabinet, a mass of metal he could grab and lighten if he needed, not that any kind of shield would fend off touches in this tight space.

"You all came." Nolan said it slowly, as if every word had a separate meaning to her.

"Of course," and Christa slid around Kate to face their enemy. "Where's Henry?"

Mark winced; Kate would have worked around to it more naturally.

But Nolan only said "Right here," and she turned and opened the inner door—but she held it just a foot open, with her body blocking them from reaching it.

Christa stepped closer to look through. Mark angled to peep between the others' heads. Beyond it were clothes… varied, multicolored clothes brighter than a Christmas tree, crowded together in long racks… and a figure slumped against a support post—

Nolan shut the door. And the air beyond it breathed, whispered, hummed to life into a shifting dull roar of indoor wind that resonated with the sheer size of the space beyond.

"That's because there's no need for them to overhear us yet." A hint of a smug smile touched her lips.

Christa glared back at her. "They're all there. Is that the combination lock Sasha mentioned? You keep another anklet on Henry so you can take him over whenever you want, and you make him unchain himself out and lock himself back up whenever you're done." The words had sharp edges, but she kept them controlled. "So you could leave them alone, but manage them without setting foot here."

"I did what I had to." Standing in front of the door, Nolan folded her arms—a swinging motion that made Christa draw back from her fingers. "Or that anklet means I could put him in a coma with a thought."

"We agreed you'd release Henry," Kate said, calm and insistent. "We already let Mark's father go, so it's Henry's turn, and we can discuss the others. Are you saying you're changing the terms?"

Nolan's eyes, and her whole body, shifted to focus on Kate behind Christa. "That girl in there is the only bait that can make Winton come to us."

"You're sure of that?" Kate said. "That he needs her?"

Christa shouldered Kate aside to face Nolan. "Are you letting Henry go or not?"

"And if I said no?" Nolan barely glanced at Christa before turning back to Kate.

Mark cut in "Please, no more threats!"

He had to force the words through the others ahead of him… but he held his place by the file cabinet, with one eye watching his father—

He raced on "You keep saying Winton needs Sasha's body, and you're probably right. But your only answer is using her as bait? That's what split us up before: we were hunting Winton together, but then you sent Rafe to, what, torture Sasha? Don't you see, it's that kind of ice-cold move that keeps turning us against each other."

Nolan sniffed. "I'm showing you what I have to do to survive. I'm fighting an enemy who could be anyone around me, and I can't even *see him* when he takes control. And nothing *any* of you do seems to get ahead of him."

Any of us? Mark's eyes flicked to his father, but the man didn't react to his boss's contempt. Mark looked back—

Nolan took the slightest step to the side. On the wall behind her, he caught one glimpse of a picture, a little girl with a face like hers. Then her shoulder blocked it off.

Focus. He said " 'Show us' what? That kidnapping and threats are the only way we can hunt Winton, and if we'd just admit it we could all be slapping prisoners around together?"

"That would be one answer," Nolan nodded. "If I could trust you. You're the ones who keep turning against me."

Christa spat "You locked us up, to hide what you did to Irene!"

Mark studied Nolan's face a moment. She'd always been paranoid… but still, he had been the one who broke away first. "You know we didn't turn *against* you," he said. "Today I stopped my father because Winton threatened Dennard and Christa, and we needed time for them to get out of his sight. And because you'd grabbed your own prisoners."

Nolan's eyes narrowed. "So it's that easy for Winton to make you do what he wants? Did he even have to possess someone to scare you? All of you are simply triggers waiting for him to pull."

Dennard's deeper voice pushed back: "Trust goes both ways." He stepped forward, past the ranks of the others to stand in front of Nolan. "Like he said before, this partnership was already breaking when you doubled down your pressure on Sasha."

"And your response was to call the police?" Nolan shook her head. "How could you think any of this belongs on the record?"

"I called the police because you killed Irene—"

That presence, *Angie!* She was within the block and closing.

"—or are you saying the police *shouldn't* be aware of a murder?" Dennard finished.

Police. Angie had been following them, her return could mean they had circled back too... but Mark held his face immobile, tracking her, grateful for Dennard and Kate sheltering him from Nolan's too-sharp eyes.

"Irene tried to blackmail me," Nolan said. "Never mind that she could have gone over to Winton too—"

"So you killed her?" Dennard flung back. He was little more than a foot from Nolan and her deadly touch, but he rushed right on "Is that your answer to anyone who knows too much? Then what does it mean that you grabbed Sasha, and pulled her mother into this too?"

"It means we have to know where they stand, and we have to be sure. You don't have to be raised in magic to know how *one word* in the wrong place could go world-wide. One word from anyone who knows more than they should."

A hiss of breath came at Mark's elbow, from his father. This was how Nolan protected her secrets—the way she'd hunted down Rafe's magic-enhanced gang, and killed Irene—so what would she do with a self-serving weasel like Bryan Petrie when she was done with him?

The thought came: *he can sense Angie too, and he's said nothing.*

"In other words," Kate said slowly, "everything you've done has been to defend yourself and the magic. And you pay the price for it. I saw your friend Zeke helping you with the police outside, and I couldn't miss how it must be taking its toll on you both."

"Now you're going to *judge* me?"

Silent behind the others, Mark tracked Angie as she reached what had to be the edge of the warehouse... and settled somewhere on its wall...

Kate answered "All of this began with Winton trying to uncover forms of magic to add to his own, and manipulating us for our secrets. But, do you even know what that power is? Does your weather magic come from some kind of spirit, or from another world, or is it something even more exotic?"

"Do you expect me to answer that?" A frown darkened Nolan's voice.

"I only have guesses about mine, and I wouldn't be surprised if you aren't much better off. I think the truth is that we all *lost* the real answers, and they're answers to something the world has been talking about for thousands of years... and I think I can understand why we lost them."

"Oh, do you?" The guardedness in Nolan's voice was still there.

And Angie moved, she dropped forward from her perch to settle downward and be swept to the side, in what had to be Nolan's indoor wind. She'd found a way inside the warehouse? That couldn't be to warn them about police. Mark locked his features stone-still.

Kate went on "The explanation is all around us, in the way we're treating each other here. Suspicion, kidnappings... everyone in this room is tearing each other apart over how to respond to *another* man's greed for our knowledge. Or else, we survive by digging ourselves into holes so deep we forget there are other 'spellkeepers' around us at all."

"It's not so easy. I... had a brother, who should have inherited the power—"

Mark searched for the family picture he'd seen on the wall, but the others ahead of him blocked his view.

Nolan went on "What happens when you do everything right, and Ethan still dies from a stupid accident?" Her voice hardened again. "What happens is, you learn to make no mistakes."

"I... see." Kate took a slow step toward her. "I have to confess something. I came back to this city hoping I could help resolve our problems and then slip away again. But now, I hope I can stay and work out what all of us seem to be becoming... in dealing with magic, enemies, public attention, and all."

"After you ran away once? No, twice, years ago! You let your power get into the hands of a street gang, until I stopped them. All because you let your ex take it up, and that man *called the police* on me. That's a lifetime of looking over my shoulder for me, even if we keep the rest of this war out of their sight. Because of *you*," Nolan sighed.

"I know. Those are responsibilities I haven't carried well. And I'd like to try to do better. But," she added, "can you consider one thing, Olivia Nolan?"

"What?"

"We've told you how our gravity magic can affect our minds. My parents used to travel just to spend time away from its supply, and even with that safety valve my father ended up destroying our house and dying afraid to face what he'd become..."

Her shoulders slumped, her head lowered a moment. Then Kate straightened again:

"Now you've begun using the Winton possession magic. In light of my example, and now what Winton's done to us, have you just... considered... that this energy of his might be making you more suspicious than you're aware? Have you thought about that?"

A jolt of cold went through Mark, and he edged over a step to see Nolan's face—tight control, but with tiny tremors moving the muscles underneath. *My God, to tell a woman who's already paranoid that she should fear what her new power's doing to her... Nolan* can't *ignore that.*

And yet, the warning felt wrong. Mark had talked to Winton over the years, and he'd seemed all too convincingly sane. But as long as it made Nolan doubt what she'd done—

And all the time that Kate's talking about building trust, Angie is creeping around her building and I've said nothing. Hell, I'm even trusting my father *to keep his mouth shut.*

"Do you believe that?" Nolan said, softly. "That magic makes us all unstable?"

Kate shrugged. "I don't know. That may be the point: this possession power is a force none of us knows about. And as long as we stay isolated, we have no way to know, until we look out for each other. But we do have a place to start, with freeing Henry."

"And what about the girl who wants to be on Winton's side? And her mother, you know a way to keep her from running to the police?"

Dennard tensed, the faintest movement gathering his weight on slightly bent knees, his arms edging up closer to being ready a strike. Mark thought he caught a low warning rumble from him.

Kate said "We have to make it clear what's at stake now. They both need to understand that we aren't the real enemy."

She motioned to the door behind Nolan.

And just like that, Nolan nodded, and swung it open.

Mark had a glimpse of the long aisles of tight-packed clothes, hangers clattering and rippling in Nolan's wind… but that wind was already dwindling, fading down from a leashed roar to a hiss, a whisper.

Angie's presence drew his gaze toward a row of plastic boxes, that she must be crouching behind—just a row away from where Henry sat chained to a wooden support post, watching them file in.

At another post, Sasha's mother demanded "Who are all of you? Please, just let us go!" She and her daughter were chained to that post together. A heavy combination lock held each prisoner's chains around them.

—And none of them mentioned seeing an owl scuttling around. Maybe Angie's presence wouldn't matter at all, if Nolan was listening now.

"Are you alright?" Christa stayed back with the group, but she looked straight at Henry.

"Fine." The word sounded forced, with the bloodless look on Henry's face. The chains would have been long enough to let him stand, but he kept his place on the ground. "I never knew getting shot could hurt so much, but they bandaged my arm and gave me pills…"

"So what is it? Are you going to let us go or not?" Elizabeth Lawrence really did look like an older—and stronger—version of her pale, dark-haired daughter next to her.

"Please!" Sasha added. She had only her jeans and a light shirt on, and huddled at the support's base with a bundle of clothes in her lap. Had they searched her and chained her before tossing her outer layers back?

Nolan took a step ahead of the others, waving them to hold back. "I'm sorry it came to this, Sasha. But you need to understand the danger you're in."

"Danger?" Sasha's mother retorted. "And that's why your man shot at us, and chained us up? To *protect* us?"

"Because of your faith in Winton. It might be the only way to keep you rushing to him the minute he calls."

That's her idea of reassuring them? Mark edged to the side, to start moving around her to the prisoners.

"Roger Winton?" the mother said. "What does that make this, some kind of demented *intervention?"*

"Please, Ms. Lawrence," Kate said. "Can you hear us out first?"

Mark locked his eyes on Sasha. "Intervention might be the word. Sasha, believe me, we tried to stop them grabbing you, but… I know Winton's persuasive. He did me a couple of favors and fooled me for years—"

Sasha spat at him. "I thought you were on my side, not hers! And stop lying about the man who did so much for me. He *gave* me the key to his magic. The book even said something about living forever—I owe him everything!"

Mark sighed. He felt Angie shift in her hiding place, still up to something.

Before he could start again, Nolan moved in front of him. "Sasha, I've already told you I've seen the state his body is in, even after months. He needs to make a permanent transfer into a new shape. Your getting to use his magic must be to prepare you for that, some-how—why else would he give it to someone like you?"

"You're all insane!" Elizabeth Lawrence said. "And you, what is 'someone like you' supposed to mean? That's my daughter you're talking to."

Sasha ignored her to glare at Nolan. "You're wrong! I know he didn't pick me for that—or for any other sick reason you're thinking of—he did it because he believed I'd use his gift right."

Mark shook his head. "I'm sorry. But I've seen it—Winton's the one who 'uses' things, and people. I've seen him kill his own messen-gers and spies, and set up 'accidents' for cops—"

"Some dangers go back further than you think," Nolan cut in. "Sasha, he killed your aunt, when she worked for him. That is, if that was your aunt, and not your mother—"

"My aunt!" Sasha snapped. "And that man would have been Mr. Winton's father, stop saying they're the same... and he didn't kill her..."

Nolan only pressed on "And yet she disappeared, after she worked for a Winton. At the same job you had—and yes, it was working for the same man. And if they were your parents—"

"That is *enough!*" the older Lawrence said. "Everything you say gets crazier every minute. And I am *tired* of telling you people the same truth: I *am* Sasha's birth mother, even besides all the years I've given to her as a parent. And my sister was alive for months after she left the Wintons."

Nolan leaned closer. "Are you sure? He wasn't simply covering his tracks?"

"I had half a dozen conversations with her—and I know my sister. Besides, Isabel didn't need murderers to get herself in trouble. She kept defending Winton even after she left, and talking some crap about ways I could live longer. I made it clear I'd had enough of her schemes, and a month later she left the state. Whatever happened then… well, old man Winton never told us she was dead."

Sasha twisted, to stare at her mother next to her. "You never told me that."

"I told you not to work for a Winton. I don't know what kind of ideas the son got from the father—"

"You *never told me!*" Sasha said.

"She said there was nothing to tell. I still heard from her after she left. And if her new scheme went bad, well, that sounded more like how she always lived than murder. Izzy always… she's not your mother, Sasha, but you take after her more than I'd like."

"What 'scheme'? What did she say?"

She shook her head. "Not that much. I don't really remember."

"What… did… she… say??"

"That's him out there!"

The voice was Mark's father, slashing through the pleas:

"Winton's controlling something in the street! He's on his way here."

Something *did* flicker out there—Mark added "He's right!"

Voices gasped, and feet shifted around him; Christa rushed to Henry, Kate turned toward Nolan. Mark tensed the power in his coat… *Are we really ready to face Winton's tricks without turning on each other first? Please, please, if I've ever gotten one wish* don't *let my father reveal Angie's sneaking around right now—*

Sasha actually laughed. "Now you'll see what he does to all of you!"

Then Nolan chuckled, a darker sound. "I should have known who you'd believe. But you're still useful as bait." She was already closing in on Sasha, and drawing out a small case from her coat pocket. Inside it glistened a syringe.

Dennard was closest to her. "No you—"

"It's just to make her sleep," Nolan said. She stretched her other hand toward Dennard, and he dodged back.

Her sleep-touch magic is ready—so why the needle—

In the moment Nolan reached the prisoners, Sasha's mother leaned out against her chains trying to stop her.

Sasha shoved her mother aside. Her other hand hugged her bundle of clothes, then she caught at Nolan's hand—

Magic twisted, from some talisman they'd somehow missed inside Sasha's clothes, to lash out at Nolan—

And it stopped, blocked by Nolan's own mind magic. The needle slammed into Sasha's shoulder with a spurt of blood.

"Bitch!" Sasha's mother yelled, but Nolan was already stepping back, warning Dennard away again.

Sasha clutched at her arm. "What was… let us go! Let us…" The last word sounded fuzzy. The drug was setting in.

Mark turned to face Nolan, keeping one eye on his own father and reining the coat's power in. It would be so easy to rush either of them, *crush* them, but the real enemy was outside.

"Bitch, that's my little girl!" he heard behind him. "She—Mr. Winton! It's a trap… a…"

Mark glanced back. Sasha hung limp against her mother's shoulder, but her power gripped the older woman and Elizabeth Lawrence was speaking her words, with the same slurring that had been on Sasha's own lips. Even reaching outside her body didn't put Sasha beyond the drug in her veins.

Magic surged, crashed against some barrier and built higher, stronger.

Then, the hardened older voice *shattered:* "Mr. Winton! Please— *Mom?*"

Kate was kneeling at her side. "Shh, relax. Sasha's breathing fine."

Mark clenched his fists and glared at Nolan… but she had a point, he could still feel Winton's grip on someone outside, already closing in on the warehouse. It winked out as he sensed it, more puppetmaster tricks.

But in Sasha and her mother now, he felt no magic at work, only heard some kind of low wailing from the older woman. Christa leaned, dazed, against the post where Henry sat. Dennard's gaze was stone-hard, fixed on Nolan. And she… she dipped her head in a small, *satisfied* nod, and turned back to the office door.

Mark's gaze swung back to Kate, to the limp Sasha and her softly moaning mother. Elizabeth's hands flailed and sent the bundle of clothes spilling from Sasha. Something silver flashed in them—the talisman Sasha had tried to use, that Nolan might have let her keep to allow whatever had just happened.

Nolan glanced at Mark's father. "Where's Winton?"

"That power's gone again, boss. You think he missed us?"

She shook her head. "No, this is how I told you he works. Winton gives someone a talisman and a reason to walk in here on their own, so he can slip in and out of their head and they never realize it. Remember, keep what you call out to me something ordinary—Winton *can't* think it's a signal, or he'll escape. And do it only right when you sense him inside them."

From her coat, she drew out a gun.

Mark's breath caught. It was the same method Rafe had tried, to simply murder whoever Winton was using, trying to send another shock back to his shattered real body—

He growled "Does it even matter who you take down with Winton?"

Coldly, quietly, Nolan answered "It's the only way." She tucked the gun back into place, ready.

Mark moved toward her, legs tense, the coat's power burning ready around him. At the edge of his vision, Dennard circled in from her other side. *Every way except hers has gone wrong, but we can't think about that.*

Nolan tucked the gun behind her back.

From the front office, a voice called "Olivia? You needed a hand?"

Nolan… froze, her arm still and her face locked in the same warning expression she'd had a moment ago. A whole second later, she called "Zeke? Stay there, I'll be right out."

Mark's father muttered to her "He's not possessed."

"Not this moment," Mark hissed, and he saw her flinch. "And what will you do when Winton does pull the string on him again? When it's someone you know?"

Her eyes narrowed until only tiny glints showed through. "Shut. Up."

She spun away and twisted through the office door before Mark could move. It clicked behind her.

That look, that voice… so Olivia Nolan did have someone she wouldn't blast out of her way? It slowed him a moment, before he grabbed at the door to follow her. Locked.

Behind him a rising, desperate mumbling came from Sasha's mother, about whatever Nolan had done to her.

"What's happening in there?" Zeke's frustration was clear, right through the door. "You never come down here. And then it's the police again, and you send me away, then call me back—"

"Please." Her voice was lower, but it stabbed past all the voices. "If you ever trusted me, I need you to stop and empty out all your pockets. Please, *now, NOW!*"

"What…"

Mark caught his breath. Such a simple solution, if Zeke listened and Winton only waited a few more seconds before peeking through him again. All they needed were seconds.

The woman behind him moaned again. His fingers hovered over the doorknob. One twitch of Winton's magic and he'd have to smash through it, and somehow stop Nolan, save Zeke.

"How'd this get in here—" came Zeke's voice.

"Just put it down—"

Then, she added softly,

"Thank you."

Air rushed back into Mark's lungs. With the talisman removed, Winton's threat was disarmed, everyone safe for now. He heard Nolan asking Zeke to wait a moment, felt one quick brush of her magic… sure, Nolan would rather have Zeke asleep than let him hear any more of the sobbing back here, but at least that kept them all safe.

Bryan's face looked stretched out of shape, struggling with what had to be shock at what she'd done. *Priceless*—Mark grinned back at his father's confusion. Yes, Olivia Nolan did have a merciful side, and that might be the first step to reconnecting with her, no matter what she'd done to Sasha.

Mark's gaze swung back to the others. Kate was walking away over to Henry and Christa; Sasha's mother had grown quieter.

No, that was Sasha in that body, even without any feel of magic. Nolan's injection had left her own body too weak to keep control of another's… but she'd *abandoned* her own drugged form, she'd moved her mind permanently into her mother. And Nolan had left her that talisman, and chained her beside her mother, like she had planned it all…

"Hey—"

Christa's cry was all the warning he had. He saw Henry had unlocked his chains to shove past her, rushing right at Kate.

Dennard moved to cut him off. "Why are you—"

Mark had one thought of *Winton got Henry, wait, it's* Nolan *who put a talisman on him,* before the possessed Henry spun around and lunged straight at Mark.

He leaped back. He had only a fleeting sideways glance to get a sense of the long rack of clothes to his side, but he shot clear over it. He arched high toward the warehouse ceiling, leaving her below and catching one long floating look at Dennard rushing for the office where Nolan had gone and Angie winging into view behind him—while Mark's own father moved ahead of them. Sasha/Elizabeth shrieked, Christa shouted some kind of warning.

The floor rushed up. Mark wrenched at power to brake and came down half sprawled over a pile of hard-cornered boxes. This *couldn't* be Nolan attacking them, why would she turn on them now?

The row of clothes behind him clattered and parted. Henry shoved through them.

Now Mark had his glimpse of the layout in his head. He was springing sideways before Henry stepped clear of the racks, and he stretched the leap into a long arching path that would bring him toward Dennard and Angie to join their attack on Nolan's office.

His father reached the door first.

And Bryan Petrie smashed it open and charged inside, and Mark neared the door in time to see him deliver a solid kick to where his "boss" lay. Mark slammed to a halt at the doorway behind Dennard. At his back he heard Henry's footsteps falter, at the moment that the pain of that kick rocked the body controlling him.

His father reached down, and clawed at Nolan's coat. When Bryan stood up, one hand held her gun, the other pocketed her case of needles.

"Found my antidote, bitch—"

Nolan's eyes opened. Bryan Petrie froze.

Oh no...

Nolan's new pawn let the gun fall, and turned... He had the same expressionless look Henry had worn when he had been possessed, but he took whole seconds to turn toward them. Off to the side, Dennard grabbed Henry's arm and yanked him back, out of the way.

A pulse of gravity magic drove the puppet straight through the air at Mark.

A clumsy leap; Mark made a light hop aside that lifted him clear as his father sailed on by and away, leaving himself still just one spring back to the door. *My father was right, I only have to hit Nolan's body hard enough...*

Instead he saw Nolan rising to her feet, searching for the gun she'd dropped for herself. Mark grabbed the doorway to pull himself back, as her hand closed on the weapon.

A body tackled Nolan from behind. A man, Zeke, if Zeke's smooth, clean-cut features could ever be warped into the sneer they had now. His hands scrabbled for Nolan's throat, and she struggled to keep them away.

Winton woke Zeke up, he had a second *talisman hidden on him—*

Mark sprang into the room, reaching toward the file cabinet he'd noticed on the way in. If he could lighten it enough to stun them both—

Angie soared into the room. Her fragile wings beat in the air barely out of reach of the struggling two.

Mark let the cabinet drop. Nolan flailed to catch at her friend's savage hands, but all the while her lips were moving.

Zeke spasmed. Mark felt the magic move... not in a quick blow of sleep or a possessing grip, instead the mind energy *streamed* out from Zeke into Nolan, flowing into a space in her pocket. Drained from him.

"Liv?"

Zeke's word was a feeble gasp, with confusion breaking into horror within the space of the one sound.

Before that pain could take full shape, power surged from her, and he slumped into merciful sleep again. Nolan leaned back with a long sigh of relief.

Another Sasha-scream tore loose, and Christa's voice shouted "Behind you!"

Mark sprang for the doorway. His father was struggling with Christa, fighting in what looked like trying to shake off her tackling him. Nolan's blank expression was back on his father's face.

Magic smashed into Christa. She crumpled to the floor.

"No, no, no, *why??*" Mark moaned, as his body dropped all too easily into a dodging crouch again. Dennard moved up behind Nolan's living weapon, but how could any of them touch him?

His father sagged where he stood.

Mark glanced back to the magic's controller. Nolan was no longer leaning back and sending her will out, now she reared up from the floor, thrashing out to force a small gray shape away from her face. Angie twisted clear, blood on her claws, darting free of the office.

Nolan slammed the door shut to close herself in.

Another moment and she'll take control again. Mark lunged for the nearest plastic crate, anything to fend off his father's touch. He lightened it as he snatched it up and spun to face the fight.

Bryan Petrie was charging toward Sasha/Elizabeth, where she huddled whimpering against the post. Mark sent the box sailing after him, leaving it light enough to reach… but it only bounced off his shoulder and made him turn. Featherweight weapons were useless.

Dennard and Kate closed in around the puppet, fanning out to opposite sides of him as if the two exes had never been out of each other's sight. Mark moved to cover a third side—the more they surrounded his father, the better the chance someone could blindside him without Nolan jumping into them in turn. If one of their fists could be faster than her thought.

Or if the fist hit harder. The power Mark wore burned around him… enough to make any scrap he picked up fall like an avalanche… one firm move could get rid of Nolan's pawn and even strike at the woman inside him, both his poisonous father and their backstabbing "partner"…

That's the magic's fever again.

The first step of his fierce charge stumbled to a halt.

And his possessed father leaped past Dennard, straight at where Sasha's mother crouched behind the post burbling screams from her daughter's mind. A hand caught her flailing arm. She crumpled.

No— Mark took a slow step in, the fastest he could risk with the magic roaring in him. Dennard and Kate, the only others left on their feet, circled in again with sudden motions and halting lunges that kept his father's gaze darting between them trying to pick a target.

But a puppetmaster only needed one touch. Mark stared around for a better weapon.

Something brushed his shoulder from behind.

Feathers beat in his ear. Talons pricked through leather—

Flying, spinning, lost in the world of the mind, battered by currents and yet blasted through by one single stream that sought him out, flooded into him—shapes and sounds, a man and a woman, struggling, familiar—her mouth moving, sounds, sounds that the images forced into him again and again—

Angie pulled away. The solid world crashed back around him. She flew past him, and something fell from her claws to his feet. The images snapped into place too: memories of Nolan and Zeke fighting and how it had ended.

He looked up. His father, with Nolan's emptied-out expression on his face, was reaching toward Dennard. "This is for... my brother," and he spun for Kate.

Mark crouched. He snatched up the bit of silver Angie had dropped as he dove forward, the smallest, lightest hop toward his father. All it needed was a touch, if Angie had given him Nolan's words right.

He landed on his father's back. *"Tomishua... zazda tomi zazda shua..."*

At the first touch, Nolan tried to buck him off her puppet, and he clamped his grip down harder. With the second word he heard her trying to speak the words herself, but the silver flood of *power* began to flow, sharp and bitter and unstoppable as he sucked the magic from the anklet talisman into the silver and jade in his own hand. The other voice faltered. Nolan's grip on his father faded, and the body collapsed.

Slowly, Mark pulled himself to his feet. Blood was roaring in his ears, but it eased as he looked around, enough to make out Dennard's words: "What did you do?"

He shook his head, and looked down at the talisman in his hand. A simple locket of silver, that must hide a bit of jade inside it; Sasha could have gotten most of it from some jewelry store. This was the one hidden in her clothes that she threw away, that Angie must have snatched up—

And it's ours now. And so are the words, *the key that can drain another mind talisman or fill this one. Fill it with enough power to block possession.*

Or free Angie.

Mark shivered. His mouth opened, but he couldn't find his voice. He looked at Dennard and Kate; were the guarded, dawning expressions on them the beginning of hope? The flicker of Angie's power drew his gaze to the feathered genius who'd seized her answers at last.

"Olivia, stop it!" Kate shouted across the room. "You attacked us—why, for this 'brother' we never met? I thought we were finding common ground here. We, all of us, could be the first time that spellkeepers have really found each other again, and it doesn't have to lead to *this!*"

"Not the first time."

The anger in that rough voice barely sounded human, until Mark followed the sound and the power to see Henry sitting up. Nolan's control had left people's faces blank before, but now the stolen eyes blazed at Kate.

"No, Ethan never met you. He died training himself to hunt our enemy."

"Hunting? Then we can finish that if we find Winton together—"

"You still think my enemy has to be him, don't you? I'm not let-ting you flyers go again."

Hearing that malice in Henry's voice was unbearable. Mark flung himself across the room and clamped his hands onto him. *"Tomishua zazda tomi zazda shua."*

The tangled rhythms of the words felt burned into his memory after so long seeking them, and they tore the power out of Henry's anklet and broke Nolan's control. The rage faded from Henry's face, leaving confusion and the paleness from his wound.

Mark whirled toward the office door.

As he leaped, a scream of wind erupted through the building. His flying body hurtled back like a leaf, before a surge of gravity slammed him to a stop.

"Now it's raw power against power? You lose!" he yelled into the storm. He sprang forward again and rammed the coat's strength into the motion itself—for a moment he clung to the momentum like hang-ing onto a truck's bumper as it bore through a hurricane.

Slamming to a stop just short of the door made his head ring. But he heard what had to be Dennard closing in behind him, no time to waste. He grabbed at the doorknob—locked—and slapped a hand on the wood to pour weight into it. Wood creaked, metal hinges moaned, until the door wrenched free and crashed to the floor in fragments.

On the other side, Nolan was gone.

He leaped for the far door, flying past Zeke's unconscious body. A voice far behind him moaned *Christa won't wake up,* one more breath to stoke the power and rage. The door rushed up.

It flew open onto a mad swirl of white and gray. *Snowstorm! Where* is *she?* Mark clutched the doorframe and glared up and down through the night. Shouts of surprise, faint shapes in the dimness, si-rens closing in—Nolan couldn't have run far—

A hand fell on his shoulder. A breath hissed out through his teeth; why would Dennard want to *stop* him?

Behind Dennard was his father. "She's gone. You run out in that and all you'll get is caught."

Another breath hissed from him, and he stopped. *Control the magic, don't let the fever win. Not in front of* him.

CHAPTER NINE

BODY COUNT

How long did they have, before Nolan or Winton sent some new attack at the warehouse? Or the police came to it again?

Mark barely had a moment to marvel at the mind talisman in his hand, and how Angie had finally found the words that powered them. Then he was wrestling with the coat's magic to split the chains off of Sasha's unmoving body, and from her mother's—the body that Sasha stared out of, shaking like a frightened child. But Christa wouldn't wake at all.

And they had to get so many people away in time, without trying to hold onto them all in the sky or being seen parading down the street. The mismatched group stumbled into some kind of coordination.

Henry, still pale from his wound, swayed on his feet until they passed him a strip of gravity-charged leather. But he pulled Christa's limp arm over his shoulder as if he meant to carry her by himself, until Kate took her other arm.

Mark and Dennard could move faster. Mark scooped up Sasha's body and Dennard coaxed her mother's to her feet.

Then Mark's father chuckled "Why's it always the girls who need to be carried?"

Like when you let Mom drown herself in your drugs—

Before Mark could spit an answer back, Henry grumbled "Sasha was the one helping me walk last night. After you *shot* me."

Kate motioned Henry back, then stepped in to whisper something to Bryan. Whatever it was, he stumbled back with his eyes wide, and fumbled out his keys and handed them over. "My car's just up the left corner."

Kate and Henry brought Christa out the front door.

Mark led the others out the back, the long way through the snow and the night to where they'd left their own car.

They'd asked him to pick a way between the backs of the industrial buildings, but almost at once he sensed Angie taking a place ahead of them. Her course twisted them among the snow-dimmed shapes, rushing past what moving figures they glimpsed before anyone could react. Magic let Mark run ghost-light across the snow, hopping fences as if Sasha's silent body in his arms was nothing. He could feel Bryan stumbling and clattering along behind him, but at least his father knew the power enough to keep up. Dennard was slower, more practiced with magic but clumsier keeping his balance with his frightened passenger.

Their twisting path had just come in view of the side street where they'd left the Subaru, when Mark felt another presence. One of Winton's or Nolan's puppets, moving on the street toward them. Dennard was half a block back... but the enemy's path headed toward where Kate's group must be. The slowest, most vulnerable group, with only Henry's sense to warn them.

"You feel that? Go help them!" he waved his father toward the others. *Our car has to be close ahead.*

Here and there a car chugged along the street, and Mark couldn't shake the fear of some driver looking over in the snow and noticing him carrying Sasha. But long seconds later, he closed in on where the Subaru waited. He fumbled the back door open and laid Sasha in the seat, safe.

But the magics around him... his father's was moving toward Dennard at the end of their own line, not heading out for where Henry and Kate needed him, where the enemy presence closed in.

No time to argue, damn him. Mark bolted down the sidewalk in the longest hops he dared, faster than the cautious shapes on the street. The enemy slowed, a block away. He felt Henry's magic ahead now, and he scrambled up the blocks.

Several outlines stood on the sidewalk ahead—Henry and Kate with Christa hanging between them, and a small man blocking their path.

"How is *that* just her getting drunk?" the man was saying. "I can't smell a thing."

As Mark came to a stop, he searched the magic again. That small pulse must be his father—closing in on them now, leaving Dennard?

"You never smell it, now that she's discovered vodka." Kate waved off the passer-by, her voice thick with what sounded exactly like years of suffering support for a friend.

"Let's just get her home," Mark added.

All they had to do was keep moving, screened by Kate's voice, and soon the well-wisher fell behind. That moved them up the street—

to the Bug—

until they drove back toward their other car, picking up Mark's father along the way.

When they reached where they'd parked, Dennard lay asleep in the snow. His eyes opened when Mark shook him, but the car, Sasha, and her mother were gone.

* * *

Don't swear. Don't blame, don't wonder what happened... Mark could feel the same pressure building between the others around him—

six people crammed into his father's damn *Beetle*—

Christa's breathing still so slow—

until they reached a quiet side street at the other end of town and wrenched the doors open to spill out.

"You could have gone after them." Dennard glared around at the silent storefronts, not meeting the others' eyes. "I had Sasha and her mother right with me. I just had to watch the sky for one minute—still got blindsided."

Mark sighed "We could have tried chasing them." Instead Nolan had recaptured them… or since the power had dived down like a spy-bird, more likely it had been Winton making his move to take them. Mark watched Henry slide out from holding the still-limp Christa on his lap to set her in the passenger seat. "But…"

Kate said "But we're in no condition for another fight. And we finally have the words to begin bringing Angie back," and Mark let the presence on the roof above draw his eyes to the owl. Kate finished "Besides, those can help with our most immediate need. Christa."

"Alright," Dennard said. "First we wake her up, then we can find the others again. Now we've got Mark, Henry, and Bryan to search for—"

"Do we?" The words burst out of Mark. "Now we're taking *him* in?" He waved a hand toward his father, and saw him flinch. *Sure he attacked Nolan when her back was turned, but he's tried that with* everyone.

"Stop it, stop it…" Henry sprawled over the open car door. "Look, can we just wake Christa up now?"

Kate held up a hand. "We need to use this carefully. We don't know how fast trying to wake her will use up the talisman; we could empty it before we can help her. What happens if we do that and then we find we only know the words to move power between mind talismans, but we can't fill up an empty one?"

Henry glared at her, face screwed tight.

"I've got this." Mark summoned up a smile for Henry. "I've seen how these hate being opened in the light. And I bet these words will work." He stole another glance up at where Angie perched.

His fingers found the catch on Sasha's locket, her version of how Winton's talismans had been built to open. *I hope Winton or Nolan catching Sasha doesn't mean they have a way to take control of Sasha's creation too...* The first step for recharging it seemed to be putting it in total darkness—before he could hesitate, he pulled off the stiff coat and then stripped off his outer shirt to wrap it around his hand and the bit of silver, tight as he could. Layer after layer went around them, while his bare arms trembled in the cold.

When the shirt was wrapped tight, he probed with his fingernail for the locket's catch. For a moment his blind fumbling seemed to miss it, and then he felt it click open.

The jade inside the silver was exposed, but shielded from light. He leaned close and breathed Angie's words onto it.

The talisman *pulled*. He felt it slowly stirring, like a breeze around him softer than the icy air, like watching water begin to trickle down a crack—water he could only feel around him because the "crack" itself was inside his grasp. Only the tiniest trickle, but it would slowly build into an invisible whirlpool of gathering energy.

"It feels hungry," his father said. "This means we can make them ourselves?" The greedy edge in his voice pulled Mark's gaze up.

"We can. We really can." His shaking, freezing hands couldn't seem to work the locket closed again, but then it shut and fastened, and the gathering power halted—for now. *We* have *this*. "Yes. We know the magic that can sustain Angie, and turn everything around. We can..." He turned to Christa.

"So do it," Henry said.

Mark yanked on the coat and flashed one more grin up at Angie, then marched to Christa.

Christa simply lay in the seat, eyes closed. Her breathing was weak, but the only thing that felt truly wrong was when his hand closed on hers and it didn't stir.

The possession magic rose through him at a thought.

So simple, the swirl of power that forced away flesh, cast him hanging in something other than space—wild currents surging through what was *him*—keep steady, feel for the other—a sense of stillness there, he reached for it, tried to shake it awake, but his touch flowed through it with no purchase—

In another place, his body swayed where it crouched—

Push, pull, feel for that binding power to drain away, but there was none—push, search and strain and make it happen—do it, do it...

The locket slipped from exhausted hands. He slumped against the car seat, head filled with mush, Christa's hand still limp.

"I... don't get it," he gasped. Was she *gone*—or just something he couldn't fix... *It can't be. This magic is the secret we spent months fighting for, and it still isn't enough.*

"It might be we need to know more." That was Kate, looming over him with a voice solid enough to anchor him in the real world again. "Sasha wanted to get Winton's book back, and that may still have the answers. Ironic: after all my arguments against feeding these feuds, we still have to get that back."

Then Henry sighed "Or Christa just wakes up on her own. Or she never does."

Mark dragged his head around to look. Henry stood back from the others, and his head and shoulders sagged with something that looked heavier than exhaustion.

Dennard reached for his shoulder. "One try doesn't mean—"

"No." Henry pulled back, and he seemed to curl in around himself. "What if there's just nothing left of her? What if we chase down the witch who did it and still... should we even be fighting her? Nolan keeps saying she's only trying to protect herself from Winton..."

"You're giving up?" Mark said, then swallowed. His saying it made the idea more real than when Henry did.

"We've been trying... We keep looking for Winton like we can stop him too, and help Angie... now we've got the magic but we can't even wake up someone who never wanted to be part of this."

Softly, slowly, Dennard said "Is that what you want? To back away?"

Mark's father broke in "Hold on, you can't walk away now—that woman put *poison* in me, remember?"

He pushed in between them, holding up the syringe case he'd pulled off of Nolan.

"Poisoned me! She said I've got maybe one day to live without one of these shots—if the real stuff's even in here—and what happens after it's gone? You going to help me or not?"

And he looked straight at Mark.

Mark locked his jaw shut, not sure what he'd answer—

Henry snarled "So we dump you with the police. You tell the hospital to run some drug tests… considering the way you've lived, that sounds like karma."

"And when Nolan finds out I'm with the cops? She'll kill me faster than the poison!"

Dennard said "Both of our enemies *have* shown they can find us there. And there are only you three Petries who can spot their magic, so they both want you eliminated or with them."

Mark forced himself to his feet. The voices, his father's and the others, pushed in on all sides, and he had to step away from their pressure. His gaze went to Christa, then to Angie, watching on the roof.

His father said "So I'm screwed, is that it?" The words lashed out, fear swallowed in anger.

"I can think of one way to help you," Dennard said. "If we can learn fast. And I'm afraid we need a guinea pig."

Mark said "I can do that. Sure," and he winced at the drained sound in his voice.

Dennard took the talisman.

* * *

It was approaching midnight when they entered Grace Hospital. Henry wouldn't leave Christa, so Dennard, Kate, and Mark and his father slipped in separately to avoid the night shift's attention.

"Hospitals," Mark breathed to himself. "If we could just stop coming back to *hospitals…*" But even if the fighting ended, they'd have to come back to this very place to free Angie. At least the owl herself was still circling above, staying close.

The glaring fluorescence hurt his eyes, an island of forced brightness after the night they'd been moving through. And the nurses, doctors, and security clustered in their posts and marched the corridors, too crowded and too alert to cut Mark any slack about how long he had been holding himself awake.

Finally, Kate found the office they needed. *Dr. Jorgenson*, the door said, the night supervisor for the lab.

Mark saw Dennard give a slow sigh—but he could get the results Mark couldn't, while Kate refused to trust herself with any magic, and none of them would trust Bryan with this. Kate and Dennard walked into Jorgenson's office alone.

From outside, Mark could hear a single "What? What is it now—" before he felt the flow of power.

Slowly, ponderously, Jorgenson stepped from the office. He was a big man even without the fat he'd packed on, but even with that Mark could see Dennard's clumsiness in keeping the unfamiliar body balanced. And the squint of repulsion in those eyes for what the new puppetmaster had to do.

His first steps were slow, and the hospital staff simply flowed past him with a few odd looks. Mark trailed behind him just close enough to see.

One of the techs stepped in Mark's way, and she said "What are you—"

"Jorgenson" snapped at her "You, I need you with me!" Her mouth actually fell open at the sudden words… but all she could do was let Mark go and follow.

Mark watched Dennard march the body into the humming center of the lab rooms.

"All right! All of you—we've got a new top priority!"

Heads turned. Doors opened, heads peeped out.

"What priority? I've got—"

The possessed hands held up a vial of Bryan's blood, and another with a fraction of the liquid from Nolan's syringe. *"This* sample is from a case of poisoning. We need to confirm that, and if *this* contains some kind of temporary antidote to it."

"What's the background? Is that in the request—"

"That's all we've got. Move! Come on, which of you can make me a list of likely substances?"

The techs began to move, and "Jorgenson" shuffled back, toward his office again. Mark trailed behind him.

His father was waiting just a turn back. "You think they'll do it? We make him say something and they all just fall in line?"

He didn't ask if they'll find *the answer, and keep him alive. But that's still fear in his voice.* Mark said "They have to, for now. Dr. Jorgenson may not sound like himself, and he's probably breaking a dozen lab rules, but they can still see it's *him* giving the order. So right now that just leaves us hoping they can do their jobs."

Bryan whistled. "You've seen it work, haven't you? Play your cards right with that power and you could get anything from any-where, long as you don't hit the same place twice."

Mark nodded, but he couldn't meet the man's eyes. Dr. Jorgenson would probably spend the rest of his life arguing that tonight was some temporary insanity, and there could be other patients at risk be-cause they'd shoved Bryan Petrie to the head of the testing line... *At least I kept the words whispered when I recharged the mind talisman, so a petty crook like this can't run off and make his own.*

Step by clumsy step, Dennard's puppet led them back to the office. With a few words of *Do not disturb,* he shut the hospital outside, and slumped behind his desk in sleep.

Mark looked around the small, functional-looking room they had to wait in. Dennard was already rising to check the doctor's breathing, face impassive but his hand eagerly quick to set the talisman aside on the desk. Kate stood silent, and Bryan glanced around at them all, a nervous look he'd been using more and more.

At least Mark had one value here. He felt again for any magic from Nolan or Winton that might have discovered them. He checked his phone and traded texts with Henry, still outside but safe.

And he's alone with the helpless Christa, while all I can do is keep watch.

"So he's only asleep?" Kate asked Dennard. "And you're alright, after doing all that?"

"I have to be."

Mark heard Dennard's determination, and wished he could take a turn with the mind magic. Kate wouldn't even offer to.

Dennard went on "Just… Tell me, why do you think Nolan double-crossed us back there? You looked like you were getting through to her. In spite of me pushing her about her crimes," he added.

Kate shook her head. "I thought I was. I thought she saw how the struggle between us was going to escalate. Between Winton, the police attention, and losing us as allies, it should be clear that she can't keep going like we were. I didn't realize she was already planning beyond that."

"What's that mean?" Bryan said.

"She had that drug ready for any excuse to use on Sasha. She kept her chained near her mother, and let her keep a talisman. Everything was ready, to force Sasha to make a permanent jump into another body. Now Nolan's seen that, and she thinks she can take any risks she wants with her own identity, and then just abandon it."

"Just like Winton," Mark growled. "And she's got Sasha and her mother now. Or it's Winton who does, but they can take either body if they—wait, you said Nolan 'thinks' she can?"

"It's only a theory I have." Kate lowered her voice. "I'm still looking through the evidence. But it may not be that easy to take a permanent body yet."

Mark moved closer, and the others drew around as he said "Why not? Wait, because Sasha would have walked into Winton's hands any time if he'd asked? And I still saw him in his Winton body, so weak that he needed a puppet to carry it away? You think he's still too weak to jump?"

"It's possible," Kate said. "Or it may be it was never easy. Sasha only promised she'd help Angie once she got Winton's book back."

"Because she needed it to save her?" Mark tried to remember. "She never said 'need,' but she *wanted* it enough. But then we saw her hop into her mother, when her own body was drugged."

"And Winton did it, once," Dennard added. "Or are you saying Roger Winton isn't Edward Winton after all?"

For once, Kate actually looked away. "I'm not sure yet. Only that there's a chance that Sasha and her mother may be better off than we feared."

"As long as we can find them in time," Dennard nodded.

" 'We'?"

That was Mark's father, and the note of selfish denial stabbed through Mark. *While we're saving your life too!* He saw the man break off and wilt under the others' cold glances, but that didn't ease the shame.

But then Kate turned to her ex. "Is that your answer, to always keep pushing? You might want to think how much the other people around us are able to give. I didn't say I *knew* those women are still out there to be saved. And if I'm right, I don't know what it means for helping Christa, or—"

She stopped, but the unsaid words were already crashing through Mark.

"Or Angie." He felt his throat go tight. "But you *can* bring her back, right? She can do it, she already made the jump to the owl—she got us the words to make it all possible, now you're telling me we can't help her?"

"What she said was," Dennard cut in, "that she's not sure about anything. And whatever it is, we deal with it."

His jaw was set, his voice didn't show one instant of hesitation.

No wonder he can make the mind magic obey, and I can't.

Mark glanced at Kate. Why had she been picking at Dennard's determination like that? It was the only thing that could get them through this.

The stillness began to lengthen, and Mark stepped back to let it settle around them. All he could do was face each moment, each second, the same way as he had the last moment—not thinking about how long they might have to wait, or how much he'd already failed, or Henry out there beside a body that might never wake up.

Deal with it.

Like Angie's own motto, *there's always a way.* Both Dennards could get up no matter what hit them.

Except, Angie was still circling above them, trapped in feathers and out of reach. They hadn't brought Christa back either, he'd failed her too.

Finally Jorgenson's computer beeped an answer. The report came in.

Dennard scrolled through it, and turned to Bryan. "It was a neurotoxin, alright. And the rest of the antidote should keep you going a while. Nolan was lying about one thing, though: what she gave you would just make you sick at first. Looks like chemicals that really could kill in one day but get held off by shots aren't things Nolan could just get her hands on."

"But… taking this shot *will* help me." Bryan's tone sank toward a hush.

"For a while," Kate said. "And there have to be ways to get more of it; Nolan did."

"So… you saved…" He broke off his words, as if gratitude was something to hide away.

Dennard leaned over the doctor one more time. "His breathing seems strong, not like Christa's and certainly not like Sasha's. You're sure most people this power put to sleep woke up on their own?" He looked at Mark.

"They… always seemed to, almost all of them. You did tonight."

"Then we've done what we came here for," Kate said. "We need to go."

As they stood, Mark caught up the silver talisman from the table, before Dennard reached for it.

Then the four of them marched out into the corridor, pushing through the hollowed, night-muted corridors, watching the quick flare-ups of medical urgency rush by them, and feeling the scattering of suspicious eyes.

Mark trudged on at the rear, watching for any feeling of other magic. The thought swam in his head: his taking the mind talisman himself was pointless, they had no time… All he had to do was take one step after another, same as how Dennard pushed on through it all. *And we can, we still can.*

Angie soared and circled beyond the roof. This roof, of Grace Hospital.

Everything they needed was here, and yet they were leaving. That awareness swelled inside him in a wave of pain. The door out was looming closer ahead.

When they stepped out into the night, he broke into a run. Kate was walking ahead of him, and he lunged forward to whisper "I'll catch up!" to her before he twisted away down the pavement.

As long as he ran, everything felt better—the cold air that told him the coat's magic hadn't melted his wits, the long walkways and turns of the hospital complex that mapped out in his head, the ground-eating stride he'd had months to learn. And Angie, swinging around toward him from the moment he'd begun to move.

—One cluster of late-shift staff on the pavement made him slow, and the thought crept back about how reckless he was being, even just with a test. But he had to know.

Then he skidded to a stop at the corner of the looming building. That spot was shelter enough from anyone who might see, this deep in the night. He leaped upward into the welcoming dark air, slipping from the unknowing voices below and blinking to keep his eyes focused on each row of the windows he passed. Second floor from the top.

Above, Angie had to have guessed what was inside. *I have to try, even if nothing's gone like we thought it would.*

The window was clamped tight, of course. Mark's fingers trembled in the cold. Still, he'd had weeks to research how this one window worked from the outside. The bolts only resisted his pocket knife for a moment before they turned. The window opened.

He gripped its frame as he floated beside it, and drew out the talisman. He waved Angie down.

She wheeled away.

He gasped in a breath of knife-cold air. "I can do this! It's just a test!"

He felt her path in the darkness tilt, the faintest fraction toward him.

"I swear I can! I need to try."

She circled, circled… hung in the sky a moment more before she slid down and perched beside him on the frame. Mark pulled himself inside.

Even with his body nearly weightless, his first footstep down in the half-lit hospital room *felt* louder than the humming breath-machines, louder than muffled voices out in the halls that might have been in another world.

The silent woman in the bed looked just the same as when he'd brought Sasha here. Her sunken face was nothing like Christa's—but he couldn't wake her either—

My father had it wrong, he thought. *It's not "always the girls" that get hurt, it's Angie and Dennard and Henry and* everyone *else while I always escape.*

Softly, he sat on the floor behind Melissa Davis's bed, out of view from the door out. Angie was still standing on the window's rim.

"This is your chance to try possessing her," Mark whispered to the owl. "Just test it—don't try to figure out a real transfer now. Just see if you can connect."

Angie didn't stir a feather. What was going through her mind, at a moment like this?

He reached up to grip the body's wrist, dry and limp. He laid his other hand on the bed, waiting, palm-up to show Angie the talisman in it.

"I don't know how any of this works. But… always a way, right? Together?"

Her wings beat once, twice, and she flapped toward him through the sound of the machines. Her feathers didn't even whisper in the air, not until the last moment when she settled onto his hand.

The buzz of the machines vanished.

Spinning, flung in wild directions—don't fight for balance, these must be thoughts, his and hers and something of the body's—too fast, that darting self far beyond had to be her, searching—but why around that faintness, so thin and nothing like the soul he'd failed to wake before—failed, failed, and now his partner danced and pushed and wrestled with the empty space—have to make this possible—

Nothing, like she can't touch her at all—

He heard the motor that carried the woman's breath—

Push, push—with his every move they still drew further away, so tired—have to reach them—close in, fight, but she couldn't—

Magic sparked, somewhere floors away—

Hurtling to them, he willed the world to steady, to let him join them—flow, like he'd moved the power itself once, help her move and flow and join—

She flowed, she *spattered* and fell away, not even touching the space—she drew together again—

You don't have to. That thought wasn't him, it was her, drawing away—

She lifted from his hand.

Real, solid vision blurred in around him as she flew away. He tried to turn his head, but his neck felt numb, unresponsive, and he lay still against the bed. So why did he feel two possessions near…

White cloth filled his sight. A nurse in whites, but so close—

Her eyes locked on his as she leaned in.

Winton. It had to be him, his words from the woman's lips that hissed through the blurriness: "You risked it? Show me—"

Mark lurched away. His legs wouldn't move, the magic left him heavy and helpless. The possessed nurse leaned closer, reaching for him.

All Mark could think was his suddenly-free hand and the piece of metal in it. He flung the talisman at the nurse's face, and Winton jerked back, tumbled backward and fell over.

The owl's scream tore the air. A streak of gray drove at the nurse's face—of course Angie came free ready to fight. The nurse crouched lower.

"Was that a bird—"

Voices in the corridor made the nurse's head swung away. Mark felt his legs responding now. A flick of magic let him kick backward in the air and find the window.

He dove through it into the night—*gravity magic's* still *only good for ducking out of trouble*—

Falling into the night air helped him focus. He felt Angie soaring out behind him, and he lifted upward to let the row of windows drop away past him, until he passed the roof and eased the magic back to let the breeze carry him over it.

Winton's presence was gone, with no other possessions lurking around either. What had said, *show me?*

And he'd lost Sasha's talisman. His fingers flexed; he'd had it right in his grasp, and his only thought for escaping was to *throw it away?*

He glanced at his phone. It was already jagged with warning texts: his father and Henry had sensed the magic, and now they were all pulling back from the complex.

He looked up toward where Angie flew in the dark, trying to find words to apologize. She was already gliding away.

He'd lost the mind talisman, and he'd shown their enemy their best hope of helping Angie. And they still failed.

Show me, Winton said?

He tried to focus on his leap, across to another hospital building where one side looked quiet. The magics that his father and Dennard carried moved along the pavement, safe. But why was Angie flying away?

Mark slipped to the ground and trotted across the pavement, toward the lot where Henry's magic waited. Here and there in the night around him, cars moved.

Why, why, didn't the mind talisman work for him? Nolan at least had years of practice with her own magic, but Dennard picked it up in a night, and even Sasha…

Henry was standing beside the Bug, where Christa still lay on the seat inside. "So one of them was waiting." His glare wasn't an accusation, just a sad truth.

"Winton." Mark couldn't look at Henry. "I… I just wanted to see if we could start helping Angie. And, I lost the talisman. I *threw the thing away* like some panicky fool. But," and he made himself look up, "at least we can make others now."

Henry only said "Sure. I started recharging the ones Nolan put on us. But aren't those the ones we shouldn't touch, in case Nolan can get control of them?"

"Right. I tried using one of Winton's once, and he almost—" Mark slumped again. "Every time we think we get closer to answers, it gets worse."

"That's right. That's exactly right," Henry sighed.

Mark's gaze sank to the pavement. He couldn't dredge up a reply, so he stayed in place, tracking as the other three moved in across the lot. And Angie circled up to a height where she wasn't even trying to hear them.

Finally Kate, Dennard, and Bryan joined them at the car.

Kate spoke first. "Winton and Nolan can't track magic without our help. Whoever was here, they may have only spotted you."

"Was it Nolan? Did you look for her?" Dennard asked. "If it's her and she's here herself, we could get a shot at her. But we aren't up for another fight now."

Mark said "That could be what Angie's out looking for—wait, she's heading back—"

The thought fell into place.

He rushed on "That was Winton in there, not Nolan, the way the 'nurse' talked I know it was him. He saw Angie with Melissa Davis, and he blurted out *show me*. What's that mean, that even he doesn't know all about leaving a body?"

And he wanted Angie to *show him?* That couldn't be right, what would it mean for her? He tried to push down the swelling cold shock in his body.

"So get out of here," his father said.

Cold eyes gleamed in the dim lot.

"Go disappear somewhere, you and her," Bryan Petrie said. "We all do it, and we don't come back. Because if all this is some kind of payback for what they've put you through, that's a sucker's game. You don't win those, you walk away."

Coward! Mark's fists clamped tight. The coat's power blazed through him, fierce and ready.

But it was just what he'd begged Angie to do, long ago...

He saw Kate open her mouth, then close it unspeaking. Henry turned away and pulled open the car door to settle beside Christa.

Dennard gave Bryan a slow, measuring look. "If you want. You know some of the risks here, and nobody should be facing them if they aren't willing to."

" 'Willing'? Why would anyone sane be here? Let those two kill themselves over their secrets—we've already got all the power we need to live anywhere. You can go fix your owl somewhere they won't be—"

"You get out of here!"

Mark spun to face the withered man that had his face, and his hand swung up… he reined the motion in to only jabbing a finger at him.

"Go, now! We found your antidotes for you, that's all you need, right? If you think this is just about *revenge…"* He stabbed his finger again, feeling how one touch could toss this man into the clouds. "Someone's still got Sasha and her mother, remember? Winton's hiding in this city twisting lives like he has for years, and now Nolan's starting to do the same thing. And we haven't stopped them, we let her get her hands on this same power—and you think this is just a grudge?"

"I think…" His father swallowed, and looked Mark in the eyes. "I think you've got no way to win."

Mark's hand shook in the air… but the rage soured and stuck in his veins, burning.

"We'll keep looking," he answered, but the words only came out tired. "We will, no matter how long it—"

SHREEEE!

Angie's shriek was the loudest she'd ever made. Mark swept his gaze around and searched for enemy magic, but the only possession he sensed was Angie herself settling onto the next car. She stood hunched forward, feathers ruffled up in warning, with her gaze boring right into him.

Stopping me.

His father laughed "See, she's sick of it too—"

Mark shot one glance over. Whatever was in his glare made his father seize up and step back, but that brought him no satisfaction now.

He looked at the others for support. Angie's father was pulling up his dropped jaw, trying to hide surprise of his own. Her mother's face had stiffened to let nothing show.

A moan came from their car—Henry, a cry of raw pain.

Mark looked for what must have struck him, but he only saw Henry slumped against Christa, gasping for breath.

Then Henry stepped back, teetering against the car door. Something fell from his hand, one of Nolan's talismans. His face was white and hollow.

Christa's eyes opened.

She stirred, she turned her head. Her hand came up, trying to smooth her hair.

Then they were all crowding in. Mark rushing forward beside Dennard, but Kate stepping in front of them all to let the two breathe. Angie chirruping joy. Henry—staggering, exhausted Henry who'd somehow found the strength to wake her—clinging to Christa and whispering something.

When Henry turned back to them, his voice was an empty croak:

"I've had it! No more risks—we get out now, we let Nolan and Winton see who's crazier—"

Christa cut him off:

"Don't you dare let them win."

CHAPTER TEN

COLD COMFORTS

Low voices pulled Mark awake. In the dreams that broke apart, he'd floated up after Angie and demanded to know why she'd cried out against them continuing the fight. If she'd given him an answer, he couldn't remember.

Now he lay crowded into the hotel bed beside Henry, hearing Christa's whispering from the corner.

He reached down to touch the coat on the floor. Its magic showed the real Angie was keeping watch above them, out of reach. No other magic lurked beyond the room.

"I know what I saw," Christa was saying. Mark lifted his head to see her advancing on the shadows the table threw in the corner—Dennard and Kate, his muzzy vision showed him. The window beside them was still thick with night.

The bed shifted under him, Henry pulling himself upright to watch the three. Over by the door, Mark's father sat quiet, watching without a word.

"You should all go back to sleep," Dennard said softly. "We can tell you when we're all rested."

"How can you *say* that? We've been kidnapped, cursed, we can't even agree whether we're fighting back, and now you're *keeping secrets from us—*"

Christa cut off her voice as it gathered force. Stillness fell around the room again, a trembling stillness of distant roads' cars and the tiny hummings and creaks of a hotel at night. Sounds soft enough to hint that her words hadn't been overheard.

Then she closed in on Dennard and Kate's corner. Henry shuffled up behind her, and Mark and his father moved in as well. Even in the dimness, everyone's awkward movements and blinking eyes were clear at these close quarters.

Kate sighed "I was saying, the evidence isn't positive yet. This is a theory I wanted to share yesterday, but it wouldn't have affected our pleas to Nolan. But now, it might fit some patterns we've seen about when someone makes a permanent body transfer. And it affects whether Sasha and her mother are still alright."

Mark stumbled closer. "And what Winton said to me and Angie last night?" *When I tried to match her with a body and failed?*

"Most of my findings are in here." Kate turned to the wall and unplugged her phone from the charger to hand it to Dennard. "I want to be sure I have the software settings right."

Dennard's voice hitched. "What? These?" He tapped at the screen, his face a glimmer in the shadows.

Mark leaned in. "What? You've got something on Winton? We *need* to know…"

He stopped, lowering his eyes from the others' gaze on him, so close. He'd already endangered their whole plan for Angie by rushing off to Melissa Davis's bedside while Winton could see it, and it had gotten them nothing. He could make out Henry's glare, stern even when Christa glanced back at him. There was Kate's silent reserve, and Bryan Petrie lurking a step back from their crowd. And Angie couldn't even hear them up in the sky. *How long can we stay together when we're already split up like this?*

"It's still going to take a while," Kate said. "I'd prefer we all catch up on our sleep."

Christa shook her head. "I've had enough *sleep.* Look, the sun isn't up yet. I'll go get the other car, the one you left on the way to that warehouse. And some breakfast for us." She reached past Henry to scrabble at the table, where flyers for restaurants had been spread.

Henry slid the flyers out of her grasp. "You're not going anywhere—" She turned a fierce glare on him, but he went on "I mean, you'd be blind on your own. You can't sense Winton or Nolan out there."

The two stared at each other, their rising breathing the only sound in the stillness.

"Mark should do it, on his own." Dennard's voice washed over them, calmness with no hint of doubt. "He's the fastest. We need a second car, and he can recharge the coat on the way. He'll make it quick."

Right after Mark had run off into Winton's sights, Dennard trusted him to go out again? Mark's throat went tight with gratitude. He waited for the others to shoot the idea down, but nobody did.

"Okay." He threw on the rest of his clothes, too embarrassed to meet their gazes. The door was just within reach.

The air outside was warmer, but some of the stars still shone in the dark sky; he had less night left than he'd thought. He stepped out onto the wide, dim parking lot, ready to break into a run. High above, Angie swung around to watch him.

"Hey!"

His father's voice slammed him to a halt. *Already I'm letting my guard down.*

Mark turned, watched the shifty-eyed shadow of himself trot up to meet him. "What is it?" he said, and managed to hold most of the contempt back from his voice.

"I saw you watching Henry and his girl. Like it hurt to see them fight."

Mark said nothing. Bryan Petrie barely knew him, he *couldn't* be picking out the most uneasy parts of him from a few careless glances...

His father gave a small, smug smile. "What I'm saying is, I didn't know that owl up there meant that much to you. But if you want to stay and fight for her, you need someone else who can track Winton down."

You said there was no way to win, now you want to help? Mark let a breath in, out, in again, before he said "You should go back inside, before they think you've run off." *While I'm the one they still trust.* He couldn't resist throwing that at his father.

"Maybe I should. Since each time you fuel that silver, you whisper so I never know how to make the stuff. That's no way to treat one of your own. How about, you want my help, you show me how the floating power charges up?"

"How... about..." Mark said through his teeth, "you go back to the room right now, if you *ever* want those people to forget what you really are."

He spun away and strode across the snowy asphalt, his eyes flicking around the lot and the street ahead. Deserted.

Behind him, he felt his father's talisman moving after him. *Sure, we can sense each other—but all you've got for power is one fragment of leather Nolan let you carry.* Mark shut his eyes and flung himself up through the cool, clean air into the sky.

The talisman below shrank away—and broke off moving, to his pleasure—and he eased the magic back and let himself float hundreds of feet up, where the city lights blurred in a soothing network of lines, and the upper breeze bore him away.

Mark curled his body tight against the familiar chill. Leaping away wasn't the kind of hard-hitting answer he'd really wanted to give his father, but it made his point. Bryan Petrie would *not* be coming along to grab some fix on the way, or watching how he pulled in the power that let him fly.

And that's not getting my own kind of fix?

He clenched his eyes tighter… but he'd been balancing that worry for months. "As long as I can still think about putting the magic down, I'm fine." So, no taking in the scenery—"Just collect the power and the car," he promised himself.

Angie drifted near him. Following him.

"Are you with me now?" he called out into the breeze. "Or you still want us to quit?"

But she only held her place, gliding some hundred feet away from him. She couldn't *answer*.

He dropped to the city at a quiet back corner, and settled into an easy trot that lightened him only enough to keep moving—even the coat's broad sheath of energy felt thinner and more drained now. It had to be six in the morning, from the scattered rumble and shine of lights that stirred in the streets, no longer quite so silent.

Using just enough power to keep weight off tired legs wasn't enough to keep the worries out of his head. All this time they'd been fighting for two goals. But now they had the magic that should give Angie her life back, and it still hadn't helped her… had *she* given up on them? As for shutting down Roger Winton and his killings, that kept being pushed back by all the damage Nolan did. *And so we've got a cheap crook in the middle of us calling it nothing but revenge.*

Three blocks later he passed the cleared space where the Dennards' house had been, burned down by Rafe and the rest of Winton's manipulations. Angie didn't even wheel to give it a second glance. The green stillness of Rosewood Park itself waited across the street, if the early Summer Street traffic would open up for a moment.

New magic moved in the air.

A spybird, *here* again? It was blocks ahead up the street but coming fast, and Mark shot a glance at the traffic, but no, not clear enough to dash across. And every time Winton saw him come back to the park it stripped away more and more of the magic's secret.

Mark dropped and slid under a parked car. The presence was still far ahead—far enough to promise him a long wait, with pavement below and metal above him squeezing cold into him. Angie's flight didn't turn, *because she and Winton can't sense each other's power, they each seem like one innocent bird in hundreds if they don't draw each other's eye.* Mark tracked the enemy closing slowly, slowly, his shivering muscles begging it wouldn't stop and circle back...

Finally it passed by beyond his range. Mark meant to lie still and count a few breaths longer to be sure, but instead he squirmed to his feet the moment it vanished.

The street was finally clear, and he scrambled across. Snow over the ground was a half-melted crust, all too eager to capture his footprints; he kept to the sidewalk along the edge and bolted for the block's north corner and the easiest way inside. With all Winton's interest in their magic's secret and now how he'd looked at them in the hospital, the fewer signs he left here the better.

As he swept toward the snack shack ahead, he saw motion behind it, that had to be someone ducking out of sight of his approach, prowling around. Rosewood at night had never been free of dangers, even when Dennard had been patrolling it as a park guard. Mark could only dash past the building and on to the corner parking lot.

The spybird moved into range again—on the far side of the park now? But it was still too far to see him, and too low to see over the trees... Mark flung himself forward, shooting across the empty lot with a step too light to leave any prints in the snow. Winton still had no reason to notice Angie in the sky either.

Nobody else in view. He vaulted the chain fence to drop beyond it and crouch in the shadows of the trees.

Snow chilled his face, and bracken rustled against his legs when he pressed lower. The bird flew closer, but too late to have seen him before he reached cover. Was it crisscrossing the park, looking for signs that Mark always had to come back here? How had it gotten from the south to the west side so quickly?

Stay low. It can't hear me if I lie still, it can't see my frozen breath under the trees.

The bird passed on by again. Its simple, straight course promised it had seen nothing, it only flew on toward the street—

It swung down toward where the snack center would be; Mark knew it without looking up. The magic twisted and jumped from the bird's path onto a grounded shape.

Someone shouted. Sharp, urgent, a half-formed voice that broke off with the sound of… were those running feet?

A gunshot split the night. Mark wrenched his head up to peer through the dim growth to the open park. Another shot boomed out, and he locked his legs to keep from jumping to his feet. A man dashed across the parking lot, away from whoever the magic gripped. Some ragged, petty park mugger.

Is Winton daring me to save that man, to prove I'm here? I can't reach him in time—

A third shot sounded. The man fell without a sound.

And a second figure, the one possessed, walked toward him, so slowly, deliberately. His gun rose to center on his victim. To finish him off.

I can't! I can't show myself, he sounds like he's already dead— Mark felt his legs drawing in to spring.

A siren howled. The possessed shooter froze, whirled, dashed away deeper into the park.

One officer, a black uniform against the night, ran to the body… and stood up only a sad second later to charge after the shooter. Mark felt the magic steer its pawn across the grounds for another second, then release him.

The magic jumped to the bird again.

The spybird circled above. Police voices called through the night. And Mark inched backward, fighting *not* to think of the two crooks who had been dragged down by Winton's scheme—or Nolan's scheme, but it seemed like the original puppetmaster—maybe just because Winton *guessed* he might be at the park again.

Each time the bird passed to the far side of its orbit, Mark crept further through the brush, silent as he could move. It finally turned and left the park, and he reached the invisible core of magic on the side of the small slope. The crack between worlds, or the ley-line crossing, or whatever it was that Angie's family had discovered long ago.

"Zha-Daruath."

Power blasted through him. Cold and exhaustion ripped away, smashed away by the flood of lightning-fierce *possibility* that poured into the massive coat, the belt, the leather trinkets in his pocket. His mouth opened for a roar—

No. I can't let the magic get to me, not when I've got this one chance.

The spybird was blocks away at the edge of his range. He scrambled through the brush and vaulted to the open again, into Angie's view.

He stabbed a finger after the enemy. "Winton's getting away! Please, he's still got Sasha—"

For one frozen moment he remembered, Angie might not believe in him anymore. But in the next heartbeat, she twisted and darted off in the bird's direction.

Mark dashed to follow. He locked his focus on the killer's magic far ahead, and on keeping behind the distance and the outlines of the buildings between them that kept him hidden. All the advantage he'd need.

Angie's presence drew closer behind Winton. Mark felt her sweeping low and twisting behind one tall building. She wasn't closing in above to dive and cut the bird down, she was following Winton. To trap him, maybe free Sasha, find his real body. Or just not risking his touch.

She might be right. Mark scrambled down the predawn sidewalk, forcing himself to hang back and not let the coat sweep him across the blocks. He dashed across one street, darting between a gap in traffic, then through a second. Then Fulton's stream of cars made him slam to a stop.

And it could still be a trap, and I said I wouldn't run off alone. Mashing the light's Walk button, he grabbed out his phone.

"We've got him!" he told Dennard. "We're tailing Winton!"

The voice that answered was Henry's, its usual scratchiness turned harsh. "You went after him? Again?"

"I know! But we're keeping our distance, he doesn't know. Is Dennard there? Can you help us?"

"We're all here," Dennard said. "What's your location?"

Mark shot off a position ping from his app, then saw the light change and bolted forward. Winton was still in range, with Angie keeping up low behind that presence. Gasping, Mark said "We've gone so many blocks, but we could be closing in on…"

The streets, the direction, clicked in his head. But that couldn't mean anything, Winton would never go back to his own home.

Henry's voice was rasping just out of his earshot. He drew the phone in close again to hear "…told you we can't do this! But you're still charging off all by yourself!"

"I'm not going after him! We're *tracking* him, that's all—"

A shape parked up the street caught his eye. That couldn't be the same Subaru that Kate had brought them. But as he drew nearer—

"That's the car! The one Winton took Sasha in!"

"Mark, wait for us!" Kate said.

Us. The word was warmer than the coat's power around him. They were still together, at least when they caught a chance like this to trap Winton. *Angie* was still with him. If he didn't waste their edge by letting the killer see him.

By the next block the buildings had lowered and dwindled, and the first streaks of true sunlight peeped between them. Winton's neighborhood lay ahead, but Mark held down the hope that it would be that easy. They'd searched his townhouse before. Angie twisted lower and lower among the buildings to stay below their target's view.

Then Winton's bird slanted downward. Mark halted in the snow, but the killer was still more than a block ahead. Its power dove at the ground, and halted there at street level.

It was grabbing another human body, Mark realized. Slowly, shivering without the run to keep him warm, Mark maneuvered around the far side of blocks to keep them between himself and the possessed pawn, until he felt it enter Winton's townhouse.

He peeped at it around the corner, watching the sunlight hit the building's windows. He'd crept around the blocks on every side of here in the past, starting with the time he'd first felt one of Winton's birds flying out from this place.

Christa's voice asked "What did you find now?"

"It's Winton's home alright. Why would he come back here? Because it's where Sasha worked for him?" Mark fought the urge to steal another glance at it.

Angie flew in. He felt her soar to the building, settle against its upper side—right where Winton had gimmicked one of his vents, so he could let himself in or out as a bird. The owl could have flown out there the night it became Angie.

A car hummed by on the street, and Mark moved back from the corner. *They say I take risks, but Angie dives right in.*

Winton's pawn vanished.

Mark's eyes went wide. In one instant Winton's control vanished from inside the building, and reappeared off behind Mark in the sky. Winton had jumped his control back to the spybird he'd left, and the bird must have wandered off in the meantime—

And Winton was searching the street again. Mark flung off his thoughts and glanced around. A tree thick with snowy branches spread over a driveway only three long steps away; he dove under it and pressed himself against the wooden fence. Its shadows had to be enough to hide him.

"Mark? Mark?" came Henry's voice.

The bird sailed by above, making only a simple sweep and not a proper search through the neighborhood's cover. Mark felt Angie creeping slowly along the far wall of the townhouse, or already inside it.

Winton's grip winked out again, and reappeared within the building.

Mark stepped out onto the sidewalk. No lights came on in the windows around him, no car passed by in the early light to spot him hiding from something in the sky. Lucky.

"Winton made another search outside," he told the others. "Then his focus jumped back into the building—he already grabbed someone off the street, and he must have put an extra talisman on them."

Dennard said "So he can 'glance' between keeping watch outside and what he's doing in there, at just a thought. Watch yourself."

"But, what *is* he doing in there? Why did he grab someone?" Mark stared at the building's windows, where the rising sun blazed against the glass. He could feel Winton's stolen body inside, and Angie sneaking closer… and he was still only *watching*.

Kate's voice was softer. "You found the car he took with Sasha and her mother?"

"Right. A few blocks from here."

"Then those two may be safe for now. That's what we've been trying to confirm since you left, and we may finally have these pictures right. I'm sending them over."

Image files arrived on the screen. Mark flicked the first two open—screenshots of Roger Winton's face and his father Edward's. Both were from familiar news shots, but these images had the faces isolated on some kind of software grid. For them to analyze.

"Is this about how one Winton took over the other? Don't tell me you figured out what he needs to make a permanent jump. If he's got that covered now, he'll bail out of his broken body in a minute—" *He could be taking over Sasha right* now— "Wait, are you saying we were wrong, he *didn't* take over his son?"

Dennard said "We're saying those kinds of transfers could be harder than we thought. That's what Kate found, and if we line up the face-recognition software just right…"

New images arrived, aligning the two Winton faces to the same angle.

"We know the older Winton ended in that fire, and the younger one needed parts of his face rebuilt after it. He looks less like his father than he did before… but if we factor out his reconstructed nose and a couple of other changes… See?"

One more image slid into view. The face was Roger Winton's, with labels beside the features:

Forehead, 100% match.

Jaw, 100% match.

Eyes, 100% match.

"WHAA—"

A motion at the corner of his eye made Mark choke off his gasp. A young man across the street was staring at him, drawn to his voice.

Mark pulled the phone in close, *huddling* around it in the sudden cold he felt creeping in. "You're saying what? He *didn't* take his son over?"

Kate said "The evidence is that that body was always the father's. It also says that he doesn't age, which may be what taking the Roger Winton identity was trying to hide."

"Whaat?" Mark heard himself repeating. "His magic can do *that?*"

"We don't know," Kate sighed. "But it may mean that he can't leave his body as completely as we feared. Last night he did blurt out…"

" 'You risked it', to Angie and me," Mark filled in. "And he *was* still trapped in his old body even when it couldn't walk, I saw that…"

His thoughts whirled.

"So he stayed trapped. Like Angie's trapped, like we can't get her out *ever*—" He heard his voice rising in a roar and tried to hold it down.

Christa was saying "No, no, remember we saw Sasha move to her mother. Wasn't that what Nolan was testing with her?"

"I… guess…" He sucked in a breath of cold morning air. "Sasha proved it can happen. And Angie made it into the owl, so she can make it out. Maybe it *is* just risky, like Winton said—and now Sasha and Angie have done it, but what's Winton want with them, is that why the car that took Sasha is here—"

Clickclick-click!

The owl's sound yanked his gaze upward, but the first brush of surprise was already fading as he sensed Angie, saw her settling out of the sky toward him. He halted, watched.

She dropped onto his arm. One foot closed around his hand.

Cold and sidewalk and flesh fell away. The whirling, wild openness of the mind swept around him—

Tightness. A sense of cramped space, impossible in this world that had no space, but there it was—a *sense* of narrowness imposed on it by her mind, for him to feel.

What did that mean? He struggled to remember where he'd been, what she'd been doing. She'd gone through the hidden entrance—that could be the narrow place, and a dim one too, and the thought opened up a feel of scuttling talons on the shaft, then the floor, until she could see—

Shapes? Two figures? No, those had to be three. With that guess the shapes resolved, half from her image and half from his understanding: a younger figure lying too still, the older woman that resembled her and stood stiff with fear, and facing her was the man that in any form must be the enemy—

Uncertainty, hesitation, that filtered how her eyes took it all in.

Angie, *hesitating?*

With that thought the trance fell away. Weight and breath crashed back into him, and Angie flapped over to settle on the wooden points of the fence.

"I thought," he heard himself stammer, "I thought you didn't want us fighting Winton anymore. But you're here, but now…"

Angie's head tilted to the side—on a human face it could be amusement, but he couldn't *know*. Even her mindtouch had only given him more questions.

Sound was coming from the phone in his hand. What he'd seen fell into place.

He brought the phone up again and reported "Angie spotted Sasha in there, and her mother. Winton's got them! I think he's poking around at how Sasha transferred. He did call it a risk."

"He's what?" Dennard said.

"He's trying something on them. I think right now!"

Henry said "You wait for us! You can't just go in there."

"I have to! If I don't come out… you tell the cops, or something…" Mark started across the street.

There was simply no time. He could feel Winton's stolen body up on the second floor, as he marched over the street slush and the scattered cars or faces that could be watching him. The coat's power thrummed ready to sweep him along, but he clamped down on the urge to run faster than his thoughts could form. Angie circled above.

The townhouse's front door waited ahead. He gathered the magic as he closed in, searching for the precision that could drag the lock down and rip it open without making more noise.

It was unlocked.

Mark flinched back. A trap?

Angie circled higher. She'd made the transfer Winton hadn't, he might want to catch her too.

Mark stepped inside.

Months of midnight searches here rose in his memory: same quiet corridor, same doors to Winton's rooms, the same orchard scent of a place that had been kept soaked in cleansers for its master's return while Winton stayed in hiding. But this time the enemy's power really was lurking in the floor above again. Mark dove in a floating arch toward the stairs—the fewer places his feet touched, the less chance he'd step on a talisman trap.

Second floor, third door. The power behind it was clearer than following a voice. Mark lurched to a halt to focus on the doorknob, for the tiniest flicker in it that might strike out and seize him. It felt clear to touch.

He gave the door the softest nudge open.

There they were. Elizabeth Lawrence—no, she was still shrinking back and hesitating, that was still Sasha in her—stood by the bed, while Sasha's body lay motionless on it. Facing them both was a haggard, aging man in a jogging suit, clutched by Winton's power. Already turning to the doorway, alert.

That's the body he just grabbed—if it was his real one I'd crush him right now.

Instead, Mark stepped forward. The bedroom was wide enough, he could start toward one woman then lunge around to scoop up the other instead.

Winton shifted to block the bed. His stolen hand was up, ready to strike. Mark felt the coat's power throbbing, eager to lash out, to bring bone-crushing power down on the enemy. But with Winton ready and the jogger's body as a hostage—

Sasha/Elizabeth gasped "What are you *doing?* Mark?"

From somewhere in his chest, a calm, sure voice replied "Don't you worry. Be ready to run."

"No!! She— my mother— Mr. Winton, he's going to pull me out of Mom and make us alright again!"

Mark's breath whooshed out, helpless. He kept his eyes on Winton, but Sasha wasn't finished.

"You don't understand, I have to trust them!"

He found his voice. "Trust *Winton*— he's just making you a lab rat. No, it's more than that."

"See, he, Mr. Winton said he could save her! Why d'you want to screw this up anyway?" She motioned to the bed. Sasha—her body— lay still, eyes glazed, empty.

"Save you? Sasha, he saw me trying the same thing tonight, and he was… he said…" Mark shook his head. "Look, we can get you both out of here."

Winton shook his head. "And what good does that do any of you? No, you should watch me work. And, shouldn't Angie see it too?"

"Don't you talk about her." Rage clenched his throat and he had to force the words out.

He reached for Sasha, but she pulled back. Away from him, away from Winton too—but then she turned toward the killer. She took his arm.

And Winton simply looked at her, and him, the face hiding secrets just like someone used to hiding his whole *self* in anyone he chose… except, something flickered in those eyes.

At least Angie stayed at her own altitude, far out of reach.

Mark drew out his phone, still on.

"Everyone?" he growled. "If you hear any trouble, send the police. We know how much Winton hates attention. But if anything about this transfer isn't what he says…"

He looked straight at Winton's stolen face.

"One trick, and all of you go straight to Nolan and tell her every last word about our gravity magic. Then she can search the whole world for more people who can use it to hunt Winton down—and we all know she will. Got that?"

"Got it." Kate's voice over the speaker was clear and firm.

Sasha stared at him. "Will you please stop—he's trying to help us, can you just back off and let him?"

And Winton's smile softened, but it still lingered at the corner of the possessed mouth, just one hint of a smirk. "It's alright, Sasha. Some people are always seeing the worst in us."

He reached into his pocket, and drew out a disk of silver.

Sasha held up a hand to slow him. "Before we start... Mom's just going to deny it again, but she said that when my aunt worked for the family, she sent some 'weird' message back about some opportunity here. Did... did you want her to know about magic too?"

She said "you." She knows they're the same Winton now—did he tell her?

Winton nodded. "We tried to tell her. Your mother... was never willing to listen."

Mark felt his breath catch. Smooth as Winton was, those words sounded like a lie hid in them somewhere.

"Oh. Well, we... we can fix that too," and Sasha's voice went soft before she added "Just bring us back."

She stretched out on the bed, next to her rightful body. Mark saw how the mother's shorter hair had begun to slip from the pins that held it. It looked more like her daughter's than ever, the way Sasha's hair pooled around her pale face, with nobody inside to care for it.

She said "I guess I'm ready. I wish I knew a real way to... well, thank you," she said to Winton, as he moved toward the bed.

And I have to be ready, for whatever he tries.

Winton said only "Now, relax..."

He set his left hand, the hand with the talisman, over the mother's hand. His right hand went on the daughter's. He closed his eyes.

Mark held his breath. If all Winton needed was a touch, Mark couldn't miss one twitch of what the magic did. For Sasha's sake, for Angie's, for everyone.

Power, quicksilver possession power, swirled in the silver disk. It streamed, flowed, Mark fought to follow every trace of how it moved—

Or I can grind Winton into the floor and see if that finishes his real body, but right now that would risk both women as well as his host. Focus!

Magic flowed, from one form to the other, but how, what was it doing…

Footsteps sounded behind him. He spun, stared at Kate as she walked up beside him.

"He can't fool us both," she whispered. "Shh."

The magic stilled. The younger Sasha was already raising her head, looking at her mother.

"You did it, you really did it, thank you thank you forever ohmygod…"

Her voice choked, and she gasped for breath, while her hand nudged her mother.

Except for a faint breath, Elizabeth Lawrence didn't stir.

"Alright, now you can wake her up too," Sasha said, but her voice hesitated.

Winton set his hand back on the still woman. Power swirled again, and Mark strained to follow it.

She didn't move.

"Mom?"

Such a soft word, hollow in the empty room.

"You try it!" Mark flung the words at Sasha, anything to stop the horror spreading over her face. "Maybe that's how it worked with Christa, it was the person who was closest to her who could wake her up—"

Sasha was already clawing at her mother's coat, yanking out a talisman from the pocket that had been hers a moment ago. She pressed it to her mother's hand, to her heart. Magic surged and flailed out from it, and her face twisted in concentration.

But Elizabeth didn't move, never responded even with her daughter's hands shaking her. Slowly, Sasha went still, slumped down beside the bed, and her breath collapsed into sobs.

Then Winton spoke, a gentle tone just louder than her own had been: "It's not your fault. You can't wake her, because she's not asleep—I think she was already gone."

Sasha stared up.

He went on "I… *hoped* I was wrong. But it looks like a complete transfer is too much for the receiving body's original mind. There's nothing left of her."

Sasha breathed "Mom… Mom said all of you were trouble…"

Mark drew down to kneel beside her.

She shot to her feet. "That Nolan *bitch!* She drugged me, she made me do… I never meant… *she did it!* I'll kill her!"

Nolan did it, she said? Mark closed his eyes. Nolan had pushed her, but Sasha's own eagerness to use magic had made her take the leap—and now blaming her enemy was easier than facing who had finally destroyed her mother.

"Kill her!" Sasha said again.

And Winton, *Winton,* said "That's not the way we live."

"What??" Sasha screamed at him. "I'll get her—and, I'll get her magic, I'll kill her, I'll destroy her every way she used me!"

Winton shook his head. "Sasha… for now, we stay away from her. If she has a weakness in her defenses, it'll take time to find it—"

"So you don't believe in me at all! How can I wait, she *killed my mother!* And you!" She whirled and stared at Mark, fury slashing across her face. "Don't you care? You told me how much she's killed people—you want to let her go?"

Mark reached inside, for something to offer her. "I… the last time I lost someone, I charged right out to get my payback. That ended up with Kate finding me stranded on a roof, pretty much out of my mind." He glanced over at Winton, daring him to smirk at what he'd driven Mark to once. *What's Winton up to here? He's got to be pushing Sasha into this rage, and yet he keeps pulling her back.* "Trust me, you need to cool down before you think about—"

"Think about what?" Sasha said. "You can't even *say* she needs to die!"

Another voice, calmer, firmer, rolled through the room: "Sasha, look at me."

Sasha's head turned, to Kate.

"You've just been through a shock, one nobody should have to endure. You've never had another experience as painful as this. Or have you?"

"Like *this?* No!" Sasha howled.

"Then—look me in the eye—can you honestly tell me that this minute is the best time for you to go after your enemy?"

Sasha's face trembled. Her mouth opened, tried to speak.

Then she slumped in place. "No."

Kate nodded. "There's no rule that you have to do everything at once, you know. You're still just beginning to learn about magic, and you've just seen the dangers it can lead to."

Then Winton turned to Sasha. "Here, let me help you with your mother—"

"I've got her!" Sasha waved him away. "I mean, she's still breathing… maybe you're wrong, the doctors can do something… And, this is *my* job. I have to do it right, don't I?"

She moved back to her mother, with slow, clumsy steps. Mark felt his frustration twisting, but everything he had said was only driving Sasha away. This was what Winton did, he wormed into people's lives.

Gently, Winton said "If that's what you want, Sasha. And I will be looking into Nolan, but please take your time. Leave studying her to me, just for now."

Sasha glanced back to him. "You… you won't take away my shot at her?"

"Not if it means that much to you. Soon."

"Soon. And thank you, for everything you did."

Winton gave Mark, Bryan and Kate a glance... a single glance at them all as if that was all they deserved. Then he walked his stolen body away without a word.

For long moments, none of them moved. Mark felt Winton moving through the rooms, heard the front door thump shut.

At that sound, Sasha burst out "You! Why'd you have to screw this up? If you didn't smash in and try to turn this into a fight..."

Mark heaved out a sigh. But all he could say was "I... you don't know how much he's done."

"Shut up! He's trying to help me—and you attacked him! He couldn't save Mom but he did switch me back. I..." She held up her hands. "A few minutes ago these weren't even *my* hands, and he gave me my life back."

If Winton could *do that for Angie*—

He crushed down the thought. "Did you hear him about your mother? He 'hoped he was wrong'? He's done this before—"

Kate said "That's enough."

"He knew it wasn't safe—maybe your aunt was—"

"Stop it!!" Sasha screamed.

Kate reached toward her. "Please—"

"Stop, just leave me alone! Just... let me..."

She waved them away, and sank, slumped, to her knees beside her mother. She leaned over her, and her talisman hand settled on the still, faintly-breathing form. Its magic flickered to probe for anything left in within her.

Sasha's breath hitched and swung between straining and sobs.

Then Kate was beside her. The woman who refused to use magic laid her hand over Sasha's, and the two strained and searched together until at last Sasha sagged, defeated, into Kate's arms.

CHAPTER ELEVEN

MISMATCH

Mark backed out of the stilled, too-clean rooms, moving weightless as a shadow to not disturb Sasha's grief. She was still crying something to Kate, but he wondered how long it would be before she went after her revenge on Nolan. If Winton let her get that far.

His fists couldn't stop clenching, even with the killer he hated most gone. Dennard reported that the borrowed jogger's body was simply awakening on the street again, left to wonder why he'd "blacked out." Henry could sense Winton's spybird flying away, but he also refused to try following it. And Mark felt his father moving *toward* the townhouse, and Angie flying back from checking on the jogger to perch above its roof—as if now that the puppet and Sasha were safe for the moment, she had no interest in Winton. No matter what other lives the puppetmaster took.

He'd begun walking away from Winton's townhouse when Sasha's voice made him whirl:

"Don't you talk about 'sorry'—you *were* the one who dragged us into Nolan's trap. Mom was fine until you grabbed us!"

She was at the front door, facing down his father. Mark rushed toward them, to hear Bryan saying "...did you try it on your mother? Think."

"I told Mr. Winton everything, and he couldn't bring her back. Now go away!"

"Alright. And, sorry again." Bryan Petrie backed away.

Mark glanced between the two. His father trying to apologize, or help Sasha? Neither sounded real.

And he's down here, after he offered to help me catch Winton. If he'd kept his word and tried to track the bird flying off, we might have had something.

Sasha headed back in alone, as Kate walked out to join them. Dennard brought the Bug around to meet the three of them.

"Never got that food for us, did you?" his father said.

"Before we do that," Kate said, "we have one stop to make: Sasha mentioned the talismans she set up around her home. I want to gather those up."

"To bring to Sasha? Or keep them away from her so she won't go after Nolan?" Dennard frowned at her.

Right, Kate had tried taking the belt away from Mark too, to destroy it. And she'd tried keeping it from Dennard at the end of their marriage.

But Kate only said "Sasha asked me to get them for her. Then, we all need to talk."

* * *

The Valen Street apartments were a cluster of noise and figures, with the morning rush to work and school still going on. Mark eyed the patches of onlookers and felt Angie flying by doing the same.

At least his father looked uncomfortable, in the place where he'd kidnapped three people and taken one away to her death.

"So where are they?" Dennard said.

Mark glanced up toward the side of the apartment block, and the invisible pressure he felt. "Tied under the buildings' eaves. I guess it's so they're out of reach of people, and split up so they can draw in power from different areas. Not as strong as the one Winton put deep in that factory, though."

Kate asked "You think you can get them down, in daylight?"

"I can try." He looked at the streams of residents, and the edge of the rooftop. With magic to keep him from falling, he could "climb" up and pull down the talismans. Would any onlookers really think he was any more than a repairman, if he didn't give them time to get in his way?

Angie glided down and perched on the overhang. He tried not to stare; she'd tracked Winton to Sasha, then let Winton's bird go, and yet she was helping here? Was she still with them or not?

But in seconds Angie had crawled under the eave, and the current of drawn-in magic stilled. Then she was flying past them, and a bundle of cloth dropped into his hands.

He worked his fingers under the folds. The fabric seemed like the same idea he'd improvised to test Sasha's other talisman: layers to keep all light out while the talisman was opened to charge it. Angie seemed to have closed it tight, so he drew it out. Another locket of silver, with what would be a bit of jade inside—Sasha really could have had these talismans made quickly, though the design didn't feel as sturdy as the ones Nolan and Winton used.

Angie was already flying on. Mark trotted around scattered people after her, wondering if she'd already spotted all the talismans with just her eyes.

She only missed one.

* * *

The diner's booth was so grimy Mark thought he saw his father's lip curl, and the burgers didn't look much better. But it had *coffee.* The six of them were all but alone here, with only a few voices and clinks from the kitchen to disturb them.

He felt Angie perching unseen up on the roof, like she was babysitting them. Or trying to shoo them out of town.

Sitting opposite Mark, Kate began with "Sasha won't listen to me. She means to destroy Nolan, and I think she's only holding back because Winton told her to wait."

Mark forced down his bite. Someone had carved random lines on the table's wood, and he traced them with a finger. Whoever'd felt that urge to cut something up, right now he sympathized.

"Then when the situation blows up, we'll be caught in the middle. Can we…" Christa took a glance around at the empty tables, and lowered her voice further. She set one of Sasha's lockets on the table. "We all need to defend ourselves from possession. Is it safe to use Sasha's talismans? Or can we make our own?"

Next to her, Henry shook his head. "Defenses? You keep trying to make plans, but is any of this our fight?"

"Henry, please…"

"Is that what you want?" Dennard asked. "You've done your part. Now it's time to move on?"

Mark's eyes widened; Dennard sounded *ready* to let him go.

Henry took a slow look around the table. "I'm *scared*. I mean, all of us get shot and kidnapped and—"

A bell rang at the door behind him, and Henry flinched, until the customer walked past them and on to the counter.

When Henry spoke again it was just above a whisper, and his eyes shifted between each of the others, searching for something. "I mean, we know Sasha's alive now, and it looks like we can't do any more for her mother. We've still got two enemies, not one. And we have the basics we need to help Angie. You say you're doing this for her," and he looked right at Mark, "but *she* wants us to get out safe. You could have years to figure her cure out—or don't you think you can?"

And what if I can't? The familiar thought was a half-closed wound, that Henry jabbed right at. Mark could only hold his face calm: "I'm sure there are ways. And, I'm sure we can beat Winton—and find his real body, and every note he's stockpiled about getting this transfer right."

Softly, Kate said "I don't think there will be any clues on him. Not about this."

"No? I thought you couldn't imagine any spellkeeper not keeping some notes. And there's the book Nolan took—"

"Mark, you're forgetting those pictures we sent you before we arrived. I said a complete transfer seemed harder than we thought. His face shows that's still Edward Winton's body—"

"So he never did take his son over?" Mark shook his head, not sure if he could shake loose a horror Winton might *not* have done. "He, what, killed him just to have a younger identity? Or you think the real Roger found out too much?"

Christa shook her head. "That's not what Kate found. It would be handy if the evidence from his 'death' told us more about him, but…"

Kate pursed her lips. "For the last month, my son and I moved around Europe. Roger Winton supposedly grew up far away from his father, and he was raised in different places that made him genuinely hard to track. Until his father's body died in that fire, we thought."

Kate held up her phone, and the research she'd mentioned earlier.

She went on "The records about Roger Winton only become solid after that point, when they treated him for burns and rebuilt part of his face. His fingerprints were burned off too."

Chills twitched and probed through Mark's nerves, not sure what to steel him for. "What are you saying?"

Kate sighed. "After I spent a month trying to trail his life, I don't think there ever was a Roger Winton. All the traces of him are so shallow… the person who knew him most was a tutor who helped him in the last months of his education. But Roger was never in a school, and she could never meet the tutors he said he had before that. The whole Roger Winton identity seems to be counterfeit, until Edward stepped into it."

"So he just… a whole identity? He could do that?"

"With his mind control?" Henry glared at him. "Of course he could—if that wasn't enough, we've seen him kill people who know too much. And why would anyone suspect? It would mean he doesn't even age, and who'd think of that? But if his face hasn't really aged, that could be *why* he needed a new name, and he could have been doing it for generations. And you want to fight *this?*"

Christa sighed "It… does look harder."

Mark stared at her, at her gaze lowered to the table. "Christa? You're giving up too?"

She squirmed. "Not 'giving up.' Just, how can we cope with someone like that?"

"We *have* to!" He raised a fist, then caught himself and settled for pressing it hard on the table, instead of hammering it. "You saw what he did to you, to all of us!"

Dennard sighed. "You sound like Sasha, right now."

Mark stared. "You too?"

Dennard raised a cautioning finger. "I mean, you need to think about what you're choosing. We all do."

Mark pressed the fist down harder, leaned toward his cousin. "I said we have to! We can't leave him out there, and every note we can find with him will help us get Angie right—"

"Forget about the notes." Henry's scratchy voice sounded like tired feet shuffling on gravel now. "Don't you get it? Winton did all that instead of taking a younger body. And the last time you saw him, his body was so weak he had someone drag it to the car, and he *still* hadn't left it."

"Because he was too weak… or…"

"Because he's *never* made a permanent jump. He didn't know how, until he helped Sasha today. The only ones who've made the jump are Sasha, and Angie."

So Winton couldn't… Mark shut his eyes. Winton used to *text* him, promising he could put Angie in a body. All of those were more lies? He whispered "So there's no secret left about helping her? It's just up to us now?"

"We don't know that," his father said softly. "What was Winton saying about what happened with Sasha's mother?"

"Winton doesn't know," Henry said again. "And now that we can make his magic, we're closer to the answer than he ever was. Kate understood this from the beginning: we just go far enough away that we don't have to look over our shoulders, and we start building real lives again. Besides, if Winton wants to know how Angie left her body, this keeps her away from him too."

Mark locked his eyes on his cousin, and opened his mouth.

Henry added "Isn't that what *she* wants?"

Mark slumped. Why did Henry keep throwing that at him, why couldn't he let him *think?* There had to be something else, some other reason or some way…

Kate said, just above a whisper, "That may be true. But it's also true that Winton and Nolan will be free to keep killing, and Sasha's still in the thick of that. Nolan said we were all 'spellkeepers,' and I told her that gave us an obligation to pull each other back from the brink. I couldn't do that with her, but I can at least try to limit the damage when we fight. I won't be running away again."

Dennard coughed, then shook his head. "And I think… we ought to cool down a moment and be sure of our facts, before any of us makes a decision. The pictures and the rest suggest Winton never made a permanent transfer, but Sasha did—"

"Only when she was passing out from Nolan's drug," Bryan added.

Dennard nodded. "There's that. Then Winton helped her switch back, but her mother couldn't wake up. Unless Winton put her to sleep while he did it."

Mark shook his head. "I didn't sense anything like a push into sleep. And I've seen that enough to know."

Kate added "I don't believe he did. Her mind felt more like what Winton said: like there was nothing left after Sasha crashed into it. We couldn't even make her body move again."

"There was… nothing in there?" Mark said. "Wait, like Melissa Davis? Like when we were trying to put Angie in a comatose body, and nothing worked then either?" He remembered the stillness inside the woman's head. Was that the key, did making Angie human again mean they needed…

A body with a live, healthy mind… for her to destroy…

His fingers were numb on the table. His ears caught only scraps of what people said.

"Possible… one explanation why she couldn't wake…" That was Kate.

"But how'd you help Christa, Henry?" His father, oddly thoughtful.

"Just… needed it to work, I think…" Henry's hand on Christa's, all white knuckles and her flinching. "Or it was the connection between us. It should be easier between Sasha and her mother, since they're related. If it's our Petrie family that lets us sense magic, maybe transfers only work along bloodlines too—"

Henry stopped short, and his eyes flicked from Bryan Petrie across to Mark. Silence fell around the table.

They had to be reading his father wrong, Mark thought while his stomach clenched. *The bastard destroys lives on a small scale, he's not twisted enough to take me over—*

Then Dennard laughed, and the tension blew away. "So what kind of genetics did Angie need to get into that owl?"

"But that didn't work the same as when Sasha was trapped in her mother." Henry snorted. "God, listen to us. How did we get to comparing things like *that?*"

"Henry—" Christa began.

"No, wait, let me finish matching up the insanity. When Sasha merged with her mother we couldn't feel any magic from her, but Angie in that owl wasn't a proper fit, so she's still leaking that bit of power we pick up—"

"It's an *owl.*" Dennard shook his head. "Genes can't be the problem here."

Mark finally pulled in a slow breath. "So. Maybe we do have what we need to bring Angie back…" *If it's not about the right body. If we can do it.* "But, Winton and Nolan are still out there."

"Out where?" Christa motioned around the walls, the city beyond them. "I want to stop them too, but we've never been able to find Winton."

Henry scowled. "Sasha. She's the game piece both of them want—but that's if you're willing to keep watch over her forever, until one of them comes after her. Is all that worth it?"

Dennard said "Finding Winton isn't impossible. He's still in that crippled body; we know more than ever how trapped he is now. And Mark, when Bryan was hunting him, he sent out that decoy in the ambulance?"

Mark nodded.

"Instead of fleeing himself. Sounds like his real body's too vulnerable to move again, but he thinks it's safe enough wherever it is."

Henry cut in "So you're going to *kill* him." The word was a low, warning rasp. He glanced around the diner's wing, still empty. "That's what we're always talking about. It's not bringing Angie back, or him holding Sasha. You're staying to kill Winton."

Kate nodded slowly. "We may have to."

"Or," and Christa pointed at the locket in front of her, "we can make mind-talismans now, to protect us from his touch. If we can touch him, doesn't that mean there's a chance we could disarm him, and lock him up? At least, if we got the chance to. And if we can find him."

"It's possible," Dennard said again. "We've tried guessing how far away he might move his body, after his last escape."

"And what then?" Mark waved an angry hand. "We just watch for his power to show up?" The city was simply too big, unless Dennard had some new breakthrough.

But Dennard only said "Or there are other tactics. Look for Nolan. Keep watch over Sasha."

Henry shook his head. "Christa, please! Can we just get away? Kate, tell her—what are you doing?"

Kate was pushing her chair back. "I'm calling my son. I won't be coming back to him for a while."

Mark gave her his widest smile. "Thank you."

For taking the risk, anyway; Mark's anger burned and shifted inside him, but he was less and less sure what to aim it at. Not with Angie herself pulling back from the fight.

Angie. Still perched on the roof.

"Christa? Can I have that locket? Angie drained her magic trying to tell me about Sasha. We've got the right words now, so we can start giving power back to her."

A smile glinted at one corner of Henry's face. "Of course we can. It's just the start of what we can do now. As long as we stay alive." He slid the silver shape over from Christa to Mark.

Mark set down some cash and turned to the entrance, glancing around the diner's stillness. They could have planned mass murder here, and the two men at the counter and kitchen wouldn't have ventured close enough to hear them.

As he started for the door, his father slid around the table to move ahead of him. *What's he want, to hear the mind words I'll need with Angie, so he can start making his own possession magic?* They'd all have to deal with his father sooner or later.

But for the moment, Mark swerved toward the back wall, where Kate was standing apart with her phone.

He opened his mouth, but she was already looking up at him. "My son wanted to talk to you."

"He did?" Mark took the phone from her. Their conversation seemed to be keeping Bryan Petrie back for now.

"Hi." James's voice sounded level, too mature for his twelve years—or trying to be, again. "So you're still keeping up the fight against, well, them?"

"For now." Where had that doubt in his voice come from? Mark felt Kate's eyes on him.

"I wanted to say… I'm sorry again. For my actions while I was in the city. For trying to trick you, so I could make myself a part of the fight."

"It's fine. We got out of there okay."

"Because you got me out. And now that I've been investigating the Winton history with my mother, I'm starting to understand the real dangers you deal with. I should never have interfered on my own."

"I said it's fine." Mark made himself smile. James's only thoughts were to apologize for himself, as if he couldn't imagine that his mother was still in danger?

"She tells me, you're using the mind secrets now? Does that mean you can send out your own animal eyes?"

"We… could try," Mark said. "It's not as easy as it sounds, but it gives us a lot to think about." And if the pictures of Winton were right, it could somehow stop them from *aging?* That couldn't be right, it was too big. He shoved that thought aside for another lifetime.

"I bet you'll win. Always a way, isn't that it? And, can you tell my sister I'm rooting for her?"

"Alright. In fact, I'm just about to go see her. And I hope it'll be safe for you to meet her soon. Now, I'm putting your mother back on."

Kate took the phone, but she paused to look right at Mark. "Thank you for being gracious with his apology. Also, can you give Angie one from me?"

"Um." For cutting herself out of her daughter's life and starting a new family, all to keep herself away from magic? For leaving the city and never knowing how much danger Angie was in? "I'll… try."

A small door stood in the middle of the back wall. Mark felt his father's talisman moving closer behind him, and grabbed the door. *Dodging him is only putting this off, but do I have to deal with everything at once?*

He stepped out into the morning sun. A wide, half-full parking lot spread around him, and he felt Angie launching from the roof as he moved. Her magic did feel thinner, the price of all the messages she'd given him. The silver in his hand was the answer to that.

His father neared the door behind him. Mark lunged across the lot with a magic-light stride over the slush, and Angie swept down the air ahead of him.

Faces turned toward him, up and down the lot. He held his pace down to a gliding sprint as his father moved to follow.

Angie twisted ahead, a shape of brown and gray veering toward the back corner of the next building. Mark realized his feet had already fallen into a path behind her.

Around the corner lay a small pocket between buildings, only half-open to the street, where not a single person stood to see them. Angie beat at the air and flew almost straight up along the wall. Mark flung himself to the rooftop after her.

Below he glimpsed his father stopping at the corner. Running from that man was only temporary as long as they could sense each other's talismans… but just for now, there was so much more satisfaction in staying out of his reach.

Angie perched on the roof's rim, just a few steps away.

"I brought some power for you," and he held up the mind talisman. "We can finally keep you as strong as you need. Oh, and your mother wanted to apologize, for… everything."

At least Kate was doing more to back that up than the man down below was. His father was already turning away.

He reached the talisman toward Angie. "We're all working on this, on how to get you a real body. I swear, we can do it. And we really *can* make Winton pay—"

Kee-yak!

The owl twisted from his hand with a quick flap. She sailed just above the rooftop's open space, an easy speed for her. Mark raced after her. Her cry had sounded, what, eager?

Her head twisted once to glance back, then she shot toward the roof's edge.

If it's a race— Mark hurled himself at the edge and the next roof across, magic's power blasting him past beating wings. In midair he stole a moment to look down to the ground and around the streets; only a few people stood in view, and none of them looked up. *But I just took that leap in broad daylight before I thought of being seen.*

He didn't feel the lightheaded madness of magic getting in his head. Only…

Angie *chirruped* and darted across the roof's left. He leaped after her, with soft skips and minimal weight to keep from skidding on piled-up snow. She dived down between two huge air-conditioner blocks, but he sensed her twisting left behind them and he leaped across ahead of her.

"Bring it on!" He held up the mind talisman. "I can keep up, like I can save you—"

She rushed straight by him. Her claws plucked the silver from his hand.

He lost a moment in shock before he thought to follow. But this wasn't like when she grabbed that talisman he almost gave Nolan… it felt nothing like it, not with her playful calls buoying him up. He dashed after her.

Roof after roof shot by. In scattered moments he thought of the faces that might look out through those windows, or the people on the street—but of course each building she picked was only a short distance from the last, a leap that a human could have cleared.

Angie's dodges used every scrap of cover, every foot of space a roof gave her to double back on a wingtip. Mark leaped and skittered and caught at gravity to lock himself in place for instants before rushing on. Anything to keep his human bulk keeping up with the owl that moved like a part of the air.

Danger and regrets fell away. He was simply nineteen… or somewhere younger.

Then—

"I said I *can!*" He saw her start to spin and read the angle she'd have to take, and dove across ahead of her. "I *know* I—" She flipped away behind his back, still easy to sense and move ahead of. "I *can* save you—"

She swung out over the open street. After so many moves staying out of sight on the roofs, she changed the rules and ventured where he couldn't go.

A flash of silver, arching high up and away from her. *She'd thrown the talisman away?*

Mark stared. He couldn't see it now, couldn't sense it from here, couldn't leap out over the street even if he did, why would she...

Angie swooped down. He saw, felt, the streak of gray rush across the sky to scoop down and spin away, in a move that could only be catching the talisman as it began to fall.

He couldn't move. He stood frozen on the edge of the roof, breath gasping, for the endless instant it took her to arch around and reach the roof. At the last moment she braked, and dropped lightly onto his arm.

The talisman slid back into his palm. And he finally had the words to share its power, because she'd found those too.

With his softest breath, he whispered *"Tomishua zazda tomi zazda shua."*

Magic wakened. The energy roused at the words, loosened, and his thought sent it flowing—not gathering power from the air or draining another talisman, but this time streaming from his into the bit of silver on Angie's foot. That magic swelled, pooled...

The thought-space opened between them.

Their breath and pounding pulses should have faded away—but instead they surged through the void like a message, her message. Soaring, twisting, the thrill she'd led him through, that had to mean flying.

Words flickered too. Unclear sounds, but he caught glimpses around them of daylight streets, windows by night, spreading from early autumn to biting winter air. Too much too fast to follow the language, but the tones were uneasy, worried, angry—all the shades of trouble and discontent around the city, plucked and gathered out of the months by her restless mind. She saw so much, followed it all.

The voices changed. A new flood of memories poured out from her—a smiling face, a woman running with smooth steps, a family looking up wistfully at the sky they'd never touch. Faces of joy.

Like our chase.

The world of the mind fell away. An owl's pale face hung just before him.

"We can… we can fly for real, once you have a real body…" he said, from a hollow throat.

She dropped off to soar away.

Mark shivered, slumped, sat clumsily down in the snow.

They'd been fighting to set Angie free. But what if…

What if she already was?

* * *

Danger after danger that they faced… and how Angie faced what she'd become, and yet now she had helped him in finding Sasha but nothing more… the thoughts turned and spun in Mark's head, no matter how he tried to settle them.

It was only when he came in view of the others that he looked up.

And realized his phone was vibrating.

The call was routed from a tip line they'd tried to bring in signs of Winton, but they hadn't used it in a month… then he remembered who he'd last shown the number to.

"Mark? You said I was trusting someone I shouldn't." Zeke's tone was thick, like the words were stones he had to force out of his mouth. "Ms. Nolan just went into Coberson Medical Supplies, and then an ambulance pulled up and they won't let me in."

"I'll be right there. Anything else?"

Zeke only hung up.

The others were closing in on him, with Dennard eying the phone in his hand.

"That was Zeke, Nolan's assistant. He's got a tip about Nolan—"

"Or a trap?" Dennard finished his thought.

"Maybe. But after the warehouse, he must have questions. And it did sound like him, and too reluctant to just be possessed—"

"Look, that's enough," Henry broke in. "You can't just get another clue and drag us all into danger again. You go if you want. I'm not. Christa?"

He gave a long, pleading look to her.

Christa looked back, tried to meet his gaze. "Isn't there any… do you have to…" She glanced over at Kate.

Then she slumped where she stood, and moved to Henry's side.

* * *

Leaving the car and dashing on ahead was nothing like feeling Angie beating through the air. His magic stretched his stride out and carried all his weight, and he only needed to hold his balance and slam to a stop when someone stepped in his path. But above him, Angie never fell behind.

He felt the magic stirring ahead, just before he cleared the corner and saw the lights outside the low, pale Coberson building.

"Ambulance, alright," he said to his phone. "And Nolan or someone is working power inside there. Be ready for anything."

Dennard said "You be ready. Without Henry, we may have to keep circling in case they make a break for it."

Mark dove for the door.

As he dragged his feet down to a simple walking pace, he caught a tense murmur of voices in the corridor ahead. A door swung open, and a pair of EMTs rolled a gurney toward him.

Another victim. Mark called out "What happened?" and moved to see the patient's face.

Zeke himself. Asleep.

The EMT in front gave Mark a sharp look. "Do you know him? Does he have a history of seizures, or stroke? Anything that would help us pin it down?"

The second medic added "There's already an incident here. Think!"

Incident? And then Zeke was struck down too? Mark lunged past her and laid a hand on Zeke's shoulder. "Come on, come on, I know you can hear me, come *on...*" The mind talisman churned energy in his pocket. How had Henry put it, he had to *need* it to work?

Do it! Feel it, just like Christa, you can *move—*

Hands pushed him away. "Please, sir, you're not helping—"

Mark slipped around her, leaning against the still shape. *I've only got one second, please, no more victims,* move!

His fingers fell away from Zeke, as the people shoved him back and glared warnings. All for nothing, he knew he'd only imagined any response in Zeke. Useless.

Zeke reared up.

He looked straight at Mark. "You! You leave her alone, she didn't—"

"Easy there," the EMT said. "You collapsed…"

Mark stepped back to watch them work, and tried to calm his own breathing. Zeke's gaze kept darting past them to glare at Mark. Zeke had called him here for answers, but now his first thought on waking up was to defend his boss?

The possession Mark had felt was still there, deeper inside the building. He glanced toward it… if Nolan had come here, to a medical supply outlet, she might be looking for traces of the supplies that the injured Winton needed. And putting people to sleep on the way.

There's always someone else hurt, when she goes after Winton.

"I am calm. Fine, see?" Zeke's smile beamed restraint and steadiness to the EMTs. He swung one hand up to touch his nose, then the other hand, back and forth in perfect coordination.

Mark added "He's right. When Zeke faints, it's never for long."

Zeke's gaze shot to him again… but his face stayed calm, still. Controlled.

"So he does have a history?" the EMT asked.

"Sure—even if we can't pronounce what they call the condition," Mark said. "I'll be sure he checks with his doctor."

"That's a good idea."

Mark waited, as Zeke made his reassurances and one EMT moved further inside—Mark caught something about the first patient waking. Dennard and his strength, or Kate's insight, had to be on their way here if they could just find a place to park.

Then both EMTs were gone further inside, and Zeke rounded on Mark.

"Alright, *Mister* Petrie. I admit I called because I was concerned about Ms. Nolan. But I'll give you one chance to give me some kind of sane explanation. Ever since you began associating with her there have been… honestly, drunken parties, and the police believe that? And you were accusing her of kidnapping, and *murder?*"

"I'm trying to warn you. Think, you know this is bigger than who said what. What happened to you right here?" Mark shot back. "Did you come with her to keep her out of trouble—and then she touched you and you woke up here?"

Zeke winced, looked away.

"And when your eyes opened, what was your first thought. That it couldn't be her fault? Or relief that you didn't wake up strangling her again?"

"So you *were* there, in the warehouse!" Zeke's hands shot out and clamped onto Mark's coat, his face pale. "Talk! Now!"

Mark held himself still, ignoring Zeke's grip. "First: how long have you known Olivia Nolan?"

"Forever! Since North Star was formed. Most of the events we've ever done, it's like I can't pick the place if she can't help pick the day…"

Zeke faltered into a weak laugh. Mark nodded; sure, Nolan could "pick" a day when she could bring any weather she wanted.

Zeke's hands pulled back from Mark, but his fists stayed up. "I said talk! Why are you trying to destroy her life?"

"I…" Mark took a breath, tried to let all the secrets and warnings find some kind of shape Zeke would listen to. "I think she's in a situation you can't help her with. And she wants you to be safe—"

"Olivia?" Zeke's gaze swung past Mark's shoulder.

Mark spun. Of *course* Nolan stood there, stepping through the door to the interior, eyes narrowed in cold fury at him.

Then she turned to Zeke. "Now you're with the enemy?"

"NO!" Zeke scrambled past Mark to reach her side. "But… if you *have* an enemy, couldn't you have told me?"

"Some things you can't watch for." Nolan gave Mark a hard glare, then started past him for the exit, Zeke behind her. "This is an enemy that could move against me any time, and use just about anything to do it."

Mark moved after them.

"And your response is to accuse *me* too?" Zeke said. "I… I can't wrap my head around what happened in that warehouse, but it *can't* mean that I was attacking you."

"Zeke—"

She laid a hand on his cheek.

A moment later she resumed walking, with only a single warning look at Mark. To Zeke she said "I know it's been hard on you. I hope you'll only have to wait a little longer, and then we'll be back to hosting banquets. But for the moment, the only way in the world you can help me is to stay safe away…"

The two passed through the front door, and Mark slowed to let them go. If Olivia Nolan did have this one soft spot, Zeke might be the one way out of her obsession with Winton.

He felt for magic—

Angie was rushing through the air toward him. He glanced around, but the building behind him was quiet, clear of power, while Nolan and Zeke were walking toward the parking lot. But Angie swept up along the street, from something beyond his range.

Then it charged in: a possessed mind down on the street, gathering speed, passing under Angie and weaving with the clumsy grace of a car twisting through traffic… up the block and closing fast, he saw the black compact barreling toward the building.

Nolan and Zeke. In Winton's sights.

Mark lunged toward them, flinging a "Look out!" ahead as he ran.

Zeke stepped in his path, fists curling. Seizing gravity for an instant broke Mark's momentum and let him dodge around Zeke toward Nolan. From the corner of his eye, the car was closing on the curb.

Nolan's hand swung up to block him—Mark cut his weight and leaped back from that possessing touch—but a blast of wind caught his weightless form and sent him spinning away.

She anticipated me—but can't she see *the real danger?*

Some huge dumpster-shape rushed up behind him, and he grabbed at power to slow himself.

Slamming into hard, blinding metal… he fought to clear his head, make his legs move. Magic cut through the flashing lights in his sight—what wind was Angie riding that sucked her in past the attacker…

His eyes cleared. Across the lot, he saw Nolan running past the green wall of the building with Zeke behind her. The black car bore down straight for where they were against the wall. But, one door stood ahead of them along that wall.

Mark forced himself to his feet.

Nolan seized the door. It stayed still, locked.

Zeke caught at her arm.

Nolan collapsed where she stood, and Zeke—driven by her control—charged straight for the onrushing car.

No, no—Mark lunged toward them, but the jump was weak, and a parking lot sign stood in his path—

As Zeke closed on the car, Angie swept down to brush against him. Mark caught the surge of power, felt Angie's magic strike and sink into and sweep away Nolan's grip as she flew by.

Zeke looked up, free, with the car only seconds from him.

Zeke froze.

Mark saw it hit, saw the ruined shape sprawl across the windshield, covering it. The vehicle rushed in at the wall, at Nolan, and she flung herself to the side with the blinded driver unable to track her.

Just as she must have planned it after all.

Winton's control vanished from the driver in the last instant before the crash. Before the hideous crumpling of metal and pinned flesh that ended in an instant, over as suddenly as… as a car hitting a wall.

All that remained was the wailing of the car's alarm, and Olivia Nolan slipping away in suddenly gathering snow.

CHAPTER TWELVE

SPARKS

The driver's cries began spilling from the wrecked car... not tight with pain, but spiraling into shrill horror as he beat the air-bag away. That shock pushed Mark away from the panicking man and the dead man slumped over the car. He charged up the street after Nolan.

Above him, he felt Angie settle on a rooftop again. *Not* guiding him.

Nolan's shape twisted in among a knot of people ahead. Mark rushed toward the outlines in the snow, trying to keep his balance in the cooling slush and ice. The figures resolved into a clump of people shivering around a corner bus stop, but Nolan was gone—was she further up the street where the snow was thickest, or one of the scattered shapes down that side street?

He dashed around the corner. Figures formed out of the whiteness: a couple, a tall man... none of them her.

Mark spun to double back.

The steel howl of a siren broke through the snow. Back on the main street where Nolan had gone, closing fast.

And he was running *away* from a crash, with the shock of Zeke's death probably branded all over his face for them to see. He made himself trudge deeper up the side street, at only a quick walk as he searched for the next turn back parallel to where Nolan might have gone. Another siren came wailing down the main street behind him.

And Angie only moved with him. Her presence shifted from one roof to the next to keep pace with him, never more than that. At least it was better than the time Winton had sent a sniper after Nolan, and Angie had tried leading them *away* from the danger.

But he did feel a different magic: the others' talismans homing in on him.

Kate's car pulled up, and a back door swung open. Mark tumbled inside next to his father.

From up at the shotgun seat, Dennard asked "What happened back there?"

"Winton happened, and Nolan made it worse. He grabbed someone to try running her down. And she just threw Zeke in the way! He never had a chance, he's *dead*… and she's up ahead somewhere. I think."

"Zeke?" Kate's surprise and the roar of the engine filled the car together. "He was the one she wanted to keep out of this. But she sacrificed him too?"

"Right." *And your daughter tried to save him, but after that she let Nolan go.*

Kate glared through the windshield. "None of us has been able to find Winton, so he's free to choose his moments for targeting Nolan. And she's pushing harder and harder to root him out before one of his plans catches her. Neither of them can back down."

Dennard added "No matter who's caught in the middle."

They twisted up the block. Mark's knowledge of the streets was their best guess for where Nolan might go, but it was still only guessing. They should be spreading out, with Mark and his father using their speed and feeling for any magic Nolan used—*Angie* should be searching—but it had already been too long.

Finally, Mark sighed "It's no good. She could be inside the mall, or down the subway by now, or… She's gone."

Kate pulled the car to the curb.

Then she touched her phone. "Henry, Christa, we could have used both of you here. Winton went after Nolan again, and this time *she killed Zeke.* To save herself."

"So you want to kill Nolan too?" Henry's voice through the speaker filled the car with thick regret. "Those two will just keep after each other—"

"She trusted Zeke!" Mark snapped. "As much as she trusted anyone. He wanted to save her from herself, and she threw him away. People will keep dying like this, why can't you see that?" Why didn't Angie see it?

"We know," Christa said. "I hate it, but… is there anything left we can do?"

Henry added "Anything that isn't hanging a target on us, again and again and again? Besides throwing *our* lives away for just one chance to stop their showdown a little sooner than when one finally gets the other? Why is stopping them our fight?"

Dennard only said "Someone has to do it."

The words, the quiet certainty, steadied the tense air in the car like its shelter against the snow outside. Mark couldn't add a word, only smiled at the tireless fighter. He kept his gaze away from his father huddled in the side seat.

Kate said, more slowly, "I think I understand Olivia Nolan. She sees her life and her legacy of magic as under attack. And Winton seems to be tied to whatever his own history is, and also to some connection to Sasha."

Mark's father broke his silence then. "You think Nolan'll go after Sasha again? To make Winton come to her?"

Mark frowned. Was his father back to trying to help again?

Dennard said "Could be. Finding her's easier than finding Winton."

"Hold on!" Henry said. "The way she talks now, she'll never let you protect her."

Mark glared at his father. "And don't you say we use her for bait. We're not that desperate, and there *have* to be better ways."

With that he reached to the window control and slid the glass down a foot, enough to stick his arm out and wave for Angie to join them. But she only held her place above, and he had to slide the glass back up before more snow blew in.

"There are other ways to find them." Dennard's calmness was a peace offering now. He held up his own phone. "Nolan may be on to something about Winton being weak. Here's a job bulletin post she probably put up—asking for 'guerilla' photos of all the bedridden patients in any hospital in town. Someone might spot him."

"Crowdsourcing her search?" Christa said. "Would that change anything? You say you've been looking for him for months."

"No, we've been *closing in* on Winton for months," Dennard said. He started thumbing through stored files. "That's how an investigation works. Every fact we follow lets us tighten the net. We have lists of shops and supplies where he could find more birds. Jewelers who'd done everything from weddings to veterans' bracelets. And we have three people here who can sense his magic."

"Right," Mark said. "It could be as simple as the three of us hopping on the subways and keep crisscrossing the city until someone finds him."

Henry sighed. "You just don't get it. You tried that too, and so did I—Nolan would have driven me around scanning until the magic wiped me out. The city's too big, and you're still just hoping to get lucky. I'm sorry, but we have to stop this."

"You aren't even starting." Mark's father scowled as if he could glare straight through the phone to Henry. "You forget the other magic we've got? We can send out our own birds, or make people do our looking for us—and that can be all six of us at once, not just three of us who can sniff around for magic. We've got the power, we should use it."

"Not like that," Kate said. "You're talking about taking over bodies that aren't ours, even if we knew how to control them."

Dennard added "Yes, I made that doctor put his lab onto that poison. But it took all I had to make him walk or talk. And birds? Don't forget, if you crash into a wall your real body can end up worse than Winton's."

"If it's so crazy, why's Sasha doing it? She saw the book and the next day she's flying parrots?" Bryan leaned forward toward Kate.

"Sasha," Kate said, "is reckless, and scared. She tries out magic because she has it, without understanding what its dangers are. We need better judgment than that."

"Then I was right—the only way left is to wait for them to come after Sasha." He looked straight at Mark. "She trusts you, *use* that. Nolan's going to grab her again, because she's seen Winton keeps coming to save her, or control her or whatever he's after. So use that! You can call it bait or protection or anything you want. You say you want to win this, you use her before they do—"

"Is that what you do?" Mark stabbed a finger at him. "Use people, let them die for you? We're trying to *stop* those two monsters from killing people, do you even understand that? Nolan threw Zeke away—and your answer is to get Sasha killed next? Hell, why are you still here?"

The words echoed and rang inside the car. He locked his eyes on his father's face, the wasted, cowardly features so sickeningly like his own.

What broke the silence was Henry's voice through the speaker. "Umm. I, I hate to leave it like this, but there's not much else we can say. We're getting out."

"We?" Kate said quickly. "Are you sure? Christa?"

No! "Listen to me—" Mark began.

His father clicked open the car door. Mark swung his gaze away as the man climbed out, back to the phone and Henry:

"Listen! I know it's all piling up on us, but you heard how close we have to be to the answer. And think, of everything Winton and Nolan put you through—kidnapped, tricked, possessed, everything. I never wanted you to take on that kind of risk. But think!"

The door slammed shut, and with the outside sealed off again he was free to force more volume, more will through his aching throat as if he could hold Henry in place by shouting him down.

"Think! If we don't finish this, Winton and Nolan will keep dragging more people into what you've been through. They'll do it to hunt each other, then to hide what they've done, to look for more magic or whatever they want next. It'll never stop! Angie knows—"

I thought *she knew that.* He clenched his eyes shut and pushed on.

"Dennard and Kate know that. We have to do this! We have to, or all we are is the people who got a look at real evil and we decided to let it get away—"

Angie dove from the roof. A part of him sensed it, he'd had been clinging tighter to his sense of her with every word that poured out. And now she dropped free, glided down.

And flew past him. She glided past the car and settled on a roof above the street corner. Where Bryan Petrie stood below, his back to them, not quite hiding the phone he was speaking on.

Bastard! Mark stared, stared through the whirling snow. *If Angie hadn't signaled me…*

"Mark?"

That was Dennard speaking, but the voice could have been miles away. Mark felt himself unfastening his coat, then his belt, before he understood why his hands were moving. But he couldn't sit waiting or try to guess what the traitor was up to, and he couldn't move in carrying even a hint of magic to give himself away. He had to know.

He slipped out onto the sidewalk. Cold air gusted and seemed to blow through his exposed shirt. Walking was clumsy, slow, with no power to hold him up if his feet slipped.

His father was forty feet away, then thirty, but still turned away and locked into his own world on that phone. Mark's fists squeezed, so fiercely tight the pressure made his pace stiff and awkward when he needed to step silently.

But Angie was still looking out for him. Twenty feet away, fifteen.

"—don't ask me how. I found him!"

His father's words tightened his fists into knots of pain. *And I've got no magic on me, no defenses, I can't even sense power.*

"Or *she* thinks she's found Winton, anyway. Nolan's sure of—"

Some footfall, some shadow, must have reached Bryan Petrie. He finally looked around at his son.

The lined face recoiled, eyes flinching shut with what might be guilt. Then those eyes blazed open to look defiantly back as he went on:

"Think, Sasha! She could be closing in on Winton right now. Where do *you* think they are? His life's in your hands." A pause, then "We'll be there. If Nolan shows up, we'll get her."

And he put the phone away.

Mark's fists couldn't seem to unclench. "So you called Sasha."

"Sure I did." He took a step toward Mark, his eyes hard now. "She's got to have a better guess where Winton is than us. And maybe Nolan *will* follow her there."

"So you… you played Sasha… to play Nolan too…"

"You're welcome, boy."

Mark edged back a step. *Is that this backstabbing cheat's way of helping us?* And they'd just said not to put Sasha in danger and he did anyway.

Mark drew away another step. He glanced upward, wishing he could make out Angie on the roof without his sense of magic.

Finally he said "Where? Where does Sasha think it is?"

"She does more than think it. She just put what's left of her mother in the doctors' system there, so maybe that'll bring Nolan to her. It's

Grace Hospital—you know, where you cured my poison and took your owl?"

God…

Melissa Davis's body… and Sasha's mother too… Winton *couldn't* be there under their noses after all this time, could he? But if Nolan thought he was, she'd tear the place apart.

He ran for the car.

* * *

The whole Grace medical complex was looming in front of them, when Mark thought to ask "Which building?"

"The main one. Guess they aren't ready to put her mother on the coma floor yet," his father added.

"She'd be safer without Sasha around," Dennard said. "Checking her in could have set off online alerts. We've seen Nolan have those waiting before. And it looks like she spotted this one."

Kate pointed ahead. "You think so?"

Around the front of the building, people circled and milled on the pavement. Too many to be normal, and instead of the proper streams of figures moving inside and out, many simply *stood* out in the cold.

And here and there in the crowd were police.

Dennard led the way up to one young cop. "What's the situation?"

His tone made the officer open his mouth reflexively, then catch himself. "Just some crowd control, sir. Some problem about the facilities, and nobody wanted any trouble."

Facilities trouble? Enough to draw a crowd?

The group pulled back, and Mark tried to feel for magic as they walked. He sensed their own talismans, Angie circling up high… was that a trace of stillness over the building?

Dennard's voice broke through his concentration. "Is it Nolan? Cutting the power and slowly freezing the place?"

Nolan's weather energy was the faintest, thin deadness to his senses, but even that hint was confirmation. Mark looked back to the others. "I, I think so. She's done it before, just not like this."

"Freezing a hospital building, to flush Winton out of it?" Kate said. "Is she that desperate?"

"Something else here," and Dennard pointed at another cop at the edge of the crowd. "They're looking for someone. I bet it'll be a person matching Nolan's description. Sasha could have put them onto her, or maybe taken a cop over to put the report in."

"Well, nobody's being controlled just now," Mark said. "Not her or Nolan, or Winton making someone drag his body out. There's just Nolan slowly freezing it all… how far do you think she'll take it? And the patients they can't move, you think they can save them?" He looked at Dennard, needing him to say yes.

"You just find her, or Sasha. We'll check the back, you keep scanning the crowd." Dennard gave him no chance to answer, already marching toward the building's rear with Kate behind him.

Mark watched them turn the corner, wanting to call them back and keep them out safe on the front, public side… but they were right, this crowd up front needed his sense to spot any possession tricks. They didn't have Henry and Christa now, only him and his father for this.

He moved along the sidewalk toward the main door. A couple in baseball jackets stepped outside, with a young nurse behind them, all rubbing their sides trying to warm up.

It was spilling out from the door—waves of glacial cold, worse than any freezer.

"—must have shorted out everything but the A/C, and that's jammed full blast—" the nurse was saying.

Some people would've burned the building, but Nolan used a cold snap…

His father's talisman was already skirting past the edge of the crowd.

Mark headed up the sidewalk. The currents of people milling about slowed him, making him step around them and peer between them for where Sasha or Nolan might be hiding in their midst.

His father stopped at one point in the crowd as Mark was just drawing close. Close enough to see Bryan had already found Sasha.

Mark closed in. Sasha was stepping away from the people and waving his father away.

"How did you know that woman would find us?" she snapped at him.

Bryan glanced over her shoulder to Mark, then looked away. Embarrassed, now?

Mark sighed, and turned to Sasha. "So… you spotted Nolan?"

She gave Bryan a hard look, the same glare she always gave the man who'd kidnapped her. To Mark she said "She has to be somewhere here. I'm sure she knocked out the power. I'm not letting her freeze my mother, or my teacher either."

"Except he's not here—none of his magic's in use, even with the place freezing." At least Mark didn't have to stop her from defending her mentor, not yet.

"But did you feel that cold? That woman thinks she can hide up the block or somewhere, and because she uses weather nobody'll have a clue what she did… or see her at all. But I can find her." She grinned, too wide.

"Find her? Sasha, she's got your magic, *and* weather, and a gun. You don't want to find her!"

"She killed my mother!" Sasha snarled. "Unless the doctors can wake Mom up—and the bitch is trying to kill that chance too!"

She stomped back toward the edge of the crowd. She stepped around the first people at the fringe, then just as Mark started to follow she sank down onto a bench. Like someone settling into a nap, she leaned back, and her legs lay out near the feet of people passing by.

One tall man passed close, and her foot stretched over to brush his ankle.

The man only flinched a moment, when Sasha seized control and her body went limp on the bench. The tall man slowed, turned, muttered something to the stouter man he'd been walking with, and jogged off toward the building's corner. He, she, gave Mark and his father a quick wave not to follow.

Mark tracked the body moving out of sight, and glanced at his father, unsure. Sasha seemed to have a plan… And if Nolan wanted to force Winton out of some hidden room in the clinic, wouldn't she be somewhere she could watch all its exits? His gaze moved to the taller buildings and their upper windows.

The possessed man walked, *staggered,* back to the main street. His steps wobbled more the closer he got to the people out front. The stocky friend he'd left behind rushed to his side with a worried shout.

"*She* did it!" The stolen voice spilled into the crowd, dousing the nearest murmurs. "I saw her, cutting wires and… and…"

"What the hell?" his friend said.

Mark's father breathed "She wouldn't…"

"I saw her! A small woman in her forties, plain, she was sneaking around—she did it, and she *hit* me…"

Right on his own cue, the man keeled over into his friend's arms. Sasha's grip jumped to him.

And her new body shouted "Hey, he's hurt… Someone *did* this, to a *hospital?* I say we find the bitch!"

A woman near him tried "Hold on, Tom—"

"Find her! This is *terrorism*—we gonna let her get away with it?"

"But—"

Sasha's pawn was already marching down the street, shouting and waving.

Mark felt a sickly feeling rising in his throat. This was Sasha's "plan," trying to start a riot and tear the whole block apart?

He looked through the ranks of the people. They were mostly confused and watching, and the shouts' outrage only roused a few scattered grumbles, like fading sparks that weren't enough to spread a fire. Down the street, he could already see the police leaving their car to close in on the disturbance.

At the back of the hospital, he felt Dennard breaking into a dash to round the building. He and Kate had heard the shouting too.

Mark moved to Sasha's body on the bench. He scooped it up to drape her arm over her shoulders and marched her up the street. Keeping her light enough to carry quickly might stop people from noticing that her feet only bobbed over the ground like some toy's, that she was not just dazed but out cold. His father followed.

Only a few heads turned toward them, with Sasha's rabble-rousing shouting away behind him. Those voices softened as he drew away, but Sasha was still fighting to start her mob, not looking back at her own missing body.

Magic moved in the air. One of Winton's birds winged toward the block—unless it was Nolan making her move…

Sasha's grip vanished from the man in the crowd, and her body over his shoulder squirmed to life. "What are you doing??"

"Getting your attention. Shutting you down." He let her pull away and stand. "You hear that? They weren't listening."

He waved back toward the crowd, half a block away now. Their voices were already fading. *And Winton will spot us any moment—*

Sasha said "So I'll get more—or she'll kill them!"

"What are the odds Nolan's even down on street level? What if she's inside, watching from three floors up? I mean, think! You know it won't work."

"It will! I'll show you!" And Sasha took a slow step toward him, with her hand reaching out.

I can jump back—no, better if I stand up to her, I've got my own mind talisman. In the moment she closed in, he steeled his will around the silver in his pocket. It had to have enough left to shield him.

"Heads up!"

Bryan's fierce shout wrenched Mark's gaze skyward, to the magic in the hawk racing toward them and Angie chasing it, too slow—even Sasha froze and stared blindly upward.

The hawk plummeted down. Mark threw his focus into the shielding talisman, sure it wouldn't be strong enough.

The bird streaked toward Bryan, easily matching his clumsy dodge and brushing past him.

Magic flicked across. The hawk pulled away with a spatter of wingbeats.

Mark locked his eyes on his possessed father. That calm, *knowing* gaze—this presence had to be Winton himself. The man who had shattered his life looked out at him from inside the man who'd broken his family… Crushing power roared in the leather around Mark, like some huge engine revving at his touch, ready to charge.

Mark forced himself backward a step.

"Hey…" Sasha looked at him, then at Winton's puppet, and back to Mark. All she said was a nervous "Don't worry, I bet he'll let your dad go soon."

Calm as he could manage, Mark said "What… do you want?" He could feel his reinforcements—Angie watching from a building's ledge, while Dennard and Kate were still at the back of the clinic, moving slower and too far away.

Winton turned away from him, to face Sasha. "Was this your plan, to use the police to find your enemy and then rouse a mob to hunt her down?" He tipped his head toward the people milling away behind them. Any anger in their voices had all but died away.

"Yes!" Sasha said. "Are you alright? Did I at least give you enough distraction to sneak out?"

"I was never here," and he sighed. "But you… you made sure everyone else was, didn't you? I've told you, the true value of possession magic is in keeping it invisible. Untraceable."

And his, Bryan's, eyes flicked toward Mark as he said the last. *Bragging.*

Sasha laughed. "I know! Nobody can connect us to what happens here—"

"Someone might still remember your face. Sasha, with the power we have, you never need to show yourself. You never need to draw any attention at all, until you find the right moment. If we keep ourselves untouchable, we can pounce on an opportunity, or simply let it all go, because we can. We are always safe, unless we give ourselves away."

"I had to! I heard about that car that almost hit Nolan... what was that, you seeing an 'opportunity'? You almost took my revenge away! I had to show you I can—"

Winton raised one finger, and Sasha stopped.

"This is how it's done," he said.

He tilted Bryan's head upward, in a slow, purposeful glance around the evening sky. His gaze slid right past Angie on her ledge, blind to the magic that could pick her out of the shadows. But that single, visible search never hesitated.

Then he spoke, to the air at large. "Angie, do you want a real body strong enough to live in? We can track down our enemy together. Nolan has to be somewhere she can observe the building. We can find her. Then I can help you."

You DARE—

Power *crackled* over Mark. And Winton had used his father's voice, the same weasel who'd made offers like that before—

"Nolan's mine!" Sasha broke in. "Please!"

" *'We'?"* Mark flung back. "Us, working with *you?* You talk about stealing someone's life for Angie, like that's a reason to let you anywhere near us?"

Winton... didn't react at all, not surprise, not shame, not denial or agreement. "We'll see," was all he said, and he turned to Sasha. "As for you, you can have as big a share of your revenge as you want, as long as it's done."

His gaze moved upward again.

"Agreed?"

Mark spat "After all your lies, there's no way we'd trust you with anything!"

Winton only waited, a slow smile moving over Mark's father's face.

Angie swooped down to barrel in on them. Mark tracked her drawing closer, closer, waiting for her to shriek defiance in the killer's stolen face.

She swept past him. She swept right past him and away over the street with a *kee-yak* that could only be an eager "Come on!"

And Winton, Bryan, turned back to the people around him. "All of you, watch yourselves."

Sasha nodded. "You know we will."

"Also, watch over these two," and he actually pointed to the body he was in, and then to Mark. "I don't get your sense for power when I jump into you, but Nolan may try a permanent jump to see if that gets her more. It might not work, but it'll still kill the mind she tries it with."

Dennard snapped "What—"

Winton's grip vanished. All that remained was Mark's father staring around.

CHAPTER THIRTEEN

PIECES OF SILVER

Winton and Angie both winged down the block. Mark traced them soaring over the street, *together* for one moment—then the two presences split to peel off over different streets.

Beside him, Sasha whispered "Is she right? Can Nolan take you over for real, and get your sense of magic?" Her voice was so low, the murmurs from the hospital up the street half swallowed it.

"Can she *what?*" Mark's father went pale.

"I don't know. Who *thinks* of moves like that?" Mark said. He tried to look at the shifting people around the pavement—at least now they all stood too far away for any to be one more possible threat now. "And... Angie isn't really making a deal with Winton. She wouldn't steal someone's life like that, you know that." *The way she flew with me this morning, I thought she'd given up on risking us for her future.*

"Later," Dennard said. "Right now, we keep our guard up."

He moved them up the sidewalk to a spot even further from any foot traffic, with their sides against with a long blank section of the wall. Passing cars rumbled, and beyond them murmured the voices standing outside the hospital complex. Every minute, Nolan's freezing put more pressure on the patients inside, all trying to force Winton's body into the open. But Winton's magic wasn't even at work inside there.

"His bird's making a wide sweep along the streets," Mark told the others. "Angie too. To spot if Nolan's out in a car ready to run, I guess."

Sasha added "I could've been with them if I'd had my parrot."

"We have another option." Kate looked at Mark and his father. "Nolan's own magic is at work here. Can you narrow down where she's controlling it from?"

"You don't know how quiet her energy is." Mark looked up and down the buildings, the streets into the hospital complex and around it. "I can try—wait. You look for it from here," he told his father, "I'll try from down the block. If we get different directions she must be close." He dashed down the pavement.

A thin layer of melted slush churned under his feet. Nolan had to be squeezing the coldest air into the hospital—was she ready to kill everyone left there all on the faint chance Winton's body was there? *Or it's to lure out Sasha, or me.* He twisted his run to swing wide and out of reach of the few people he passed.

He halted at the corner, and strained to feel Nolan's power.

The stillness, the faint emptiness her grip left on the air hung all around. But to feel through that sea of shadows to find the place she breathed it out from… Compared to that, Angie and Winton were clear beacons sweeping up and down the space where different streets would be.

And those two were flying in the same search, the same purpose now, when she'd been letting Nolan go before. Until Winton's offer pulled her back?

Or Nolan's rampage forced them all to stop her. Mark locked his fingers on the belt, felt the coat throbbing around him. He tried to force the thoughts from his head, but his eyes ached from lack of sleep. The air, the treacherous balmy air on his face, mocked him with how all its cold must be forced into the hospital itself.

And the sounds, the currents of fear and frustration in the people outside, hinting that nothing anyone did could keep the air from freezing...

Magic moved toward him. Not Nolan's or Winton's but the clearest power around: a piece of their gravity magic. Mark saw his father leaving the others and jogging toward him.

Leaving the others, the bastard. Mark dashed up the street to cut him off.

"You just left Sasha and the rest blind to Nolan's tricks," Mark said. "Just like when after we'd saved her from Nolan, and you let Winton grab her."

"Says the boy who couldn't leave them fast enough." His father's nose twitched like a nervous animal, and his eyes didn't look at Mark. "If they're that soft, why are you the one yelling at them to stay in town and fight?"

"Why?" He stopped, took a breath. "Because Angie... Is. An. Owl." Even if she flew like she was born for it.

"So you're making deals with Winton now? You don't need him."

"I'm not making any... Are you still helping us, or back to cutting and running?"

His father looked up now, straight in Mark's eyes. "You don't need Winton. And if you're staying to stop *this*—" and he waved down the street, to the crowd around the slowly freezing building— "then you stop it. You tracked Nolan down yet?"

Mark's fingers gripped the belt tighter, trying not to think of how its power could stop that voice. "Did you even try? Her power's slippery stuff."

"Shut your eyes and just find her!"

Mark's eyes squeezed closed—not obeying his father, he told himself, just to prove him wrong. Still nothing, only Angie and Winton racing over the sky. "Well, she's somewhere. Still freezing the place."

"Because she doesn't stop. That girl Sasha knows more about magic than you—she jumped into her mother—"

The world stopped. Stopped cold, for one dead instant, on hearing *that* word in *his* voice.

"—and she jumped all the way, because she had to—!"

"DON'T you talk about mothers." He kept his eyes closed, to not give the bastard the satisfaction of looking back. But the spots dancing in his eyes looked like a face, a dying face, that would be alive if that man hadn't left drugs lying all around.

"I asked Sasha. When she was crying over what she'd done, I asked her what she did to make that jump work."

"You asked her—" Fingers clenched on the belt—was the leather's corner drawing blood? So easy, so easy to look up and squash that voice to pulp.

"She said all she did was push harder, same as when Henry woke up Christa. Maybe there is no trick to keeping bodies, and Winton's trading your girl help she doesn't need. If you want to fix Angie, stop waiting for an instruction book—you're the one holding back."

Something rumbled in Mark's throat.

"And if you can't find Nolan, that's you holding—"

He walled the words out. He walled everything out, everything but the power in his head.

The air's magic was still. Barely moved at all. But not as still as the hospital behind him.

And that space to the side.

He looked toward the trace, across the street. One longish, three-story building of old masonry… with a clear open view of the block and the hospital… somewhere in there was a patch of weather magic at work. Controlling the rest.

"Well?" Bryan Petrie's face split into a smile, like a window opened to give a room a glimpse of real, actual sunlight. "You get something?"

Mark stepped past him, toward the others. When his face was turned away his lips were free to shape a *thank you,* and he put no voice behind it to make it carry. Not to *him.*

He remembered to walk, not run. Nolan was staying in that building so she could keep watch outside, and any urgency he showed might give away the fact that he'd spotted her. His head ached like he'd beaten down barriers with just his skull.

As he and his father neared the group, he felt Winton closing on them above. He reached the others and stood with his back to the building, to hide when he hooked a thumb back toward it. "Nobody look. She's in there."

"My turn!" Sasha said. "There's got to be someone I can grab, and get a crowd ready to go after her—"

"Don't." Dennard cut in. "No riots. They don't work anyway."

Mark felt Winton passing above the building, a hundred feet above and too small for the eye to see. The bird made one sweep high along each wall. Then it dropped to the street somewhere behind the building, and the power moved to someone on the ground.

"Winton grabbed a body," he said. "I think he spotted Nolan in a window. He's going in."

"Then we keep her distracted." Dennard swung out his arm in a wide gesture toward the spaces beyond the hospital.

Mark waved in the other direction; let Nolan see what looked like an argument between them. He sensed Angie closing in too, circling above. Winton's pawn was moving on a slow pace that had to be working his way through the rooms.

"Now we just stay put," Mark's father grinned. "She can stare at us, but she'll never sense what's coming up behind her. Boom, dead."

Mark looked away. Even after Winton's crimes and Nolan's treachery, his father's casual words made it sound more ugly than ever.

He locked his gaze on the gray sidewalk and let his mind track Winton's searching movements. That presence moved slowly back and forth and further in—finding the way through, working his way closer to whichever window he'd seen Nolan in. If Winton could find her with three whole floors to lose her in, if he could take her down.

Angie dove. Toward the street outside the building, the back corner away from the hospital view. Mark turned to steal a glance toward her.

Her magic reached out.

A thin trickle of power flailed out, and he watched a limp gray shape sinking down off the shoulder of a young woman in blue. A woman who fumbled and dropped to one knee before she caught the owl. A woman stirring in the grip of Angie's control.

How, how, can she really...

Power sparked in both of them now—both a presence in the woman as unsteady as her balance, and a dim ember still clinging to the motionless owl that the woman laid to the ground. She set the bird beside a short stairway, then caught its rail to pull herself up the steps and into the building.

Mark remembered to wrench his gaze back to their own side of the street, praying Nolan hadn't seen him.

"What is it?" Kate asked.

"Angie... just possessed someone. She walked the body into Nolan's building, same as Winton did." Was that ragged sound really his voice?

"I knew it!" his father laughed. "She wants her freedom, she fights for it!"

"No!" Even the way the presence moved through what must be the corridor was so slow, clumsy. "Can't you feel how weak she is? And that bit left in the owl is her *life*. She's risking two lives just trying this!"

"Sure," Sasha muttered. "But Mr. Winton said I'd get my payback too. I can't just stand here."

Kate said "They're already closing in. The best help we can give is to keep Nolan distracted."

Sasha scoffed. "And let the owl get her body for herself? That's too quick. Angie gets what she always wanted, but the blizzard bitch needs to suffer."

Mark's head pounded, louder with each word. He looked up the street and stared at the far corner, anything to stop that one glance back that might alert Nolan. Angie wouldn't... her magic was so weak, she knew that...

Only look at the traffic light. Look at the scaffold outside the top floor, that's on the block beside them. Look at anything else.

He felt the two possessed bodies moving through the confines of the building, Winton careful and sure, Angie slow and stubborn—so slow she'd be helpless if Nolan even guessed who she was. *Look at the traffic light, look at the scaffold.* At his rear the two presences worked through one turn after another, searching.

Somewhere on the second floor, Winton and Angie's paths drew closer, then met. Mark's breath caught, but they only moved on past each other—did they even recognize each other? Where was Nolan?

Winton's control vanished.

Mark let out a whoosh of breath, and caught Winton's power reappearing down the street and winging up, searching away down the block. And Angie's puppet turned and began making her way back.

"They're both leaving, and Winton's searching," he reported. "Nolan must have slipped out."

The back door opened. The woman in blue staggered down the steps, clinging to the rail. She knelt by the limp owl, and collapsed.

The magic left her body, but the owl's power barely flickered—

Mark charged into the street. A car honked, he leaped past it to land beyond the street, to crouch beside the two figures.

They didn't move. The woman—blonde, tattooed, too young—lay still, and Angie's feathered head hung limp in the snow. Her power, her last grip on her owl's body, flickered.

He waved back at the others, waving for them to come, to bring more talismans to feed power to her own. His fingers couldn't seem to open his pocket, and the locket there felt so weak. Kate and Dennard raced into the street, waving back what cars were there. But his father hung back, he *hung back,* standing and talking with Sasha as if anything else could matter—

Mark poured fury into his gaze. Even across the street, he saw his father flinch away.

Feathers ruffled.

Angie shook herself awake. She flapped upward, smooth and easy to settle on a ledge above, and Mark felt the vice of his headache simply open up in joy.

Sounds behind him showed Dennard was helping the woman sit up. "You alright? You passed out."

Mark flashed them a smile, then trotted a few steps up the street, toward Angie's ledge.

Soft as he could, he said "You just about killed me back there! And killed yourself too, and, and… Sasha said you must be trying to take Nolan's body."

Angie's head shook, in a *no* so hard he heard feathers crackle in the air.

The two watched Dennard and Kate help the woman to her feet and coax her through a few steps to prove she could walk. Once she was slinking embarrassedly away, Mark joined them, trying not to think about what it meant that Angie was able—and willing—to take control of people at all.

Dennard nodded across the street, to Sasha and Bryan finally crossing to reach them. "Quick, before Sasha hears!" he whispered to Mark. "You see Winton's body anywhere? Or feel him moving it?"

"Nothing. The whole chase here got us nothing," Mark said as the stragglers reached them.

"She really got away?" Sasha said.

She? Sasha still thinks Nolan's the only one worth hunting.

Kate said "If Nolan's running, can she keep freezing the hospital? It looks like it's calming down over there."

She turned up the street. The motions and sounds and the number of flashing lights clustered at the hospital entrance did look calmer than before.

"But we're back to the same problem: how do we find her?"

Sasha gave a short, cold laugh. "We tried it your way. All your senses and traps and everything, and she's still gone. I've got a better idea."

"Oh?" Dennard frowned.

"Simple. Bryan here used to work for her. So *call* her."

"Hold on—" Kate began, but Bryan Petrie was already keying his phone, and handing it to Sasha.

Mark glanced between the two, trying to think what they were up to. And Nolan wouldn't just pick up—

Sasha broke into a wide smile. "I thought you'd answer. This is Sasha, and I've got a deal I think you'll like. Because you'll never find Mr. Winton when you can't sense his magic. What you need is Bryan Petrie back—you can make him work for you again, or see if sticking your mind into his brain for real lets you scan like he does."

She didn't *just give away...* Beside him, Dennard's breath caught.

"That is if you dare to try that yourself, now that you finished testing it by *killing my mother—*" She stopped a moment and tried again. "Well, I want to see which of us is stronger. I'll bring him, you bring Mr. Winton's book and whatever you wrote up about your own power. Name the place, and we'll see who survives."

All the dazedness was gone, washed away in cold shock. Sasha actually was standing there, smugly brushing her hair back as she offered some kind of *duel* to Nolan herself. And his father, her bait for it, hadn't moved at all…

Sasha added "Of course Mr. Winton isn't in on this. My other friends might be, but this is about me beating you myself. But if you don't think you read me right? or you're afraid you can't beat me? Then just don't come. Isn't that how spellkeepers like us should

fight—no rules, we just use everything, starting with how well we figure each other out?"

For a long, long moment, the street was silent.

Then she hung up.

"At the end of County Route 12, in two hours. I said I had a plan,"
she smirked.

Softly, Kate said "That's your plan? To send her a challenge?"

"It makes her bring the books, no matter where she hid them. Then
we just have to outsmart—"

"No."

Kate's single word snapped like a chain breaking, like something
that had been coiling around them all until she spoke.

"Sasha… first, you can't wager Bryan's life."

Mark's father said "Hold on, if it works—"

Mark blinked, stared. *He* was sticking his neck out?

But Kate was already going on: "We know the priority isn't getting
anyone's books of magic. What we need is to win this fighting before
someone else is dragged in, and then start healing. Besides, I doubt
there's ever been a situation where letting an enemy prepare against
you ended well. Letting Nolan pick the place gives her every advantage."

"Anything could happen," Dennard added. "From her sending the
police to planting a bomb. Or she'll think of us considering all of
those, and she'll never go there at all unless she's got a move to top
every one of them. There's simply too many ways it goes wrong, and
they all cost us everything."

"Or go wrong for her," Sasha said. "If she thinks she's got the
edge, we can finally win this, we can get the books and… well, show
the person who believed I deserved this power…"

"But we don't know what Nolan's thinking; we can't play that
game. But, we could use your challenge for something else."

Mark heard the shift in Dennard's voice. Before Sasha could refuse
he asked "What's that?"

"You want a risk worth taking? There's a chance Nolan will be out there—but *no* chance she'll bring the real books, because she doesn't need to. So we don't go there at all, and we use the time to search her home again. It may not be the priority, but it's something."

The books... one thought stabbed into Mark's soul and wouldn't let go: *if we get Winton's book of mind magic, maybe my father's wrong, there* is *some secret in there that can fix Angie for real...*

"Besides," Dennard added, "Nolan might come running back at the alarm and we can ambush her on our terms. That makes two ways this could put us ahead."

Sasha swallowed. Slowly she nodded.

* * *

Sasha called for one stop on the way. The mind talisman in Mark's pocket only had a trickle of magic left to restore Angie, and when that was drained Sasha said "There's more we can pick up. I got these from a jewelry store, and I made the owner do some more work for me. If we do meet Nolan, I want to see her *try* blocking a whole shop-full of lockets that have had days to power up."

When they settled in their cars, Mark found himself with Dennard and Kate while his father drove Sasha—he tried not to think what might be connecting those two now. Instead plans, memories, and worries chased around and around Mark's head, and he stayed in the passenger seat as Kate drove. Attacking Nolan's electric lines again would still limit her house's alarms, if he got the backup generator too. Would the books be there? Would she?

The jewelry shop was a small place, shuttered tight in the night. But Sasha didn't try to go inside. She walked out from Bryan's car alone, along the rustic old stone wall around the shop, and Mark sat watching her dig talismans out of its crevices.

Having more magic wouldn't hurt... but he felt the real pressure on himself, on them all to keep a step ahead of Nolan. *We did chase her off.* But if they could get Winton's book, get one more advantage in helping Angie, and use Winton's and Nolan's secrets against them both…

Here we are back at our first attack plan again, and alongside Sasha, only this time we're keeping my father where we can see him. No matter what Sasha says, Nolan and Winton have to be stopped.

Angie perched on the parking meter beside their car, never moving. Mark slid the window down for her to hear him try to work his thought out.

"If an alarm brings Nolan back, we want to catch her on the way in. So Angie should be keeping watch outside, right?"

"Right," Dennard said.

"And then…" But that was it. All the rest of the planning needed his father and Sasha, and for him to stop worrying over what had brought them this far.

Instead, he brought out his phone and called Henry.

"Hi. You still in the city?"

"On the road." Henry spoke slowly, like he was straining to feel connected to the people he'd left.

Mark switched to speaker. "Watch yourselves. Winton, and now Nolan too, they just got the bright idea that taking a permanent body that can sense magic might give them that sense themselves. We're all fine, but you watch yourself."

"Us? *You* be careful, all of you."

Kate said "Is Christa there? Are you sure you both want to leave?"

Christa answered "I think so. Every time I think about what you've done, I think I was never that useful to you anyway."

"That's not true," Mark said.

"It is true. I wish we could make our enemies disappear too, but Henry and I just don't think like you do under pressure, and we only get in your way. Maybe if we go where we don't have to look over our shoulders, we can do some of what Kate did. You know, look for information, and help you keep looking for Winton."

"Great. Unless Sasha talks us into letting him go, or… something." He slid the window up again, trying not to look at Angie. She really had tried out Winton's method and risked a bystander's life.

"Nobody's letting Winton off the hook," Dennard said. "Never."

"Yeah. And, I get that Nolan's a bigger danger this minute, threatening a whole hospital and all. But why's that mean Angie has to search beside Winton… she says she's not trying to take Nolan's body, but…"

"Whaaaat?"

Mark lowered his voice. "I don't even see how she wanted to give up, I thought she'd never do that—now she keeps letting Nolan or Winton get away, and then whenever things go to hell she turns around and helps us again. Even my damn father keeps saying he's trying to help now. Says he's willing to be bait for Nolan."

"My uncle said *that?*" Henry was silent a moment. "He's got some kind of trick there, I guess. But understanding Angie is simple—and your father might be trying the same thing."

"Simple?" Mark clenched the phone, stared at the bird outside the glass.

"She can't let you get hurt. Mark, I'm sure she hates anyone else getting caught in this too, but it's you, and her father and mother, that she's really trying to save now. Before one of you has your luck run out."

"But… She's the one trapped in…"

Except Angie flew like the air was her home.

"You really think… we started this fighting for her sake, but she's looking out for us?"

He remembered Dennard and Kate then, and glanced at them both. Angie's father had a small smile, and her mother gave him the faintest nod. Like there was no doubt in their minds.

"But then she—hold on, you said *my father* might be trying the same thing, like he'd do that for me? The same bastard who raised me on drug money, until my mother…" *Until my uncle and then Henry took me in. But* that *man, caring about anyone else?* "Him?"

"I don't know," Henry said. "Maybe it's a scam. Or maybe he's decided he has to do something right for you."

"Him??" Mark said again.

"I don't know. Did you give him a chance?"

"I…"

"What's Bryan doing?" Dennard's words snapped out.

Mark's head jerked up. His father's Beetle was rolling away down the street, at the speed of a quick jog—

Sasha dashed down the pavement to it, leaped in the open door. The two drove away.

Mark stared, stared, with only one thought able to form in his head: *nobody's possessed, they were both moving at the same time, so my father* wanted *to go with her.*

Kate brought their engine to life. "Sasha and her *plan.* We all know where they're going."

* * *

The Bug couldn't lose them… but Bryan and Sasha tore through the back streets as fast as evening traffic allowed, daring Kate to cut them off. All their calls went unanswered, leaving them nothing but the roar of the engine.

At the first red light that actually stopped them, Mark had just steeled himself to climb out and crush something vital on the maddening vehicle, when the light cleared and it roared away. Then the chase twisted onto the highway, and traffic thinned away to sparse motions within the flat dimness, while the Bug raced on faster and faster. Angie fell behind, back out of his reach and gone.

Again and again, they drew in behind their target, and Mark gripped the door handle and wondered if he could leap across and stop them… but he could only imagine what shattered machinery would do to a car at that speed, or the people inside it. Each change of roads narrowed the lanes, stripped the roads of more traffic, and brought them nearer to their destination. The sky deepened to twilight.

Finally the bug slowed. It settled to a stop, and a small figure that must be Sasha dove out and dropped to the roadside—and the car moved on.

Ten seconds later, it reached the equally narrow route that the road met, and ended at. Mark's father pulled the car across the intersection and climbed out on the field beyond it.

Kate settled their car behind the Bug. Dennard lowered the window and called out "Alright, so we're here. Want to tell us what you two are planning now?"

Bryan Petrie only walked forward. His head turned side to side to search the broad, starlit openness around.

"We're here!" he shouted out. "So where are you?" The sound spilled outward and vanished in the night, meeting nothing but grass and air.

A gunshot boomed.

Mark froze, glanced around. No magic out there, no motion…

Something moved, rising up to reveal a figure crouching just behind one shallow little hill in the dimness. Then she dropped flat again, and Nolan shouted "Walk over here, just you. Or the next ten shots won't be warnings."

"Are you crazy?" Bryan said. "I'm the one you need alive!"

Nolan laughed. "You don't need your knees. And Sasha, where are you? You'll never get your book back this way."

Mark's father raised his hands and began walking in, already beaten.

Maybe sixty feet of open ground between him and her… Nolan lay behind what must be the only hint of cover for hundreds of yards besides their cars…

Mark dropped to the ground. Even in the open, Nolan could only look so many directions at once.

He pressed flat, spread his arms and legs wide. Cutting his weight let his sprawling limbs lift his belly just clear of the spongy dirt and still scurry him through the dimness, fast and low. *If I can get around out of her view, I can risk jumping up and onto her, and maybe nobody has to die.*

His father drew closer to Nolan. A passing thought: did she even need her magic here, with the gun and her position? He scuttled faster, and he felt Dennard's magic creeping around the other way, more slowly.

Another magic moved. Something possessed ran toward the field, back from where Sasha had slipped away—it headed for Nolan, some tiny shape his eyes couldn't catch in the dimness. If it reached her, Sasha just might break Nolan's mind before she knew what hit her.

Bryan slowed, from a reluctant walk down to a trudge. He had his own talisman, he must feel Sasha's advance too and want to buy her time.

Mark crept on. He could just see the sheltered side of Nolan's hill.

The animal streaked for Nolan, low and small.

Its speed must have caught Nolan's eye. Magic sprouted beside her, and a possessed figure rose from beside her, throwing off some blanket that had masked its outline. The man stood up and tossed the blanket down to trap Sasha's creature.

Her magic vanished from it. Nolan's man raised a gun and blasted shots at the blanket, no doubt tearing some squirrel apart, but a moment too late to catch Sasha.

Mark's father leaped away, one quick leap that swept him clear of Nolan and let him land flattened to the ground.

More shots boomed, a deeper roar—from Dennard's gun, at the other side of Nolan's hill.

Wind slashed the air, so sudden and sharp it made the nerves spasm and flinch away. Dennard fired once more, before the snow rushed in to fill the air with whirling madness.

Mark's eyes slammed shut against the biting fragments of cold. For a moment he struggled to peer out through it, then gave up. Instead he crouched and leaped blindly, locking his motion against the wind and aiming for the space above Nolan's possessed body.

His power began pushing him through; he clenched his fingers against creeping numbness. The storm had to be stronger than Nolan had ever used, but her borrowed body still crouched somewhere in the whiteness ahead. *I just grab the real Nolan and get into the sky before she takes me over, then force her to give up and hand over the book.* She couldn't take him over and try learning to fly in the *seconds* before she hit—his one move could pull this back from the brink.

Somewhere far in the world of wind, a voice sounded.

"Who's here… ice storm… have to get inside…" A strange man's voice.

Far away, peeking through the snow, Mark caught a glimpse of what might be a blocky shape beyond the field below. A house, people, still too close.

Another presence started across the ground, another of Sasha's creatures.

The wind went still.

Mark's face ached in relief, but the cross-cutting blurs in the air settled into simple down-drifting snow. Nolan had used this trick before: suddenly she could see.

Mark had one glimpse of the stranger running toward her hill, a hunter's cap splashing orange through the night, a long gun in his hands. Closing on the squat hill, where two shapes lay limp and the man she controlled swung up the pistol.

Four shots rang out, five. The hunter jerked and twisted as he dropped.

Dizziness washed through Mark, and he could only feel himself drifting higher.

Kate's voice shouted through the still air, from back at the cars. "Is that how you fight? Shoot everyone and hope Sasha's in one of them?"

The wind thrashed to life again.

Mark huddled in the sky, arching higher. *The storm's so strong, and Nolan ought to be tired... is that why she has the other bodies?* Did working weather only tire the body she was in right then?

And his path still hadn't brought him near her. He saw he'd launched on too high an angle, too eager to get above her sight, and now it left him too slow to move across to her.

Sasha's new animal crept across the ground toward her, slowed by the wind as well.

And further back up the road, another presence closed in—Angie, fighting through the air.

The wind cut out again.

During one breath it blasted against his body, in the next there was only stillness and Nolan's voice: "I thought you wanted revenge for your mother! But you destroyed her yourself, didn't you?"

Sasha's magic on the ground flicked away. Far down the road, her real body shouted "You're dead..."

Nolan laughed, a harsh, sneering sound. "Not me. I'm not the one you killed, because you can't control what you have. I bet your aunt got a taste too, and she couldn't survive either—and Winton *still* sees something in your family? *Why?*"

Bitch!

Nolan was preying on Sasha's guilt and pride, trying to work her into a frenzy... but, Mark felt the magic reappear at the point where Sasha's animal had crept. Instead of rising to more taunts, she was closing in on her target again.

Kate's shout came from the cars. "What did *your* family see in you? What would your brother say—"

Shots blasted at her. Kate dropped behind the car—moving too smoothly for her to be hit, he told himself.

Other shots pushed back against hers, louder and more rapid, from where Dennard lay on the ground. Mark huddled tighter, hanging in the open sky where he could only trust that the bullets would rush by below him. Dennard's barrage drove Nolan's borrowed body down behind her hill. The wind roared up again to cover the air in shifting snow.

I'm just about over her spot... please let Dennard be done shooting for now...

Mark dropped. The ground was lost in the twilight and the blizzard, but he could judge distance from feeling Nolan's possession below. He slowed to settle and drop flat on the soggy ground. He'd passed partway behind Nolan's hill; Sasha's animal was closing in—

Angie twisted down through the storm. Mark felt her veering for Nolan's possessed body... past that, toward another figure lying beside them. Angie's power reached out, seized.

No, she's too weak—

She gripped at the other sleeping body, her control hauled him to his feet, and she sent him lurching toward the smallest of the shapes lying on the hill. Toward the real Nolan.

Then her energy buckled. It spasmed, shook, and the kick she swung at Nolan flailed. She staggered, and the man Nolan controlled slammed a punch into her.

She spun away, away, he felt her presence snap back into the tiny bird shape that the wind flung across the air... *please let her be safe!*

The air clamped to stillness again. Mark pressed himself flat, trying to look like a piece of ground in the twilight.

"...was a shot..."

Someone across the silent air, another voice was calling out. More people, more witnesses for Nolan to pick off.

Mark drew his arms and legs in, gathering for a leap at Nolan.

The wind and snow slammed down. He gritted his teeth, but the whiteout couldn't hide her magic's grip on the body she was using.

Another presence scrambled up to crouch beside him. Right in his ear, his father's voice chuckled "She just dropped the books."

Books? He's watching for Winton's book? Mark muttered "How'd Sasha talk you into this?"

"You finish this! Being bait was my idea."

More lies.

"And I got Sasha talking, sounds like her aunt—"

Wind swallowed the rest, as Mark crawled away and crept around toward the side. All he needed now was to come at Nolan from outside her view.

Bryan Petrie was in the air. A single, clean leap straight across rushed him past Nolan's borrowed body to snatch up something from the ground. He slid past it, clear.

Magic struck. A hidden talisman's power burst from the book Bryan had caught up, seized control of him. Nolan's will vanished from the body she'd been holding, and her new pawn took a step back toward the hill, toward her real body—as Mark dove at that helpless shape.

His father lunged in front of him, fingers lashing out. Mark wrenched himself *up*—brain-numbing force kicked him up clear into the sky out of reach, but he'd pulled too far up—

Away across the ground below, Sasha's voice screamed "Shoot him! Shoot him before she does it!"

Bryan Petrie leaned down. Olivia Nolan reached up.

The power surged, once.

Then the grip of control was gone.

"…shoot? Who's out there?" The voices, the people who'd heard them, were closing in somewhere in the storm.

Mark dropped. The snowscreen below him thinned to show his father raising a gun, aiming straight toward the one patch of ground where Sasha's animal was watching, and pouring bullets after it. *Not my father—not a puppet any more, I can't feel any control on him—*

The gun swung up. Right at Mark's spot in the sky.

No no nonono—Mark rocketed upward, like he always did, so easy to leave people behind and get *away*...

The storm shrieked and tore at his flesh. Sounds flew through it, gunshots and voices below, too many for the wind to swallow up.

The other pulse of gravity power, Dennard, drew back from the fight. Dennard was retreating, so that had to be the only choice, and Angie moved with him... Mark let his power ease back and leave himself only feather-light, letting the wind do the work of tossing him away, away.

The magic that had been his father's fell back behind him. Mark rode the wind for a few frozen breaths—he forced himself to breathe—then settled toward the ground.

One more time, the wind faded. Off behind him, he heard Kate's car roaring away. And a voice, *the* stolen voice, calling out "Anyone seen my niece? The shooting must have her scared out of her mind..."

From the shadows right nearby, Mark heard Sasha's "More *niece* cracks? Just you wait—"

She was rising to her feet. Beside her a patch of ground shone pale, strewn with what must be a small heap of some kind of food. To draw in animals, the ones she had sent after Nolan.

For all the help they'd been. But he saw her crawling back toward the magic, the voices, behind them. Still thinking she could fight.

Mark charged at her. She gave a short yelp, but he caught her up and leaped away down the road.

"Put me down!" she sputtered. "I have to get her—she killed my mother—"

"And killed my father."

But you dragged him here... no, he did it to help me... the damn conniving cheat wanted the risk... he got it...

Mark skipped across the ground, but his balance crumbled. His feet slipped from under him and he toppled, spilling Sasha over the grass.

He lay still and tried to breathe. He could still feel Angie flying towards him, but he had to move...

She dropped something from her claws. So close, the wind whipped it right onto his chest—a sheet of paper.

He clutched numbly at it. Even in the dimness, it looked unmarked, blank.

Nolan had never brought her "books" at all. Bryan Petrie had only grabbed at a trap.

Sasha's voice mused "So Nolan's finally got your senses, with that body? That idea was right after all?"

Her words were wrong.

Mark dragged his head around and spat "And *you* told her." But the blame that thickened his voice was aimed at the wrong target. Sasha wasn't the one speaking now, not with that power gripping her.

"And the girl sent him straight into our enemy's reach. I thought she'd do better than this."

Winton. So... at some time he'd slipped a talisman onto Sasha herself, always pulling the strings...

Mark glared into the stolen eyes and tried to point the blame back at Winton. "And her aunt failed too, when you knew *her?* You ever think you're not much of a teacher—except at getting people killed?"

Sasha, Winton, shook her head slowly. "Sasha led Nolan and you to me... she tried raising a lynch mob at the hospital... now she's handed Nolan the weapon to track me down... Some people simply can't be taught. That was her last chance."

A threat.

And what did it mean when Winton bothered with threats?

After death after death, after people Mark had *wanted* dead that left him swamped in regret... he clung to the night in the police station, Winton threatening Dennard and his father too, and how Dennard had seen through his front. "You, you're telling me for a reason. You want me to do something, or else you'd just get rid of Sasha—so what is it now? What's the price for her life?"

"No. She is the price."

"What?" Mark squinted and stared, sure the wind must have muddled those words.

"Before we finish Nolan, bring Sasha to the Darrow Clock Tower, at midnight; I should be ready then. Sasha getting her own mind back inside her never damaged her brain. Her body should be just right for Angie."

He didn't… Winton didn't just make Sasha say…

Angie only hung in the sky. No answer, no denial.

"I'll see you there," Winton said.

Mark forced out "You really think we believe you? Trust *you,* with Angie? Trust you with *anyone* when you use people like this?"

"You should. This stupid girl here doesn't deserve her head. She k…"

The killer's power let go after the next words, and those were soft, too faint to make out.

Or they would have been. But Mark had heard his father starting to share what he'd coaxed out of Sasha—before he'd turned his back on that last message. That and the taunt of Nolan's that had hit home with her. Sasha's aunt, Isabel Lawrence, the first to know the Winton family.

And "Winton" had defended Sasha for so long, and tried to defend her mother too. But…

"She killed my sister."

CHAPTER FOURTEEN

MIDNIGHT DEADFALL

He couldn't move.

Sasha stared around the night, with no idea what her own voice had just condemned her to, while Angie still hung in the air above them… Mark opened his mouth again and again, but each time the weight of it all only pulled him deeper in. His father, Winton's truth and the trap for Sasha, Angie's silence.

Then the car found them. His father's car.

"I don't think they saw us leave," Dennard said as he waved them inside. "But we can lose this car back in town." Kate sat behind him. And, there was nobody else to wait for.

"Leave?" Sasha jumped into the passenger seat. "Can't we circle around and follow Nolan? Let Angie watch her and find when we can attack again."

"We can't!" The words tumbled out of Mark. "Didn't you see? With Nolan taking… taking him over, she can sense Angie or any of us with power. She did it back there, she's got his eyes because she *killed him…* "

As he sank into his seat, a burst of wingbeats carried a small shape inside to settle on his lap. Angie's talon pricked his leg below the heavy coat, and he heard more pages from Nolan's decoy rustling. The car started rolling.

Beside him, Kate said "Ah." Her sympathy, her look straight at him, made him want to push away.

Instead he rushed on "If she, he, can sense Angie and keep twisting the winds, then she can track her flight and smash her out of the air, Angie can't go near her ever again—"

Sasha said "Then we need another way to get—"

"Get these?" He shoved the pages Angie had snatched toward Sasha. "They're blank, see? Nolan didn't bring the real ones—if we even need them anymore. My father said we never did, but he made a grab for them anyway!"

"But—"

"And they weren't even here! You think Nolan would follow some rule about playing fair? She just brought some fake and hid a talisman inside it—of course she put her trap on it, because you made the whole setup about betting over the damn books. No, about that and how she could use *his* body, and now he's gone."

"That's not just on me, she must have figured it out herself—"

SHREEEE!

Angie's voice cut off Sasha, an explosion that smashed through the enclosed car and turned it into a shell of buzzing echoes.

She leaned in against him, nestling her head against his chest with a soft croon.

But she couldn't reach the knots inside him. *Most of my life, I had to steel myself just to mention my father around her, to the girl who had the real life... now I got to watch him conniving against every side, but he died trying to help me, and his murderer's taken his face...*

Sasha added, more softly, "I'm... sorry, about your father. I guess he's like my mother now, all empty. I know how you feel."

No you don't. And you're the one who told Nolan she should take him.

Winton might have the right idea about you.

His head sank into his hands.

Then the Bug stopped rolling.

Kate's own car stood beside it. She stepped out to it, and as she did Angie squirmed from Mark and flapped out to join her. Mother and daughter climbed silently in... it was almost their first moment together since she was a little girl.

He didn't feel Angie reaching out to Kate's mind. Her magic felt so drained, she might have nothing to do but sit beside her for the whole drive back. And it was Sasha in this car who still had the talismans that could restore her, and Mark hadn't even thought to ask... Too late now, as the two cars started up.

Sasha still sat right in front of him, thumbing through the empty pages, still blind to what Winton had planned. He tried to find some warning for her, but his throat seized up.

He slumped in the seat. Instead of thinking of her, or his father, he poked at Winton's words: *Killed my sister.* If that did mean Sasha's mother, then "Winton" was Sasha's own lost aunt, who'd stolen Edward Winton's life long ago—so the killer, he wasn't Winton at all, or even a "he"—

No, I have to think of my enemy the way I knew him. Something has to be simple, after my father and Angie and Winton's plan for Sasha...

A flicker of magic sparked in Sasha. For one heartbeat, the figure in the seat in front of him twitched to steal a glance around. "Winton" was keeping watch on them through her eyes, with tiny glances Mark could have missed... and Sasha still didn't know...

His throat clenched. He had to warn Sasha, but Winton could take control of her anyway with the talisman he'd given her. Her blind trust, Angie's silence, Winton's power—he stared out at the dim countryside, as clear and open as their choices were narrowing around them.

Finally, the safest words he could find seeped out: "So, how do we stop Nolan?"

"Mark..." Dennard said slowly. "You need to rest—"

"How??" The word tore out of him, and he clawed out his phone and brought Kate in. They had to make Nolan pay, and still save Sasha and keep Angie clean and…

Dennard sighed, and his voice settled into the firm rhythm Mark needed to hear. "Nolan will be busy explaining about her empty body, and having a gun with all those shots fired."

"And about the two men she brought that she woke up to 'body'guard herself," Sasha added. "I saw those through my animals' eyes."

Kate said "I don't doubt that Nolan has a whole set of excuses prepared. And if the others are neighbors she scooped up for her use, she only needs to make one 'wake up for a moment' to verify that she was the one defending them."

"But she's *got* to be—"

For one instant her voice faltered, *Winton* flickered inside her, then gone—

"—stopped," she picked up again. "How about if we go after her real body. She'd have to defend that if she wants to come back to it— oh. She doesn't need it anymore."

Winton peeked in again, as—

Dennard said "I know. If any life she has gets too hot, Nolan can take over a new one now. She'd still find it easier to do what you did and go back to her own body, but she can keep moving all she wants too. We already thought Winton had done that for generations, right?"

"Right." Mark's voice came out far too calm, with Winton himself peeking in and out right under Dennard's nose.

Generations of Wintons… except it was all Sasha's aunt inside Edward Winton, still clinging to that body even after Angie broke it… what was all the rest, *tests* about how to escape it?

Mark looked at Sasha again. She knew about her aunt now; Winton might have risked telling her before "he" pulled her out of her mother. And Sasha was still hiding that from them. Except that one backstabbing, scheming crook had conned the truth out of her as a gift for his son.

Sasha only leaned back, keeping the secrets she thought were hers. "Nolan can live forever now. Nice try, Kate—did you really think talking with her about your 'spellkeeper history' would make her back down and go back to a normal life?"

Kate didn't hesitate. "I admit it, I never understood her. And I've been letting the rest of you do all the fighting for too long."

Mark took a breath, tried to keep his words casual. "Sasha? Maybe you should take your talismans off when you don't need them. I know mine start to get into my head," and he slid the coat off his shoulders. Once she cut herself off from Winton, he could let her know the truth.

"Not a chance," Sasha said. "These are my future. Because of my aunt and—well, I'm the one Mr. Winton picked to help him beat his enemy. I'm not going to lose."

Liar. You know you're just "Mr. Winton's" family, not his favorite. And it's not saving you: now that you've disappointed him, he's picked you for something else.

It would be so easy to say that, to lash out at Sasha's blindness and the noose around her neck… Mark locked his jaws shut. And now that he'd brought up the risks of magic himself, his only move that wasn't suspicious was to set his coat and belt beside him on the seat. He was blind to Winton.

Dennard said "Once Nolan makes her excuses, I expect she'll go back to hunting Winton, the one she sees as the real threat to her. And everything she's already investigated, she can narrow down with her new sense."

"Agreed," Kate added. "Mark? I can ask Henry and Christa if they can help. I can tell Henry about your father for you."

"No. It's my family."

Bringing Henry into the call was simple, familiar.

"Mark? Stop worrying." His cousin's voice sounded odd, still un-scarred by the last hour. "We're still safe."

"Yeah. My dad wasn't so lucky—"

His throat closed up.

Gone. My father's really gone—why does it hurt to lose the man who taught me how to hate, even after I thought I'd lost the girl who taught me something else... But he's dead...

Somewhere far away, he heard Dennard and Kate giving the details. How his father had risked himself for Sasha's plan—and somehow leaving out how reckless the scheme was and how desperate his father must have been to make it work. And none of them knew the last secret Bryan Petrie had stolen from Sasha.

Finally, Henry said "So he's really..."

Mark heard himself answering "Nolan killed him. He took the risk—isn't that what Dennard says about us staying? Our own choices?" Somehow he kept his eyes off the man in the driver's seat, to force out a few more words before the tears could start. "You're making yours too. You two think you'll get in the way here, so you're probably right, and I'm glad you're staying where you're safe."

Safe. What would that be like, to run off with them? Let Winton give Sasha what she deserved for getting people killed, let Winton and Nolan wipe each other out. He, Kate, and Dennard would just turn away, Angie would be safe and flying free...

Kate was saying "We could still use your help, wherever you go. You've got our findings about where Nolan might look next?"

Christa answered "I... Mark, I'm so sorry about your father. But if you really want help, all we can think is that Nolan might go on searching medical sites for Winton. And that could mean anywhere."

Anywhere? She doesn't mention how we're *still trying to hunt Winton ourselves.* Was that her, and Kate, not trusting Sasha?

Henry said "You really want us to stay away? After this?"

After his father, Nolan, Winton, Angie? *"God, yes!* You stay safe!"

Sasha added "This fight is no place for people who want to pitch in and then walk away. If you want to survive, you need to believe you can do this forever." Her voice sounded firm, but Mark caught a quaver in it; who was she trying to convince?

Mark shut his eyes. Sasha could go on about what she owed Winton, never knowing the killer had turned against her... but it looked like she'd sacrifice anything for her traitorous aunt.

Or sacrifice anyone?

Would Angie?

Like I wanted to for Angie?

* * *

No police cars disturbed their path back to the Lavine city limits. Mark guided Dennard to one of the factories in the industrial edge. His past glimpses from above had seen cars there at night, and an unenclosed, unwatched lot they could slip into. They'd have some time before anyone reported his father's car.

Once they parked, Dennard began wiping fingerprints from the Bug's controls, handles, and seatbelts. Sasha watched him closely, but Kate lingered in her own car updating Henry and Christa.

Mark pulled on his coat and studied Sasha, watching Winton peek in and out of her and trying to think of ways to make her believe the danger she was in. While he thought, he shot a secret text over to Kate:

Sasha knows Winton's her lost aunt

we need to tell her W will

—He couldn't finish, only glanced at Sasha again.

Kate only sent back *I'll check*

They had little more than an hour to midnight.

He stepped over to Sasha's side. "About your talismans? Angie used up too much power, and I think she's barely hanging on. Please."

"Oh, the magic you didn't want me holding in the car, now you want it?" Sasha frowned. "But, here." She handed over one of her lockets.

Mark turned and held out his arm for Angie. She was already flapping toward him. *Please, please, try to talk to me. What are you planning for Sasha?*

A light needle stab slid around his cuff. He brushed the locket against the silver at her foot, spoke the words, poured power back into her.

And the torrent of thought swept through them.

—Reach out, to greet her in the wild space by offering whatever he had, all what she'd always known, but stretching out his fear of what she might reach into—racing on, her endless rushing and soaring and twisting in both her frantic thought and the glimpses of the world outside shooting by, never resting, staring below and so frightened for the ones she knew best, the people she guarded—

—He had to reach out, beside her, under her to offer a place to perch—*let me find a way, don't surrender*—

—On and on she raced, heart flailing, small and desperate and never ever slowing—

A *slash* tore away the trance. He felt his body again as he staggered. The pain in his hand was nothing, compared to feeling her fly away into the night…

She couldn't be off to the Darrow Tower, to join in Winton's trap, she couldn't be. Her magic felt barely brighter than before, and her body was so always so light. But the fierce spirit he knew would never take a body at this price.

Time to have some faith in that.

He stood still, trying to breathe the thought in and out, until Kate climbed from the car. She called "Henry said he might have some news."

Sasha said "Hold on. I want a moment with Mark, to apologize."

Dennard glanced between them. "Alright. A moment."

He and Kate walked away. As their footsteps receded, Mark turned to where Sasha had settled under one of the lot's glowing lights. So it was Sasha herself who was giving him the perfect opening to bring her to Winton's meeting, or stop it.

"I really do understand about your father." She folded her arms awkwardly, and her eyes slid to look just past him. "I mean, I just lost my mother too. I guess, all I can say is that we have to keep doing whatever it takes to win this."

"Anything? At any price?" *When Winton said* you're *the price?*

"Of course—"

Her voice halted, her mouth... slowed, as Winton's control twitched in her—

The moment passed, Winton left her herself again, with her still ignorant of his spying.

How long before he won't let her go? Mark said "How many talismans do you have? Can you show me, right now?"

Her surprise flickered, then faded into a proud smile. "See, I got everything the store could turn into one. And this one, from Mr. Winton."

Mark felt himself rocking nervously on his feet as she went through her pockets. Gray silver lockets glinted in the lamplight above, topped by a smaller, thicker disk. She cupped them all in her hands.

He took the locket she'd given him and laid it on the pavement. "Can you put them all on the ground, now?"

"Huh?" That was irritation stinging her voice.

"Please!" he rushed on. "Listen, I know about Winton being your aunt, but there's more—"

"What? What is it?" Her fingers tightened on the jewelry.

"As soon as you put them down— please, just do it!"

Her eyes squinted, she drew back a step from the center of light. "You... you think I'll hand over my power? I get it, you think I can't handle it, and you're making stuff up—"

"It's not about you! Winton took—"

Winton's power gripped her, Mark wrenched his words around—

"—everything, everything depends on us keeping it together—"

Winton vanished again. *He still thinks we're having an ordinary conversation—*

Mark snapped "Feel that? That second you just thought you missed what I said? He took you over! And those moments in the car—"

His hands itched to reach across to her, the one thing he didn't dare, knowing Winton could strike again.

He added "And, when I carried you out tonight. Remember waking up there, missing time?"

Sasha's pale face twisted in confusion, but he couldn't slow down.

"He used you to speak to me. I know your mother was his sister, because he told me. And he said you killed her, and he wanted your body for Angie, so you have to put those talismans down before he—"

"Liar!"

Sasha—still Sasha, from the outraged sneer he saw so clearly—lunged at him, hands clenching magic.

He darted back with an easy, lightened hop. Sasha charged at him, running through the pool of light, mouth opening ready to scream.

Mark shot upward. Away from her, away from the ground, the factory, from all the stupid words he'd *had* to try rattling Sasha with when he could have just kept begging her to drop the talismans.

She'd never listen to him now. And far below, Winton was already peeking through her again.

And I can only fly away—like when I broke our deal from Nolan to save Sasha, but this time without even saving her. And Kate and Dennard were still down there.

Floating in the cold, clean space above the city lights, he dug out his phone.

His finger must have touched the wrong thing. The voice he heard was Henry's: "Winton's her aunt? Is Kate sure about that?"

"Listen! Winton—" *but not Angie, it couldn't be, but why am I telling this to Henry*—"is planning to kill Sasha. He's been using her talismans, he can take her over any time, but she won't listen to me. All I could do was…"

His voice cracked.

"…was nothing, except make enemies, it doesn't matter how hard I try, I still…"

He ran out of breath, out of words. The cold air rippled and whispered where he hung in place. Still.

Henry's words drifted through the night:

"…maybe, maybe you can get to him first. See this?"

A picture spread over the screen. A hand, scarred, with some kind of ID bracelet around it. Hadn't he seen that before?

Henry was saying "You said Winton needed to hide his body somewhere safe, somewhere that could keep him alive. If he used to be Isabel Lawrence… this is a veterans' home she used to work at. She'd know it. And they use these ID bracelets."

He knew that gray sheen.

"You… think that's a talisman?" he said.

"There's a lot of them there, if you look at the news pictures. Like some donor paid for them all, all for his own reasons. It's on Fall Street—"

Henry's words touched the memory. The place would be west, about…

The edges of the phone dug into his fingers. That couldn't be it, Winton himself wouldn't simply *be* there.

But the pictures show silver, they could be disguised talismans. The site would have medical care for Winton's body. It's familiar to him—to her, to the past life that my father died to find out.

Please let this be right.

Mark swept a gaze around the blocks below. The Fall Street Veteran Center would be north; he dropped down, down, into the space between the lines of light. Less than an hour before when Winton expected to get at Sasha—or whatever time he really had before the killer's other schemes.

The lash of night air on his body slowed, ended when his shoes hit the roof, and he leaped into it again in a lunge toward the highest roof on the next block. Magic held his path straight, arrowing over the few nighttime lights moving on the streets below.

The wide shape he closed in on slid toward his side—his aim would leave him flailing in open space, with only open, visible streets to drop down to. He loosened the power to leave him coasting, and the wind's pressure softened as it drew him into its current and toward another roof, until he could drop to it and leap again into the teeth of the cold.

Leap by leap, watching the light-lined fingerprints of the city shift with each block as he moved through them... so many miles around him, and he was gambling everything on one spot—

Don't think it. He locked his thoughts on cutting through the air, on reaching "Roger Winton" and destroying him. *Killing him, Henry would remind us.* And condemning Angie to a lifetime of perching on branches... and flying with the joy he felt in her, or, they'd find another way... but he was taking the choice from her—

A web of power lines loomed ahead as he touched down, he twisted up to hop over and bound on—

All this to save stubborn, power-greedy Sasha... or to save the memory of the loyal, fearless Angie that should never be so worn down that she'd agree to steal another's life... *except she already risked one woman's life chasing Nolan...* He leaped faster, tearing through the air to race past the last time he'd be free to worry. Finish it.

The buildings stood below.

A snowed-over park with a line of cages, dog kennels. A small garage where a single ambulance waited. An old house in the back. A long building in the center. All with only the faintest light on.

He sensed no magic. Less than twenty minutes to midnight. *Winton wouldn't be steering any puppets here, his focus will be on his way to where he expects Angie. If his body is here at all.*

Only the center building was large enough to really hide Winton; one leap brought Mark down to its door. Dogs—comfort animals for the patients?—burst out barking. Mark gripped the door's hinges, and a surge of gravity wrenched them down from the frame.

All that mattered now was speed. He dove into the corridor with the light, long stride Angie had taught him—*don't think of that.* Through the soft after-hours lights, he lunged through room after room, dodging examining tables and heavy, locked drug cabinets. The dogs' voices scrabbled against the stillness outside. Room after room flew by, with nothing but cabinets and posters on the walls—the one door that led further in ended in a single room with only a hulking medical machine. No bedridden puppetmaster.

Brighter lights shone around the turn ahead, as he charged on. Voices stirred somewhere behind the dogs' barking.

For an instant, he thought he felt Winton's magic sparking somewhere, then gone. Nowhere close.

He rounded the corridor into the light, into view of the open doorway and the men sitting in a circle. *What, some late-hours therapy group for night terrors?* No time to flinch—he gave the leader a passing nod, glanced around to find only a door at the back that must be only a few feet of closet space before the outside wall, and he walked on out, ignoring the voices rising behind him.

The building's end must be close. He moved on, nudging open doors in search of something, *anything.*

The last door short of the night-shadowed entrance opened onto a flight of stairs down.

Its swinging open triggered a *Hey, you can't!* from the gathering shouts behind him. No time to trip on stairs or leap blind; he sprang down to float into the basement's shadows. One heartbeat, three, five, seven—

His hands touched the wall, he glanced around. One light flickered in the space's center, but at its edges he thought he saw only walls, shelves.

"Dead end."

The voice—angry, *honest,* it sounded—flooded through the base-ment from above, and the main lights clicked on. Mark blinked to focus, but he knew what he saw: no doors or openings or anything but rows of supplies. On the stairs, two, three men started down to trap him.

Winton's power moved outside.

Not in the air, on the ground—the thought brought back his glimpse of the complex's layout, and the simple house behind this building. Out there.

The thought was all he needed. The men were halfway down the stairs, and Mark hurtled in a high leap over their heads.

In another breath he reached the corridor above and flung open the door outside. Winton's presence was gone again, and the shrill shock of the voices behind him reminded him he'd shown those men a leap that shouldn't be real.

But the outside gave him shadows and open space to move again. He slowed as he moved for the building's corner, just enough to let the men behind him see him there. The dogs barked louder. He spun around the corner, out of sight, and leaped for the roof.

He'd only have moments, before they might think he'd double back. He glared at the back building, some old house still on the prop-erty, discolored in the moonlight.

Two taps of his phone brought up Dennard and sent a location ping. "Winton's here, I think."

"Listen, Nolan's freezing the whole—"

"No time!"

He shot down for the house's door. In midair he felt Winton's magic move within it—right inside, but fainter now, and why was Winton still paying attention here? Mark landed by the door and shoved it open.

Dust touched his nose, faint but still there. He shut the door and fo-cused on what light slipped through the windows—a desk, shelves, had someone tried to keep the house for some administration work for the center, then given up?

Faint light shone from one corridor, right where Winton's magic moved, muted. That muzziness in its sensation would be from mind talismans drawing in power around it; he felt that whirlpool swelling around him as he closed in.

Magic let Mark move softly as a shadow. He slipped through the doorway toward the glow. The dogs' barking faded behind him.

Beyond another turn, a door hung open to let a few inches of dim light shine through. Peeking through it showed only a wall, but he could still feel the enemy's grip through the pool of power.

The door felt heavy at his first touch, but it swung out easily.

The room was windowless, filled with shadows and mustiness, but he saw nothing human. He brought up his phone's glow—had the lights really been set so dim?—to confirm what he saw.

Ten steps across, *no people,* no doors leading any deeper. A birdcage with a silent, slender hawk inside—the cage looked like some of Sasha's, latched so that a spybird could let itself in or out. Winton's control had left it, Mark could still make that out through the waves of the mind talismans around him.

A small, empty bed. A table, laid out with…

A board creaked as he closed in. A thick, businesslike ledger lay on one end, but next to it stood two photos; one with two little girls, with the childish writing *Izzy* and *Lizzy* under them, another with two grown women, sisters, one of them Sasha's mother.

Beyond them, a set of smaller pictures of Roger Winton… or Edward Winton, father and son, but essentially the same face whatever fashion the people around him wore. A certificate from some far-off school, with no pictures of the boy himself, the boy who'd never existed. A half-folded chart of Lavine, with spots around Rosewood Park circled.

Mark shook himself, held up the phone to send pictures to the others.

As he brought it up, the phone's reception cut off.

A soft electric sound was humming, right at the door.

He spun, leaped, but the door was already closing on its own. He caught one glimpse of the same too-familiar face as the pictures, and the wheelchair the man sat in, before the door sealed with a heavy *thunk.*

"I'm sorry, Mark."

A frail breathlessness hollowed out Winton's sigh.

Mark slapped his hands on the door. *One wrench and I've* got *you!* Raw power flooded out from the huge talisman he wore—

The door held, the frame held… something shifted in the *wall,* in the ceiling above.

"You don't want to do that," Winton said. "A reinforced door, in an ancient house…"

Mark pulled back. No wonder those pictures had been laid out; he'd stepped straight into the trap.

Somewhere far, far away, the scattered sound of dogs' voices was fading.

"You… you're not Roger Winton," Mark said. "Or Edward Winton, you were Isabel Lawrence before you found out how to take his body, right? And there was never a Roger Winton—you really don't *age?"*

"Your magic heals you." The puppetmaster's voice was soft, a steadier whisper now. "Even a little. Mine is different, ever since I found magic's secret of sleep. Every day I sleep, I don't age at all."

"Sleep? What's that mean?"

"I set my plans, I rest, and then I wake to see how they've done. Every day in the world takes its toll, so some days are worth having, and some are not. Like some people," he added softly.

"You expect me to accept that? After everyone you've destroyed?"

"No I don't. I did want your healing too… but I will settle for Angie and Sasha giving me one more test of a complete transfer. I've only been through that the one time. But I guess even when I have only one chance to tell someone, it's still pointless."

Angie... He dragged his hands back away from the door. "And when you're done, what happens to her—"

The lights went out.

He's got them rigged too—Mark blinked, stared around at the sudden blackness. The only ember was the glow of his phone, back on the table, too weak to shine far.

Something rattled in the darkness. A soft sound just breaking above Mark's pounding heartbeat. The magic that moved it was swallowed in the vortex of feeding power, but he knew the sound had to be right where the hawk's cage stood.

It's coming for me.

The trapped room. Winton *warning* him about the door.

"You don't need Angie after that." His words rushed out. "You need *me,* once you're ready to risk a real jump. Just like you told us, you take over my body so you get my sense to track Nolan down, isn't that it?"

Not a sound, except the scratching behind him. Winton was done explaining himself.

Mark gasped in a dusty breath and bellowed "HELP! IN HERE, HELLLP…"

He pulled in air for more shouts—and heard another voice outside. A shout with the same desperation he'd used, not answering but calling for help for himself. Drawing anyone else away.

"You're controlling them too? What, every ID bracelet here is one of your talismans?"

Another scratch at the birdcage behind him said Winton was back to closing his trap. Mark blinked in the dimness, knowing he should try to stay clear of the creature, but instead he kept talking.

"Did you lure me here? What, I'm your hostage to make Angie go through with your test, and then you get rid of both of us? Or am I just your way out of that chair?"

Finally, Winton spoke:

"I *am* sorry. I did like your drawings."

No, no no no…

Tricked.

Helpless.

And the killer was only a few thoughts away from putting him to sleep, then flicking back and forth to use him against the others…

Mark clutched at the doorframe, straining to push his power through to the hinges on the other side. Instead the whole frame creaked, and something rattled above.

The only way to go… he floated up until his hands pressed blindly against the plaster. If cracking the door brought down the ceiling… how much power did he really have?

Magic surged, thundered, blasted up, tearing through his heartbeat and singing in his fingers as wood shifted, caught in the spreading web of force. *Wider, stronger, pour it out, rip through it all or there's nothing left.*

Walls and roof groaned, all around him.

His sight washed away in light.

Those fingers on the ceiling went numb. A memory of sky-deep ozone flushed through him, but that wouldn't be here, yet if he could only reach that sky…

He felt his heart beat again.

He knew it, because the magic dwindled and died, and he heard one whine of a wheelchair motor bearing Winton to safety.

The world crashed down.

CHAPTER FIFTEEN

FLY BY NIGHT

A distant, hollow ringing, somewhere deep inside his ears.

Grayness lay over the world.

Something jabbed within him, every time he tried to sneak a breath.

His arm lay numb, cold, dissolving his impulse to move it into weak twitches. If he had any other arms or legs, they felt nothing at all. Something wet dripped over his face.

One sound, then another, filtered in. The ragged noise of dogs, broken here and there by a voice. And closer than all that, pulling away, the whine of Winton's wheelchair. Still alive, still free, still ready to trap Angie and then the rest…

He forced his hand down against what felt like splintered, broken wood. The pressure pushed the dimness back; a sky of soft silver moonlight formed above him. The *keekeekee* of what must be the caged hawk sounded, somehow alive too. Shadows to his side resolved into mounds of wood with metal lines—pipes—poking out of them like exposed bones. Stripped skeletons.

His arm could ache when he moved it; his lungs bit on every breath, but was there any more to him? His head could loll to the side, but something blocked it from looking down toward how much of himself he couldn't feel, and that was a comfort.

But to the side… that slow, rolling shape was Winton, gliding down the walkway—Mark couldn't find one spark of his own magic left to sense the enemy's power at work.

Just try and take my body now, it's more shattered than yours…

The grayness welled in his head. He pushed his hand against the rubble again, anything to force the darkness away, but he'd lost it all.

What moved in the night should be beyond any seeing. But he'd tracked that motion so many times: its pathway down from the open sky, the soundless blur that closed in an instant, that could be nothing else but her.

Winton never even looked up, in the single frozen moment when the shape struck his face.

Stabbing into his eye.

Winton went limp.

Never even saw it coming.

Then the dimness closed over Mark; aches and sounds faded away. Whatever he'd seen would have been a dream, some last wish that Angie had never gone across town to wait for their enemy's trap…

The ground was gone, up and down were gone, floating in a perfect sky where the air was never cold. Dust still tickled him, but that was fine, it made no difference what had been wrecked behind him or who might have seen it… it must have been heard for miles… and he still had the dream that their enemy might be gone…

Feathers brushed his face. Soft, *real* feathers.

And the frantic way they rubbed against him, driven by some will outside of his own fading senses…

Of course. Angie never went to Winton's trap, she'd never steal Sasha's life or anyone's. She'd tricked Winton, bought more time to search for him, and the crumbling house had brought her right to him.

His eyes opened. A laugh stirred and broke through him, tearing at somewhere in his lungs, but he couldn't stop.

The pale shape drew back from his face. Her talons pricked his chest, yes, sharper than she'd kept them a day ago, honed into true weapons.

Kee-yak? she said, and he heard the question and the concern in her.

"Look… at us," he forced out through the stillness. "We won. You killed Winton."

The words should have lifted something from him, but instead they dug deep into his ruined bones. His thoughts shied screaming away from trying to look downward; Angie's tiny form had to be more than he had left.

The white disk of her face blurred in the night. He thumped knuckles on the debris, trying to hold on. Numbness pressed in.

Cold…

Dim…

Push…

Cold…

Cold in his *face,* deeper than the rest of his body. The noise, shrill and sharp and whistling off the remains of the building, wind. Something wet fell across his face, too cold to be blood.

Another howl moved in the distance. A siren, that was it, there should be sirens for a fallen house.

Snow. What did snow mean, when it broke out this suddenly, when the clouds gathered above to swallow the moonlight? Why was Angie leaning over him, wings spread over his face in some bird-boned, birdbrained attempt at protection?

A sound came, closer now. A voice, calling *Anyone here?* and *Police, is anyone hurt?*

Angie drew back, feathers sliding over Mark's cheek. He strained his neck around to watch her hop up on a chunk of rubble and peer across the snow.

He couldn't see the ground. But, a shadow settled through the air above… to land in the open? No, if that was someone flying, they'd drop onto or behind the main building, out of sight.

"Who's there? Police!" the voice called again. An older, confident man, the officer sounded like.

Angie's wings hunched and mantled, like a boxer crouching to lunge.

Why… how did the cop spot someone who moved in from the sky…

A shriek of wind tore through the air, with a gunshot inside the same moment—timed too perfectly, the wind must be to disguise the sound and the shooter must be Nolan.

Mark couldn't even move.

The winds dwindled to a simple wail. In that hush came the cop's voice: "Looks all clear. I'll look around and check in later."

That had to be Nolan in control, but she would never risk possessing the police… or had that changed, now that she could abandon a body all the way? She could take any risk now, knowing she could skip out if the traces led back to her?

And—who had she shot at?

Angie hopped into the air. One stroke of her wings and she was gone. He didn't even have the magic left to track her.

The storm tightened again, louder and shriller. The air darkened. Dimness crept in—

No! Mark beat his hand on the rubble to fight the shadows back. Closing in through the wind, he heard footsteps.

The wind paused. Nolan's cop called out "Winton's dead. Or did he get to another body?"

"Dead?"

The voice came from somewhere across the grounds, shocked. Dennard.

"Are your friends listening?" Nolan's puppet said. "Mark and Henry, you get down here—I won't have your scanning interfere with my confirming Winton is gone. Get down here, or I'll have to freeze them all."

No answer came.

The wind sprang up, and this time it smashed at the rubble, then paused for one quick twist of the air and hammered down from a different angle, sending wood skittering away over snow. Nolan was flinging the winds around the way she kept birds grounded—*and she could sense Angie now, and chase her out of the sky—*

And Angie and Dennard must still be here, or Nolan would have eased up. But they could have slipped away before, why…

Dennard's searching for us. He and Angie are both staying because of me.

He sucked in a full breath, fighting through the wet, clogged feeling in his chest:

"Let them go—"

The wave of pain cut his shout off. Teeth clenched, hand flattened on wood and metal…

A dim silhouette loomed over him. Only for a moment, then it shuffled out of view.

"Mark's here," Nolan's puppet called. "He's got no magic left, and he's not going anywhere. That just leaves Henry—and three of you as hostages until he helps me finish the search. Yes, three, Angie too."

Stupid, stupid—

"Henry won't be coming." Dennard sounded close, for all the good that did. "He and Christa wanted a life. And we all know you'll just kill us."

The air bit deeper. It seeped into Mark's face, colder than the numbness in his body. The wind slashed around once, and he thought he heard a shriek from Angie somewhere within the gale. Helpless.

Mark strained his will to float the boards away—just empty, flailing thoughts, with the coat and belt bled dry of power. His working arm scrabbled in the rubble. Flesh tore, pulling fingers clear of some frozen bit of metal, a stretch of pipe from the house.

And... something else cold and smooth, deep under the ruin. A small square shape he knew would be silver.

The wind stilled a moment to lash around again. As it did, more gunshots roared somewhere beyond him. Nearer to him, something gave a weak, defeated cry.

Winton's caged hawk.

The world shrank to Mark's ice-stiff fingers. He couldn't *feel*, but where one finger moved and another met resistance... he could picture Winton's talisman turning in his hand, and knew when it had clicked closed. Ready.

The voice of Nolan's puppet sounded in the wind, some lie about not needing to kill...

Going dim...

No, no, NO. The talisman was Mark's anchor, and he thrust his will into its power to reach for the matching silver that would be on the hawk.

Nothing answered, the magic rose to carry his thoughts but it had nothing to touch, cut off and useless as his buried body...

No. Hot rage shot through him—*all this time I've worried whether any talisman of Winton's was still under his control, and now that he's gone I grab the only one that he* didn't *connect to that spy-bird's...*

The thought dissolved, thrashing. Teeth gritted, lungs heaved, a hand beat on the half-buried pipe again. Metal clinked against metal, so weak, but he felt an idea behind his impulse...

Gray silver magic... soft gray... don't think about graying out again...

A corner of the silver bent, snapped off. The bulk of the talisman settled behind his lower fingers, with the fragment pinched between thumb and forefinger, and he lifted his arm clear of the rubble. Nothing left to do but the hardest part of all.

He tried to sit up.

With no idea how much of his body would respond, he wrenched his back, dug his elbow down, curled his head in to steal one glimpse down toward the hawk's cage—falling back even as he moved, his arm swung out to loft the broken-off corner of silver toward it.

One more time throwing mind talismans away.

He flopped back in skewers of pain, *blind* as the bit of magic flew, and clutching everything he had around the remaining square of metal and its trapped power matching the flying piece that might... might...

Touch.

The swirling thought-world burst through him to feel another mind there, even a tiny unknowing thing—

There's no trick to it, my father said. Just don't hold back. Another swirl of raw power beside it to suck him into—

Wholeness.

The feel of complete muscles, four real limbs and a shifting sense of balance, tore a shriek from him... still too many legs straddling back between forms. And cold, the wind tearing through his feathers...

He strained his head around. The cage bars felt bent, but the latch was still...

Grayness crept in, pulling at his hold back on the other form, making him sway between them...

He clamped his beak—*beak?*—on the mechanism, again and again until he caught the bit of metal that slid over and let him step free. Air battered at him, and he crouched down low and crawled between wood and snow and endless noise, toward the larger power clenched in the broken shape ahead that still bled his strength away.

Don't black out, don't black out, don't look—

A claw closed around the hand, and the talisman. There was nothing left, only to pull free.

Like breaking an embrace to say goodbye, like sliding out of a torn coat too battered to keep, like pulling a foot free from sucking mud and leaving more than a shoe behind but turning away to *LEAP*—

When the wind paused again, he moved the sprawling broad things that would have been his arms, and stroked them down against the air.

He spilled upward—for an instant he thought of some swinging motion carried by his arms—but balance tipped over and air spilled between fingerlike feathers… He caught at the air and fought to level off as he shot up away from the ground.

The world was a *sea* of grays. His gaze flailed against the night, until one shape moved below and his head clicked toward it. Dim, half swallowed in the shadows, but nothing could hide how that one patch of motion was where Nolan had to be.

He tilted and dove, screaming fury.

The blur twisted around, with what had to be an arm swinging up. He flung out wings trying to angle up—the aim was off, he slid away… *my fault, I should have kept my mouth shut, until I did she wasn't sensing me like she did Angie…*

She can't sense me, I made a clean jump so I'm just a bird now.

I'm… a bird…

He hung in the air, dangling from the wings he'd bound himself to.

Then that air smashed against him, sent him tumbling sideways and lashing back at it for balance.

The air twisted again. He shoved down hard in the moment it changed and pulled himself higher. He had to twist his head back to see, but he caught the motion streaking past Nolan that had to Angie, and the enemy crouching low for shelter with the ground.

The ground was Nolan's weapon, and height was shelter and speed for himself—Mark beat harder to wrestle his way upward. The world still lay dim all around; one motion had to be Dennard pulling back around a corner, away from Nolan.

He swung around. Each twist of the wind tore at his balance—his skin bristled with feathers that ruffled with every change.

A man-shadow cut through the air, arcing toward Nolan.

The wind spun again. Mark saw the floating shape pull upward, spotted the tiny figure of Angie scuttling over the ground toward the base of some wall—

Mark wove closer. True flying seemed to move like floating, but without willing the belt to fight the air for him… instead only his arms, his wings, could pull him up or twist him away, and yet every inch of the sky was space that he could "jump" against or simply ride…

The next slash of the wind dragged the floating shape closer to Nolan. It struggled, dropped—Mark saw it topple where it hit the ground.

Nolan stepped closer. "Now drop the gun—"

She froze.

Mark stared harder. That grounded figure was too small for Dennard—was that *Kate?* He flicked his head around, looking for blotches in the lines of shadow. Another shape crouched low beside the wall, where Dennard could have crept in.

And back at the building's far door, a woman-sized figure slipped inside. The cloud of long hair about her made her Sasha.

"Henry! Where are you!" Nolan shouted, her gun on Kate.

"Is he the one you really want dead?" Kate couldn't seem to stand, and pain gritted in her voice. "He's had only days as a spellkeeper. *I'm* the one who knows how you think."

Mark battled his way closer. The darkness still masked the distance to the ground, that held him back from striking.

"Who else did you tell about magic?" Nolan demanded. "Never mind, at least you understand that much."

"I do. But tell me: all of this is to track down whether Winton's dead? How long will you search until you're sure he didn't escape?"

"Until I'm *sure.*" Nolan's words smashed like her winds, like a whole restless world stirring itself to toss aside what didn't align with its fears.

Mark shifted in the air again. Dennard was staying low, but… a door opened in the building behind Nolan. A man-sized shape peeped out.

"Then here's my offer," Kate said. "Let the others go, and keep me—*and* when they're free I'll tell you how to replenish the flying belts. You've got a long search ahead, and the minute you use them up you'll blind to his tricks again. That secret can die with us. This is the only chance you'll ever have."

Behind Nolan, the figure took a step toward the crumbled building. Toward Winton's body in its wheelchair outside.

Nolan's voice softened. "The only…"

The man behind Nolan charged straight at her.

He had only a few dozen feet to cross, and Nolan stood like she was fixated on Kate.

But Nolan's body *slumped,* just for an instant—

Then it rose and whirled around. Quick and sure as if she'd seen him all along, she swung her gun up, and fired.

The attacker's head burst. In the moment he began to topple, a hoarse, ragged shriek tore from the building behind him.

More shots burst through the night: Dennard blasting at Nolan, at her stolen, policeman's body. That body dropped for cover, un-touched—like Dennard hadn't aimed for it, only wanted to break off Nolan's attack. Too late.

Too late for that man, and for whoever else screamed.

The air bucked around Mark, savage as the thoughts tearing through him.

That scream—was that what Winton did when Angie killed a hawk with him inside it? Sasha went in one end of the building, that man rushed out…

Nolan's body did *slump, just before sensing the attack. That's not my father's body out here, she has to flick back into him to sense mag-ic. She can't sense all the time—*

And I'm the one she can't sense at all—

He drew his wings in and streaked down.

Air slashed past him; these new eyes didn't need to blink. Another twist of wind made him twitch a wing to spin off it, sweeping in off-center but close—if he read the distance to that shadow right—

Talons swung out. They swept by through empty air—

A yell of pain made him glance back. Another shadow, Angie, raced past the stolen body, and *her* course shook from impact with her target.

Shots roared again. Dennard was firing in the air, and as the body flinched he charged at her.

The cop's body collapsed.

Dennard shot him? No, they'd forced Nolan to bail out—

Where's her real mind, where's my father's body—

The air smashed straight down.

Mark tumbled and spun, flailing for some gap in the currents to slip through. So much *power*... Kate's voice shouted something that the storm crushed into nothingness.

Mark felt the current break at last and twisted away in a sidedraft; the brutal ground leaped up and skidded by just below. Stroke after frantic stroke dragged him upward again, but the wind lashed around—

His head followed it. That tiny shape by the wall, Angie—Nolan was twisting the wind to root her out from her cover.

No good, no good! Mark flipped and twisted higher, gambling a better vantage would do something. But all he saw was the great murky soup of shadows below—*I'm a hawk trying to see at night, why couldn't it have been another owl left in that cage?* He could guess at what the blotches meant, and catch any movement, but nothing moved down there except the shapes he knew.

Nolan had his father's sense, her winds could chase Angie any-where. She could track their power, but they had nobody left who could sense where she hid.

Because I'm a hawk. Because I gave up my body, I'm just a bird...

The air kicked him over once, twice. Cold bit through his feathers. Nolan could be *anywhere,* and all he saw below were Dennard staring around, and Kate trying to shelter Angie with her own body.

Down by the grounds' street entrance, two more people forced their way through the storm. Mark bobbed and wove in the winds until he could dip closer to them. From their sizes and how close they stood… Henry and Christa, and they moved straight toward the Center building's door. Dennard moved around to join them.

Part of Mark caught that direction and thrilled to what it meant: Henry *could* sense Nolan's powers, they could still root her out.

And behind that thought, a simpler one: *They came back. My family's with us after all.*

He tucked down through the currents and made for the open door. A glance over as he dove saw Kate lying still, holding her leg; it must be injured from when Nolan grounded her. Angie slipped from her grasp to make for the door.

Sirens sounded back behind the wind.

Shots fired… police… only minutes to run Nolan down…

Inside the doorway lay the wind tunnel. Dennard, Henry and Christa struggled forward against it, Kate limping up with them, and Mark dropped into the sheltered space behind their bulk and pressed flat on the too-smooth tiles. Talon-tips couldn't even dig in; he scuttled forward, trying not to think what the wind would do to him if he left their bodies' protection in this tight space.

No wonder Angie spent so many fights stuck outside the buildings, rather than give up the safe, open sky. But she pushed along behind him now—*nothing* would make them miss this.

Dennard led them through the corridors, always one turn ahead of the others and waving them to keep back. Of course; Kate had been flying with his belt so Dennard had no magic on him, and Nolan might only be tracking the group behind him…

At one doorway, he stopped, and motioned them inside.

In a simple office chair, Sasha sat. Her arms hung still at her sides, a talisman fallen at her feet, her head slumped… and the rictus of pain on her face brought a new kind of shiver.

Dennard checked her pulse, but Mark could already picture her sitting down to take control of some man she'd found here… then sending him out to spot Winton's body and rush Nolan's puppet… Did she think she was avenging her aunt? Instead she'd sent that man to his death, and the shock had…

"She was just a child," Kate said. "She never had a chance. Not once."

"But Nolan…" Henry faltered, then pushed on. "Look, she's the one who killed her, killed both of them. And Bryan's gravity talisman says she's… just *that* way." He pointed along the corridor, angling his finger trying to show the spot his mind must see. "I think about forty feet. And she can sense mine too."

Dennard raised his gun. "But not me. Before the police get here, I'm ending this. Now."

He gave them one solemn wave to stay put, and he crept into the corridor.

Mark followed. The wind twisted again, but he pressed low at the base of the wall, and tried to keep close. Dennard watched the doors ahead.

One flapped open, and he moved closer.

That would be the large meeting Mark had seen. But Henry had said forty feet… Mark looked at the door, back at the room where they'd been, and remembered the months he'd been sensing magic and trying to map it onto streets and doorways…

Forty feet was too far. But there had been the door at that room's back, a closet door. It had to be there.

Softly as he could against the wind, he called *Keee.*

Somehow, Dennard stopped. He looked down, and Mark gestured with his head, along the line he pictured to where the closet door would be inside the room.

"That way? You sure?" was all Dennard said.

Mark bobbed his head.

Dennard reached the doorway.

Then he dove straight through it. If Nolan *was* any closer and watching…

But no shots cut Dennard down. He shouted "You're trapped! I'll give you one chance to come out."

Nothing answered. But the wind slowed, died away.

Mark edged up to the doorway. Dennard was crossing the—uninhabited—room, dashing for the far corner of the closet door's wall… off to the side and out of the line of fire if Nolan shot through the door.

He could have fired through it himself… no, not a former cop shooting through a closed door, not with the thought of the real police closing in.

Standing back beside the door, he flung it open.

Inside, a stranger lay slumped against the shelves, asleep. Not Bryan's body, but his talisman *must* be there—

Mark tried to shriek *trap,* but the hurricane swallowed it.

Savage winds ripped him from the floor. He spun into the room, glimpsed the death-hard wall rushing at him… something soft caught him. Hands folded around him, Dennard's hands.

All around the room, furniture toppled, papers shredded. The *cold* stabbed deep, even with Dennard's body sheltering him. A voice sounded somewhere in the maelstrom, torn to meaningless sounds.

This is Nolan's full *strength again, throwing everything her body can stand and then using others' endurance.* And she could be anywhere.

Dennard struggled to stand, and slumped to the floor.

"What—"

A single word. But he *heard* it, heard the howling falter around him. The wind faded, chased away by the sounds of some struggle.

Mark dropped from Dennard's arms and flapped across the room. Nolan could smash him down any moment, but he couldn't waste the chance.

The door across the corridor hung open. Two, three people struggled, and more lay scattered over the ground. Mark's father—Nolan—jumped back, away from some smaller man, and Henry.

Something glinted in Henry's hand—Sasha's talisman. He'd found the bodies Nolan used to power her winds, and begun waking them.

Christa moved in behind Nolan. Nolan spun around and reached a hand for her, and Christa jerked back.

Nolan slumped in place.

Mark stared around, looking for the next attack. How many bodies did Nolan have ready—

Behind him, a new pair of scrambling feet sounded clear. He turned to see the decoy from the closet standing up, drawing back his arm.

Something arched through the air. Mark's hawk eyes saw it perfectly in the moments it flew past: a scrap of black leather, the talisman Nolan still needed to track them.

Dennard shouted *get down*. But the talisman reached his father's stolen body as it stood up, snatched the leather from the air. All three talismans were back in the same hands.

Mark dropped flat an instant before the storm exploded. The gust flung them all away.

An instant later it stopped, and he felt the air begin to swing around. Not to push them away down the corridor, but pulling.

Nolan hopped from the floor. Hawk-clear sight saw the moment that her weight vanished, and her winds swept her away up the corridor.

Easy as that, she's combining all three magics again. And in the end, she only thinks of preserving herself—as long as she's got my father's body and some gravity magic left, she can dodge police and stalk us any time she wants.

Then the wind caught Mark's spread wings to snatch him along in her wake.

The far wall shot up, *so fast* as his heart hammered, calling him a fool and bloodthirsty and about to *die*... the wind slowed, Nolan kicked the door open, and Mark wrenched at the air and slid out after her.

Angie flew right behind him.

They moved under open, clear sky again. Mark knew what that meant to Nolan now, and he slammed wings at the air trying to climb.

Nolan sprang upward. Angie rushed in with a twist of her wings to arc up, straight at the enemy's face.

That face—*my father's face*—glanced toward her, sensing her coming. Wind blasted out. Angie tumbled away.

Mark kited around the edge of the blast, curved his momentum up, and shot at his target.

His father's face didn't turn toward him; Nolan couldn't sense him. But when Mark's talons closed on the leather in those fingers, Nolan's reaction clamped that grip on the magic tight.

Right where I need it.

As Mark felt his momentum yanked around, he let his will, his rage, his need burst into the flying talisman in one command: *down.*

Nolan slammed for the ground.

Mark hung on for whole heartbeats, pounding at the magic and feeling the motion and the air tearing at him, until his poor frail claws gave out and broke from their grip. Muscles burned fighting to open his wings again...

He heard the body hit below.

His own landing was a slower, drawn out pain. All he needed was to hold his wings out, keep his balance, and let the soft, cool snow soothe the fires.

Above him, Angie shrieked, again and again. Voices and feet moved in the night, toward him, and feathers brushed and mingled with his own.

Some of the voices loomed over him:

You got her.

Mark, is that you…

We'll get you some…

It's over.

Over.

BIRD'S EYE VIEW

Still playing hide and seek…

The clock over the bank showed the meeting would be soon. Mark caught the breeze and glided over the blocks, glad the sun was setting.

The open streets and low buildings made this coastal town easier to study, but harder than most cities to find his way around. He kept his neck twisting, searching the streets and people for signs of problems to point out later. Most of all, he scanned the sky and the corners and crevices of the buildings. Even today she'd make him work for it. Especially today.

A sweep through the structures around the hospital found there simply *was* nowhere she could hide, and he sank down to perch on the ledge opposite the window. The fading sun left an odd warmth in its concrete.

The moment his talons touched down, Angie slid into view from wherever she'd been. She settled down at his side.

Henry was sliding the window open, looking around for where her energy was. Naturally; he'd replenished their talismans only this morning, and he took his place as their lookout seriously.

Rose Sarita chinned herself up toward the window, and Christa pulled their daughter back. The child had no fear of heights at all, and Mark could only wonder how much she'd already noticed about her family's secrets at age four.

Those three stepped back from the opening. Beyond them, the teenage James motioned inward, moving with the same hesitation he always had for this. He'd waited so long to meet his half-sister on the terms he expected…

But there by the bed, Kate herself couldn't seem to face the window. The weight of these attempts might be taking its toll after all.

Behind her, Joe Dennard seemed to notice, and his hand moved partway to her shoulder before he yanked it back.

Angie's wing brushed against Mark's.

He sent to her *Do you think this time will be different? Or should we try telling them there's no hurry?*

They've worked at it long enough, her thought answered. *They deserve the ending they can appreciate.*

You see your parents there? Maybe after they get us walking they'll finally open up to each other.

She gave a warm *chirrup*.

Then she dropped into the air, Mark behind her. They glided toward the lit opening below, both owl-silent, and the voices inside faded to a hush.

The woman on the bed looked more withered than most they'd seen. She had neatly-brushed hair that might have been a dirty blonde color to human eyes. Her still form under the blankets looked too tall to be a new Angie… but they'd said they'd worked out the medical challenges so there'd be dozens of others to try after this one, for both of them.

Angie settled slowly on the bed. None of the others would catch it, but Mark saw her hesitate. Some failures behind them, some changes ahead, were things anyone would fear.

She stepped in among the pillows.

She gripped the woman's hand, and Mark waited for her fingers to move.

*****

Keep reading for a look at the Shadowed Steps series in:

Shadowed

PREVIEW from SHADOWED

The pigeons *moaned*. It was the only word for their frantic cooing from the cardboard box he'd crammed them into. Even winter had its uses, at least it made the birds desperate enough for food that he could net half a dozen within walking distance of Quinn's building. And as that brick shape came in sight, Paul stopped to pour more seed into the box to quiet the birds again.

He left the cooing box halfway up the block, in the alley behind the buildings, and moved forward to Open and study his target again. Same dog, same window and alarm, and he waited until he could just make out the guard still patrolling inside.

Alright then.

First, he walked under the window and along the alley, back and forth, scuffing his feet around until the still-light layer of snow looked as if a whole gang had marched through it; a clumsy camouflage, but he could hope the guard wouldn't look too closely. And with any luck, this would be finished before enough snow fell over those to make his later tracks clear.

Then, he hefted the biggest discarded bottle he'd been able to find, and flung it straight through Quinn's window.

An alarm shrilled and the dog exploded into barking, both sounds ringing down the streets through the window's broken pane. The dog fell silent again, almost at once… too well-trained to keep going when nothing more was happening.

When the alarm cut off and Paul could hear the guard moving inside again, he darted up the block with the box of pigeons. Then he waited in the cold until the guard had made his sweep around the building and settled back inside. *I thought some of those wires were in case someone broke the window. But that's all I need for now.*

He poured another helping of seed into his cardboard pigeon-coop and began easing the four-way overlap of the top flaps open. With all the care he could manage, he parted them just enough to reach both hands in—wishing he could use his thicker winter gloves when they pecked at him—and pulled out one struggling bird before closing the top again. He placed that pigeon in his second, smaller box, and carried it under his arm to the fire escape and up.

The dog stood right under the window, a brown and black brute that looked like a Doberman but seemed a bit heavier than most. It growled but didn't bark yet, and for a moment Paul wondered if his plan would work.

Then he raised the box up to the high window-pane he'd smashed, and popped the pigeon through the hole.

The dog went mad. The bird beat its wings to catch itself in the air and fluttered around the room with the dog chasing it and barking in a frenzy. The animals hopped from one desk to another as the pigeon circled but couldn't turn tightly enough to stay airborne within the walls…

Paul slid back down to the alley and ducked around the corner. He strained his hearing to focus past the barking and the echo of his memory, praying that the trick would work.

Not that he had any trouble hearing the guard's "What in *hell*…?" Paul could imagine him watching as the dog and bird chased around the room. A moment later, the barking ceased and Paul caught one wild flutter of the pigeon. It was outside again, having finally squeezed back out the broken window.

Paul followed the guard's cursing all the way to the window and heard it grow louder still the longer he stood there. When he stomped away again, Paul could only wait in the cold, and found himself envying the other pigeons that could huddle together in his box for warmth. But the guard didn't come back to cover the window; the top pane he'd smashed would be difficult to block, as Paul had hoped.

Carefully, Paul pulled out another bird from the box, trying not to think of the one slip of his hand that might let the struggling flock burst free and ruin his whole night's work. Again, he sent the bird inside and then dropped back out of view as the dog's barking split the night. When he heard the guard enter again, he grinned wickedly; since the window was broken, was it so odd that birds would try to get to the warm room inside?

Then he heard a loud metallic *cough* sound, a "Damn!" and then one more cough, and then the dog hushed. As the footsteps moved away, Paul realized what the guard had done.

He'd shot the pigeon. He'd blown it apart so they could get back to work, and he'd done it using an illegal silencer and an ominously good aim.

Paul crouched down in the dark, chilled through with a cold deeper than the winter. He'd always maneuvered far away from armed guards, targeting secrets or at least strategies that kept him away from real physical danger. He chose his own cases, sometimes selecting unsavory types—but he'd never dared go up against a real criminal like this loan shark. Arthur Quinn seemed more dangerous by the hour.

Quinn's *They'll pay it all* echoed louder than ever in his mind, and Paul wondered how many ways Quinn made his enemies "pay."

Paul shook his head, trying to clear it. Dangerous or not, Quinn's words were all he knew about that night and whatever memory was blocking his power. *And if Quinn was part of that night, maybe I've always had to stop him.*

The next pigeon seemed to tremble a bit more than the others when he pulled it from the box. Paul tried to hold onto his city-bred contempt for the "winged rats," how there were always more of them and more pigeon droppings everywhere they flocked. But the more the bird thrashed in his hands, the harder it was to keep his touch from Opening to feel its panicked heartbeat.

This pigeon was luckier than the last; the guard shot once, then swore and walked away, letting the dog chase it out the window again.

For the pigeon after that, the guard didn't come at all. *Finally.*

Carefully watching the alley's corners and windows for observers, Paul took his last bird and other tools up the fire escape. The dog stood just behind the glass with its teeth bared, waiting.

But this time, Paul peered at the window, looking from the hole at the top on down to the latch and then to the tiny, hidden sensor along the jamb inside. Even while Opening sight, he could barely make out its wires there along the side of the frame, against its mate on the window itself. He unwrapped a sliver of metal from his pocket, his gloved fingers careful of the sharp edge on one side.

He stared harder at the tiny switch, struggling to push back the shadows that pooled around the wires. From the design, they should be about *there* and *there*, and he'd done this many times before. But this time…

He Opened to listen again for the guard, took a deep breath, and strained past the thunder of *I'm sure they'll pay it all.*

They won't pay.

Paul started, looking around the alley below. But nothing had stirred except the drifting snow; the thought was another memory. *They won't pay,* Quinn had said that night. Paul knew it now. *They won't pay.*

But he must have said "They'll pay!" Which one was it?

He gritted his teeth. Gripping the metal piece as firmly as he could through the glove, he Opened to the shape in the shadows along the window, fighting to ignore the two memories so he could just *see* the wires, *know* the distance…

In one move, he reached down through the broken pane to stab the metal's edge into the wood below, pressing its length between the sensors at just the proper angle. Nothing snapped, no alarm blared… and he yanked his hand back up as the dog snapped at him.

The metal stayed in place. He tried to Open his hearing to follow if the electrical path had changed, but all he heard were Quinn's words and the dog's thwarted growls.

Time to find out.

The dog watched his every motion now, so he took the last pigeon from his box and slid it through the hole. The dog barked as the bird fluttered by, but this time, it turned right back to the window as Paul reached in again to flip the latch.

He pulled his hand back in time, but the dog kept barking, and Paul could only hope the guard was still sick of false alarms. *And that the other alarm here...*

The window slid up, just three inches for now. No bells rang, but the dog snarled and snapped just beyond that gap.

And Paul raised the pet store's spray bottle and squirted cleaning fluid into its face.

The dog yelped and pulled back, giving Paul a moment to fling the window up. As the dog started toward him again, he gave it another spray, then caught up the bird net and flung it over the beast.

Paul grabbed the bottle again and leaped through, into the room.

A few desks and cabinets stretched around him in the dim light. He turned back to see the dog already shaking off the thin net, as expected. He stepped back and pumped the spray as the dog charged— but it squirted once and then the trigger clicked in without pumping any liquid. He back-pedaled and pumped more slowly, but now the spray only made the dog flinch back a moment.

The inner door's this way—Paul took a step, and his hip bashed the edge of a desk. The dog lunged.

He spun around the desk and threw himself at the door. For one frozen moment, he wondered if he'd ever heard the guard open it. *What if it's locked?* Then he seized the handle and wrenched it open, which sent a spasm through his injured arm.

As he stepped through, the dog came up behind him. Paul ducked sideways and gave the spray bottle trigger one hard squeeze. The spray drove the dog back only a step, and Paul pumped wildly, felt the trigger catch on nothing—He smashed the bottle into the animal's head, knocked the dog away, then leapt back out through the door and slammed it shut.

Gasping for breath, he listened to the dog's muted barking for a moment. The spray bottle had split open in his hand, and he set the its remains quietly on the floor.

Paul looked past the desks to the office's little file cabinet and then marched back to slide the window shut and gather up the net. That left him in the space between the alarms, with the dog trapped, and the guard tired of checking out all these noises.

"Alright, what *now*?" the guard growled, as the outer door's lock clicked open. Paul dropped flat, behind a desk just as the light came on.

He heard the guard march in as the dog in the side room kept barking and scrabbling at the door. He tried to Open his hearing to track the guard better, but then broke off as the memories of Quinn's voice almost deafened him. Somewhere up near the ceiling, he heard the pigeon still fluttering around.

The guard stomped down to the inner door and paused in front of it, listening to the dog trapped behind it. "How did you pull *that* off, boy?"

Oh God, when he lets the dog out— Paul peeked over the desk at the path around the furniture to the outer door. He'd only have a moment while the guard was distracted—

He heard the pigeon flap toward his hiding place, saw the guard start to turn his way and ducked down again by reflex. The bird landed right on the desk, and Paul held his breath, but he couldn't hear the guard move. *Please, please...*

"Yes, sir?"

A phone call, now? Paul strained to hear the voice on the other end, but heard only *they'll pay it all, they won't pay, they'll pay...*

"Thor got into the back room, sir. Someone broke a window here, and he's been chasing the birds that keep flying in…"

The guard's voice stopped so suddenly that Paul knew his boss had cut him off. Paul tensed, waiting.

At last, he said, "Understood," and walked away from the door. The dog kept growling behind it, but he said, "Sorry, boy, that's enough excitement for you."

Then Paul heard a faint beep and looked out to see the guard pushing a combination on the alarm control panel. Paul *threw* his thoughts toward seeing that keyboard, but the mocking memories choked off his concentration.

The guard turned away and Paul remained crouched down until he heard him finally walk out and shut the door. *Gone. I'm safe.*

Safe? No, Quinn must have told the guard to leave 'Thor' in the back room…

Paul struggled to fit the pieces together. So now Quinn knew about this latest disturbance himself, but the guard hadn't told him about the others? *Of course*, their alarm system must have left the inside of this main room clear for the dog to patrol but kept a silent alarm in the back room. *That* was what Paul had triggered by knocking the dog in there, and what the guard had shut off now… and that alarm was the only one that signaled Quinn personally.

So now Quinn is awake—maybe even on his way here, if he's suspicious enough. And I just shut the dog in with the only things Quinn made sure to monitor himself!

Paul scowled at the net he'd gathered up; it had barely slowed the dog down before. He glanced around, looking for something else to use. Maybe a chair, to fend the beast off or hit it… no, if he missed once, the dog would drag him down. But what if Quinn *was* on his way, and time was running out? This might be his last chance to learn what was haunting his power…

Paul yanked off his coat and moved to the door. He spread the coat out in both hands and crouched down, feeling for a moment like a baseball catcher with some flimsy, two-handed mitt. The dog barked louder, scrabbling right at the door.

Twisting the knob, Paul kicked the door open and turned that step into a crouching lunge forward, springing to meet the dog and wrapping the coat around it. They crashed to the floor together, his arms clutching Thor in a bear hug.

The brute writhed in his grip; he felt its jaws straining to rip free from the few layers of cloth that kept them from his captor's chest and throat. Paul crushed the coat around it, desperate to keep the dog from getting leverage. With all his weight, he pressed the dog to the floor.

His injured arm burned and the dog's nails ripped at his thighs as the jaws fought to get their grip. Paul could only hold on, thinking *Tighter, I'm still twice your size, dog, and I* need *this...*

After an eternity, the dog's thrashing stilled. Paul hung on a little longer, his muscles aching, his heartbeat settling as one fear faded to another.

His hands fumbled around the dog's sides and he Opened to feel for its breathing, but felt only the flood of Quinn memories now. As he let the power fade, he caught a weak stirring within the dog. It was alive.

Relieved, Paul staggered to his feet and dragged the limp body outside the room, then closed the door to leave himself in the dark. For one long moment, he felt every tremble in his gasping body. Sweat soaked through him and his new injuries flared with pain that was almost worse than the throbbing of his abused arm.

He felt weakly along the wall until he could work a light switch and then looked around.

The room was tiny. A few posters lined the walls. Instead of a desk, it had a small, empty table, set between a well-padded chair and a TV set. Nothing else.

Paul gazed around the near-empty room, struggling to hold off exhaustion. The place was set aside for resting, not for work and secrets...

But Quinn put the extra alarms here for a reason, he must have! Paul glanced numbly at the table and fumbled his hands up and down the chair, searching for anything hidden in its cushions. He turned to the TV and glanced at the only other objects in the room: four posters of different vacation spots around the world.

He ripped the posters down but saw only simple wood paneling behind them. Unless… he gingerly rapped on the walls where the posters had been, straining to hear any whisper of hollowness. But he couldn't be sure…

His battered left arm could barely move now, could barely pull off the glove from his shaking right hand. But slowly, slowly he laid the backs of his fingernails against the wall, hoping he could keep enough control not to brush the surface with his fingers' pads and leave prints.

Now. Now, or never. He Opened his touch.

I'm sure they'll pay it all… they won't pay… they won't pay… Quinn's words about the hospital boomed through his memory again—both versions—and with them Paul felt the *need* to face down schemers and secrets like Quinn. The need shook him, stronger even than the trembling in his fingers or the agony that tore through the body, the pain he tried to focus away from. *They won't pay, they'll pay…*

He'd fought through to Quinn's own room, and he couldn't get past just the memory of the answers? *No.* Paul gritted his teeth and pressed… not forcing his fingers against the wood but pushing all his focus, all his will, and all his need into his awareness there.

Fingernails glided over wood, but felt only wood. He focused harder and brushed it again. Again, again… he felt the finer shapes of the boards, and brushed again, clutching for more sensation. He shut his eyes, gave up his hearing to feel the wooden lines. Up and down, side to side along the wall…

He felt his eyes open, hearing the catch he'd clicked and watching the soundproofed panel swing back. Within the compartment lay two huge envelopes—and bundles of cash. There were thousands, maybe tens of thousands of dollars.

Paul knew the faint line next to the hinge was one last alarm, already triggered. He snatched up the envelopes—

And stared at the money. How many contacts could that buy? Maybe even a peaceful cabin away from the world. And every dollar taken would weaken Quinn, too…

I didn't get this power to steal! He slammed the panel shut and ran for the door.

The dog stood waiting. But as Paul rushed forward it whined and crouched down low, and Paul snatched up his coat and ran for the window. In a few more motions, he smoothly slid it up, stepped through, and dropped down from the fire escape to the alley below.

His injured arm struggled to clasp the packages, but all he had left to do was trot away through the snow, twisting his way up and down the blocks and trying not to feel the cold as he worked to hide his footprints. At last, he reached his bike and took the time to pull his coat on, but that made little difference with the holes the dog had torn in it, or the shocked exhaustion within his flesh from what he'd forced himself through.

A colder wind began blowing. The snow drifted as high as his bicycle wheel rims, sometimes twice that, and Paul pushed the bike along through it, in no shape to ride it without it slipping out from under him. He could only keep walking, more and more slowly, watching the last of the city night fill up with paler shadows.

They'll pay… they won't pay…

Somewhere on his long trudge, a little more of that memory fell into place. Quinn *had* said both things that night. And since it was in that place, he must have been talking about Lorraine's mentor and trying to offer his "help" with the bills. But… but…

Even with dawn beginning to shimmer in the air, Paul grew colder with every step. By the time he reached the Side Alley, he was shivering wildly and certain that whatever had happened that night was much more than Quinn's schemes or any simple locks and guards.

He threw himself down on his bed, knowing he should sleep. But instead, he could only huddle in his blankets as he began poring over Quinn's envelopes.

Sure enough, he found pages with long, handwritten rows noting loans and the payments made. They had only initials to mark them, but Paul flipped back to the long-ago June 13th that the Schuman boys had been raised to curse, and sure enough, he saw "K.U., $60,000."

K.U., Ian Schuman's initials if they're moved two letters forward on the alphabet—Paul's hazy thoughts dredged that fact up from some of the codes he'd tried to keep his own notes in. And with the code's key, he could check every other entry for anyone interesting... *When I wake up...*

But instead of letting himself drift off, he flipped ahead a number of Septembers, for one glance around the date when he'd heard Quinn at the hospital. Not much stood out, except...

There on the next page, in slightly larger letters: "K.U., 750,000."

It's a different I.S. It has to be. But no other initials were written quite so large. Paul stared at the letters; in among all the other, smaller rows, those initials seemed to crow Quinn's triumph at bringing "the one that got away" into his debt—again.

If that was a new loan, it had been made in the months after the hospital cover-up had failed, after discovering the firm's fax that branded Schuman and Son a family of backstabbers. The exposure must have hurt the business far worse than anyone had known...

No wonder Dad hates whoever handed over that fax. And if he thought it was Paul instead of Quinn...

Not Quinn.

Wrapped tightly in his blankets, Paul felt a new kind of cold wave sweep out of his memory. Whoever had added the Schuman name to Paul's exposé, he somehow *knew* it wasn't Arthur Quinn. And whatever had really happened, why it wasn't Quinn... *that* was the real memory he was letting Quinn's voice block out, even now.

Was it something he'd tried to stop... something worth risking *everything* to stop, even his family? Or something someone had done. Something just too *wrong*...

When Paul slept, none of his dreams were pleasant.

ABOUT THE AUTHOR

"Whispered spells for breathless suspense."

Ken Hughes dreams of dark alleys and the twenty-seven ways people with different psychic gifts might maneuver around each corner. He grew up on comics and adventures before discovering Stephen King and Joss Whedon, and he's written for Mars mission proposals and medical devices, making him an honorary rocket scientist and brain surgeon. Ken is a Global Ebook Award-nominated urban fantasy novelist, creator of the Shadowed Steps series, the Spellkeeper Flight, the Mirrorman, and many more series of supernatural thrills.

Don't get him started on puns.

Find more books and join the Overview newsletter at:

KenHughesAuthor.com.